James H. Graff, Edmund Hodgson Yates

A Righted Wrong

A Novel

James H. Graff, Edmund Hodgson Yates

A Righted Wrong
A Novel

ISBN/EAN: 9783337349400

Printed in Europe, USA, Canada, Australia, Japan

Cover: Foto ©Andreas Hilbeck / pixelio.de

More available books at **www.hansebooks.com**

A RIGHTED WRONG.

A Novel.

BY

EDMUND YATES,

AUTHOR OF
'BLACK SHEEP,' 'THE FORLORN HOPE,' 'BROKEN TO HARNESS,' ETC.

New Edition.

LONDON:

TINSLEY BROTHERS, 18, CATHERINE ST., STRAND.

1871.

JOHN CHILDS AND SON, PRINTERS.

CONTENTS.

A RIGHTED WRONG.

CHAPTER I.

HOMEWARD BOUND.

'GOOD-BYE, again; good-bye!'

'Good-bye, my dear; perhaps not for ever, though: I may make my way back to the old country once more. You will tell my old friend I kept my word to him;' and then the speaker kissed the woman to whom he addressed these parting words tenderly, went quickly away, and was hidden from her in a moment by all the bewildering confusion of 'board ship' at the hour of sailing.

He had not waited for words in reply to his farewell; she could not have spoken them, and he knew it; and while she tried to make out his figure among the groups upon the deck, formed of those who were about to set forth upon the long perilous ocean voyage, and those who had come to bid them good-bye, some with hearts full of agony, a few careless and gay enough, a suffocating silence held her.

1

But when at length she saw him for one brief moment as he went over the side to the boat waiting to take him to the shore so long familiar to her, but already, under the wonderful action of change, seeming strange and distant, the spell was lifted off her, and a deep gasping sob burst from her lips.

A very little longer, and the boat, with its solitary passenger, was a speck upon the water; and then she bowed her head, unconsciously, and slightly waved her hand, and went below

There was no one person in all the crowd upon the deck of the good ship Boomerang sufficiently disengaged from his or her own cares to take any notice of the little scene which had just passed—only one amid a number in the great drama which is always being acted, and for which a ship with its full complement of passengers, at the moment of beginning a long voyage, is a capacious and fine theatre. Selfishness and self-engrossment come out strongly in such a scene, and are as excusable under such circumstances as they ever can be.

She was quite alone in the little world of the ship; in the great world of England, to which she was going, she might find herself alone too, for who could say what tidings might await her there? in the inner world of her heart she was still more surely and utterly alone. In the slight shiver, in the forlorn glance around, which had accompanied her gesture of farewell to the man who had escorted her on board, there was something expressive of a suddenly deepened sense of this solitude.

In the cabin, which she shared with her maid only, she found this sole and newly-selected companion making such preparation as she could for the comfort of her mistress. The girl's face was kind and pleasant and handsome; but the sight of it did not lessen the sense of her solitude to Margaret Hungerford, for the kind and handsome face was also strange.

Rose Moore, whom she had engaged to act as her servant during the voyage, was an orphan girl, who wished to return to Ireland to her 'friends,' as the Irish people, with striking inaccuracy of speech and touching credulity, designate their relatives.

When Margaret Hungerford had lain down upon the little crib, which was to serve her for a bed during a period which would sound appalling in duration in the ears of a world so much accelerated in everything as our world of to-day is, she thought of Rose Moore, and of the difference between her own position and that of the girl who was to be her companion.

'She is going home to friends,' she thought, 'to a warm welcome, to a kindly fireside, and she is bringing money with her to gild the welcome, to gladden the hearth; while I—I am returning alone—oh, how utterly alone!—and destitute—ah, how destitute!—I, to whom not even the past is left; I, who do not possess even the right to grieve; I, to whom life has been only a mistake, only a delusion. I am returning to a home in which I was regarded rather as a trouble than anything else in my childhood, and which I was held to have disgraced in my girlhood. Returning to it, to feel that the judgment I set aside, the wisdom I derided, was right judgment and true wisdom, and that the best I can hope is to keep them from ever finding out how terribly right they were. The only real friend I now possess I am leaving behind me here; and I am glad it is so, because he knows all the truth. Surely no one in the world can be more lonely than I.'

Margaret Hungerford lay quietly in her narrow bed, while the ship resounded with all the indescribable and ex-

cruciating noises which form a portion of the tortures of a
sea-voyage.

She did not suffer from them, nor from the motion. She
was tired, too tired in body and mind to care about discomfort, and she did not dislike the sea. So she lay still,
while Rose Moore moved about in the little space allotted to
the two, and which she regarded as a den rather than a
' state-room,' looking now and then curiously at her mistress,
whom she had not had much previous opportunity of observing.

The girl looked at a face which was not less remarkable
for its beauty than for its expression of weariness and
sorrow, at a figure not more noticeable for its grace and
suppleness than for the languor and listlessness which every
movement betrayed.

Margaret Hungerford was tall, but not so tall as to be
remarked for her height ; and her figure, rounded and lithe,
had still much of the slightness of girlhood remaining. Her
face was not perfect ; the forehead was too high and too
heavy for ideal beauty ; there was not enough colour in
the clear pale cheek ; there was not enough richness in the
outline of the delicate mouth. Her face was one in which
intellect ruled, and thus its beauty served a master which is
pitiless in its exactions, and wears out the softness and the
fineness and the tinting in a service which is not gentle.

But it was a beautiful face for all that, more than beautiful for those who looked beyond the deep dark colouring of
the large gray eyes, deep-set under the finely-marked brows ;
who looked for the spirit in their light, for the calm and
courage which lent them the limpid placid beaming which was
their ordinary characteristic. It was not a perfect face ; but
it had that which very few perfect faces possess—the capacity

for expressing feeling, intelligence, the nobler passions, and utter forgetfulness of self.

To look at Margaret Hungerford was to feel that, however faulty her character might be, it at least was noble, and to know that vanity had no share in an organization which had no place for anything small, whether good or evil. It was a magnanimous resolute face—not strong, in any sense implying roughness, hardness, or self-assertion, but evincing a large capacity of loving and working and suffering.

And she had loved and worked and suffered. The bloom that was wanting to her pure fair cheek, which touched too faintly and grudgingly her small, well-curved, but ascetic lips, had vanished from her heart as well; the slight white fingers, too thin for beauty,—though the hands, clasped over her breast as she lay still with closed eyes, were curiously small and perfectly shaped,—had been unsparingly used in many and various kinds of toil in the new land, which had been wild and rough indeed when she had come there.

The girl looked at her admiringly, and with a sort of pity, for which she had no reason to give to herself except that her mistress was a widow. Explanation enough, she would have said, and naturally; and still, there was something in the face which Rose Moore felt, in her untaught, instinctive, but very acute fashion, had been there longer than three months, which was the exact period since Mrs Hungerford's husband had died.

Who was she going to? she thought; and did she like going home? and what was she leaving behind? Not her husband's grave, the girl knew, and felt the knowledge as an Irish peasant would feel it. No, she had not even that

consolation; for her husband, who had been a member of
one of the earliest-formed exploring parties who had undertaken to investigate the capacities of the unknown new
continent, had been killed in the Australian bush. It was
better not to think what the fate of his remains had been,
better that it was not known.

What, then, was this pale young widow, who looked as
though her sorrow far antedated her weeds, leaving behind
her? Rose Moore was not destined to know. What was
she going to? the girl wondered. In the short time she had
been with her, Mrs Hungerford's kindness had been accompanied with strict reserve, and Rose had learned no more
than that she was returning, probably, to her father's home;
but of even that she was not certain.

Thus the 'lone woman' seemed pitiable to the gay and
handsome Irish girl, and the thought of it interfered with
her visions of 'home,' and her exultation in the money she
had to take thither, and the love she was going to find.

Pitiable indeed she was.

As the long low banks of Port Phillip faded from the
sight of the passengers on board the 'homeward bound,' not
a heart among the number but yearned with some keen and
strong regret, too keen and strong to be overborne by the
gladness of hope and the relief of having really begun the
long voyage. Not a heart, not even that of Margaret
Hungerford; for she had looked her last on the land where
she had left her youth, and all its dreams and hopes; where
love had died for her, and truth had failed; where she had
been rudely awakened, and had never again found rest.

At such a time, at such a crisis in life, retrospection is
inevitable, however undesirable; however painful and vain, it
must be submitted to. The mind insists on passing the
newly-expired epoch in review; in repeating, in the full and

painful candour of its reverie, all the story so far told; in returning to the old illusions, and exposing their baselessness; in summoning up the defeated hopes, which, gauged by the measure of disappointment, appears so unreasonable—weighed in the balance of experience, seem so absurd.

Can I ever have been such a fool as to have believed that life held such possibilities? is the question we all ask at such times; and the self-contempt which inspires it is only as real, and no more, as the pain which no scorn or wonder can decrease.

So, like one performing an enforced task, with what patience it is possible to command, but wearily, and longing for the end, and for release, Margaret Hungerford, during the early days of the long voyage from Australia to England, gazed into her past life as into a mirror, and it gave her back a succession of images, of which the chief were these which follow.

CHAPTER II.

PAGES FROM THE PAST.

THE woman who was now returning to her native land after a long and painful exile looked back, in her retrospective fancy, upon a home which had external beauty, calm, and comfort to recommend it. She was the daughter of a gentleman named Carteret, a man of small but independent fortune, and whose tastes, which had been too extensively and exclusively cultivated for the happiness of his son and daughter, led him to prefer a life of quietness and seclusion, in which he devoted himself to study, and to the pursuit of natural history in particular.

Mr Carteret, who is an old man now, might have been the original of 'Sir Thomas the Good,' whose wife, 'the fair Lady Jane,' displayed such becoming resignation on his death. Mr Carteret, like the worthy knight, 'whose breath was short, and whose eyes were dim,' would 'pore for an hour over a bee or a flower, or the things that come creeping out after a shower;' but he was sadly blind to the subtle processes of the human heart in the development of the human beings under his own roof, which were taking place around him.

He had lost his wife very soon after the birth of his daughter, and when his son was three years old; and within little more than a year, a resolute young woman, who had long made up her mind that a pretty little country place within easy distance of London,—for Mr Carteret lived in Reigate, — a fair position in the county society, and a comfortable income, were desirable acquisitions, married him.

People said Miss Martley made all the preliminary arrangements, including even the proposal, herself; and though that statement was probably exaggerated, there can be little doubt that the suggestion, that it would be an advisable and agreeable circumstance that Miss Martley should become Mrs Carteret, originated with the lady.

She was rather young, and rather pretty; and there really was not so much to be said against the match, except by Mr Carteret's servants, who naturally did not like it. They liked it still less when the new mistress of the establishment, emulating the proverbial new broom, swept them all away, and replaced them by domestics of her own selection.

The novel state of things was not a happy condition for Mr Carteret. He was a gentle-natured man, indifferent, rather cold, and indolent, except where his particular tastes were concerned; he pursued his own avocations with activity and energy enough, but his easy-going selfishness rendered him a facile victim to a woman who managed him by the simple and effectual expedient of letting him have his own way undisturbed, in one direction,—that one the most important to him,—and never consulting his opinion or his wishes in any other respect whatever.

Mr Carteret might spend time and money on 'specimens,' on books, and on visits to naturalists and museums; he might fill his own rooms with stuffed monkeys and birds, and indulge in the newest form of cases for impaled insects, and even display very ghastly osteological trophies if he pleased; his wife in nowise molested him. But here his power was arrested—here his freedom stopped. Mrs Carteret ruled in everything else; and he knew it, and he suffered it 'for the sake of a quiet life.' He had a conviction that if he tried opposition, his life would not be quiet; therefore he never did try opposition.

The new Mrs Carteret did not actually ill-treat the children of the former Mrs Carteret; she only neglected them—neglected them so steadily and systematically that never was she betrayed into accidentally taking them, their interests or their pleasure, into consideration in anything she chose to do or to leave undone.

The servants understood quickly and thoroughly that if they meant to retain their places they must keep the children from annoying Mrs Carteret, from incommoding her by their presence, or intruding their wants upon her. They understood as distinctly, that if this fact were impressed by any misplaced zeal upon the attention of Mr Carteret, the imprudence would be as readily repaid by dismissal; and as they liked and valued their places,—for Mrs Carteret, provided her own comfort was secured in every particular, was a liberal and careless mistress,—the imprudent zeal never was manifested.

Thus the two young children grew up, somehow, anyhow, well-fed and well-clothed, by the care of servants; but in every particular, apart from their mere animal wants, utterly neglected. People talked about it, of course; and just at first the neglect of her husband's children threatened to be a little detrimental to the popularity which Mrs Carteret ardently desired to attain. But she gave pleasant garden-parties, at which neither husband nor children 'showed;' she dressed very well; she was very kind to the young ladies of the neighbourhood who were still on their preferment; her well-trained household were discreetly silent; and she had no children of her own.

This last was readily accepted as a very valid excuse; no one thought of the total absence of wifely sympathy and womanly tenderness which the argument conveyed. Mrs Carteret could not be expected to care about children—no one really did who had not children of their own 'to arouse the instinct,' as a foolish female, who fancied the phrase sounded philosophical, remarked. So the neighbourhood consented to forget Mr Carteret's children, and that contemplative gentleman consented to remember them very imperfectly, and things were very comfortable at Chayleigh for some years.

But Haldane and Margaret Carteret grew older with those years; the little children, who had been easily stowed away in a nursery and a playroom,—judiciously distant from drawing-room, boudoir, and study,—were no longer of an age to be so disposed of. The boy must either be sent to school or have a tutor,—he and his sister had passed beyond the rule of the nursery governess, — the girl's education must be attended to.

The latter ease was especially disagreeable to Mrs Carteret. It forced upon her attention the fact that she was no longer in the first bloom of her youth. A rather young and rather pretty stepmother is capable of being made interesting, if the situation be judiciously treated; but Mrs Carteret had never treated it judiciously, and now it could not avail.

She had nearly exhausted her *rôle* of young matronhood at thirty-seven, and Margaret was then twelve years old. True, there would be a revival of its material pleasures, its gaieties and dissipations, when Margaret should be ' brought out ; ' but Mrs Carteret found feeble consolation in the anticipation of the pleasures and importance of chaperonage. They can only be reflected at the best ; and Mrs Carteret cared little to shine with a borrowed light.

In the mean time, she had no notion of having a gawky girl, as she called Margaret in her thoughts, always about her at home, growing old enough to interfere, and perhaps to attract her father's attention unduly and put absurd ideas into his head. Margaret Carteret was not at all gawky ; but even then, at the least beautiful period of life, gave promise of the grace and distinction which afterwards characterized her.

Mrs Carteret made up her mind, and then informed her husband of the resolution she had taken, and the arrangements she had made. He acquiesced, as he always did ; and when Margaret, startled, confused, not knowing whether to be frightened at or pleased with the novelty which the prospect offered, asked him if it was really true that she was going to school at Paris, and was not to return for a whole year, he said placidly,

' Certainly, my dear. Mrs Carteret has arranged it all ; and I have told her to be sure and ask the school people to take you to the Jardin des Plantes.'

Then Mr Carteret, who never perceived that his daughter was no longer a baby, sent her away with a pat on the head, and turned his attention to investigating the structure of a 'trap-door spider's abode,' which had reached him the day before, having been sent by a friend and fellow-naturalist from Corfu.

The education of Haldane Carteret had been differently provided for. It chanced that the one human being besides herself for whom Mrs Carteret entertained a sentiment of affection was her cousin, James Dugdale, a young man who had no chance of success in any active career in life, being deformed and in delicate health—anything but a desirable tutor for a delicate retiring boy, like Haldane Carteret, people said—a boy who needed encouragement and companionship to rouse him up and make him more like other boys. But Mrs Carteret evinced her usual indifference to the opinion of 'people' on this occasion. She chose to provide for her cousin a mode of life suitable to his mental and physical constitution.

James Dugdale came to live at Chayleigh. The deformed young man had much of the talent, and all the unamiability, which so frequently accompany bodily malformation, and he inspired Margaret Carteret with intense dislike and repulsion—with admiration and some respect, too, child as she was; for she soon recognized his talent, and succumbed to his influence. James Dugdale taught Margaret as much as he taught her brother; he implanted in her the tastes which she afterwards cultivated so assiduously; but the boy learned to love him, while the girl never faltered in her dislike. When she found her lessons easily understood and soon learned at school, she knew that she had to thank her stepmother's cousin—her brother's tutor—for the aid which had rendered them light to her; but she never could bring herself to thank him in thought or word. The girl's heart was almost void of love and gratitude at this time of her life. She hardly could be said to love her father; her stepmother she neither loved, hated, nor feared; for her brother alone were all her kindly feelings hoarded up. She loved him, indeed; and, next to that love, the strongest sentiment in her heart was dislike of James Dugdale.

Time passed on, and Margaret grew up handsome, with a strongly intellectual stamp upon her face, and, in her character, self-will and impulsiveness prevailing. She liked the Parisian school—for she ruled her companions, some by love, others by fear and the power of party—and she cared little for her home, where she could not rule any one.

Her father was not worth governing; her stepmother she treated with a studious and settled indifference, forming her manner on the model of that of Mrs Carteret, but never attempting to gain any influence over that lady, who was, however, not without a misgiving at times that when Margaret should come home 'for good' she might find it rather difficult to 'hold her own.' Holding her own, in Mrs Carteret's case, rather implied holding every one else's, and that privilege she felt to be in danger. It was, therefore, with but a passing reflection on the fatal obstacle which such an occurrence must offer to her maintenance of the 'young married woman's' position in society, that Mrs Carteret, when Margaret was fifteen, began to speculate upon the chances of getting Margaret 'off her hands,' when she should have finally left school, by an opportune marriage.

A year later, and, much to the surprise of his father, and indeed of every one who knew him except James Dugdale, Haldane Carteret proclaimed his wish and intention of entering the army. His father did not oppose; his stepmother and his tutor supported him in his inclination; the

interest of a distant relative of his mother's was procured ;
and thus it chanced that, when Margaret came home 'for
good,' at a little more than sixteen years old, she found her
brother in all the boyish pride and exultation of his com-
mission and his uniform.

Then Margaret's fate was not long in coming. The first
time her brother came home, and while she had as yet seen
little of the society in which her stepmother moved, he
brought a brother officer with him, a handsome young man,
named Godfrey Hungerford, with whom he had contracted
a friendship—the more enthusiastic because it was the first
the lad had ever experienced.

And now active antagonism arose between Margaret
Carteret and James Dugdale. The girl fell in love with the
handsome young officer, whose bold and adventurous spirit
pleased her ; whose manifest admiration had a pardonable
fascination for her ; who raised even her father to animation ;
and for whom Mrs Carteret thought it worth while to put
forth the freshest of her somewhat faded graces.

Haldane paraded and boasted of his friend according to
the foolish hearty fashion of his time of life, and was delighted that his sister felt with him in this too.

But the ex-tutor, who, it appeared, was to remain a
fixture at Chayleigh, conceived a profound distrust and dislike of the brilliant young man, whom he quietly observed
from his obscure corner of the house—and of life indeed
—and who had no notion of the scrutiny he was undergoing.

Was James Dugdale's penetration quickened by the
hardly-veiled insolence of Godfrey Hungerford's manner to
him—insolence which sometimes took the form of complete
unconsciousness, and at others of an elaborate compassionate
politeness ? It may have been so ; at any rate, he made

PAGES FROM THE PAST.

15

his observations closely, and, when the time came, he expressed their result freely.

The time came when Godfrey Hungerford asked Margaret to become his wife; and then James Dugdale, for the only time during his long residence in Mr Carteret's house, spoke to that gentleman in private and in confidence.

'Insist on time, at least,' he urged upon Margaret's father; 'think how young she is; think how little you know of this man. You have no guarantee for his character but the praise of an enthusiastic boy. For the girl's sake, insist on time; do not consent to less than a two years' engagement; and then rouse yourself, and go to work as a man ought on whom such a responsibility rests, and find out all about this man before you suffer him to take your daughter away from her home—a girl, ignorant of the world and of life, in love with her own fancy I know Margaret's real nature better than you do, and I know she is incapable of caring for this man if she knew him as he really is. It is a delusion; if you can do no more, you can at least secure her time to find it out.'

'Find what out?' asked Mr Carteret, fretfully; 'what do you know about Hungerford?—how have you found out anything?'

'I know nothing; I have not found out anything,' said James Dugdale. 'I wish I had, then my interference might avail, even with Margaret herself; but I have only my conviction to go upon, that this man is not fit to be trusted with a woman's happiness; that Margaret is not really attached to him; and, in addition, the suggestion of common sense, that she is much too young to be permitted to settle her own fate irrevocably.'

The latter argument seemed to have some weight with Mr Carteret, and James Dugdale saw his advantage.

'Do you think,' he said, 'if her mother were living, she would permit Margaret to marry at her present age? Do you think, if you knew you would have to account to her mother for your care of her, you would listen to such a thing?'

This reference to his dead wife was not pleasant to Mr Carteret. He was growing old, and he had begun of late to think life, even when surrounded by specimens, and enlivened by numerous publications concerning the animal creation, rather a mistake. So he assented, hurriedly, to James Dugdale's arguments, and the interview concluded by his promising to prevent Margaret's marriage taking place for two years, when she would be nineteen.

But Mr Carteret and James Dugdale both knew that the real decision of that matter rested not with them, but with Mrs Carteret, and that, if she decreed that Margaret should be married next week, married next week she inevitably would be. So the ex-tutor addressed himself to his cousin, with whom he adopted a different line of argument.

'I know you don't care about Margaret,' he said; 'but I do; and I know you admire Lieutenant Godfrey Hungerford, which I do not; but you care what people say of you, Sibylla, as much as any one, I know; and you will get unpleasantly talked about if the girl is allowed to marry, so young, a man whom you know little or nothing about, and who is a scoundrel, if ever there was one, or I am more mistaken than I generally am. Take care, Sibylla, your husband is notoriously under your guidance, and you will have to bear the blame if this marriage takes place too soon; it is a serious thing, and you have never been a fond stepmother, you know.'

Mrs Carteret loved her cousin, and feared him; she also had a great respect for his judgment; and he had gone to work with her in the right way. The result was satisfactory to the ex-tutor, who took himself to task concerning his own motives, but found no room for self-condemnation.

'If I could suppose for a moment,' he thought, 'that I am insincere in this thing—that I am actuated by any selfish feeling or hope regarding Margaret—I should hesitate; but I know I am not: my heart is pure of such self-deception; my brain has no such cobwebs of folly in it. Separated from him finally,—if I can contrive to part them,—held back from her fate for a while, by my means, at all events she will only dislike me the more. And my conviction respecting this man,—is that prejudice?—is that an unjust dislike?—is it pique, because he has good looks, and grace, and good manners, and I have none of these? Is it spite, because he has been insolent to me when he dared, and, in a covert way, more insolent still, when these simple people did not understand him? No; I can answer to myself for single-mindedness in this matter. I might not have seen so plainly had not Margaret's happiness been at stake. But I do see; I do not only fancy. I do judge; I do not only imagine.'

So James Dugdale carried his point. Margaret resented his interference bitterly; she learned that his arguments had induced her stepmother to take the view to which her father had acceded; and she raged against him and denounced him as insolent, presuming, intolerable.

But she liked the idea of the long engagement, too. She was romantic and imaginative, and her bright pure young heart—all given up to what was in reality a creation of her fancy, but in which she saw the dazzling realization of her girlish dreams—was satisfied with the assurance of loving and being loved.

The presence of her lover was happiness, and his absence was hardly sorrow. Had she not his letters? Were there ever such letters? she thought; and while she exulted in all the delicious exclusiveness of the possession of such treasures, she almost longed that the world might know how transcendent a Agnes was this gallant soldier whom she loved.

She was glad that Godfrey felt so much disappointment at the delay; and the impertinence of any one who interfered to prevent the fulfilment of any wish of his, no words could adequately describe. But, for all that, Margaret was extremely happy, though she did hate James Dugdale.

Her lover encouraged her in this feeling, and when he and her brother had rejoined their regiment she restricted her intercourse with the officious ex-tutor to the barest acknowledgment of his presence. James Dugdale took this mode of procedure calmly, and applied himself to the task of finding out all that was to be ascertained concerning the circumstances, character, and antecedents of Lieutenant Godfrey Hungerford.

CHAPTER III.

DISCOMFITURE.

WHEN the engagement between Godfrey Hungerford and Margaret Carteret had lasted six months, during which time James Dugdale had contrived to learn several facts to that gentleman's disadvantage, Haldane Carteret made his appearance unexpectedly at Chayleigh. Margaret's first look at her brother revealed to her quick instinctive fears that his errand had in it something unfriendly to her love. With all the selfishness which comes of an engrossing feeling, she was insensible to any other impulse of alarm.

Margaret was right; her brother was come to unsay all he had said of Godfrey Hungerford—to tell his father that he had been deceived in his friend—to try to undo the work he had helped to do.

'He drinks and gambles, Margaret; for God's sake, don't marry a man with such vices,' said Haldane eagerly to his sister.

Her father roused himself, and warned her too; but the girl was obdurate. She only knew of such things by name; they had no meaning to her as terrible realities of life; and then she had her lover's letters—the priceless, charming, incomparable letters—and they told her that her brother had come round to Dugdale's way of thinking, and had turned against him because he had interfered to keep him out of some boyish scrapes.

The strongest and most spurious of all arguments too, used to a loving foolish girl, were not wanting. If even he were guilty of some follies, granting that he was not a perfect being, could he fail to become so under her influence—could he resist such perfection as hers, become the light and guidance of his home? It is needless to repeat the flimsy foolish strain of the arguments which bewildered and beguiled the girl. She met her father and her brother with vehement opposition, and replied to everything they urged, that she alone knew, she only understood Godfrey, and she was not going to forsake him to serve the turn of interested calumniators.

This taunt, aimed at the brother, did not hit the mark. He had not the least notion to what it referred. The young man spoke frankly and gently to the infatuated girl, lamented his own easy credulity which had at first betrayed his judgment, and finally left the matter in his father's hands, only entreating him to be firm, and to take into consideration, in addition to what he had told him, certain circumstances which had come to the knowledge of James Dugdale. For himself, the pain of enforced association with his quondam friend would soon be at an end. The brigade of Royal Artillery to which he belonged was then under orders for Canada, and this was to be his farewell visit to his home.

The brother and sister parted, in sorrow on Haldane's part—in silent and sullen estrangement on Margaret's. The girl's heart was full of angry and bitter revolt, and of the keen indignation which inexperienced youth feels against those who strive to serve it against its will. They were trying to protect her from herself—to save her from the worst of evils—the most cruel of destinies; and she treated them as if they had been, as indeed she believed them to be her worst enemies.

But they were not to succeed—Margaret was not to be saved. The girl's life at home—though no one molested her—though her father, if the matter were not pressed upon his attention, took no notice—though her stepmother was, as usual, coldly but civilly negligent of her—though James Dugdale maintained his inoffensive reserve—became intolerable to her; intolerable through its loueliness—intolerable by reason of its cross-purposes. The one thought, the one image, the one hope for which she lived was not only unshared, but condemned by those with whom she lived. The one name precious to her heart, delightful to her ears, was never spoken within her hearing—the little world she lived in ignored him who was all the world to her.

When Haldane Carteret had been three months in Canada, Godfrey Hungerford was dismissed the service for conduct unbecoming an officer and a gentleman; and in another month, Margaret Carteret had clandestinely left her home, joined her lover, and become his wife.

The shock to her father was very severe. It was the first misfortune of his life, including his first wife's death, to which 'specimens' offered no alleviation. It was not an

evil which brought finality with it; and Mr Carteret therefore found it difficult to bear. If Margaret had died, her
father would have grieved for her, no doubt, but there
would have been au end of it; now, though no one could
foresee or foretell the end, it was easy to prognosticate evil
as the result, and impossible to hope for good.

Like all men of his sort, Mr Carteret had a great horror
of the openly violent and aggressive vices of men. He was
incapable of understanding the amount of suffering to be
inflicted upon women by the supineness, selfishness, indo-
lence, imprudence, or eccentricity of their husbands and
fathers; but the mere idea of a woman being in the power
of a man who actually got drunk, lost or won money at
cards or dice, used bad language, or had any stain of dis-
honesty on his name, was terrible to his harmless, if value-
less, nature.

Mrs Carteret was extremely indifferent. Of course it
was an unpleasant occurrence, and people would talk unpleasantly about it; but she had never pretended to care
much for, or interfere with, Miss Carteret,—and no one
could blame her.

Of all those who had shared her life, who had seen her
grow from childhood to girlhood, James Dugdale was the
only one who had made Margaret Carteret's character a
subject of close and loving study—the only one who understood its strength and its weakness, its forcible points of
contrast, its lurking dangers, its unseen resources. He
knew her intellectual qualities, he knew her imaginativeness,
and understood the danger which lurked in it for her—a
danger which had already taken so delusive and fatal a form.
With all the prescience of a calm and unselfish affection, he
feared for the girl's future, and grieved as only mature wisdom and disinterested love can grieve over the follies and

illusions, the inevitable suffering and disenchantment, of youth and wilfulness.

'She has a dreadful life before her,' said her misjudged and despised friend to himself, as he left Margaret's father, after the two had discussed the letter in which the misguided girl had informed him of her marriage; 'a dreadful life, I fear, and believe; but, if she lives through it, and over it, and takes it rightly, she may be a noble and strong woman yet, though never a happy one.'

For some time Margaret Hungerford's communications with her family were brief and infrequent. She said nothing in her letters of happiness or the reverse, and she made no request to be permitted to revisit her former home. She never wrote to or heard from her brother.

After a while a formal application was made to Mr Carteret by Mr Hungerford for pecuniary assistance, as he had determined to try his fortune in Australia. To this Mr Carteret replied that he would give Margaret half the small fortune which was to have been hers on his death, but required that it should be distinctly understood that she had nothing more to expect from him.

Mr Carteret went up to London and drew the sum he had named, 500l., out of the funds, and availed himself of that opportunity to make his will, by which he bequeathed to his son all his property, a life-interest in the greater part of which had been secured to his wife by settlement. This done, and provided with the money he had named, he went to see Margaret and her husband. The meeting was brief and final. Mr Carteret returned on the following day to Chayleigh.

Godfrey Hungerford and his wife were to sail for Sydney in a fortnight, he told Mrs Carteret, in reply to her polite but quite uninterested inquiries. Nor was he much more communicative to James Dugdale.

'How does she look?' he asked.

The father made no reply, but shook his head, and moved his hands nervously among the papers on the table before him.

'Already!' said James Dugdale, when he had softly left the room, and then he went away and shut himself up alone.

CHAPTER IV

THE IDEAL AND THE REAL.

IF it were possible to linger over the story of Margaret Hungerford's life—if other and later interests did not peremptorily claim attention—how much might be said concerning it? On the surface, it had many features in common with other lives; and the destruction of a fancy, the awaking to a truth, terrible and not to be eluded, is the least rare of mental processes. But the individual history of every mind, of every heart, has features unlike those of all others—features worthy, in even the humblest and simplest lives, of close scanning and of faithful reproduction. Margaret Hungerford was not an ordinary person; she had strongly-pronounced intellectual and moral characteristics, and her capacity, whether for good or evil time and her destiny alone could tell, was great.

The very intensity of her nature, which had made it easy for her to be deceived, easy for her to build a fair fabric of hope and love on no sounder foundation than her fancy, made it inevitable that the truth should come with terrible force to her, and be understood in its fullest extent and in its darkest meaning—that most full of terror and despair.

The external circumstances of her life subsequent to her marriage did not affect Margaret Hungerford so much as might have been anticipated, in consideration of her delicate nurture, her previous life of seclusion, and her habitual refinement. She was destined to encounter many vicissitudes, to endure poverty, hardship, uncertainty, solitude of the absolute kind, and of that kind which is still more unbearable—enforced companionship with the mean and base, not in position merely, but in soul.

She had to endure many actual privations—to do many things, to witness many scenes which, if they had been unfolded to her in the home of her girlhood, uncongenial as it had been, as probabilities lurking in the plan of the future, she would have merely regarded with unalarmed incredulity, would have put aside as things which never could have any existence.

But these things, when they came, she bore well—bore them with strength and patience, with quiet resolution and almost indifference, which, had there been any one to contemplate the girl's life, and study her character at that time, would have revealed the truth that worse things than privation and hardship had come to her, and had rendered them indifferent to her.

Worse things had come. Knowledge and experience, which had outraged her pride and tortured her love, crushed her faith, scattered her hopes, and left her life a desert waste, whence the flowers of youth and trust had been uprooted, and which lay bare to be trampled under-foot of invading foes.

Margaret's delusion had lasted so short a time after her marriage, that the first feeling her discovery of the utter worthlessness of the man into whose hands she had committed her fate produced in her mind was dread and distrust of herself.

Was this fading away of love, this dying out of all respect, of all enthusiasm, this dreary hopelessness and fast coming disbelief in good, was all this inconstancy on her part ? Was she false to her own feelings, or had she mistaken them ? Was she light and fickle, as men were said to be ?

But this dread soon subsided : it could not long disturb Margaret's clear good sense. The fault was not hers; she was not inconstant, though she no longer loved Godfrey Hungerford. The truth was, she had never known him; there was no such person as her fancy had created and called by his name.

She had believed herself to be doing a fine heroic thing when she married a disgraced man, a man unjustly judged of his fellows, one against whom the world had set itself— why, she did not quite know, but probably from envy— and who therefore needed her love and fidelity more than a prosperous man could need them. It was a foolish, girlish, not unnatural delusive notion of grandeur and self-sacrifice, and, added to the fascination exerted over her by Godfrey Hungerford's good looks and artistic love-making, it had hurried Margaret to her doom.

The girl married, as she believed, a hero, with a few follies perhaps, all to be forsworn and forsaken when she should be his, to guide and inspire every moment of his life, and whose unjust penalties her love was to render harmless. What did she not believe him to be ! Brave, true, generous, devoted, clever, energetic, unworldly, poetical, high-minded, and pure—the ideal man who was to disprove those horrid sayings of disappointed persons, that

the lover and the husband are very different beings, and
that 'man's love is of man's life a thing apart.'

They would prove it to be their 'whole existence.'
Could any sacrifice be too great to make for such a prize
as this? No. The sacrifice was made by him. Who
would not have loved and married Godfrey Hungerford?
She did not believe that any one could be so bad as to
believe the accusation brought against him by a low mean
clique, a set of men who could not bear to know that he
was cleverer at card-playing than they were—just as he
was cleverer at anything else—and who did not know how
to lose their money like gentlemen. Of course, as he never
could be secured against meeting persons of the sort, it
was much better that Godfrey should make up his mind, as
he had done, never to touch a card after their marriage.

And then how great was his love for her! How delightful was the scheme of the future, according to his casting
of it! So Margaret dreamed her dream, and when the
waking came she blamed herself that she could dream it
no longer, and could not be lulled to sleep again.

Godfrey Hungerford has no place in this story, and there
is no need to enter into details of the life he led, and condemned his wife to. He proved the exact reverse of all she
had believed him. Base, mean, cowardly, in the sense of the
cowardice which makes a man systematically cruel to every
creature, human and brute, within his power, though ready
to face danger for bravado's, and exertion for boasting's sake,
or either for that of money—a liar, a gambler, and a pro-
fligate.

He laughed at her credulity when she quoted his promises
to her, and ridiculed her amazement and disgust as ignorance
of life, girlish folly, and squeamishness. In a fitful, 'worthless' sort of way, he liked and admired her to the end; but

the truthfulness that was in her prevented Margaret from taking advantage of this contemptible remnant of feeling to obtain easier terms of life. She had ceased to love him, and she never disguised the fact—she let him see it; when he questioned her, in a moment of maudlin sentiment, she told him so quite plainly ; and her tyrant made the truthfulness which could not stoop to simulation a fresh cause of complaint against her.

What Margaret suffered, no words, not even her own, could tell; but the material troubles, the grinding anxieties of her life, deadened her sense of grief after a time. They were always poor. Money melted in the hands of her worthless, selfish husband. Sometimes he made a little, in some of the numerous ways in which money was to be made in colonial life, sometimes he was quite unemployed. He was always dissolute and a spendtbrift.

It was hard training for Margaret, severe teaching, and not more full of actual pain, privation, and toil than of bitter humiliation. They moved about from place to place, for at each Godfrey Hungerford became known and shunned.

Villany and vice were loud and rampant indeed in the New World then, as now; but he was not so clever as the superior villains, and not so low, not so irretrievably ruffianly, as the inferior ruffians, and it fell out, somehow, that he did not find any permanent place, or take any specific rank, among them. Of necessity, suffering, both moral and material, was his wife's lot, and it was wonderful that such suffering did not degrade, that it only hardened her. It certainly did harden her, making her cold, indifferent, and difficult to be touched by, or convinced of, good, or truth, or honesty.

Of necessity, also, her life had been devoid of companionship. Too proud to tell her sorrows, and unable to endure

the associations into which her husband's evil life would have
led her had she been driven by loneliness to relax in her
resolute isolation, she had neither sympathy nor pity in her
wretchedness.   But at length, and when things were going
very hard and ill with her, she found a friend.

Time, suffering, and disenchantment had taught Margaret Hungerford many hard and heavy, but salutary, lessons,
before the days came which brought her fate this alleviation;
and she did not regret it, because it had been procured for
her by the care and solicitude of James Dugdale.

Her love had died—more than died; for there is reverence and pious grief, with sweetness in its agony, and
cherished recollections, to modify death and make it merciful
—it had perished.   So had her dislike of James Dugdale.
He had been right, and she had been wrong; and though
he could never be her friend, because she never could admit
to him the one fact or the other, she thought gently and
regretfully of him, when she thought of her old home and
of the past at all, which was not often, for the present
absorbed her usually in its misery and its toil.

When, in the course of their wanderings, the Hunger-
fords went to the then infant town, now the prosperous
city, of Melbourne, Margaret sent home one of her infrequent letters to her father.   Thus James Dugdale learned
that the woman whose fate he had so unerringly foreseen—
the woman he loved with calm, disinterested, clear-sighted
affection—was at length within reach of his influence, of his
indirect help.

An old friend, schoolfellow, and college chum—one Hayes
Meredith, a younger man than James Dugdale by a few
years—had been among the first of those tempted from the
life of monotonous toil in England by the vast and exciting

prospects which the young colony offered to energy, industry, ability, and courage.

Hayes Meredith possessed all these, and some capital too. He had settled at Port Phillip, and was a thriving and respected member of the motley community when Godfrey and Margaret Hungerford arrived to swell the tide of adventure and misery. To him James Dugdale wrote, on behalf of the woman whose need he divined, whose unhappiness he felt, with the instinct of sympathy.

Hayes Meredith responded nobly to his old friend's appeal. He befriended Margaret steadily, with and without her husband's knowledge; he won her affection, conquered her reserve, softened her pride, and, though her fate was beyond amelioration by human aid, he succeeded in making her actual, everyday life more endurable.

When Margaret was sought out by Hayes Meredith, release was drawing near, release from the tremendous evil of her marriage. Godfrey Hungerford, by this time utterly incapable of any steady pursuit, and seized with one of the reckless, restless fits which were becoming more and more frequent with him, joined a party of explorers bound for the unknown interior of the continent, and, regardless of Margaret's fears and necessities, left her alone in the town.

For months she heard nothing of him, or the fate of the expedition; months during which she was kept from destitution only by Hayes Meredith's generous and unfailing aid.

At length news came; a few stragglers from the party of explorers returned. Godfrey Hungerford was not among them; and the remnant related that he had been murdered, with two others, by a tribe of aborigines.

Hayes Meredith told Margaret the truth; he sustained and comforted her in the early days of her horror and grief;

he counselled her return to England, and provided money for her voyage. He secured her cabin and the services of Rose Moore. It was he who bade her farewell upon the deck of the Boomerang—he of whom she thought as her only friend.

Margaret had little power of feeling, love, or gratitude in her now, as she believed, and that little was exerted for the alert, kindly-voiced, gray-haired, keen-eyed man who left her with a heavy heart, and said to himself, as the boat shot away from the ship's side, 'Poor girl! she has had hard lines of it hitherto. I wonder what is before her in England!'

CHAPTER V

CHAYLEIGH.

A BRIGHT soft day in the autumn—a day which appealed to all who dwelt in houses to come forth and taste the last lingering flavour of the summer in the sweet air—a day so still and peaceful that the sudden rustle of the leaves, as a few of their number (*ennuyés* leaves, tired of life sooner than their fellows) detached themselves, and came, gently wafted by the imperceptible air, to the ground, made one look round, as though at an intrusion upon its perfect repose—a day which appealed to memory, and said, 'Am I not like some other day in your life, on which you have pondered many things in your heart, and looked far back into the past without the agony of regret, and on into the future undisturbed by dread—a restful day, when life has seemed not bad to have, but very, very good to leave?'—a day on which any settled, stern, inexorable occupation seemed harder, more unbearable than usual, even to the least reasonable and most moderate idler—a day on which the house which Margaret Carteret had forsaken looked particularly beautiful, tranquil, and inviting.

The orderliness of Chayleigh was delightful; it was not formal, not oppressive; it was eminently tasteful. Inside the house and outside it order reigned, without tyrannizing. The lawn was always swept with extreme nicety, and the flower-beds, though not pruned down to a tantalizing precision, bore evident signs of artistic care.

The house stood almost in the centre of the small grounds, and long wide French windows in front, and bow windows in the rear, opened on smooth grassy terraces, which fell away by gentle inclines towards the flower-garden in front, and at the back towards a pleasaunce, with high prim alleys, and bosquets which in the pride of summer were thickset with roses; and so, to some clumps of noble forest-trees, behind which, and hidden, was the neat wire-fence which bounded the small demesne.

On this soft autumnal day, the three bow windows which opened on the terrace at the back of the house were open, and every now and then the white curtains faintly fluttered, and the leaves of the creepers which luxuriously festooned the window-frames gently rustled. Far above the height of the central window, an aspiring passion-flower, rich in the stiff, majestic, symbolical blossom, stretched its branches, until they wreathed the window just above the centre bow, and aided an impertinent rose to look into the room. They had looked in ever since the one had blossom and the other leaves, but they had seen nothing there that lived or moved.

The middle room, above the suite of drawing-rooms—whose rosewood furniture, whose Ambusson carpets, and whose sparkling girandoles formed the chief delight and

pride of Mrs Carteret's not particularly capacious heart—
had not been used since Margaret Carteret had left her
home to follow the fortunes of her lover.

That such was the case was not due to any sentiment on
Mr Carteret's part, or any spite on that of his wife. If the
former had happened to want additional space for any of his
drying or 'curing' processes, he would have invaded his
daughter's forsaken room without the slightest hesitation,
and, indeed, without recalling the circumstance of her
former occupation, of his own accord; while it was quite
safe from interference on the part of the latter for another
and a different reason.

Mrs Carteret's rooms were perfectly comfortable and
sufficient, and she never had 'staying company.' She knew
better. She was quite sufficiently hospitable without in-
flicting that trouble on herself, and she had no notion of it.
Indeed, she never had any notion of doing anything which
she did not thoroughly like, or of putting up with any kind
of inconvenience for a moment if it were possible to free
herself from it; and she had generally found it very possible.
Life had rolled along wonderfully smoothly, on the whole,
for Mrs Carteret. She possessed one advantage which does
not always fall to the lot of supremely selfish and heartless
people—she had an easy temper.

It is refreshing sometimes to observe how much utterly
selfish people, whose sole object in life is to secure pleasure
and to banish pain, suffer by the infliction upon themselves of
their own temper. But Mrs Carteret was bucklered against
fate, even on that side. She took excellent and successful
care that no one else should annoy her, and she never annoyed herself. It would have afforded a philosophic observer, indeed, some congenial occupation of mind to divine
from what possible quarter, save that of severe bodily pain,

discomfiture could reach Mrs Carteret. She was very well off, perfectly healthy, wholly indifferent to every existing human being except herself and her cousin, had everything her own way as regarded both objects of affection, had got rid of her stepdaughter, and had a very comfortable settlement 'in case anything should happen'—according to the queer formula adopted in speaking of the only absolute certainty in human events—to Mr Carteret.

This seemingly-invulnerable person had no need of Margaret's room then, and when James Dugdale said to her,

'If you don't want that middle room over the drawing-room for any particular purpose, I should be glad to have the use of it for mounting my drawings, and so on; the light is very good,' she said at once,

'O yes; you mean Margaret's room, do you not? I don't want it in the least. I will have it put to rights for you at once; it's full of all her trumpery.'

No third person listening to the two would ever have discerned that any matter of feeling, or even embarrassment, had any connection with the subject under mention, still less that the 'Margaret' in question had so lately left the home of her girlhood on a desperate quest, which the woman who spoke of her complacently believed to be desperate.

'Yes, I mean that room,' said James Dugdale in a careless tone; 'but pray don't have anything in it touched. I will see to all that myself; in fact, presuming on your permission, I have put a lot of my things in there, and the servants would play the deuce if they meddled with them. I may keep the key, Sibylla, I suppose?'

'Of course,' replied Mrs Carteret; and from that moment she never gave the matter a thought, and James Dugdale had the key of Margaret's room, and he did put some sketch-books, some sheets of Bristol board, and other adjuncts of his favourite pursuit on a table, and thus formally constituted his possession and his pretext. But he seldom unlocked the door ; he rarely entered the apartment, even at first, and more and more rarely as time stole on, and all his worst fears and forebodings about Margaret Hungerford had been realized.

Sometimes, when all the house was quiet, on moonlight nights, his pale face and bent figure might have been seen, framed in the window, between the branches of the passion-flower which he had trained. There he would stand awhile, leaning against the woodwork and gazing into the sky, in whose vastness, whose distance, whose sameness over all the world, there is surely some vague comfort for the yearnings of absence, uncertainty, even hopeless separation, or why is the relief of it so often, so uniformly sought?

Sometimes, but not often, he wrote in Margaret's room ; one letter which he had written there had exerted a great influence upon her fate, how great he little knew. All the girl's little possessions were in the room, just as she had left them.

Tidy housemaids, with accurate ideas of the fitness of things, had come to and gone away from Chayleigh since the sole daughter of the house had taken her perilous way, according to her headstrong will, and had been disturbed, and even mutinous, in their minds concerning the ' middle room.' But on the whole they had obeyed orders; and James Dugdale, who had long ceased to be the ' tutor,' and was supposed to be Mrs Carteret's stepbrother by the servants of late date in the establishment, enjoyed undisturbed possession of the trumpery water-colour sketches; the little desk with a sloping top, with ' Souvenir ' engraved in flourishes on a mother-o'-pearl heart inserted over the lock; the embroidery-frame, the bead-worked watch-pocket, and the little library which occupied two hanging shelves, and chiefly consisted of the

'Beauties' of the poets, and a collection of 'Friendship's Offerings' and 'Forget-me-nots.'

James Dugdale's thoughts were busy with Margaret Hungerford that sweet autumn day—more busy with her than usual, more full of apprehension. The time that had elapsed had not deadened the feelings with which he regarded the wilful girl, who had scorned his interference, scoffed at and resented his advice, but been obliged to avail herself of his aid.

He knew that she had done so, but he knew nothing more. And as he roamed about the garden, and the terrace, and the pleasaunce, and rambled away to where the forest-trees stood stately, idly treading the fallen leaves under his listless feet, so lately in their green brightness far above his head, he sickened with longing to know more definitely the fate of the absent girl.

'She hated me then,' he said with a sigh, as he turned once more towards the house; 'and she is just the woman to hate me more because she has found out for herself that I was right.'

He little knew how fully, to how far greater an extent than he had discovered it, Margaret had learned the worthlessness of Godfrey Hungerford.

As he crossed the garden, a woman-servant came towards him, and asked him for the key of 'the middle room.' The request jarred upon him somehow, and he asked rather sharply what it was wanted for.

'We are getting the cleaning done, sir; master and missus is to be home on Saturday.'

James Dugdale handed the key to the housemaid, and entered the drawing-room through the open window.

'I may as well write to Haldane,' he muttered. 'The Canadian mail leaves to-morrow.'

When James Dugdale had written his letter, he went out again; but this time he took his way to the village, intending to post the packet, and then pursue his way to a 'bit' in the vicinity from which he was making a water-colour drawing.

As he passed the inn which occupied the place of honour in the hilly little street, the coach which ran daily from a large town on the south coast to London was drawn up before the door, and the process of changing horses was being accomplished to the lively satisfaction of numerous bystanders, to whom this event, though of daily occurrence, never ceased to be exciting and interesting.

James Dugdale glanced carelessly at the clustering villagers and the idlers about the inn-door, of whom a few touched their hats or pulled their hair in his honour; observed casually that two female figures were standing in the floor-clothed passage, and that one of the ostlers was lifting a heavy trunk, of a seafaring exterior, down from the luggage-laden top of the coach; and then passed on, and forgot all these ordinary occurrences. He took his way to the scene of his intended sketch, and was soon busily engaged with his work.

When the autumnal day was drawing to its close, and the growing keenness of the air began to make itself felt, quickly too, by his sensitive frame, James Dugdale turned his steps homewards, and, taking the lower road, without again passing through the village, he skirted the clumps of forest-trees, and entered the little demesne by a small gate which led into the pleasaunce.

He had almost reached the grassy terrace, when, glancing upwards, as was his frequent custom,—it had been his habit in the time gone by, when Margaret's light figure and girlish face had often met the upturned glance,—he saw that the window was wide open, and some one was in the room ; saw this with quick impatience, which made him step back a little, so as to get a clearer view of the intruder, and to mutter, as he did so,

'Those confounded servants! What can they be doing there up to this time?'

But, as he murmured the words, James Dugdale started violently, and then stood in fixed, motionless, incredulous amazement. The window of the middle room was wide open, and against the woodwork, framed by the blossoms and foliage of the passion-flower, leaned a slight figure, in a heavy black dress.

The slender hands were clasped together, and showed white against the sombre garb; the pale, clear-cut, severe young face, lighted by the last rays of the quickly-setting autumn sun, looked out upon the tranquil scene ; but on every feature sat the deepest abstraction. The eyes were heedless of all near objects, fixed apparently upon the trees in the distance ; they took no heed of the figure standing in rapt astonishment upon the terrace.

Not until James Dugdale uttered her name with a faltering, with an almost frightened voice, as one might address a spirit, did the face in the window droop, and the eyes search for the speaker. But then Margaret Hungerford leaned forward, and said, quite calmly,

'Yes, Mr Dugdale, it is I.'

CHAPTER VI.

HALF-CONFIDENCES.

'You cannot surely be serious—you do not really mean it?' said James Dugdale, in a pleading tone, to Margaret Hungerford, as, some hours after he had discovered her presence at Chayleigh, they were talking together in the drawing-room.

'I do mean it,' she replied. 'You never understood me, I think, and you certainly do not understand me now, if you think I shall remain here dependent on my father, having left his house as I did.'

James Dugdale did not speak for some minutes. He was pondering upon what she had said. He had never understood her! If not he, who ever had? Unjust to him she had always been, and she was still unjust to him. But that did not matter: it was of her he must think, not of himself.

The first bewildering surprise of Margaret's arrival had passed away; the mingled strangeness and familiarity of seeing her again, changed as she was, in the old home so long forsaken, had taken its place, and James Dugdale was looking at her, and listening to her, like a man in a dream.

Their meeting had been very calm and emotionless. Margaret, in addition to the hardness of manner which had grown upon her in her hard life, had felt no pleasure in seeing James Dugdale again. She had not quite forgiven him, even yet, and, though she was relieved by finding that the first explanations were to be given to him, and not to her father or Mrs Carteret, she had made them ungraciously enough, and with just sufficient formal acknowledgment of the service which James Dugdale had rendered her, in securing to her the friendship and aid of Hayes Meredith, as convinced her sensitive hearer that she would rather have been indebted to the kindness of any other person.

On certain points he found her reserve invulnerable; and he was not slow to suspect that she had made up her mind exactly as to how much of her past life she would reveal, and how much should remain concealed; and he did not doubt her power of adhering to such a resolution. She had briefly alluded to her widowhood, acknowledged the kindness she had experienced from Hayes Meredith, said a little about the poverty in which he had found her, and had then left the subject of herself and all concerning her, as if it wearied her, and with a decision of manner which prevented James Dugdale from questioning her further.

Her questions regarding her father, her brother, and all that had occurred at Chayleigh during her absence, were numerous and minute, and James answered them without reserve or hesitation. They chiefly related to facts. Margaret dealt but slightly in sentiment; but when she asked James if her father spoke of her sometimes, there was a little change in the tone of her voice, a slight accession of paleness which she could not disguise.

'At first, very seldom; in fact, hardly ever, Margaret, for I see you wish the whole truth, and nothing but the truth; but more frequently of late. Only the day before he and Mrs Carteret went to Bath, he—you remember his way —was showing me a peculiarly repulsive specimen of some singularly hideous insect, and he said, "How pleased Margery would have been with *that*." Quite a hallucination, if I remember rightly, but still pleasant to hear him say it, and showed me that he was thinking of you. You see this as I do?'

'O yes,' she answered with a smile that was a little hard and bitter, 'very pleasant; indeed, the pleasantest possible association of ideas according to papa. And—and Mrs Carteret?'

James Dugdale hesitated for a little, and then he said,

'You remember what Sibylla is, Margaret, and you know she never cared much for you, or Haldane—'

'Particularly for *me*,' she interrupted, in a tone whose assumed lightness did not impose on James. 'Well, she need not fear any intrusion or importunity from me. I have come here because I must—I must see my father once more, before I have for ever done with the old life and begun with the new.'

'Are you going away again, Margaret?' said James, astonished. 'Going away, after having come home through such suffering and difficulty! Why is this?'

And then it was that Margaret asked him if he were really serious in supposing she had any other intention.

The truth was, she had very vague notions of what she should do with herself. The pride and self-will of her nature, which the suffering she had undergone in Australia had somewhat tamed, had had time for their reawakening during the long voyage; and it was not in the most amiable of moods that Margaret reached her former home.

'Whatever my fault may have been, I have fully expiated it; and I must have peace now, and forgetfulness, if it is to be had,' was the form her thoughts took.

She had not been recognized at the village inn, where she had left Rose Moore and her scanty luggage, and the servant who had opened the door of her father's house to her was a stranger. He might fairly have hesitated to admit a lady whom he did not know; but Margaret's manner of announcing herself permitted no hesitation within his courage. His master and mistress were not at home, the man said, but she could see Mr Dugdale when he came in. So she walked into the drawing-room, and James was sought for, but not found.

What agony of spirit the young widow underwent, when she found herself once more in the scene of the vanished past, none but she ever knew. The worst of it had passed away when James saw her leaning out of the window, a picture framed in the branches of the passion-flower.

The hours of the evening went rapidly by, though the talk of the strangely-assorted companions was constrained and bald. Margaret was resolute in her refusal to remain at Chayleigh. James Dugdale, she argued, might believe that her father would gladly receive her; but he could not know that he would, and she would await that welcome before she made her old home even a temporary abode. A few sentences sufficed to show James that this determination was not to be overcome.

' At least you are not alone,' he said; and then she explained to him that Hayes Meredith had engaged an Irish girl, named Rose Moore, to act as her maid during the voyage, and that the girl, having become attached to her, was willing to defer her departure to Ireland for a few days, until she, Margaret, had made some definite arrangement about her own future.

' I got used to Irish people at Melbourne,' said Margaret, ' and I like them. I have half a mind to go to Ireland with Rose. I suppose people's children want governesses there, and people themselves want companions as well as here; and I fancy they are kind and cordial there.'

' You must be very much altered, Margaret,' returned

James gravely, 'if you are fit to be either a governess or a *dame de compagnie.* I don't think you had much in you to fit you for either function.'

'I am very much altered,' she said; 'and what I am fit for, or not fit for, neither you nor any one can tell. There is only one thing which would come to me that would surprise or disconcert me *now.*'

She rose as she spoke, and drew her heavy black cloak, which she had only loosened, not laid aside, closely around her.

'And that is—' said James.

'Finding myself happy again, or being deceived into thinking myself so,' she said quickly and bitterly.

This was the first thoroughly unrestrained sentence she had spoken in all their conversation, the first clear glimpse she had given James Dugdale into the depths of her heart and experience.

They went out of the house together, and she walked by his side—he did not offer his arm—to the village. The night was bright and beautiful, and some of its calm came to the heart of Margaret, and reflected itself in her pale steadfast face. The road which they took wound past the well-kept fences and ornamental palings of a handsome place, much larger than Chayleigh, which, in Margaret's time, had been in the possession of Sir Richard Davyntry, whose good graces, and those of Lady Davyntry, she remembered her stepmother to have been particularly anxious to cultivate.

Mrs Carteret had not succeeded remarkably well in this design, and her failure was conspicuously due to her treatment of Margaret; for Lady Davyntry was a motherly kind of woman, much younger than Mrs Carteret, and whose own childless condition was a deep and unaffectedly-avowed grief to her.

As Margaret and her companion passed the gates of Davyntry, she remembered these 'childish things,' as they seemed to her now, and she paused to look at the stately trees, and the fine old Elizabethan house, on whose gilded vane the moonlight was shining coldly.

She asked if Sir Richard and Lady Davyntry were staying there just now, adding, 'As I remember them, they were not people who, having a country house and place combining everything any one can possibly wish for, make a point of leaving it just when all is most beautiful.'

'No,' said James Dugdale, 'they certainly are not; and Sir Richard stuck to it, poor fellow, as long as he could; but he died nearly a year ago, and not at Davyntry either—at his brother-in-law's place in Scotland.'

'Indeed!' said Margaret. 'I am sorry for Sir Richard, and more sorry still for Lady Davyntry; she is a widow indeed, I am sure. Perhaps she wants a lady companion. I might offer myself: how pleased Mrs Carteret would be!'

'Margaret!' said James Dugdale reprovingly.

He spoke in the tone which had been familiar to him in the days when he had been 'the tutor' and Margaret his pupil; and she laughed for a moment with something of the same saucy laugh with which she had been used to meet a remonstrance from him in those old days. James Dugdale's heart beat rapidly at the sound; for the first time, her coming, her presence seemed real to him.

'Well, well, I won't be spiteful,' said Margaret. 'Is Lady Davyntry here?'

'Yes; she has been more than a month at Davyntry. Her brother is with her, and a remarkably nice fellow he is. I see a good deal of him.'

'I don't remember him. I don't think I ever saw him,' said Margaret absently. 'What is his name?'

James Dugdale did not note the question, but replied to the first part of the sentence.

'I don't think you can have seen him. He was abroad for some years after his sister's marriage; indeed, he never was here in Sir Richard's lifetime—never saw him, I believe, until he and Lady Davyntry went to Scotland, on a visit, and he died there.'

'Is he here now?' Margaret asked in an indifferent manner.

'Yes,' returned James; 'I told you so. He comes to Chayleigh a good deal. He is nearly as fond of natural history as your father, and nearly as fond of drawing as I am; so we are a mutual resource—Chayleigh and Davyntry I mean.'

'And his name?' again asked Margaret quietly.

'Did I not tell you? Don't you remember it? Surely you must have heard the name; it is not a common one—Fitzwilliam Meriton Baldwin.'

'No, it is not common, and rather nice. I never heard it before, that I remember. We have arrived, I see; and there is Rose Moore looking out for me, like an impulsive Irish girl as she is, instead of preserving the decorous indifference of the truly British domestic. You will let me know when my father arrives. No, I shall not go to Chayleigh again until his return. Good-night, Mr Dugdale.'

She had disappeared, followed by her attendant, whose frank handsome face had candidly expressed an amount of disapprobation of James Dugdale's personal appearance to which he was, fortunately, perfectly accustomed and philosophically indifferent. Fate had done its worst for him in that respect long before; and he had turned away from the inn-door, and was walking rapidly down the road again, when a cheery voice addressed him.

'Hallo, Dugdale! Where are you going at this time of night? and what are you thinking of? I shouted at you in vain, and thought I should never catch you. Are you going home? Yes?—then we shall be together as far as Davyntry.'

The speaker was a young man, perhaps six-and-twenty years old, a little over middle height, and, though not remarkably handsome, he presented as strong a contrast in personal appearance to James Dugdale as could be desired. He had a fair complexion, bright-blue eyes, with an expression of candour and happiness in them as rare as it was attractive, light-brown hair, and a lithe alert figure, full of grace and activity. In the few words which he had spoken there was something winning and open, a tone of entire sincerity and gladness almost boyish; and it had its charm for the older and careworn man, who answered cheerily, as he linked his arm with his own:

'It is always pleasant to meet you, Baldwin; but to-night it's a perfect god-send.'

CHAPTER VII.

THE OLD FAMILIAR FACES.

THE communication which James Dugdale made to Mr Carteret on his arrival at Chayleigh was received by that gentleman not altogether without agitation, but with more pleasure than the ex-tutor had expected.

Mr Carteret had missed his daughter, in his quiet way, and had occasionally experienced something which approached remorse during her absence, when he pondered on the

probabilities of her fate, and found himself forced to remember how different it might have been had he 'looked
after' the motherless girl a little more closely, had he extended some more sympathy to her and exerted himself
to understand her, instead of confining his fatherly fondness
to occasional petting and careful avoidance of being bored
by her.

Mr Carteret was easily reconciled to most things, but he
had never succeeded in reconciling himself thoroughly to
Margaret's marriage and her exile, and he heard of her
return with equal pleasure and relief. These feelings ex-
panded into positive joy when he learned the delightful fact
of Godfrey Hungerford's death.

In the first vague apprehension of James Dugdale's
news, he had imagined that Margaret had left her husband
and come home, and even that he hailed with satisfaction.
But to know that his son-in-law was safely dead was an
element of unmitigated good fortune in the matter. And so
strongly and unaffectedly did Mr Carteret feel this, that he
departed from his usual mild method of speech on the
occasion, and delivered himself of some very strong language indeed.

'The infernal scoundrel!' he said; 'he made her miserable, I've no doubt. She'll never tell us anything about it,
James, if I am not much mistaken in her, or she is not very
much changed; and so much the better. I don't want to
hear anything about him; I should like to think I should
never hear his name mentioned again as long as I live!'

'Most likely you never will hear it mentioned, sir,' said
James. 'If you like, I'll tell Margaret you would rather
she did not talk about him.'

'Do, do,' said Mr Carteret eagerly. He hated explanations, and would never encounter anything he disliked if he

could at all decently avoid doing so. 'The only good or pleasant thing that could be heard in connection with the fellow, I heard when you told me he was under the sod, and there is no use in hearing bad and unpleasant things. Of course, the child knows she is welcome home; and the very best thing she can do is to forget the scoundrel ever existed.'

The ignorance of human nature, and the oblivion of his wife's peculiarities, which this speech betrayed, were equally characteristic of Mr Carteret; but James Dugdale could not smile at them when Margaret was concerned.

He determined to say nothing to the young widow's father about her expressed resolution of leaving Chayleigh again, but to abandon that issue to circumstances and the success of the mode of argument he intended to pursue with Mrs Carteret. He would go and fetch Margaret home presently, when he had spoken to his cousin. He thought it better her father should not accompany him, and Mr Carteret, who had some very choice beetles to unpack and prepare, thought so too.

He delightedly anticipated Margaret's pleasure in exploring the extended treasures of his collection, and was altogether in such an elated state of mind that he had consigned the whole of Margaret's married life as completely to oblivion as he had forgotten the partner of that great disaster, by the time James Dugdale passed before the windows of his study on his way to fulfil his mission of peace and reconciliation.

It never occurred to him to think about how his wife was likely to take the news of Margaret's return. Mrs Carteret had not given him any trouble herself, or permitted other people to give him any trouble, since Margaret and Haldane had gone their own way in life, and he was not afraid of her departing now from that excellent rule of conduct.

'Margaret is not a child now, and they are sure to get on together,' said the mild and inexperienced elderly gentleman, as he daintily handled some insect remains as reverently as if they had been mummies of the Rameses; 'each can have her own way.' He had forgotten Margaret's 'own way,' and he knew very little about Mrs Carteret's.

It was rather odd that his wife did not come to talk about the news that James Dugdale had communicated to her. He wondered at that a little. He would go and find her, and they should talk it over together, presently, when he had put this splendid scarabæus all right,—a great creature!—how fortunate he had secured it, just as old Fooster was on the scent of it too!

And so Mr Carteret went on, and the minutes went on, and he had not yet completed his arrangements for the adequate display of the scarabæus, when two figures, one in heavy black robes, passed quickly between him and the light. A window-sash was thrown up from the outside, and Margaret Hungerford's arms were round her father's neck.

Under the roof of Chayleigh, on that bright autumn night, there was but one tranquil sleeper. That one was Mr Carteret. He was thoroughly happy. Margaret had come home, Godfrey Hungerford was dead, and she had never mentioned his name.

He felt some tepid gratitude towards Hayes Meredith : of course he should at once repay him the sums advanced to Margaret, and it would be a good opportunity of extending his correspondence and his scientific investigations — the Australian fauna had much to disclose.

He had experienced a slight shock at observing the change in Margaret's appearance; but that had passed away, and when Mr Carteret fell asleep that night he acknowledged that everything was for the best in the long-run.

Mrs Carteret had behaved very well. She had met Margaret kindly, with as much composure as if she had been away from home 'on a week's visit; had inquired whether 'her maid' would remain at Chayleigh; had added that 'her things' should be placed in her 'former' room; and had evinced no further consciousness of the tremendous change which had befallen her stepdaughter than was implied in the remark that 'widow's caps were not made so heavy now,' and that Margaret's 'crape skirt needed renewal.'

The evening had passed away quietly. To two of the four individuals who composed the little party it had seemed like a dream from which they expected soon to awaken. Those two were Margaret Hungerford and James Dugdale.

One slight interruption had occurred. A note had been handed to Mrs Carteret from Lady Davyntry. She had heard of the return of her former 'pet' to Chayleigh—the expression was as characteristic of Lady Davyntry as it was unsuitably applied to Margaret, who was an unpromising subject for 'petting'—and hoped to see her soon. Mr Meriton Baldwin would forego the pleasure of calling at Chayleigh that evening, as he could not think of intruding so soon after the arrival of Mrs Hungerford.

Mrs Carteret threw down the letter with rather an ill-tempered jerk, and her face bore an expression which Margaret remembered with painful distinctness, as she said,

'Very absurd, I think. I don't suppose that Margaret would object to our seeing our friends because she is here.'

The speech was not framed as a question; but Margaret answered it, lifting up her head and her fair throat as she spoke, after a fashion which one observer, at least, thought infinitely beautiful.

4

'Certainly not, Mrs Carteret.   Pray do not allow me to interfere with any of your usual proceedings.'

And then she went on talking to her father about the habits of the kangaroo.

The thoughts which held Mrs Carteret's eyes waking that night were anything but agreeable.   She did not exactly know how she stood with regard to her stepdaughter. If she determined on making the house too unpleasant for her to bear it, she might find herself in collision with her husband and her cousin at once, unless she could contrive that the unpleasantness should be of a kind which Margaret's pride—which she detected to be little, if at all, subdued by the experiences of her married life—would induce her to hide from the observation of both.

Margaret should not live at Chayleigh if Mrs Carteret could prevent it; but whatever means she used to carry her purpose into effect must be such as James Dugdale could not discover or thwart.   The thing would be difficult to do; but Mrs Carteret had well-grounded confidence in her own power of carrying a point, and this was one which must be held over for the present.   It was agreeable to be able to decide that, at all events, Margaret was no beauty, that she was decidedly much less handsome than she had been as what Mrs Carteret called 'a raw girl.'

And this was true, to the perception of a superficial observer.   Margaret looked very far from handsome as she sat in a corner of the bow-window of the drawing-room, her small thin hands folded and motionless, her head, with its hideous covering, bent down; her pale face, sharpened by the angle at which the light struck it, and her whole figure, in its deep black dress, unrelieved by the slightest ornament or grace of form, pervaded by an expression of weariness and defeat.   She might have been a woman of thirty years old, and who had never been handsome, to the perception of any stranger who had then and thus seen her.

But, three hours later in the night, when Margaret Hungerford was alone in the room which had been the scene of her girlish dreams and hopes, of the fond and beautiful delusion so terribly dissipated—in the room where her dead mother had watched her in her sleep, where she had read and yielded to the lover's prayer which lured her from her home—when she was quite alone, and was permitting the waves of memory to rush over her soul;—no one would have said, who could then have seen her, that Margaret was not handsome. Her face was one capable of intensity of expression in every mood of feeling, and as mobile as it was powerful. The wakeful hours of that night passed over her while another crisis in her life was lived through—another crisis somewhat resembling, and yet differing from, that which had marked the first hours of her voyage.

She had sent Rose Moore away as soon as she could, but not before the girl had imparted to her her conviction that English people, always excepting Margaret, were ' quare.' She could not understand the tranquillity of the widowed daughter's reception at Chayleigh. The reception awaiting her in the ' ould country ' would be of a very different kind, ' plase God,' she added internally; and the extent and importance of the business of eating and drinking among the servants had gone nigh to exasperate her.

Rose was devoted to Margaret, but she thought the sooner she and her mistress turned their back on a place where servants sat down to four regular meals a day, and did not as much as know the meaning of the ' Mass,' the better.

· She 'll never do for these people,' the girl thought, as she waited for Margaret in her room ; she's restless with sorrow, and it's not a nice nate place, like this, with the back parlour full of spiders laid out in state, as if they were wakin' them, and little boxes full of bones—nor yet the drawin'-room, all done out with bades, and a mother, by way of, sittin' in it that 'ud think more of one of her tay-cups bein' chipped than of the young crayture's heart bein' broken —that'll ever bring comfort or consolation to the likes of her.'

The thoughts which had put themselves into such simple words in the Irish girl's mind had considerable affinity with Margaret's own, but in her they took more tumultuous form. The strong purpose, half remorse, half vain-longing, which had brought her home, was fulfilled.   She had seen the place she had left, and thoroughly realized that her former self had been left with it.

The few hours which had passed had made her comprehend that her life, her nature, were things apart from Chayleigh; she could not, if she would, take up the story of her girlhood where she had closed the book.   Between her and every former association, the dark and miserable years of her married life—unreal as they seemed now—almost as unreal as the illusion under which she had entered upon them—had placed an impassable gulf.

Wrapped in a dressing-gown, and with her dark hair loose upon her shoulders, Margaret paced her room from end to end, and strove with her thoughts.   She was a puzzle to herself.   What discord there was between her—a woman who had suffered such things, seen such sights, heard such words as she had seen, and heard, and suffered—and the calm, well-regulated, comfortable household here!   If she had ever contemplated remaining an inmate of her father's house, this one night's commune with herself would have forced her to recognize the impossibility of her doing so. The stain and stamp of her wanderings were upon her ; she could not find rest here, or yet.

Her father's dreamy ways; the selfishness, heartlessness, empty-headedness of Mrs Carteret; the distaste she felt for James Dugdale's presence, though she persuaded herself she was striving to be grateful;—all these things, separately and collectively, she felt, but they did not present themselves to her as the true sources of her present uncontrollable feelings: she knew how utterly she was changed now only when she knew—for it was knowledge, not apprehension—that the home to which she had found her way of access so much easier than she had thought for, could never be a resting-place for her.

Was there any resting-place anywhere? Had she still to learn that life's lessons are not exhausted by one or two great shocks of experience, but are daily tasks until the day, 'never so weary or long,' has been 'rung to evensong'? She was a puzzle to herself in another respect. No grief for the dead husband, the lover for whom she had left the home which could not be restored, had come back to her. No gentle tender chord had been touched in her heart, to give forth his name in mournful music.

In this, the truth, the intellectual strength of her nature, unknown to her, revealed themselves. No sentimentality veiled the truth from Margaret. She had said to herself that it was well for her her husband was dead, no matter what should come after, and she never unsaid it,—not even in the hours of emotional recollection and mental strife which formed her first night under her father's roof.

Standing by the window at which James Dugdale had first caught sight of her the day before, Margaret clasped her hands over her head and looked out drearily. The moon was high, the light was cold and ghastly. She thought how she had seen the same chill gleam upon the shimmering sea, and upon the grassy wastes of the distant land she had left; and the fancy came to her that it was to be always moonlight with her for evermore.

'No more sunshine; no more of the glow, and the glitter, and the warmth—that is done with for me. There's no such thing as happiness, and I must only try to find, instead, hard work.'

There was another wakeful head at Chayleigh that night. James Dugdale was but too well accustomed to sleepless nights, companioned by the searching, mysterious pain which so often attends upon deformity—pain, as if unseen fingers questioned the distorted limbs and lingered among the disturbed nerves; but it was not that which kept him waking now.

It was that he, too, was face to face with his fate, questioning it of its past deeds and its intentions for the future—a little bitterly questioning it, perhaps, and yet with more resignation than rancour after all, considering what the mind of the man was, and what a prison-house it tenanted. Among the innumerable crowd of thoughts which pursued and pressed upon each other, there was one all the more distinct that he felt and strove against its unworthiness.

'I am so thankful she is at home—so glad for her sake. Nothing could be so well for her, since the past is irrevocable; but nothing could be so bad, at least nothing could be worse, for me. No, nothing, nothing.'

And James Dugdale, happily blind to the further resources of his destiny, felt something like a dreary sense of peace arising within him as he assured himself over and over again of the finality to which it had attained.

CHAPTER VIII.

MRS CARTERET IS CONGRATULATED.

'I AM positively dying to see her—I am indeed; you have no notion what a darling she is. I am sure you would be delighted with her, Fitzwilliam!'

These gushing sentiments were uttered by Lady Davyntry, and addressed to her brother, Mr Fitzwilliam Meriton Baldwin, while they were at breakfast together, on the morning after Lady Davyntry's note had been received at Chayleigh.

Lady Davyntry was given to gushing. She was a harmless, emotional kind of woman, who had led a perfectly discreet and comfortable life, and had never known a sorrow until the death of her husband.

Lady Davyntry was a very pretty woman—as pretty at her present age, thirty-five, as she had been at any time since she had turned the corner of extreme youth. Her mild, lambent blue eyes were as bright as they had ever been, and her fair, rather thick skin had lost neither its purity nor its polish.

She had been rich, well cared for, and happy all her life; she had never had any occasion to exert herself; the 'sorrows of others' had cast but light and fleeting 'shadows over' her; and her sentimentalism, and the romance which had not been much developed in the course of her prosperous uneventful life were quite ready for any demands that might be made upon them by an event of so much local interest as the return of Mr Carteret's daughter, whose marriage was generally understood to have been very unfortunate.

She was interested in the occurrence for more than the sufficient reason that she had liked and pitied Margaret in her neglected girlhood. Perhaps the strongest sentiment of dislike which had ever been called forth in the amiable nature of Lady Davyntry had been excited by, and towards, Mrs Carteret.

The two women were entirely antagonistic to each other; and Lady Davyntry felt a thrill of gratification on hearing of Margaret's return, in which a conviction that that event had taken place without Mrs Carteret's sanction, and would not be to her taste, had a decided share.

She had favoured her brother—to whom she was very much attached, and who was so much younger than she that he did not inspire her with any of the salutary reserve which induces sisters to disguise their favourite weaknesses from brothers—with a full and free statement of her feelings on this point, and he had not strongly combated her antipathy to Mrs Carteret. The truth was, he shared it.

Mr Baldwin had risen from the breakfast-table, and was standing, newspaper in hand, by a large window which commanded an extensive view, including the precise angle of the little demesne of Chayleigh in which the rear of the house and the window of Margaret's room, with its frame of passion-flowers, could be seen—not distinctly, but clearly enough to induce the eyes of any one gazing forth upon the scene to rest upon it mechanically.

His sister rose also, as she repeated her assurance that Margaret was a 'darling,' and joined him.

'Look,' she said; 'you have sharp eyes, I know. There is some one leaning out of the centre window. I see a figure; don't you?'

'Yes,' said Mr Baldwin; 'I see a figure, all in black,— there's a flutter of something white. Who is it?'

'I'm sure it's Margaret,' said Lady Davyntry, 'and the white thing must be the strings of her widow's cap, poor child. How horrid it will be to see her sweet, pretty little face in it! Ah, dear! to think that she and I should meet under such similar circumstances!' and Lady Davyntry sighed, and a tear made its appearance in each of her calm blue eyes.

'Similar circumstances!' repeated her brother, in some surprise. 'Ah, yes! you are both widows, to be sure; but the similarity stops there; if what Dugdale said, or rather implied, be true,—as of course it is,—you and Mrs Hungerford wear your rue with a difference.'

'We do, indeed,' said Lady Davyntry. 'Give me that field-glass, Fitz. I must make out whether that really is Margaret.' And then she added, as she adjusted the glass to her sight, 'And I pity her for that too. I cannot fancy any lot more pitiable than being forbidden by one's reason to feel grief. Yes,' she went on, after a minute, 'it *is* Margaret. I can see her figure quite plainly now. Look, look, Fitz!' and she held out the glass to him. But Mr Baldwin did not take it from her hand; he smiled, and said:

'No, no, Nelly, I could not take the liberty of peeping surreptitiously at Mrs Hungerford. You forget you are renewing your acquaintance with her; mine has to be made.'

'That's just like your punctilio,' said his sister. 'I declare I feel the strongest impulse to nod to her, this glass brings her so near; and you are a goose for your pains. However, when you do see her, I prophesy you will agree with me that she is a darling, a delightful girl.'

'Well, but,' said Mr Baldwin, who was amused by his sister's enthusiasm, 'you forget how long it is since you have seen this paragon, and that she is not a girl at all, but an unhappy and ill-treated wife, who has lately had the good fortune to become a widow.'

' That's true,' said Lady Davyntry; ' but I'll not believe that any change could interfere with Margaret's being a darling. At all events, I am going to see for myself this very day.'

' So soon ? ' asked Mr Baldwin, in a surprised tone.

' So soon ! why not ? You don't suppose Margaret has any tender confidences with Mrs Carteret which must not be broken in upon, and, as for her father, I am sure he is as much accustomed to her being there, since yesterday, as if she were one of those horrid specimens *en permanence*.'

Mr Baldwin laughed. ' I don't suppose the meeting has been very demonstrative,' he said, ' considering the parties to it whom I *do* know, and Dugdale's account of the party whom I *do not*. According to the little he said, Mrs Hungerford's firmness and reserve are wonderful—more wonderful than pleasing, *I* should consider them.'

' Never mind Mr Dugdale, Fitz,' replied his sister. ' He never liked Margaret either, I believe : I know she quarrelled with him at the time of her love-affair. It is very likely he does not like her coming home ; she may make things unpleasant for him now, you know, which she could not when quite a girl. Don't you mind *him*. Take my word for it, the young widow is a darling.'

' Take care, Nelly; that is rather a dangerous thing to insist upon so strongly, except that you know I have a prejudice against widows—always excepting *you*,' he added, as she raised a warning finger.

' Nonsense,' said Lady Davyntry ; and then she left the room, and her brother resumed his newspaper ; but, as he folded it and prepared to read the leading articles leisurely, he thought, ' I wonder if she is really nice. Certainly Dug-

dale did not convey to *me* any impression that he did not
like her, or that her coming was contrary to his convenience,—rather the opposite, I think. This must be a
fancy of Nelly's.'

'Am I right? Did I say too much of Margaret, you
incredulous Fitz?' asked Lady Davyntry of her brother,
when the gates of Chayleigh had closed upon them at the
termination of an unusually protracted visit, during which
Mrs Carteret had endured the mortification of seeing Lady
Davyntry in a character of affectionate neighbourliness,
which had never been evoked by all her own strenuous and
unrelaxed efforts.

'Did you ever see a nicer creature?' persisted the impulsive Nelly, 'and though of course she's changed, I assure
you I never thought her so handsome when she was quite a
girl; and her quiet manner—so dignified and lady-like—not
cold, though: you didn't think it cold, did you, Fitz?'

'Not cold to *you*, certainly,' replied Mr Baldwin, who
was glad to escape, by answering this one, from the more
direct question his sister had put to him at first.

'No, no,' she went on; 'quite cordial; and I told
her how I looked at her with the glass this morning, and
how you were quite too proper and precise to follow my
example; and she blushed quite red for a moment—her
pale face looked *so* pretty—and just glanced at you for an
instant: it was when Mr Carteret was bothering you about
the articulations of something—and I'm sure she thought
you very nice and gentlemanly, and——'

'What *I* thought of Mrs Hungerford is more to your
present purpose, Nelly,' said her brother, in an embarrassed
voice. 'I quite agree with you in thinking her very charming, but she looks as if she had gone through a great deal.'

'Yes; doesn't she, poor dear?' said Lady Davyntry,

who simply did not possess the power to comprehend even
the outlines of Margaret's life ; ' but now that she is at
home it will bo all right ; I shall have her with me as
much as possible, and she will soon forget all her troubles.'

Mr Baldwin did not reply. There was something in
Mrs Hungerford's face which forbade him to believe that
Davyntry and its mistress would prove a panacea for whatever was the source of that expression. It was not grief,
as grief is felt for the dead who have been worthily loved
and are fitly mourned.

It was an utter forlornness, combined with suppressed
energy. It was the expression of one who had been utterly
deceived and disappointed, and was now crushed by the
sense of bankruptcy and defeat in life. The quiet manner
which had been so satisfactory to the shallow perceptions of
Lady Davyntry did not impress her brother in the same way.

'That is a woman,' he thought, 'who has gone peril-
ously near to the confines of despair.'

When he had seen Lady Davyntry into the house, Mr
Baldwin turned away from the door, and went a long
ramble through the fields. His wanderings did not take him
out of Chayleigh ; and once he stood still, looking towards
the window where Margaret's figure had been dimly seen
by him that morning, and thought,

'What does this woman mean to me ? Not a mere
passing interest in my life ! What does this woman mean ?'

' I suppose you don't see much change in Lady Davyntry ? ' Mrs Carteret said to Margaret, after the visitors
had departed. ' She is as nice-looking, in a common way,
and as full of herself as usual.'

' Lady Davyntry was always very kind to me,' replied
Margaret gravely. ' In that she is certainly unchanged.'

' Oh yes, she's kind enough, in her empty way,' said

Mrs Carteret; 'but for my part I don't care about those
violent intimacies. I never would be led into them—they
are quite in her way. If I would have responded, there
would have been perpetual running back and forward between Davyntry and Chayleigh ; but that sort of thing
does not suit me—I consider it vulgar and insincere.'

Margaret did not exactly know, but she suspected, quite
correctly, that her stepmother was endeavouring to disguise
a considerable amount of pique under this depreciation of
undue intimacy. She therefore made no reply, and Mrs
Carteret continued :

'I dare say she will be taking you up violently, for a
while, until she tires of you. The fuss she makes with her
brother is quite absurd. He is a nice-looking young man,
and nothing more. Don't you think so, Margaret ?'

'He is nice-looking, certainly,' said Margaret; 'but I
have seen too little of him to pronounce any further.'

'He has the great attraction of being very rich,' said
Mrs Carteret, in a sharp tone; Margaret's cautious and
reasonable reply irritated her. 'If he dies without heirs,
his sister will have all the Scotch property; it is worth
fifteen thousand a-year, and entailed on heirs general. It
is a wonder some manœuvring mother has not made a prize
of him long ago. He's rather a soft party, I should say.'

'Should you ?' said Margaret. 'Mr Baldwin looks
firm as well as gentle, I think—not the sort of man to be
married by anybody without his own unqualified consent.'

'Of course he's a great catch,' said Mrs Carteret, 'and
I understand he is terribly afraid of ladies. He thinks
every woman who looks at him is in love with himself or
his acres.'

'Indeed,' said Margaret—and there was a tone of polite

incredulity in her voice—'I should not have taken Mr Baldwin to be a vulgar-minded man.'

'I dare say not,' returned Mrs Carteret; 'he is rather prepossessing than otherwise to strangers; but then, you know, Margaret, your judgment of men has been rather rash than infallible hitherto. Dear me! I had no notion it was so late—time to dress for dinner!'

Mrs Carteret rose, laid aside her everlasting fancy-work, and left the room. Margaret rose also, but lingered for a few moments. As she stood with her hands pressed upon her temples, and her pale face drawn into a look of pain, she thought:

'I wonder, if James Dugdale had heard that speech, would he think I could possibly stay here.'

CHAPTER IX.

WHAT THE WOMAN MEANT.

A MONTH had elapsed since Margaret Hungerford's return to her father's house, and had brought with it certain changes in the situation of things at Chayleigh, which, though they could not have been understood by outsiders, were very keenly appreciated by the actors in the small domestic drama there.

It had brought to Margaret more calm and peace. It had not changed her intention of leaving Chayleigh, of seeking some independent means of providing for herself; but it had decreased her anxiety to put this intention into immediate, or even into very early, execution. The main element in this alteration was her perception of her father's pleasure in her society.

'It is not much to bear for *his* sake,' she said to herself, 'to put up with Mrs Carteret. I have had worse things than that to endure without the power or the prospect of escaping from them either, and I will stay for six months with papa. James Dugdale thinks it the right thing, and, if Mrs Carteret is convinced that it is to be only for six months, she will see that her best policy, in pursuit of her favourite plan of making things pleasant for papa, in order to have her own way thoroughly in things she really cares about, is by behaving properly to me. I will take care she shall labour under no delusive fears about my having come to take up my abode here; and then I am much out of my calculations, and egregiously mistaken in my amiable step-mother, if she does not change her tactics altogether.'

The result justified Margaret's calculations. She took an early opportunity of informing Mrs Carteret that she did not contemplate a long stay at Chayleigh.

The intimation was received by her stepmother with much propriety of manner, but without the slightest warmth. She designed to let Margaret perceive that while she (Mrs Carteret) was too ladylike, too perfectly trained and finished in the polished proprieties of life, to fail in the fulfilment of the exact laws of hospitality, it had never occurred to her to consider Margaret in any other light than that of a guest; and that she therefore regarded the communication as merely relating to the duration of her visit.

Margaret clearly perceived her meaning, but she did not resent it, nor did it grieve her. The peace of a settled resolution had come to her. Mrs Carteret condescended to express her approbation of Margaret's determination, and her readiness to assist her in carrying it into effect.

'Nothing is more admirable in young people than an independent spirit,' said the approving lady; 'and, notwithstanding your unfortunate marriage, Margaret, I consider you as a young person still. You are quite right in considering it unjust that your father should be expected to provide for you twice over—first, in handing over the money you were not really entitled to, to that unpleasant person, Mr Hungerford, and a second time, by having you to live here.'

'My father is not expected, either by me or by any one that I know of, to do anything of the kind,' interrupted Margaret, with a slight quivering of the lips and a transient accession of colour to the pale cheeks.

'That is just what I am saying, my dear. I highly commend your very proper view. It would be quite my own. Indeed, I am sure, were I in your position, I could not endure dependence, even if my father were a much richer man than yours is. I cannot understand any one not doing anything to secure independence.'

Margaret smiled, rather a hard kind of smile, as she thought there was one thing she certainly would not do to attain independence, and that one thing was precisely what Miss Martley had done in becoming Mrs Carteret.

The elder lady continued to talk for some time longer in the same strain, and at length she asked Margaret how she intended to procure occupation.

'I have not thought about that part of it yet,' she replied.

Then Mrs Carteret allowed the truth to slip out; then she betrayed her real consciousness of the meanness she was perpetrating. She shifted her eyes uneasily away from Margaret's face, as she said,

'I should not mention the matter to any one about here if I were you, Margaret. People talk so oddly, and your father might not like it. I always think, when anything of the kind is to be done, it had better be away from home, and among a different connection.'

Margaret answered her with hardly-disguised contempt :

'Your warning comes rather late. I have already told Lady Davyntry of my intention, which she approves as much as you do. She has been good enough to promise me her friendship and interest in settling matters to my satisfaction. As for papa, he will not mind how I do it, when I can succeed in reconciling him to my doing it at all.'

Mrs Carteret felt strongly tempted to get into a violent rage, and relieve her vexation, which was intense, by saying anything and everything which anger might suggest to her, to Margaret.

That Lady Davyntry, who had taken no notice of the advances she had made towards an intimacy which would have been a social triumph to Mrs Carteret—Lady Davyntry who, since Margaret's return, had gone so near ignoring her stepmother's existence as was consistent with the observance of the commonest civility—that she should be admitted behind the scenes, that Margaret should instruct her in the *dessous des cartes*, was gall and wormwood to her. She had never been very far off hating Margaret hitherto; her quiet stealthy dislike to the girl now deepened into the darker feeling; and though she merely replied, 'Oh, then, in that case, it cannot be helped,' Margaret knew that that minute marked an era in Mrs Carteret's feelings towards her.

'Never mind,' she said to herself, as though she had been encouraging another person; 'never mind, it is only for six months. She will always be civil to me, and it can't last.'

She was right; Mrs Carteret always was civil to her. She was a woman in whom cunning and caution were at least as strong as temper, and she took counsel of both in

5

this instance. She was by no means free from an uneasy suspicion that, if Margaret had formed a contrary determination, her influence with her father would have outweighed that which she herself could have exerted.

It behoved her, therefore, to be thankful that the occasion for testing that unpleasantly-important point had not arisen, and to confine her tactics to such consistently-ceremonious treatment of Margaret as should keep her position as only a guest constantly before her eyes, and maintain her resolution by the aid of her pride; while all should be so contrived as to avoid attracting the attention of her absent-minded husband.

Mrs Carteret conquered her temper, therefore—an operation in which she found the counting of the stitches of her everlasting fancy-work afforded her a good deal of assistance—and, after a short pause, took up a collateral branch of the same subject.

Margaret had dismissed Rose Moore, and the girl had gone on her journey with a weight at her heart which she would have hardly believed possible, seeing that she was going home. But she had come to love Margaret very much, and she was very imperfectly consoled for parting with her by the distant hope which the young widow held out of a future meeting.

'You will be married, and away in a house of your own, my dear girl, very soon, and you will not care much about anything else then; but I promise you, if ever I want you very much, Rose, I will send for you. I don't think I ever *can* want you, in all my life, as much as I wanted you when you came to me; and of course you never can want me; your life is laid out for you too securely for that.'

'None of us can tell *that*,' said Rose Moore; 'who knows?'

'Well, of course no one knows,' said Margaret; 'but it looks like it. However, we shall never forget one another, Rose, and if either can help the other, the one who can will.' And with this understanding they parted.

Mrs Carteret had never taken any notice of Rose Moore, who, in her turn, had held the lady of the house in slight reverence. Mrs Carteret had a constitutional aversion to the Irish. She considered them half-civilized beings, with a natural turn for murder, a natural unfitness for domestic service, and an objectionable predilection for attending the ceremonial observances of their religion.

As an Irishwoman, then, Rose Moore was antipathetic to her; and as a devoted though humble friend of her step-daughter's, she was something more. The Irish girl's bright-hearted love and sympathy for the young widow was positively repulsive to Mrs Carteret, because there was a reproach in it.

But when Rose was actually gone, Mrs Carteret found herself in a difficulty. She disliked the idea of a successor to Rose being found, because her narrow, grasping nature was of the small tyrant order, and she could not endure that in her house there should be any one who did not owe allegiance *to her.*

Another reason was to be found in Mrs Carteret's parsimony. She was as avaricious as she was despotic, and both these passions were stirred within her when she asked Margaret, in the most distant and uninterested tone which even she could assume, whether she had yet made any arrangements about replacing Rose Moore. 'Moore,' she called her, after the English fashion, which had been a deadly offence to Rose.

'Calling you as if you were either a man or a dog,' the indignant damsel had said.

'It's the English fashion, Rose,' Margaret had pleaded in mitigation.

'Then it's like more of their fashions, and they ought to be ashamed of it, and would if they were Christians. However, I suppose English servants put up with that, or anythin' else, for their four meals a-day, and snacks into the bargain, and their beer, and the liberty their clargy gives them to backbite their masters and mistresses.'

Margaret tried to explain that neither in this nor in any other particular were the objects of Rose's indignant scorn in the habit of applying to their ' clargy ; ' but this was an enormity which she found the girl's mind was quite incapable of receiving as a truth.

Mrs Hungerford replied to Mrs Carteret's question, that she had no intention of providing a successor for Rose Moore.

'I should have thought it quite unnecessary to tell you so,' she said, rather angrily. 'You can hardly suppose I am in a position to keep a maid. Even if I were for the present, to accustom myself to any luxury which I must lose at the end of six months would be unpardonable folly and weakness.'

'You are quite right, my dear,' said Mrs Carteret, with a cordial tone in her voice, and a side-glance in her eye of intense dislike of the speaker. 'I admire your correct and self-denying principle, but I am not sure that your father will like it. While you stay with us, I am sure he would not wish you to be without a maid.'

Margaret did not take much trouble to conceal the contempt which animated the smile that she permitted to pass slowly over her face as she replied :

'Pray do not trouble yourself about that, Mrs Carteret. If papa thinks about it at all, which is very unlikely, he will know how little personal attendance I have been

accustomed to. But you and I know the fact of there being
a servant more or less in the house will never present itself
to his notice. Pray make your mind easy on that point.'

'But there's—' said Mrs Carteret hesitatingly—'there's
James, you know; he is sure to know that Moore has left
you, and to find out whether you have got any one to re-
place her.'

'Make your mind easy about *that*, too, Mrs Carteret,'
said Margaret; and the confidence in her tone was particularly displeasing. 'I will take care that Mr Dugdale
understands *my* wishes in this matter.'

So Mrs Carteret carried three points. She avoided
having a servant in the house who should not be her servant;
she escaped an additional expense; and she was exempted,
by Margaret's express disclaimer, from offering her the
services of her own maid—an offer which, had she found
herself obliged to make it, Mrs Collins would probably have
declined to carry into execution. There was one person in
the world of whom Mrs Carteret was afraid, and that
individual was Mrs Collins.

When the conversation between Margaret and Mrs
Carteret had come to an end, to their mutual relief, Margaret went to her father. As she approached the study, she
heard voices, and knew she should not find him alone.

'I suppose it is James,' she thought, and entered the
room. But it was not James; it was Mr Baldwin, who held
a large old-looking volume in his hand, and was discussing
with Mr Carteret a passage concerning the structure of
crustacea. He closed the book, and replaced it on the table
with great alacrity, as Margaret came in and spoke to him.
Then she turned to her father. 'I was going to talk to you
for a little while, papa; but as Mr Baldwin is here—'

'Never mind that, Margery,' said her father; 'Mr

Baldwin was just going to the drawing-room to see Sibylla and you. He has a message for you from Lady Davyntry'

Mr Baldwin confirmed Mr Carteret's statement, and took from his waistcoat-pocket a tiny note, folded three-corner-wise. This was before the invention of square envelopes and dazzling monograms; and female friendship, confidences, and general gushingness usually expressed themselves in the three-cornered form.

Margaret took the note, and, passing before the 'speci-men'-laden table, went to the window and seated herself on the low, wide, uncushioned ledge. She held the twisted paper in her hand, and looked idly out of the window, before she broke the seal, unconscious that Mr Baldwin was looking at her with an eager interest which rendered him singularly inattentive to the arguments addressed to him by Mr Car-teret in pursuance of the discussion which Margaret's entrance had interrupted.

The girlish gracefulness of her attitude contrasted strangely with her sombre heavy dress; the soft youthful-ness of her colourless face made the harsh lines of the close crimped cap an odious anachronism.

'MY DARLING MARGARET,'—this was the note,—'I have such a cold, I *cannot* get to you. Do be charitable, and come to me. My brother will escort you, and will see you home at night, unless you will stay.

'Always your devoted

'ELEANOR.

The renewed acquaintance with Lady Davyntry was at this time an event of a fortnight old, and the irrepressible Eleanor had to a certain extent succeeded in thawing the frozen exterior of the young woman's demeanour. Kindness, if even it were a little silly and over-demonstrative, was a refreshing novelty to Margaret, and she welcomed it.

At first she had been a little hard, a little incredulous towards Lady Davyntry; she had been inclined to treat her rapidly-developed fondness for herself as a *caprice de grande dame*. But she soon abandoned that harsh interpretation; she soon understood that, though it was exaggerated in its expression, the affection with which she had inspired Lady Davyntry was perfectly sincere.

Hence it came that Margaret had told her friend what were her views for her future; but she had not raised the veil which hid the past. Of that dreadful time, with its horrid experience of sin and misery, with its contaminating companionship, and the stain which it had left of such knowledge of evil and all the meanness of vice as never should be brought within the ken of pure womanhood at any age, Margaret never spoke, and Lady Davyntry, though inquisitive enough in general, and by no means wanting in curiosity in this particular instance, did not seek to overcome her reticence.

She had considerable delicacy of mind, and, in Margaret's case, affection and interest brought her not-naturally-bright intelligence to its aid. She had noticed and understood the changeableness of Margaret's moods. She had seen her, when animated and seemingly happy in conversation with her or Mr Baldwin (what a treat it was to hear those two talk! she thought), suddenly lapse into silence, and all the colour would die out of her cheeks, and all the light from her eyes—struck away from them doubtless by the stirring of some painful memory, aroused from its superficial slumber by some word or phrase in which the pang of association lurked.

She had seen the expression of weariness which Margaret's figure had worn at first come over it again, and then the drooped head and the listless hands had a story in them, from even trying to guess at which the kind-hearted woman, whose one grief had no touch of shame or dread or degrading remembrance in it, shrunk with true delicacy and keen womanly sympathy.

Lady Davyntry had been a daily visitor at Chayleigh since Margaret's return. She treated Mrs Carteret with civility; but she made it, as she intended, evident that the attraction was Margaret, and Mrs Carteret had to endure the mortifying conviction as best she could. Her best was not very good, and she never allowed an opportunity to pass of hitting Margaret's friend as hard as her feeble powers of sarcasm, which only attained the rank of spite, enabled her to hit her. Lady Davyntry was totally unconscious, and Margaret was profoundly indifferent.

It happened, however, on this particular day, after the conclusion of Mrs Carteret's conversation with her step-daughter, and while she was superintending the interesting operation, performed by Collins, of altering the trimmings of a particularly becoming dress, that she came to a determination to alter her tactics. She had not to dread a permanent invasion of her territory, a permanent usurpation of her place by Margaret; she would therefore profit by the temporary evil, and so entangle Lady Davyntry in civilities that it would be impossible for her to withdraw from so *affiché* an intimacy when Margaret should have left Chayleigh.

In all this there was not a particle of regard for Lady Davyntry, of liking for her society, of a wish that the supposed intimacy should become real. It would be quite enough for her that the Croftons and the Crokers, the Willises, the Wyngroves, and the Savilles should know that Lady

Davyntry was on the most familiar terms with the Carterets, and quite beyond those to which any other family in the neighbourhood could lay claim.

Mrs Carteret's busy small brain began to entertain an idea that Margaret's stay might be made profitable, in a social point of view, to her future position.

The writing of the note of which Mr Baldwin was the bearer had been the subject of some doubt and discussion between Lady Davyntry and her brother.

'Do you think it would do to ask her here, to dinner and all that, without asking Mrs Carteret, and making a regular business of it?' said Eleanor.

'Of course it would,' returned Mr Baldwin. 'If you want to have Mrs Hungerford here, and do not want to have Mrs Carteret, as I understand you that you do, you could not have a better opportunity. Now is your time. You have a cold, you can't go out, and you certainly cannot see company. Write your note, Nelly, and I'll take it. I want to see Mr Carteret. You cannot have a better opportunity.'

'Let me see,' said Lady Davyntry, biting the top of her pen contemplatively; 'Mr Dugdale is down at Oxford, isn't he?'

'Yes,' said her brother; 'gone to see his old tutor,—a fellow he is, but I forget his name,—and won't be back for three weeks.'

'Well, then, I *will* ask Margaret alone. I thought, if Mr Dugdale had been at home, we might have asked him to come to dinner. But you won't mind seeing Mrs Hungerford home, Fitz, will you? She could have the carriage, of course, and go round by the road; but I am sure she would not like that.'

Mr Baldwin was exceedingly complaisant and agreeable.

So far from growling an assent in an undertone, sounding much more like a protest than an acquiescence, as is the usual manner of men with regard to the bosom friends of their sisters, he expressed his readiness to undertake the task of seeing Margaret home with a cheerful readiness quite beyond suspicion of its sincerity.

When Margaret had read the note, she twisted it in her fingers without speaking. Mr Baldwin's attention wandered a little, though Mr Carteret had opened one of the glass cases, and taken out a horrid object like an old-fashioned brooch with an areole of long spikes, and was expatiating upon it with great fervour.

He looked at Margaret; but her eyes were turned from him, straying over the garden. At last he moved to where she was sitting.

'You will grant my sister's prayer,' he said. 'I know what is in the note. She really has a cold, Mrs Hungerford. It will be a charity if you will go to her.—What do *you* say, sir?'

Mr Carteret said nothing, for the ample reason that he had not the remotest idea of what Mr Baldwin was talking about. When, however, that gentleman explained the matter, he gave it as his decided opinion that Margaret ought to go for Lady Davyntry's sake and her own. A little change would do her good. She must not mope, the kind gentleman said; and he and Sibylla were but dull company now. She must find it dismal enough now that James was away. By-the-by, did Margaret know how Mr Fordham was? Had James found him any better than he expected when he arrived at Oxford? Yes, yes, Margery must go— she moped too much; she did not even care for the specimens so much as she used to do.

'Indeed I do, papa,' said Margaret, rising suddenly from

her seat and laying her hand on her father's shoulder; 'I
care for them a great deal more—for everything that interests you, and that *you* care for.'

Her luminous eyes were softer and brighter than Mr
Baldwin had ever seen them. She had evidently been thinking of something in the past with which her father's words
had chimed in. He was waiting her decision with a strange
feeling of suspense and anxiety, considering that the matter
involved was of no greater moment than the question
whether his sister's friend, who had seen her yesterday, and
would in all probability see her to-morrow, should make up
her mind to refrain from the luxury of seeing her to-day.

'Do you, my dear?' said Mr Carteret. 'That's right;
you will go, of course, then, and Foster shall fetch you this
evening.—No, indeed, Mr Baldwin, I could not think of
your taking the trouble.'

But Mr Baldwin insisted, subject to Mrs Hungerford's
permission, that he would see her home. This permission
she carelessly gave, and then left the room to prepare for
her walk. The two men stood silent for a minute; then Mr
Carteret said, with a deep sigh,

'Poor Margery! she has had plenty of trouble in her
time. I often wonder whether she is going to have peace
now. We can't give that to our sons and daughters, Baldwin, or get it from them either.'

There was a sad desponding tone in Mr Carteret's voice.
Now he was beginning to understand something of the
meaning and extent of the sorrow that had befallen his
daughter—now, when the indelible stamp of its effect was
set upon her changed face, upon her shrinking figure, upon
her slow and unelastic movements.

She had had time now to feel the repose, the comfort,
the respectability of the home to which she had come back,

and yet there was no change in her beyond the release from mere bodily fatigue. The wan weariness which he had not seen at first, but had seen when James Dugdale directed his attention to it, was there still, unaltered; indeed, to the eye of a keen observer, it was deepened. In some cases, mere respite from physical labour does not produce the effect of mental repose. Margaret's case was one of those.

Mr Baldwin did not reply to Mr Carteret's observation; he walked towards the window, and looked dreamily out, as Margaret had done. Presently she came back, wearing her sombre mantle and the close widow's bonnet of a period when *grand deuil*, in the Mary-Stuart fashion, was unknown.

'You will tell Mrs Carteret, if you please, papa, I could not find her.'

'I will be sure to tell her,' said Mr Carteret; 'and, Margery, I want you to observe Lady Davyntry's Angora cat very carefully, and bring me word whether she has one ring or two round the top of her tail. Don't forget this, my dear, for it is really an important point.'

'I'll be sure to remember it, papa,' said Margaret; and then she and Mr Fitzwilliam Meriton Baldwin went out through the French window of Mr Carteret's study, and took their way across the grassy terrace, through the lawn, to the little iron gate which opened into the meadow-lands, through which the 'short cut' between Chayleigh and Davyntry lay.

In the first field beyond this gate a noble clump of beeches stood.

'That is a favourite point of view of Dugdale's,' said Mr Baldwin. 'I have two sketches he made of those forest lords. Splendid trees they are. I love them.'

'And I hate them,' said Margaret.

He glanced at her in surprise. Her tone was bitter, and

her face wore an angry scornful look. But it was scorn of herself that Margaret was feeling. There, under the shade of those trees, she had come suddenly upon her brother and Godfrey Hungerford; there the first incense of her worship of the false god had been offered up. She felt his glance, and instantly began to talk of Lady Davyntry's cold.

'The idea,' she thought indignantly, ' of saying such a thing as that—of my betraying feelings to a stranger which it is impossible to explain.'

The first visit made by Margaret to Davyntry was the beginning of a series which contributed not a little to bringing about the changed aspect of things at Chayleigh, at the end of the first month of Margaret's residence there. She was beginning to feel something like a revival of her youth. The cheerful society, the sense of being loved and valued; the action of time, so mighty, so resistless, when one is young; the future dim, indeed, but still in a great measure within her own control: these were all telling on the young widow.

At first she had suffered keenly from the remembrance of the past episodes in her life, which seemed to set a barrier between her and the well-regulated, spotlessly respectable social circle to which she was restored ; a social atmosphere in which shifts, contrivances, shady expedients for the procuring of shabby ends, were as unknown, as unconceivable, as the more violent roisterous vice with which she had also, and only too frequently, been brought into contact. At first, this sense of an existence, separate and apart from her present associates, oppressed Margaret strangely, and caused her to shrink away from the manifestations of Lady Davyntry's friendship with sudden coldness, quite inexplicable to the impulsive Eleanor, whose life was all so emphatically aboveboard.

There were times when, in the luxurious and picturesque drawing-room at Davyntry, whose treasures of old china and ivory caused Mrs Carteret acute pangs of envy, Margaret felt the whole scene fade from before her eyes like a stage transformation, and some squalid room which she had once inhabited rise up in its place, with its mingled wretchedness and recklessness; a horrid vision of dirty packs of cards, of whisky-bottles, and the reek of coarse tobacco; and the refined tones of Mr Baldwin's voice would mingle strangely in her ears with the echo of loud oaths and coarse laughter.

At such times her face would harden, and the light would fade out of her eyes, and the grace would leave her form in some inexplicable way; and, if the cloud settled heavily, and she knew it was going to last, she would make some excuse to get away and return to her father's house and the society of Mrs Carteret, to whom her moods, or indeed those of any human being in existence, except herself, were matters of perfect indifference.

Mr Baldwin thought he understood the origin of these sudden changes in Margaret Hungerford; and, though he had no knowledge of the past, he discerned the spirit of the young widow with the marvellous skill which has its rise in very perfect sympathy. When his sister spoke to him about her friend's strange manner at times, he entreated her not to notice it in any way.

'She has had such troubles in her life, as, thank God, neither you nor I can understand, Nelly; and when this cloud comes over her, depend upon it, it is because the remembrance of them returns to her, made all the more real by the contrast here. Take no notice of it, and it will wear away in time.'

'She seems to me, Fitzwilliam, as if she had some painful secret pressing on her mind. I don't mean, of course, any secret concerning herself, anything in her own life; but Margaret constantly gives me the impression of being a person in possession of some knowledge unshared by any one else, and which she sometimes forgets, and then suddenly remembers.'

'It may be so,' said Mr Baldwin slowly, and looking very uncomfortable. 'I hope not; I hope it is only the effect of the early trouble she has gone through.'

'I wonder how she will get on when she leaves Chayleigh,' said Lady Davyntry.

'When she leaves Chayleigh!' repeated her brother, surprised, for the intentions of Margaret had never been discussed in his presence.

Then Lady Davyntry told him what Margaret had said to her, and how she had asked her advice and her aid.

'I could not possibly advise her to remain all her life with that dreadful stepmother of hers, could I, Fitz? You can understand what Mrs Carteret is in that relation, civil as she is to *you*. I really think she imagines you entertain a profound sentiment for her; perfectly proper and Platonic, you know, but still profound; and I don't think Margaret's naturally active mind could endure the idleness of the life at Chayleigh, even if Mrs Carteret were out of the question.'

'Idleness!' said Mr Baldwin, 'what idleness? There is just the same kind of life to be had at Chayleigh, I suppose, as women, as ladies, lead everywhere else—the kind of life Margaret was born to. I can't see the matter in *that* light.'

'I dare say not, Fitz,' said Lady Davyntry, rather proud of the chance of offering a suggestion to this infallible and incomparable younger brother of hers. 'But I can. Margaret certainly was, as you say, born to lead the kind of life which all women of her position get through somehow; but then she was taken out of it very young, and, whatever it was she did or suffered, you may be sure that it gave her mind a turn not to be undone.   Of course, I don't mean to say she wants to go back to that again, whatever it was ; but I am sure she must have some settled occupation to be happy.   I do not think, when one's heart has been once crammed quite full of anything, be it joyful or sorrowful, one can stand a vacuum.'   From which speech it will be made plain that Lady Davyntry did not cultivate her emotions at the expense of her good sense.

'You are right, Nelly; I see you are quite right.   But what does her father say ? '

'That I really cannot tell you ; but I suppose what Mr Carteret usually says, in any matter unconnected with birds, beasts, fishes, or insects—nothing.   He and Margaret have a tacit understanding that Mrs Carteret and she are not exactly sympathetic, and he has a feeble desire that his daughter should be happy.   Beyond that he really thinks nothing, and would have as much notion of the new life she wants to enter upon, as of the old life she has escaped from.'

'What does Dugdale think ? '

'That I cannot tell you.   Margaret never said a word about his opinion in connection with the matter.   I don't think she likes him.'

'No,' said Mr Baldwin, 'I don't think she does.'

'I asked her to come to me,' Lady Davyntry continued, 'and tried very hard to persuade her that I required the services of a *dame de compagnie*.   But she laughed at me, and would not listen to me for a moment, though she told me she had once suggested to Mr Dugdale that she should ask me to take her, for the commendable purpose of spiting Mrs Carteret.   "Do you think I want to *play* at independence ? " she said.   "If you do, you are much mistaken.   I won't have any more *shams*, please God, in my life. No, I am going to work in earnest." So I could not say any more. She may change her mind in six months, though I do not think she will.'

Mr Fitzwilliam Meriton Baldwin left his sister to entertain a selection of the Croftons and the Crokers and the Willises, and betook himself to a solitary ramble. The question which he had asked himself when he had seen Margaret Hungerford but once had recurred to him very often since then. Now he asked himself if he might dare to hope that he had found the answer.

He did not deny to himself now that he loved Margaret Hungerford. He was quite clear on that point: and he knew, too, that it was with an immortal and a worthy love. What did she mean? Was she to mean to him happiness--the realization of a man's best and wisest dreams? Was she to mean this to him in time, or did that sombre past in her life, of which he knew nothing, interpose an impassable barrier between her and him? He thought of Margaret's frank unembarrassed manner towards him without discouragement; he never fancied she could feel anything for him yet; he perfectly comprehended that nothing was so utterly dead for her as love.

But he would have patience, he would wait; a resurrection morning might come; he would try to *win* such a prize as she would be, not by a *coup de main*, but by slow degrees, if so it might be. In the true humility of his mind, in the perfect nobility of his soul, it never occurred to Mr Baldwin to think of himself as a prize also worth the winning.

He had often laughed with his sister about the ' mantraps ' set for him; but it was always Lady Davyntry, and not he, who had detected the devices prepared for the captivation and capture of Mr Baldwin of the Deane.

6

It rarely happened that Fitzwilliam Baldwin thought about his wealth ; his habits and tastes were simple, and his large property was well administered.　He had been a rich man ever since he had come to years of manhood, and the fact had not the same significance for him which it assumes for those who come late to a long-looked-for inheritance, whose attractions are exaggerated by the aid of fancy.

But he began to think complacently of his wealth now ; he began to see visions, and to dream dreams ; to think of the power he had to reverse all the former conditions of Margaret's life, let them have been what they might.　At least he knew she had been unhappy ; he could give her happiness, if unbounded love and respect, if the guarding her from every ill and care, if the holding her a sacred being, apart, to be seated in a shrine and worshipped, could give her happiness. This he could do, if she would but let him.

He knew that she had been poor, that she had now no means of her own.　There was his wealth, which had never been very important to him before, and could never be important again if she would not in time take it from him. How he would lavish it upon her; how he would try, without annoying her in any way, to find out some of the features of her past experience, and efface them by the luxury and honour in which he would envelop her !　Fitzwilliam Baldwin had advanced very far in a dream of this kind before the end of the month.　He had no longer any doubt of what this woman meant to him.

Shortly after, and sooner than his return was looked for, James Dugdale came back to Chayleigh, and found a letter awaiting him.　It was from Hayes Meredith.

CHAPTER X.

THE LETTER FROM MELBOURNE.

' BEFORE you receive this letter, my dear Dugdale,' wrote Hayes Meredith, ' you will have seen Mrs Hungerford, and she will have told you all the news about me, in giving the history of herself—a history, by-the-by, which has had a better ending than I expected, when first I made her out, according to your request.

' She is not much given to talking, I fancy, to any one, and I dare say she will not let you know much about her wretched life out here ; but I can tell you it was wretched ; and when I came to know her, and understand how superior a woman she is to the generality of women, such as I have known them, I was really grateful to you for giving me tho chance of serving her. I don't think I was much more obliged to you in my life, and I *have* owed you a turn or two.

' Hungerford was a regular blackguard, and an irredeemable snob as well, and she was only to be congratulated heartily on his death. The mode of it was rather horrible, to be sure ; but if he had not been knocked on the head in the bush, the chances are he would have been hanged ; and there's something to choose between the two, at all events.

' She is an interesting young woman, and I was sincerely glad to do her all the service in my power, which was not much, after all. I should like to know what becomes of her. I hope she has better days to see than any she lived through here ; and I hope you will write to me when you can.

' But my letter does not solely concern Mrs Hungerford. I have a selfish purpose in writing to you also, and the explanation of it needs some detail. You know that I am, and that I have been for some years, what I may safely call a prosperous man; and though I have a large family to provide for—five of them now (they were seven, but two little ones early succumbed to the climate)—I have never found that same very difficult to do. My children are all well, hearty, jolly, sturdy children, with the exception of our eldest boy—you have seen him, you may remember—Robert. He is not exactly sickly, but he is not strong; but it is less his bodily than his mental health that troubles his mother and myself.

'The boy is not contented, not happy, not a born colonial, like the rest; he has ideas and fancies other than theirs; he has an unruly temper, a quick impressionable brain, and a great aptitude for the graces, refinements, and luxuries of life, which—as I need not tell you it has had no chance of cultivation here—must be natural to him.

'His mother and I are not people to have a favourite among our children; it is share and share alike with them all, in affection as in everything else; but Robert is a discord somehow, and captious—in short, very hard to manage—and I have not the time to devote to an exceptional person in the family.

'He has a great notion that he is very superior to his brothers—quite an unfounded one—and thinks he should do no end of wonderful things in England, if he had the chance, by which, of course, he means the money. This I can give him; and as there is no doubt he can get a better education in England than here, and should his projects fail, or should he get tired of them, he can come back whenever he pleases, and still find a corner for himself here, I am quite disposed to let him try his own plans out.

'The others are true colonials; they have not the least

desire to see the old country until they can do so in independent manhood; but I can plainly perceive that, for his own sake, and that of all the household, Robert must be allowed to have his own way, as far as it lies in my power to give it him.

'There is some prospect of an improved and accelerated communication between us and England, and should it be realized by the spring of next year, I will probably bring the boy to England myself, and thus see you once more in this world, which I never had any hope of doing a little while ago.

'My wife does not like, nor, to tell the truth, do I, the notion of a whole year being taken out of our span of life together, which it must be if I make my proposed voyage; but neither does she like the idea of her son travelling alone to a strange country, and commencing his career without the assistance and the comfort of his father's presence and guidance in those important "first steps." We shall see, when the time comes, which of these feelings will prevail.

'In the mean time, my dear Dugdale, I rely on your friendship, aided by your experience of English life, and all the changes in public opinion and manners which have taken place since my time, to guide me in this matter, to tell me what it will be best for me to do for and with the boy.

'Robert is not ill educated, in as far as the limits of our colonial possibilities extend; but his education will aid him little in English life, and towards that his inclinations set.

'Turn all I have said over, and write to me concerning it. Then, by the time I get home, if I ever get home, and if I do not, by the time I send my boy home, you will have made up your mind, which, in a matter of this kind will be, as it ought to be, equivalent to making up mine, as to the proper course to be pursued.

'With all his faults, Robert will interest you, my dear Dugdale, I am certain; in his industry, his ambition, and his adaptive nature you will find something to admire.

'I have almost forgotten the ways of the old country, so completely have I turned—not my mind only, but my heart and my tastes—to the life of the new. I dare say you remember the days in which I was rather a ' buck,' ran heavy accounts with our common tailor, and knew, or pretended to know, a lot about good dinners and wines.

'Ask Mrs Hungerford what sort of rough and gruff old fellow I am now, and you will understand, from her description, the difficulty I should have in getting into, or even comprehending, the ways of the other side of the world again. But, remembering what I once did know, and thinking of what I have heard and seen since I ceased to know, I think Robert is cut out for success in England. Mind, he will not have it *all* to do unaided; he will have a little money, enough to keep him respectable, to back him.

'I feel I am unwise in thus talking to you so much beforehand of Robert—time enough when we meet, as I hope we shall do; but I have a notion you might hit upon some plan for him for the future more easily and successfully if you had an idea of the sort of person he is.

'If his mother could see this letter, and recognize the very moderate colours in which I have sketched her eldest son, I don't think I should hear the last of it between this and the date at which I and he are to start for England. I am such a dolt in these matters, I do not rightly know what to ask you to think about, or advise me upon; but you will know generally. Shall it be private tuition, or public school, or business life at once combined with education?

'My other boys never give me the least anxiety. I know they will take to the sheep-walk or the counting-house as readily as to their food, and plod on as comfortably and as cheerily as possible. And, indeed, while I am anxious about Robert, it would be giving you an unfair impression to say that I am uneasy about him. I am *not that;* but he is so different a stamp, I hardly know how to manage him.

'I have written all this to you with as much ease and confidence as if we were smoking together in the old quarters, velveteen-coated and slippered, as in the time I remember so well. I wonder if you—who have remained in England, to whom, at all events, life cannot have brought such physical changes as it has brought to me—remember it half so well as I do.

'There are hours even yet, when I am alone and thinking, when all that has intervened seems utterly unreal, and those old days, with their old associations, the one true and living period in my life. Do you remember the day after you, poor little shivering youngster as you were then, came to the school, when I was a great hulking fellow, and my mother, God bless her! came to visit me, and, being taken by old Maddox to see the playground, was just in time to behold me tumble from the very top of the forbidden pear-tree and break my arm?

I can see her face and hear her voice now, as plainly as if I could see the one and hear the other by going into the next room. And how you cried! Well, well, I suppose something of the boy remains until the last in every man's nature, and that more of it has the chance of remaining in our lives here than in yours at home.

'The progress of this place is extraordinary, and there are rumours of discoveries in metals, and so forth, which, if verified, will give it very great impetus. I don't mind them much ; they don't disturb and they don't excite me even in this go-ahead colonial life. I carry my old steadiness about with me, and am go-ahead in my own business only.

'There is much in the political and social world here which would interest, but little which would please you, unless you are very much changed.

'I never could arrive at a very clear notion of you from Mrs Hungerford; she was not communicative on any point, and she never told me anything about you, except that your health was delicate, which I could have told her from your letter. The sort of life we lead here is certainly calculated to give one the power of feeling acutely for a man to whom bodily exertion is forbidden; but you were always a patient fellow.'

The letter was a very long one; the above is but an extract from it. James Dugdale had recognized the handwriting of his friend with pleasure, and had opened the letter with delighted eagerness. It would tell him something of Margaret; it would give him an insight into the troubles of her life; it would give him a clue to the enigma which lived and moved within his sight and his reach daily.

But his calculations were overthrown; he perceived at once that he was destined to gain no further knowledge of Margaret's past life from Hayes Meredith. The disappointment was so keen that at first he hardly had power to feel the interest in his friend's communication which it was calculated to evoke; and, when he had read half through the letter, he returned to the earlier portion in which Margaret was mentioned, and reperused it.

'I wish he had even told me more about Hungerford's death,' said James Dugdale to himself. He was lying on a couch drawn close to the window of his own room, and he allowed the letter to drop by his side, and his gaze fixed itself on the landscape as he spoke. 'I wish he had said more about him. What *were* the circumstances of his death? The little he says here, and one sentence of Margaret's—"when I first heard that my husband had been murdered by the black fellows"—comprise all I know—all any one knows —for her father would not mention his name, and I verily believe has forgotten that the man ever existed. I wish he had told me more.'

He resumed the letter and read it again, this time through to the end, steadily and attentively.

Then he said slowly, and with a despondent shake of the head:

'I am very much afraid my old friend's son, Robert, is a bad boy.'

James Dugdale had not been more than an hour at Chayleigh when he had read Hayes Meredith's letter. His return was unexpected, and he had been told by the servant who admitted him that the 'ladies' were out. This was true, inasmuch as neither was in the house, but incorrect in so far as it seemed to imply that they were together.

Mrs Carteret had departed in her pony-carriage, arrayed in handsome apparel, the materials and tints whereof were a clever combination of the requirements of the season then expiring and the season just about to begin, with a genteel recognition of the fact that an individual connected with the family had died within a period during which society would exact a costume commemorative of the circumstance. Mrs Carteret had gone out, in high good humour with herself, and her dress, and her pony-carriage, with her smart servant, her pretty harness, her visiting-list, and the state of her complexion.

This latter was a subject of unusual self-gratulation, for Mrs Carteret's complexion was changeable: it needed care, and, on the whole, it caused her more uneasiness, and occupied more of her attention, than any other mundane object. She was by no means a plain woman, and she had once been pretty—but her prettiness had been of a sunny, commonplace, exasperating, self-complacent kind ; and now that it existed no longer, the expression of self-satisfaction was rather increased than lessened, for there was no delicacy of feature and no genuine bloom to divert attention from it.

If Mrs Carteret believed anything firmly, it was that she was indisputably and incomparably the best, and very nearly the handsomest, of created beings ; and she had a way of talking solemnly about her personal appearance,—taking careful note of its every peculiarity and variation, and bestowing upon it the minutest and most vexatious care,—which was annoying to her friends in general, and to James Dugdale in particular.

Mrs Carteret was a woman who would be totally unmoved by any kind or degree of human suffering brought under her notice, but who would speak of a cold in her own head, or a pimple on her own face, as a calamity calculated to alarm and grieve the entire circle of her acquaintance. She was almost amusing in her transparent, engrossing, uncontrolled selfishness—amusing, that is, to strangers. It was not so pleasant to those who lived in the house or came into constant contact with her ; they failed to perceive the humorous side of her character.

Her husband, who, with all his oddity and absence of mind, was not destitute of a degree of tact, in which there was a *soupçon* of cunning, and which he aired whenever there was any risk of his dearly-prized 'quiet life' being endangered, had invented a kind of vocabulary of compliments of simulated solicitude and exaggerated sympathy, which was wonderfully efficacious, and really gave him very little trouble. To be sure he was rather apt to adhere to it with a parrot-like fidelity, and on her 'pale days' to congratulate Mrs Carteret on her bloom, and on her 'dull days' to discover that it was difficult to leave her, she talked so charmingly—'but those new specimens must be seen to,' &c., &c.

But these were mere casualties, and, as intense vanity is frequently accompanied by dense stupidity, they never endangered the good understanding between the husband—who was not nearly so tired of his wife as a more clever and practical man must inevitably have been—and the wife, whose wildest imaginings could never have extended to the possibility of any one's finding her less than perfectly admirable, or her husband otherwise than supremely enviable.

In the days when Mrs Carteret had been pretty, her prettiness was of the corset-maker's model description, a prettiness which consisted in straight features, a high and well-defined colour, and a figure which required, and could bear, a good deal of tight-lacing.

Women did lace tightly in the golden prime of Mrs Carteret's days, and she was not behindhand in that or any other fashion; indeed, she had a profound and almost religious respect for fashion, and she had, in consequence, a stiffness of figure suggestive of her being obliged to turn round 'all at once' when it was necessary for her to turn at all, which gave her whole person an air and attitude of stiff and starched stupidity, highly provoking to an observer endowed with taste.

The paying of morning visits was an occupation especially congenial to Mrs Carteret's taste, and well suited to her intellectual capacity, which answered freely to the demand made on it on such occasions. She was not by any means a vulgar gossip, but she possessed a satisfactory enough knowledge of the affairs and 'ways' of all the 'visitable' people within reach, and she found discussing them a very agreeable pastime.

She was not so stupid a woman as to be unaware that she and her affairs were discussed in their turn; but her invariable conviction that, in all respects, she was a faultless being, rendered the knowledge painless.

Thus, when Mrs Carteret set out on a round of visits, in the aforesaid equipage and in her customary choice apparel, she was as happy as it was in her not expansive nature to be.

All the happier that Margaret did not accompany her, for, though Margaret's heavy mourning dress was not a bad foil to the taste and elegance, as she believed, of her own, people were apt to be too much interested in, too curious about, the young widow—always rather an interesting object—for the fancy of Mrs Carteret, who did not admire her stepdaughter herself, and to whom it was neither intelligible nor pleasant that other people should admire her.

As to Lady Davyntry and Mr Baldwin (for she had been forced to include the brother with the sister in the category of Margaret's friends), she had, as we have seen, resolved to find her account in *that* intimacy, and she did not trouble herself about it.

At the same hour in which Mrs Carteret was giving way to her self-complacent sentiments, Margaret was taking leave of Lady Davyntry. She had been at Davyntry since the morning, and was then going home.. Mr Baldwin was ready, according to his now almost invariable custom, to offer her his escort,

It was quite the end of October, a soft, shadowy, beautiful day, the air full of the faint perfume of the fallen leaves and. of the golden gleam of the sunshine, which lingered as if regretfully. Lady Davyntry accompanied Margaret to the little garden-gate which opened into the demesne, and then took leave of her.

When her friend and her brother had left her, she stood for a few minutes looking after them, then walked up the garden-path, saying to herself:

'I hope I shall be able to hold my tongue about it, and not spoil all by letting her see that such an idea has ever entered into my head!'

In many respects Lady Davyntry was a sensible woman.

Margaret and her companion went on their way, slowly. They were talking of a projected journey on the part of Mr Baldwin. He was going to visit his Scotch estates.

'I have not been much there,' he said; 'my time has mostly been passed abroad. My longest stay at the Deane was when poor Nelly was there with Sir Richard; and, of course, I can't expect her to go back to the scene of all her trouble so soon; so I must go alone.

'Can't you?' said Margaret, with a sudden flush on her cheek; 'I should have thought it would have been her greatest, her best consolation. But people feel so differently,' she said absently; and then made some remark about the beauty of the day. Her companion wondered at her strange manner. He took the hint to change the subject.

'Shall you be long away?' Margaret asked him.

He would have been only too happy to tell her that the duration of his absence would depend entirely on her pleasure—to tell her what was the truth, that he was leaving her now because he loved her, and hoped the day might come when he might try to make her love him; when respect for her position should no longer bind him to silence.

He felt he could not remain in her vicinity during the time that must elapse before he could venture to acknowledge his feelings, without the risk of offending her, perhaps

losing her by their premature betrayal, and he had determined to go to Scotland and remain there until the time
should be near when she thought of leaving Chayleigh.

Then he would return and take his chance. If she
would accept the love, the home, the fortune he had to offer
her, he almost dreaded to think what happiness life—which
had never been adorned with any very brilliant hues of imagination by him before—would have in store for him.

When she asked him, in her clear, sweet voice, whose
tones were to-day as pure and untroubled as if she had
never spoken any words but those of the gladness which
should so well have beseemed her youth, that careless question, he felt all the difficulty of the restraint he had imposed
upon himself.

'I am not quite certain,' he replied ; 'I dare say I shall
find a great deal to do at the Deane, and a good deal will be
expected from me in the way of sociability—a tribute, by
the way, which I render very unwillingly. I—I suppose
you will not leave Chayleigh this winter ? '

'I don't think my father has any intention of going anywhere,' Margaret said ; 'and I shall remain with him until
I leave him " for good "—as people say when they leave for
the equal chance of good or evil. I believe, too, there is a
chance of my brother's coming home.'

'Indeed,' said Mr Baldwin ; 'that is good news. I
didn't hear anything of it.'

'No. I told Lady Davyntry this evening, before you
came in. I should like to be here when Haldane comes '
—and her face was overcast by the mournful, musing expression he knew and loved so well. 'He and I quarrelled
before he went away—but I suppose he will not keep that
up with me *now*.'

She looked round with a forlorn kind of smile actually

painful to see. In it there was an appeal to the dreariness of her lot, to the terrible blight which had settled on her youth, against harsh judgment of the wilfulness and folly which had led her to such a doom, inexpressibly affecting.

The strong restraint, the habitual patience which she maintained over all her emotions, seemed to forsake her quite suddenly. Her companion might have taken it as a good omen for him that it was in his company alone the control was loosened; but he did not think of himself, only of her.

The forlorn smile was succeeded by an ominous twitching of the lips, and the next moment Margaret had covered her face with her hands and burst into tears.

Mr Baldwin watched her with inexpressible pangs of love and pity. He dared not speak. What could he say? He knew nothing, though he could surmise much, of the past which had given rise to this burst of emotion.

To try to console was to seem to question her. He stood by her in the keenest distress, and could only entreat her to remember that it was all over now. The paroxysm passed over as he uttered the words for the second time.

Margaret took her hands away from her face, and looked at him, and there was an angry sparkle in her eye which he had never seen before, but which he thought very beautiful.

'You don't believe what you say,' she said quickly, and walking on hurriedly as she spoke; 'you don't believe what you say. You know there are things in life which are never over—sorrows and experiences which time can never change. When you say to me that it is all over now, you say what is not true, and you know it, or you guess it; you might know it if you would. Do you think I am like other women, like your sister, for instance, with nothing but pure and sanctifying grief for the dead, to ripen my mind? Do you think I

am like her, or like any other woman, whose quiet life, however sad, has been led in decency, and has been sheltered and
guarded by the protections which may be found in honest
poverty? Do you think I can come home here, and find
myself once more among the people and places I knew when
I was a girl, and not feel like a cheat? I tell you the Past is
not all over; it will stand as long as I live between me and
other people—not my employers, for there will be no associations in their case ; but every one who knew me once,
and who knows me now. Why does no one speak to *me*, in
even a casual way, of the places I have seen, or the people
I have been amongst? Do you think I imagine it is because
they are unwilling to awaken a slumbering sorrow? No!
You know, and I know, it is because they feel that I have
seen sights unfit for women's eyes, and heard words unfit for
women's ears; and can I ever forget it while others remember it whenever they see me? No, no, no! I never, never
can ! '

She pressed her small hands together and slightly wrung
them, a gesture habitual to her in distress, but which he had
never seen before. He caught her right hand in his, and
drew it within his arm. She walked on with him, but was,
as he knew, almost unconscious of his presence.

How he loved her ! how he hated the dead man who had
caused her to suffer thus ! A young man himself, and she no
more than a girl ; and yet how little of the aspect, how little
of the sense of youth there was about either as they walked
together through the woods and fields that day !

This sudden revelation of Margaret's feelings brought a
sense of despair to Fitzwilliam Baldwin. If the spectre of
the past haunted her thus, if she were divided from all the
present by this drear shade, then was she divided from him
too.

How should he hope to lay the ghost which thus walked abroad in the noonday beside her ? Had he had a little more experience, had not Margaret been so completely a new type of womanhood to him, had he had a little less humility, he would have taken courage from the fact that she had given utterance to such feelings before him.

That he had seen Margaret as no other human being had ever seen her, ought to have been an indication to him that, however unconsciously to her, he was to Margaret what no other human being was. The time was to come in which he was to make that discovery ; but that time was not yet, and he left her that day with profound discouragement.

She recovered herself after a little, and when they reached the confines of the demesne of Chayleigh they were talking in their ordinary manner of ordinary subjects, but Margaret's arm still rested on that of her companion, nor was it removed until they reached the little gate between the wood and the pleasaunce.

As they crossed the lawn, Margaret's dress swept the fallen leaves rustling after her. She was very near the house now, and the sound caught James Dugdale's ear as he lay on his couch in the window. He raised himself on his elbow and looked out. The letter from Hayes Meredith was still in his hand. Margaret looked up and greeted him with a smile.

The next moment she was in the verandah, and he heard her laugh as she spoke to her father. Her voice thrilled his heart as it had done on the first day of her return. Her laugh had something like the old sound in it, which he had not heard since she was a girl. Good God! how long ago! She was looking better than when he went away. She was happy again in her old home.

He went down-stairs, and they had a pleasant meeting.

7

Margaret was kindly interested in his Oxford news.　Mr
Baldwin and Mr Carteret talked together.　James and
Margaret remained in the verandah until after Mr Baldwin
had taken his leave, and the sharp trot of Mrs Carteret's
ponies was audible.　Then Margaret said :

'I must go and get ready for dinner.'

And James detained her for a moment, saying :

'I have a letter which will interest you.　It is from a
friend of yours.'

'A friend of mine ? ' said Margaret, in surprise.　'Who
can it be ?　I have but two or three friends in the world.'

'A cynic would tell you you were exceptionally rich in
friends, according to that calculation.　How do you count
them ? '

'Yourself,' said Margaret, with more frank kindness of
tone than he had ever before recognized in her manner
towards him.

'*Après ?*'

'Well, Lady Davyntry.'

'And Hayes Meredith ?　That is it, is it not?　The
letter is from him.　You shall hear all about it after dinner.'

Margaret left him and went to her room.　She felt
rather vexed with herself.　When she answered James
Dugdale's question, she had *not* been thinking of Hayes
Meredith.

CHAPTER XI.

FOOLS' PARADISE.

SHORTLY after the incidents narrated in the preceding
chapter, Mr Baldwin left Davyntry.　His sister maintained

to the last the strong constraint she had put upon herself. She had seen with a genuine disinterested pleasure, for which the world in general might fairly have been excused for not giving her credit, that her young favourite had captivated her only brother.

Without being a very wise, a very witty, or in any marked way a very superior woman, Eleanor Davyntry possessed certain admirable and estimable qualities. Not the least remarkable, and perhaps the most rare of these, was disinterestedness. This virtue was in her: it did not arise from circumstances. She was not disinterested because she was rich,—the amount of wealth in people's possession makes no difference in their appreciation of and desire for wealth, —and Lady Davyntry 'had no nonsense about her.'

She thoroughly understood the value of her money as a means towards the enjoyment of the happiness which she acknowledged to be hers; but it never occurred to her for a moment to consider her own interests in the question of her brother's future. That he would probably marry at some time she looked upon as certain; and the inheritance of the Deane from one so much younger than herself would not have been a hopeful subject of speculation, had she been a person who would have speculated upon it at all. Even if she had had children, it would have been all the same to Lady Davyntry. She would not have been covetous for them any more than for herself. She had thought rather nervously, since Sir Richard's death had left her more dependent on her brother for the love and companionship without which life would have been intolerable to a woman of her disposition, of the probabilities of Mr Baldwin's marriage.

Lady Davyntry had her prejudices; one of them was against Scotchwomen. She hoped he would not marry a

Scotchwoman, therefore she had never encouraged her brother's residence at the Deane.

'It is not so much their ankles and wrists,' she had assured Sir Richard, when he had remonstrated with her for 'snubbing' a florid young lady who hailed from Aberdeen, and did it in a voice which set Lady Davyntry's teeth on edge, and made her backbone quiver, 'as it is their minds and their ways. Of course, the way they speak is very awful, and the way they move is worse; but I could stand all that, I dare say. But what I cannot stand is their coarse way of looking at things, and the hardness of them in general. And as for flirting! *You* may think it is not dangerous, because it is all romping and hoydenism ; but I don't want a sister-in-law of Miss MacAlpine's pattern, and so I tell you.'

'Hadn't you better tell Baldwin so, my dear Nelly ?' the reasonable baronet had made answer. '*I* don't want a MacAlpine importation into the family either; but, after all, it's *his* business, not mine.'

'No, no,' said the astute Nelly; 'I am not quite so stupid as to warn any man against a particular woman of whom he has hitherto taken no special notice. That would be just the way to make him notice her, and that would be playing her game for her. I am not really afraid of the fair Jessie; Fitzwilliam can see her wrists, and her ankles too, quite as plainly as I can ; and I fancy he suffers rather more acutely from her accent. I shall limit my interference to getting him away from the Deane.'

Other and sadder preoccupations soon after claimed Lady Davyntry, and Miss Jessie MacAlpine was forgotten. And now, when her brother spoke of leaving her to return to the Deane, she remembered the young woman and her mosstrooper-like accomplishments without a shade of apprehension.

'My darling Margaret has made my mind quite easy on
that point, at all events,' thought Eleanor, as Mr Baldwin
imparted to her some of his intentions for the benefit of his
tenantry and estate. 'Whether she cares for him or not,
whether good or evil is to be the result,—and I believe all
will go well with them both,—he is safe in such an attachment.'

When her brother had left her, Eleanor thought long
and happily over it all. Of his feelings she did not entertain a doubt, and her keen feminine perception had begun to
discern in Margaret certain symptoms which led her to hope
that for her too the dawn of a fair day was at hand. If she
had known more of the young widow's inner life, if she had
had a clearer knowledge of her past, Lady Davyntry would
have hoped less and feared more. But her ignorance prevented the discouragement of fear, and her natural enthusiasm aided the impulses of hope; and she saw visions and
dreamed dreams which were pure and beautiful, for they
were all of the happiness and the good of others.

Thus Margaret's sadness and silence, the gloom which
sometimes settled heavily over her, did not grieve her watch-
ful friend. If only she loved, or should come to love, Fitzwilliam Baldwin, all this should be changed. All the dark-
ness should pass away, and a life adorned with all that
wealth could lend, enriched with all that love could give,
should open before the woman whose feet had hitherto
trodden such weary ways. Lady Davyntry pleased herself
with fancies of all she should do to increase the happiness
of that splendid visionary household at the Deane.

If Lady Davyntry could have known what were Margaret's thoughts just at the time when Mr Baldwin went
away, she would have felt some discouragement, though not
so much as a person less given to enthusiasm, and to the

raising of a fancy to the rank and importance of a hobby.
She had never realized any of the painful features of Mrs
Hungerford's past life ; she had never tried to realize them.
Her mind was not of an order to which the realization of
circumstances entirely out of the sphere of her experience
was possible, and she never speculated upon them.

In a different way, and for quite another class of reason,
Lady Davyntry had arrived at a state of mind similar to
that of Mr Carteret, who regarded the blissful fact of his
son-in-law's death as not only the termination, but the con-
signment to oblivion, of all the misery his existence had occasioned.

'Of course she is low at times,' thought Lady Davyntry ;
'that is only natural.   After all, she must feel herself out of
her place at Chayleigh, with that detestable woman.   But
that will not last ; and she will be all the brighter and happier when Fitz has her safely at home.'

The world would have found it hard to understand that
Mr Baldwin's only sister—the great, rich, enviable, to-be-
captured-if-possible Mr Baldwin's sister—should desire so
ardently the marriage of her brother with a person who had
no fortune, no claim to personal distinction, and—*a story*.
Horrible dowry for a woman!   Better any insignificance,
however utter.

And Margaret ?   While Mr Baldwin was attending to
the long-neglected demands, undergoing active persecution
at the hands of a neighbourhood resolved on intimacy, and
longing, with all the strength of his heart, for the sight of
Margaret's pale face and the sound of her thrilling voice—
while his sister was building castles in the air for him to
tenant—what of Margaret ?   What of her who was the
centre, so unconsciously to herself, of all these hopes and
speculations ?

She was perhaps farther just then than she had ever been from a mood which was likely to dispose her towards their realization. She had been disturbed rather than affected by the perusal of Hayes Meredith's letter. It had immediately succeeded to the outburst of emotion to which she had yielded in the presence of Mr Baldwin, and for which she had afterwards taken herself severely to task; and it had upset her hard-worn equanimity.

She was ashamed of herself, angry with herself, when she found out how much she desired that the past should be utterly forgotten. She had had to bear it all, and she had borne it, not so badly on the whole; but she did not want any reference to it; she shrunk from any external association with it as from a physical pain. Her reluctance to encounter any such association had strangely increased within the past few weeks.

She did not know, she did not ask herself, why. Was she ungrateful because she had felt intense reluctance to read Hayes Meredith's letter? Had she forgotten, had she ceased to thank him for all he had done to lighten her lot? Was she so cold, so 'shallow-hearted,' as to think, as many a vulgar-minded woman would have thought, that her account with the man who had succoured her in a strange land was closed with the cheque which her father had given her to be sent to him, in payment of the money he had lent her?

No, Margaret Hungerford was not ungrateful; but there was a sore spot in her heart which something—she did not ask what—was daily making sorer; the letter had touched it, and she shrunk with keen unexplained anguish from the touch. She lay awake the whole night after she had read the letter from Melbourne, and it seemed to her that she lived all the old agonies of despair, rage, humiliation, and disgust over again.

It chanced that the next day James Dugdale was ill. This was so common an occurrence that no one thought much about it. James was familiar with suffering, and it was the inevitable penalty of fatigue. Not for him was the healthy sense of being tired, and of refreshing rest. Fatigue came to him with pain and fever, with racked limbs, and irritable nerves, and terrible depression. His journey had tired him, and he lay all day on the couch placed in the window of his room.

Hither came Mrs Carteret frequently, fussily, but genuinely kind, and Mr Baldwin, to say some friendly words, and feel the truest compassion for the strong man thus imprisoned in his weak frame. Hither, later in the day, and much to the surprise of James Dugdale, came Margaret. He had thought she had gone to Davyntry, and said so. She reddened, a little angrily, as she replied,

'No: I have not been out. You seem to think I must always go to Davyntry'

'Not *I*, indeed, Margaret,' said James, with a smile; 'but I think *they* do. Since I have been away, I understand you have been constantly at Davyntry, and I am very glad to hear it; it is good for you and for Lady Davyntry also.'

'Perhaps so; she is very kind,' said Margaret absently. 'At all events, I am not there to-day, as you see, and I am not going there, or anywhere, but I will sit here with you, if I may.'

She turned on him one of her rare, winning smiles—a smile far more beautiful, he thought, than any her girlhood had been decked in. She drew a low chair into the bow of the window, beside his couch, and sat down. Between him and the light was her graceful figure, and her clear pale face, with its strangely-contrasted look of youth and experience.

'Are you really going to give up all the afternoon to me?' said James, in delight.

'I really am. I will read to you, or we can talk, just as you like. I suppose you don't feel any great fancy for turning tutor to me over again, though I see all my old school-books religiously preserved on your book-shelves,' she said, glancing round at the well-stocked walls of the room, which had been the school-room in the days when Haldane and she had been James's pupils.

'I have kept every remembrance of that time, Margaret,' said James.

There was a tone in his voice which might have been a revelation to her, had she heard it, but she did not. She smiled again, and said :

'You had a troublesome pupil. I am in a good mood to-day, as I used to say long ago, and I want to talk to you about this.'

She took Hayes Meredith's letter out of her pocket as she spoke.

James Dugdale kept silence, looking at her. 'Is she going to tell me the story of her life?' he thought. 'Am I going at last to learn something of the history of this woman whom I love?'

Margaret did not speak for some moments; she looked at the letter in silence. Then she unfolded it, and said:

'I am glad you let me read this letter for myself, James' (she had dropped into the habit of calling him by his name); 'there are some hard things in it, but they are *true*—and so, better spoken, no matter how hard they may be. But let us pass them over, they are said of the dead.'

Her face hardened, and she turned it away from him. James Dugdale laid his thin hand on her arm.

'Margaret,' he said, 'you know I would not have given

you that letter to grieve you. I was thinking so much of what Meredith says of himself and his son that I forgot the allusion to—'

'I know, I know,' she said hurriedly; 'don't say his name; I never do.'

The admission was a confidence. She was breaking down the barrier of reserve between them. She trusted him. She might come to like him yet. The friendship at least of the woman he loved might yet come to gild this man's lonely life. It would be much to him to know that she forgave him; and there was something in her manner now so different from anything that had ever been there formerly, that he began to hope she had really forgiven him.

In his quiet life, James Dugdale had contrived to attain, with very little aid from experience, to a tolerable amount of comprehension of human nature, and he understood that Margaret's practically-enforced conviction, that he had been unerringly right in all he had suspected and predicted of the fate in store for her, in her marriage, had not made her more inclined to pardon the interference on his part which she had so bitterly resented. But this was all over now, he did not know why; he felt it, he did not understand it.

Was it that the natural elasticity of youth was asserting its power—that Margaret was regaining her spirits, was throwing off the burden of the past, and, with it, all the feelings which had obscured the brightness and injured the gentleness of her nature? This was the most probable explanation; if, indeed, there was any other, it did not present itself as an alternative to James Dugdale. While he was thinking thus, she began to speak again in a hurried tone:

'I should like to tell you now, James, because I would rather not have to refer to the matter again, that I know how kind you were to me, and how right in everything you said, and how hard you tried to save me. Yes, yes; let me speak,' she went on, and tears, seldom seen in her eyes, stood in them now. ' I could not again ; let me speak now. You tried, James, I know ; but you could not succeed. It was from myself I needed to be saved. Never think that you could have done anything more than you did; indeed you could not. Nothing could have saved me.'

She was trembling now, even as the hand which he laid on hers, unnoticed, was trembling. Her lustrous eyes were wet, and the emotion in her face made it quite beautiful. James Dugdale did not attempt to speak ; he looked at her, and his heart was wrung with pity.

' It *had* to be, James, and it is done with, as much as it ever can be in this world, in which there is no release from consequences of our own acts. And now '—she raised her head, she released her hand, she was regaining her composure, the momentary expansion was past, as he felt, and he had learned nothing!—' let us talk of your friend, who was so kind to me, and retains so kind a recollection of me. What do you think of all he says ? '

' I think badly of it,' said James, as he leaned back on his couch again, and adopted the tone she had given to their conversation. ' I fear Robert Meredith is a bad boy.'

' So do I,' said Margaret. ' I have seen him, though not often, and I never saw a boy—almost a child—whom I disliked so much. He is a handsome fellow, but selfish, heartless, and sly. His very cleverness was revolting to me, and I suspect the feeling of dislike between us was mutual; he has an American-like precocity about him which I detest. His little brothers, rough colonial children as they are, are infinitely more to be liked than he is. Of course you must do as Mr Meredith asks you; but if you will credit my judgment—and, all things considered, I am

rather daring in asking you to do so—you will not undertake anything like personal charge of Robert Meredith.'

'I will certainly take your advice in the matter, Margaret ; you *know* the boy. I fancy I had better urge
Meredith to bring him to England himself, if it is determined that he is to come. Tell me as much as you remember about the boy, and all the family. I remember Mrs
Meredith, a pretty, active, pert kind of girl—strong and
saucy—a capital wife for him, I should think.'

'I dare say,' Margaret answered carelessly ; 'I did not
know much of her.'

Then their conversation turned on the career and circumstances of Hayes Meredith, with which this story has
no concern. In aftertime James Dugdale remembered
that day as one of the happiest of his life. They were
quite uninterrupted until late in the evening. Mrs Carteret had carried off to a dinner-party her reluctant husband, who would have infinitely preferred to superintend
the dinner of a peculiarly fine spider—whose proceedings
he was watching just then, and whose larder was largely
provided with the last unwary flies of the expiring autumn.

Margaret and James Dugdale dined alone. She was in
good spirits on the occasion ; she had almost lost the painful impression produced by Hayes Meredith's letter, by
talking it over with James ; and between herself and him
there reigned harmony and unreserve which had had no
previous existence. James had never seen her look so
nearly beautiful ; he had never seen her so kind, so gentle
to him.

The hours passed over him in a kind of trance-like spell
of pleasure. Margaret talked as he had never imagined
she could talk. He had soon recognized that her character
was hardened and strengthened by the trials she had en-

dured; but until this day he had not known that her intellect had grown and brightened in proportion.

They read together Haldane's letters to his old friend, and Margaret found in them many a kindly mention of her. Her brother would know of her arrival in England at about this time.

'You must promise to tell me what he says, James, if it is not something very disagreeable indeed.'

And James promised.

From that day Margaret was a less unhappy woman than before. The first effect produced on her by Meredith's letter returned when she went to Davyntry, after Mr Baldwin's departure, and was more than ever warmly greeted by her friend.

'I don't think I could bear Fitzwilliam's absence if I had not your society,' Lady Davyntry said to her; and, fond and flattering as the words were, there was, not in them, but in the mood in which she listened to them, something that hurt Margaret.

The young widow's pride was for ever rebelling against the unshared knowledge of the experiences through which she had passed. Eleanor talked to her incessantly of her brother, of the Deane, of his occupations, his neighbours, and his popularity. The theme did not weary Margaret; and Lady Davyntry accepted her unflagging attention as a delightful omen.

'She misses him; I am sure she misses him,' was her pleased mental comment.

'I hardly expected Margaret to remain so long at Davyntry to-day,' said Mrs Carteret to James Dugdale, as the family party were assembled in the drawing-room at Chayleigh.

James observed the emphasis, and replied:

' Indeed ; why not ? '

' Mr Baldwin is not there, you know, and I fancy he is the great attraction.'

James made her no reply. He fully understood the spiteful animus of the observation, but he also admitted its terrible probability ; not in the present—he did not take so superficial a view of Margaret's character as that would have implied—but a thrill of fear for the future came over him, troubling his Fools' Paradise. In a little while Margaret came in, looking as tranquil as usual, and, in her accustomed manner of placid, unalterable calm,—the bearing she always opposed to the masked battery of Mrs Carteret's insinuations and insolences,—answered the questions put to her.

When James Dugdale was alone that night he took himself to task, in no gentle manner. He knew he had nothing to expect beyond the unexpected boon of kindness and confidence she had already extended to him ; and yet the thought that another might again stand nearer to Margaret than he, struck him with an anguish almost as keen as the first torment had been. He had doubted that fate could bring him anything very hard to bear again, and here was a faint sickening indication that fate intended to resolve his doubt into a fatal certainty.

But no: he would not think of it; he would not let it near him ; it could not be. He knew he was weak in shrinking as he did, in striving to shut out anything that might possibly be true—and, therefore, ought to be faced—as he did ; but the weakness would have its way, like the fainting of the body, and, for the present time at least, he would put the apprehension from him.

The days and the weeks passed by, and the external state of things remained unchanged at Chayleigh. Uninterrupted friendship, and a certain degree of confidence, were maintained between Margaret and James. The health and spirits of the young widow improved ; her friendship with Lady Davyntry remained unimpaired. The correspondence between Eleanor and her brother was frequent and lengthy, and the letters from the Deane were imparted with great frankness by the elder to the younger lady. They were vivid, amusing, and characteristic, and invariably included a message of cordial remembrance to the household at Chayleigh. Peace of mind was prevalent among all the parties concerned in the little *drame intime* with which we are dealing.

Lady Davyntry's mind was at peace, because she saw that Margaret's interest in Mr Baldwin's report of his doings at the Deane did not flag ; and, as she said to herself, 'there was no one to interfere with his chances.'

James Dugdale's mind was at peace, because Margaret seemed happier and calmer than he had ever again expected to see her ; and, as Mr Baldwin remained away, he was not to be feared ; and it was evident that the source of her renewed content was to be found in her present sphere.

Mrs Carteret's mind was at peace, because Margaret gave her no trouble, and kept herself so quiet, so completely aloof from 'the neighbourhood,' that that noun of moderate multitude,—having satisfied its curiosity by observing how Mr Carteret's daughter looked in her 'weeds,' was content to forget her existence, or ready to condole with Mrs Carteret upon her stepdaughter's strange unsociability, and to compliment the lady upon the contrast in that respect which they presented.

Things had turned out so differently from Mrs Carteret's first apprehensive anticipations—she had been able to *exploiter* Margaret so successfully ; her boasted intimacy at Davyntry had been so complacently indorsed by Lady

Davyntry, who would have gone more directly against her
conscience even than that to make Margaret's position at
home easier—that Mrs Carteret had almost ceased to wish
for Margaret's departure—had even thought casually that it
would certainly *look* better, and might possibly *be* better, if
she could be induced to remain at her father's house.

'Perhaps she may settle herself advantageously yet,' Mrs
Carteret—whose ideas were eminently practical—said to herself; and she even thought of consulting James as to
whether she had not better suggest such a solution of the
problem of the future to Margaret.

Mr Carteret's mind was at peace, because his mind had
never been in any other condition since Godfrey Hungerford's death had restored it to ordinary equilibrium, and
because his collections were getting on splendidly.

When Margaret Hungerford had been five months at
Chayleigh—when the time was approaching which she had
fixed upon as the period at which she would commence her
career of labour and independence—when eleven months
had elapsed since Godfrey Hungerford's death—when the
snows of February lay thick and white upon the earth—an
event occurred which disturbed the calm of Chayleigh.

Mrs Carteret distinguished herself in a most unexpected
manner. She caught cold returning from one of the dull
dinner-parties which her soul loved, and which no inclemency
of weather, or domestic crisis which could be ignored with
any decency, would have induced her to forego. A second
dinner-party was to come off within three days; so Mrs
Carteret denied the existence of the cold, and attended that
solemn festival. That day week she was dead.

CHAPTER XII.

DAWNING.

'You cannot conceive anything more perfect than the way Margaret is behaving,' wrote Lady Davyntry to her brother, when the first novelty and shock of Mrs Carteret's death had somewhat subsided, ' in this sad affair. Her conduct to her father is most admirable. He, poor man, is in a wretched state—more, perhaps, of bewilderment than grief, but altogether unhinged.

' " Master's put out terrible," was the account I had from one of the Chayleigh servants, and, odd and horrid as it sounds, I really think that is the best description of poor Mr Carteret's state of mind. Anything he is not used to " puts him out," and he is singularly little used to trouble or emotion of any kind.

' He wanders about in a way distressing to behold, and cannot be induced to occupy himself. "There ain't no keeping him in the study," Foster said to me; "and as much as stick a pin in a butterfly, Mr James nor Miss Margaret can't indoose him to do."

' He seems to have lost all his taste for his specimens, but Margaret has hit upon a great idea for his relief and amusement. This is no other than to talk to her father about the interest which the poor woman who is gone took in his pursuits, and how much she would have regretted his abandonment of them.

' There is a touch of pious fraud in this, for no one can possibly know better than Margaret that Mrs Carteret never took any interest in anything but herself, and was rather more indifferent to her husband's pursuits than to any other matters; but the fraud is pious and successful.

'I have just had a note from her telling me he is more cheerful, and has been watching her dusting specimens this morning. She also says—but, on second thoughts, I enclose the note.

'With all this, my darling Madge has been very candid and sincere. She has felt the awfulness and the import of the event most deeply, but she has not pretended to a personal sorrow which it is impossible she should feel, and I honour her for that—indeed, I honour her for everything, and love her better every day.

'Mr Dugdale has taken Mrs Carteret's death to heart terribly. She was sincerely attached to him, I believe, and I fancy he was the only person in the world who loved her, while he managed her perfectly, and quite understood her queer disposition. I have seen very little of him, but Margaret has told me a good deal about him.

'If you remember, we used to think that he and she did not get on well together—that she did not like him. With all her reserve, Margaret is not difficult to understand; she may keep facts to herself, but she does not disguise feelings, and I am glad to think she and Mr Dugdale get on nicely now that they are in such responsible charge at Chayleigh.

'If my letter bores you, my dear Fitz, I really cannot help it, for my head and my heart are both full of Margaret. The Martleys and Forbeses sent a strong contingent down to the funeral, and two of the Martleys stayed a week: very handsome young men, not in the least like their sister, who was very much older.

'I could not help thinking how vexed the poor woman would have been if she could have seen Henry Martley so captivated by her stepdaughter. He fell in love with Margaret with quite old-fashioned celerity, but she calmly ignored him and his love. Mr Dugdale saw it plainly, and did not like it by any means. They have all had enough of the Martleys, I fancy.

'The young men took their sister's death very easily; the eldest was evidently glad to get away; and I cannot be very much surprised or very angry. This event will make a great difference to Margaret. I have always had a presentiment—I *have*, however you may laugh—that she would not have to leave Chayleigh. Of course, she cannot think of doing so now; she must remain with her father.

'Captain Carteret is on his way home. Mr Dugdale came here yesterday with Margaret for the first time. I believe something was said about his leaving Chayleigh and going back to Oxford, but Mr Carteret would not hear of it; he clings to Mr Dugdale more even than to Margaret. So they will settle down together, no doubt. It is a good thing Captain Carteret was not here sooner; the gloom will have pretty well dispersed before he comes.

'Your account of the Deane is delightful. I think you are quite right not to refurnish the drawing-rooms just yet. Perhaps I might screw up my courage to going there in summer, and then I could choose colours, and so on, for you. You do not really want drawing-rooms at present, and I should not mind anything of the kind if I were you. You may not remain at the Deane long. Indeed, I hope you are thinking of coming back to me; I want to consult you about such a lot of things; and I hate letter-writing, and explain myself so badly.'

For a lady who hated letter-writing, Lady Davyntry indulged in it a good deal; and, with singular self-denial, devoted herself to keeping her brother thoroughly well-informed concerning affairs in the neighbourhood.

She would, priding herself on her astuteness and believing herself inscrutably clever in the performance, send him pages of gossiping details about other people than the dwellers at Chayleigh ; she would tell him about the Croftons, the Crokers, and the Willises, about friends in town and friends in foreign parts, whenever it appeared to her that her insistence upon Chayleigh was becoming too marked.

By such artful dodges did she seek to divert Mr Baldwin's suspicions that she cherished the profound design of marrying him to her friend.

Her brother, on his part, carefully forbore to point out the inconsistency between her dislike of letter-writing and the frequency of her correspondence. He understood the guileless and amiable Eleanor thoroughly, and smiled over her letters as he thought how charmingly transparent the artifice was, and how easily he could have disposed of it all, had it not precisely coincided with his own wishes.

Time hung heavily on Mr Baldwin's hands in the midst of his great possessions, and in the presence of his popularity with an assiduous neighbourhood. He had set his heart, he was ready to stake his whole future, upon winning the wearied heart of the pale-faced girl who had brought something into his life which had never been there before, and the hours and days lingered until the time should come which he had set before himself as fitting for the attempt.

Her first year of widowhood would soon have elapsed, and then he might, without offence, tell her that he loved her. So he named that time, in his own mind, for his return to Davyntry.

When Mrs Carteret's death occurred, Mr Baldwin did not alter his plan. The change in Margaret's prospects, the necessity for her remaining with her father, the fact that her sphere of duty was strictly defined now, gave him no uneasiness.

He would never ask her to leave her father. He knew Mr Carteret well. It did not take much time or pains to acquire that knowledge, and he knew he had no strong attachment to Chayleigh. If he could but persuade Margaret to come and reign at the Deane, he had no doubt her father would readily go there too.

He had a conviction, which, after all, was not presumptuous for a man of his fortune and station to entertain, that in Margaret's brother he should find a friend. James Dugdale had told him a little of the family history—had given him a vague notion of the part Haldane had taken in the circumstances which had led to Margaret's disastrous marriage; and he felt that the young man would naturally rejoice that such a total change should be wrought in the life of his sister, who had paid so dearly for her imprudence.

A man of peculiarly simple tastes and habits, of unaffected ways of thinking about himself and other people, it rarely occurred to Fitzwilliam Baldwin to take his wealth into account; but he did so now, very reasonably. 'It would not weigh with her for a minute,' he thought; 'but it will with them, and it will be pleasant to have them all for, and not against, me.'

Life at Chayleigh had settled down again. The delusive appearance of immutability which human affairs assume—human affairs which are but a shifting quicksand—had established itself. The establishment, presided over by Margaret, went on in the ordinary way, the servants highly appreciating the change of *régime ;* and Mr Carteret was beginning to dispose of the days after his old fashion, when Mr Baldwin returned to Davyntry, and Haldane Carteret arrived at Chayleigh.

The meeting between the brother and sister was frankly affectionate; the renewal of their companionship was delightful to both. Margaret thought her brother wonderfully improved. He was a handsome, manly, soldierly fellow, who had no trace of likeness to his gentle, studious, feeble father, but whose face, despite its bronzed skin and its thick dark moustache, awakened strange memories in Mr Carteret's placid breast.

A curious mental phenomenon took place in the experience of Haldane's father. A little while ago, and he was fretting for Mrs Carteret—if he had said he was wretchedly uncomfortable it would have been a more correct description of his state of mind; but he chose to call himself, to himself, profoundly miserable—and now, since Haldane came home, he had almost forgotten her.

True, he still sat mopingly in his chair, and stared vacantly out of the window, when they left him alone; but the reverie which filled those hours was no longer what it had been. With his son in his bright strong manhood, with his daughter in her womanhood—early shadowed, indeed, but beautiful—beside him, his heart turned to the past, and a gentle figure, a fair delicate face, long since turned to dust, kept him ghostly company in his solitude.

Margaret was much surprised when, shortly after Haldane's return, Mr Carteret began to talk to her one day about her mother, and spoke of her with a cheerful freshness of remembrance which she had never supposed him to entertain.

'The colours she preferred, the books she liked, the places they had visited together, certain fancies she had in her illness—the smallest things, I assure you—is it not wonderful?' Margaret had asked of Lady Davyntry, as she was telling her this strange circumstance. 'I never was more surprised, and, I need not say, delighted; I don't think poor Mrs Carteret's fancies and sayings remain so fresh in his memory. After so many years, too! The fact is, I don't believe she ever really filled my mother's place at all.'

Margaret was seated on a cushion in the bay of a great window in the drawing-room at Davyntry as she spoke thus. Her heavy bonnet and veil were thrown on the floor beside her, her pale, clear, speaking face, the eyes bright and humid, the lips parted eagerly, and the flickering light, which emotion always diffused over her face, playing on her features. Lady Davyntry stood in the window, and looked down upon her.

'I am sure she never did,' said the impulsive Eleanor; 'how could she? It is all very well for a man to marry again, as your father did, when he has little children, and no one but servants to look after them; but, of course, a second marriage never can be the same thing. All the romance of life is over, you know, and one knows how much fancy there is in everything; and, in fact, I can't understand it myself —not for a woman, I mean, who has been happy. A man is different.'

And then Lady Davyntry suddenly discovered that, in proclaiming her general opinion, she was saying exactly the opposite to what she thought in the particular case in which she was most deeply interested, and stopped, very abruptly and awkwardly, and blushing painfully. But Margaret did not seem to perceive her embarrassment. Her hands were pressed together; her eyes looked out strangely, eagerly; her words came as though she had no control of them.

'And do you think an unhappy woman—one who has found nothing in her marriage but misery and degradation —one who has nothing of the dreams and fancies of her youth left for retrospection but sickening deceit and a horrible cheating self-delusion—one who has no good, or pure, or gentle, or upright recollections to cherish of a past which was all a lie, a base, infamous lie—do you think a woman with a story like that in her life ought to marry again? Do you think—you, Eleanor, who are truth and honour themselves, and who, I suppose, in all your life never said, or did, or saw, or heard anything for which you have a right to blush or ought to wish to forget—do you think that a woman with a story like that in her life ought to marry? Do you think she ought to link her life to that of any man, however he might love her and pity her, and be prepared to bear with her, while she had to look back upon such a past, however guiltless she might be in it—do you think this, Eleanor? Tell me plainly the truth.'

She put her hand up, and caught one of her friend's hands in hers. Lady Davyntry still stood and looked at her, and, laying her disengaged hand on her shoulder, answered her passionate question.

'Do I? Indeed I do, Margaret. Tell me, are you asking me this for yourself? Are you asking me if I think, because you have had the least-deserved misfortune to have been the wife of a bad man, and you have been released from him, you are to carry the chain in fancy which has been taken off you in reality? It's unlike you; it is morbid to ask, to think of such a thing. What are you but a young girl still? Are you to do penance all your life for the sins of another? No, no, Margaret; silent as you are about your past, you are asking me this question in reference to yourself. Is it not so? Do not place a half-confidence in me. Do not let a delusion like this take possession of your mind, and blight your future as your past has been blighted.'

'There is nothing in my question,' said Margaret, drawing her hand away from Lady Davyntry, and rising; 'nothing

in the sense you mean. My future seems plain and clear
enough now. My place in the world is fixed, I fancy; but
sometimes, Eleanor, sometimes the past, of which I have
never spoken to you, of which I cannot speak, comes back
to me, not only in its own dreadful shape, but with a dim
undefined threat in it, and makes me afraid. You don't
understand me; well for you that you do not. I trust you
never may.'

She picked up her bonnet and tied it on, and was folding her shawl round her, while Lady Davyntry stood by,
longing to speak out all that was in her mind, and yet
fearing to damage her own hopes by doing so and learning
the worst, when the door opened, and Haldane Carteret
and Mr Baldwin came into the room.

Margaret was standing with her back towards the door,
and facing a mirror, in which Lady Davyntry saw her face
reflected. It was startlingly pale, and there was a wild
look of pain in the eyes, quite other than sadness—sometimes a little stern—which was their usual expression.

Lady Davyntry could hardly reply to the cheery greeting
of Haldane, so much was she struck by Margaret's change
of countenance. Margaret spoke hurriedly to Mr Baldwin.
The only one of the four who did not know that there was
a consciousness on the part of all the others that something
unusual had taken place was Haldane.

'I have come to fetch you home, Madge,' he said, 'and
then I'm going out for a ride with Baldwin, and we dine
with the Croftons, so you won't see much of me to-day.
Are you ready?'

'Quite ready,' said Margaret; and she kissed Lady
Davyntry, and took so hurried a leave of her that her friend
had not time to ask her a question. She was about to give
Mr Baldwin her hand, and bid him good-bye too, but he

said he was going their way—his horses might be taken to Chayleigh.

When she was left alone, Lady Davyntry tried to disentangle her impressions of what had occurred. At last she thought she saw the meaning of it all. Margaret had found out Mr Baldwin's not-carefully-preserved secret, even as she (Eleanor) had found it out, and she loved him. Yes, his sister was sure of it. She had all the acuteness which keen feeling and true sympathy give, and which is truer in emergencies than that of mere intellectual cleverness, and she knew that a sharp and severe struggle was raging in the young widow's heart.

She understood it all now—she understood that Margaret shrank from the avowal to herself that she had learned to love and trust again, that she had not been able to carry out the expiatory process which she had resolved—the process of loneliness and labour, of self-repression, and the abnegation of the true happiness to be had even in this world, because she had been beguiled by the false. She understood that Margaret, however believing and trusting in Fitzwilliam Baldwin's love, would feel that there was no equality between them, and that the serene and beautiful fancies of a happy girl were not for her, while all the illusion and gladness of life's early days still were his. Intuitively Lady Davyntry understood it all; the face she had seen in the glass, when her brother's entrance had surprised Margaret in one of her rare moments of emotion, had made it all plain to her.

'She will refuse him,' Eleanor thought; 'she will refuse him. These two, the most suited to one another, the best calculated to be happy of any people I ever knew—the very ideal of a well-matched pair—will be kept apart by a chimera. So the evil of that vile man's life lives after him, and he has the power to make her and others miserable, though he is in his grave. Shall I speak openly to Fitzwilliam? I cannot do harm now. No man could be more bent upon anything than he is on marrying Margaret. I may as well let him know—if, indeed, he has not guessed it—how much I wish it too.'

Lady Davyntry's nature, like her brother's, was essentially sunny and cheerful; so she soon roused herself from the depression her discovery had caused her.

'If she does refuse him,' thought Eleanor, after long cogitating with herself, 'she cannot refuse to tell him why. She is too sincere—she will not deny that she loves him, and then she will be persuaded out of this morbid fancy by degrees. After all, it will only be a case of waiting. I must have patience, and Fitzwilliam must have patience too. Margaret is worth waiting for. I shall see her at the Deane yet.'

It was a source of great satisfaction to Lady Davyntry to remember that Margaret was settled at Chayleigh, that Mr Baldwin need not fear her removal—that, in fact, he had every external advantage on his side.

'How strangely things happen!' she thought. 'Really, it seems as if that poor woman's death were quite providential. If she had lived I don't see how Margaret could have possibly stayed at Chayleigh; and now she cannot get away. Even if she had remained, she could not have been in such a pleasant and independent position.'

And then Lady Davyntry, who possessed in perfection the fine feminine facility for looking at every subject from exclusively her own point of view, came to the comfortable conclusion that poor Mrs Carteret's death was 'all for the best.'

Haldane Carteret retained all his boyish affection for

James Dugdale. His old tutor loved him, too, better than
any one in the world save Margaret; and the young man's
sojourn at home was a bright spot in the life of the older
man, whose life had in it very little brightness. All that
James knew of Margaret's story he had told Haldane by
letter, and now the subject was but rarely revived between
them.

Haldane was not a very acute observer. He rarely
troubled himself with the reflective part of life; he had
bright animal spirits, good health, and was now of an active
temperament very different from the promise of his boyhood.
The experiment of letting him follow his military inclinations had turned out admirably. His father was very fond
of him, very proud of him, and kept out of his way as
much as possible. His presence had the best possible effect
on Margaret, who was beginning to bloom again, not only
with the roses, but with the spirits of her girlish days.

Haldane was immensely delighted with Mr Baldwin. It
was a new experience to him that a man of such large
fortune, such assured position, such high intellectual attain-
ments, still young and flattered by the world, should be of
so unworldly a spirit, so pure of heart and life, and so entirely unassuming. In modern parlance, Mr Baldwin was
an undeniable 'swell,' but he never seemed to remember the
circumstance except when an act of generosity, or the exercise of privilege in the cause of good, was required.

'I'll tell you what, Dugdale,' Haldane Carteret said to
his old friend as they strolled together in the fields by the
clump of beeches which Margaret had said she hated, 'there
are not many such fellows going as Baldwin!'

James Dugdale heartily concurred in his companion's
estimate of Baldwin.

'Knocking about the world teaches a fellow to appreciate a man like that,' continued Haldane. 'It's very strange to remember how one has been taken in by people. There was that ruffian Hungerford, for instance. By-the-by,'— and Haldane stood still, and looked into James's face to make his words more emphatic,—'I think Baldwin is uncommonly attentive to Madge, don't you?'

'N—no,' said James hesitatingly; 'I can't say I noticed anything of the kind.'

'Look out, then, and you will notice it. You're not an observing person, you know—not a lady's man exactly— neither am I; but I think I know the symptoms of that sort of thing when I see them; and I don't think Baldwin is staying at Davyntry altogether on account of his sister. I say, James, what a grand thing it would be, wouldn't it?'

'What a grand thing *what* would be?' asked Dugdale in an impatient tone.

'If Madge likes him, and he likes her, and they make a match of it. It would be a fine marriage for any girl, and it would be a great thing to have all the past put out of her mind. Fate owes her a good turn, poor girl!'

And James? Did not Fate owe him a good turn? If so, he thought sadly, the debt was not likely to be paid. The change in Margaret's manner the increased frankness, the ready kindness she showed him now, had ceased to bring him any happiness. He did not deceive himself now as to its source.

He was nothing more to her than he had ever been; but, instead of the old bitterness, a root of sweetness was springing up in her heart, and its natural outcome was the oblivion of her former feelings, the remission of all past and gone offences from those who would but be doubly indifferent to her under the influence of this new motive in her life.

For a time James Dugdale yielded to the weakness which this new keen suffering produced. He felt that life had been always bitter for him—there was no mercy, no gentleness in it at all.

When he looked at Margaret and noted the change in her face—saw how the light had come back into the eyes, the roundness to the clear pale cheeks, the softness to the square brow and the small lips, and interpreted the change aright, notwithstanding the fits of heavy sadness which still came over her—he would feel very tired of life. Impossible not to envy the lot which was never to be his—the destiny of those who are dowered with love.

Never to be, never to have been, the first object in life to any one is a melancholy fate, he would think—one for which no general affection, or appreciation, not even the most intoxicating gift of fame, could ever compensate.

This was his lot, and he knew it, and did not attempt to persuade himself that it was not very hard and bitter to submit to. After a time he should be able to look at the matter from the unselfish point of view of Margaret's happiness; but not yet. He had never quite realized the nature and extent of his own fears, until Haldane's words had put the truth before him in the airy and cheerful manner related. Of course he was right; of course it would be a 'great match,' and a 'fine thing;' of course it would be the most complete reparation of all that Fate had wrought against Margaret —the most total reverse of her life which could be devised.

The love of such a man—as James, rigidly just in all his pain, acknowledged Fitzwilliam Baldwin to be—had in itself such elements of dignity and honour, such power of rehabilitation for the wounded spirit of the woman he loved, that it was an act of utter oblivion.

From the unassailable height of her position, as Mr Baldwin's wife, Margaret might look down upon the pigmy cares of coarse remark and prying curiosity, as on all the sordid and common anxieties of material life from which she had once suffered so keenly.

He knew all this—he who would, he believed, have suffered anything in the cause of her welfare. Yes, and so he would, anything but just the thing he was appointed to suffer; and he could not bring himself to bear it, not yet. He forgot how he had acknowledged, when she returned to Chayleigh, that she could not continue to live there, that the dead level of life there would be intolerable to her who had breathed the atmosphere of storm and been tossed on the waves of trouble. She was too young to find refuge in calm ; the peace which is the paradise of age which has suffered, is the prison of suffering youth.

He knew all this, and yet he murmured against the destiny that was going to release her, without penalty or price—that was going to crown her life with happiness. He murmured, he revolted, he raged ; and then he submitted, as we all must, to everything.

From this state of feeling to an intense longing to know the truth, to have it all over and done with—to be quite certain that Margaret had put the old life from her, and with it all the ties which existed between her and him ; that she was going into a sphere in which he could have no place— was a natural transition for James Dugdale's feverish, sensitive temperament.

He watched Margaret and her friend ; he understood Lady Davyntry's feelings perfectly, and owed her no grudge for them ; he rather honoured her as more large-minded and disinterested than most women. Of course she coveted such a prize as Margaret for her brother. To the rich, treasures, was the judgment and the way of the world.

He watched Margaret and her lover. Yes, her lover—he forced himself to give him that kingly title in his thoughts, and he thought, he knew, he hoped it might soon come—that suspense, at least, would be over, and nothing would remain for him but to accustom himself to the new order of things.

Full of these thoughts, he sought Margaret, one beautiful day in May, in the pleasaunce. He had seen her walking on the lawn. She had exchanged a few sentences with him as she passed the windows of Mr Carteret's study, where James was sitting, and he had promised to join her presently, when her father released him. He was anxious to tell her that he had heard again from Hayes Meredith. When he joined her he held a letter in his hand.

'Papa has been bothering you about those dreadful bats, hasn't he, James?' asked Margaret with a smile; 'I will take my turn at them this afternoon.'

'Oh no,' he said; 'but I wanted to see you before you went out, because I have a letter from Melbourne.'

She changed colour slightly, and glanced nervously at the letter.

'It is very short. Meredith merely says he cannot come to England, or send his son for some time—not for a year, indeed. There is a money difficulty out there, and Mrs Meredith is in delicate health.'

'Indeed! I am sorry for that. So master Robert must put up with colonial life for a little longer.'

'Yes,' replied James; 'and I am not sorry. The longer my responsibility as regards that young gentleman is deferred the better. Still, I should like to see Meredith. Shouldn't you, Margaret?'

'No,' she said quickly, and in a tone of decision, 'I should not, James. Not because I am ungrateful—no, indeed—but because anything, any one connected with that dreadful time I would shun by any lawful means. You don't know how I dread any mention of it, how I shrink from any thought of it. You don't—you can't—it is like a curse from which I never can escape. If'—she continued vehemently—'if Hayes Meredith came into this house, if any one from that place came, I should feel it was an evil omen—I should be sure it could only be to bring me misery. Very superstitious, very wrong, very weak,—is it not, James?—I know; but it is perfectly true, and stronger than I—

She shuddered as she spoke, and was quite pale now.

James looked at her in agitated surprise, and put the letter, which she had made no motion to take from him, into his pocket.

At that moment the footman approached them, coming from the house.

James glanced at Margaret's white face and tearful eyes, and went forward to intercept the servant before he should be near enough to discover them also.

'A letter from Davyntry, for Mrs Hungerford, sir,' said the man.

'Is there any answer required?'

'I don't know, sir.'

James brought the letter—a very thick one—to Margaret.

'Just open this,' he said, 'and see if there's an answer.'

She broke the seal of the envelope, which was directed in Lady Davyntry's hand, and drew out, not a letter from her friend, but a second sealed envelope, with her name upon it. The writing was well known to her; it was Mr Baldwin's.

9

The outer cover fell to the ground, as she stood with the enclosure in her hand, James looking at her and at it.

'There's—there's no answer,' she said. She had not made the slightest attempt to open the missive.

James Dugdale delivered the message to the servant, who went back to the house, and then he turned away down another path and struck into the fields.

CHAPTER XIII.

DAY.

It will probably be entirely unnecessary to inform the intelligent reader what was the nature of the contents of the letter which James Dugdale had handed to Mrs Hungerford. Retrospect, present knowledge, or anticipation will convey a sufficiently accurate perception of it to all the readers of this story.

The writing of that letter was the result of a long and entirely unreserved conversation which had taken place between Lady Davyntry and her brother, after the last-recorded interview between the former and Margaret.

So entirely confident was Eleanor of Mr Baldwin's feelings and intentions, that she no longer hesitated to speak to him on the matter nearest her heart from any apprehension of defeating her own purpose by precipitation.

In the doubts and fears, in the passionate and painful burst of reminiscence which had given her added insight into Margaret's nature, Lady Davyntry had seen, far more plainly than Margaret,—or at least than ever she had confessed to herself,—that a new love, a fresh hope, had come to her. The very strife of feeling which she confessed and described betrayed her to the older woman, whose wisdom, though rather of the heart than of the understanding, was true in this case

'It will never do to let her brood over this sort of thing,' said Lady Davyntry to herself with decision. 'The more time she has to think over it, the more danger there is of her working herself up into a morbid state of mind, persuading herself that she ought to sacrifice her own happiness, and make Fitz wretched, because she had the misfortune to be married to a villain, and associated, through him, with some very bad people—the more she will tax her memory and torture her feelings, by trying to recall and realize all the past. I can see that nature and her youth are helping her to forget it all, and would do so, no doubt, if Fitz never existed; but she is trying to resist the influence of nature, and to train herself to a state of mind which is simply ruinous and absurd.'

So Lady Davyntry spoke to her brother that evening, and had the satisfaction of finding that she had acted wisely in so doing. 'Don't speak to her, Fitz,' she said, towards the conclusion of their conversation; 'don't give her the chance of being impelled by such feelings as she has acknowledged to me, to say no,—let her have time to think about it.'

It was a position in which few men would have failed to look silly, that of talking over a love affair, in the ante-proposal stage, with a sister. But Mr Baldwin was one of those men who never can be made to look silly, who have about them an inborn dignity and entire singleness of purpose which are effectual preservatives against the faintest touch of the ridiculous in their words or actions.

He had spoken frankly of his hopes, and of his grounds for entertaining them, but the account his sister gave of Margaret's state of mind troubled him sorely. Here Lady

Davyntry again proved her possession of sounder sense than many who knew her only slightly would have believed she possessed.

'It won't last,' she assured her brother; 'it is a false, phantasmal state of feeling, and though it might grow more and more strong if nothing were opposed to it, it will disappear before a true and powerful feeling—rely upon it she will wonder at herself some day, and be hardly able to realize that she ever gave way to this sort of thing.'

Mr Baldwin wrote the letter, the answer to which was to mean so much to him; and Lady Davyntry enclosed it in a cover directed by herself.

'I don't think my darling Margaret can have much doubt about how I should regard this affair,' she said, as she sealed the envelope with such a lavish use of sealing-wax in the enthusiasm of the moment, that it swelled up all round the seal like liliputian piecrust; 'but whatever she may have teased herself with fancying, she will know it is all right when she sees that I enclose your letter. Some women might take it into their heads to be annoyed because you had spoken to another person of your feelings; but Margaret is too high-minded for anything of that sort, and, rely upon it, she will be none the less happy, if she promises to become your wife, that she will make me as happy in proportion as yourself by the promise.'

At this stage, the impulsive Eleanor gave vent to her emotion by hugging her brother heartily, and accompanying the embrace with a shower of tears.

Margaret remained where James Dugdale had left her standing with Mr Baldwin's letter in her hand. She did not break the seal, she did not move, for several minutes,—then she picked up Lady Davyntry's envelope, which had fluttered to the ground, and went into the house.

Any one not so innocently absent-minded as Mr Carteret, or so cheerfully full of harmless self-content of youth, health, and unaccustomed leisure as Haldane Carteret, could hardly have failed to notice that there was something strange in the looks and manner of two of the little party who sat down that day to the dinner table at Chayleigh, shorn of much of its formality since Mrs Carteret had ceased to preside over it.

Margaret was paler than usual, but not with the pallor of ill-health—the clear skin had no sallowness in its tint.

To one accustomed to read the countenance which had acquired of late so much new expression, and such a softening of the old one, the indication of strong emotion would have been plain, in the pale cheek, the lustrous, downcast eye, the occasional trembling of the small lips, the absent, preoccupied gaze, the sudden recall of her attention to the present scene, the forced smile when her father spoke to her, and the unusual absence of interest and pleasure in Haldane's jokes, which were sometimes good, but always numerous.

James Dugdale sat at the table, quite silent, and did not even make any attempt to eat. Margaret, with the superior powers of hypocrisy observable in the female, affected, unnecessarily, to have a very good appetite. The meal was a painful probation for them.

It was so far from unusual for James to be ill and depressed, that when Haldane had commented upon his silence and his want of appetite in his usual off-hand fashion, and Mr Carteret had lamented those misfortunes, and digressed into speculation whether James had not better have his dinner just before going to bed, because wild beasts gorge themselves with food, and go to sleep immediately afterwards, no further notice was taken.

It never occurred to Mr Carteret or to Haldane that

anything except illness could ail James.   Neither did it occur to one or the other to notice that Margaret, usually so observant of James, so kind in her attention to him, so sympathetic, who understood his ' good days ' and his ' bad days ' so well, did not make the slightest remark herself, and suffered theirs to pass without comment.

She never once addressed James during dinner, nor did her glance encounter his.   Why ?

It had been Margaret's custom of late to sit with her father in his study during the evening.   Mr Carteret and she would adjourn thither immediately after dinner, and James and Haldane usually joined them after a while.

Margaret did not depart from her usual practice on this particular evening, but she was not inclined to talk to her father.   She settled him into his particular chair, in his inevitable corner, and began to read aloud to him, with more than her usual promptness.

But somehow the reading was not successful, her voice was husky and uncertain, and her inattention so obvious that it soon became infectious, and Mr Carteret found the effort of listening beyond him.   An unusually prolonged and unmistakeable yawn, for which he hastened to apologize, made the fact evident to Margaret.

' I think we are both disinclined for reading to-night, papa,' she said as she laid aside her book, and took a low seat by her father's side.   ' We will talk now for a while.'

' Very well, my dear,' said the acquiescent Mr Carteret. But Margaret did not seem inclined to follow up her own proposition actively   She sat still, dreamily silent, and her fingers played idly with the fringe which bordered the chintz cover of her father's chair.   At length she said :

' Papa, what do you think of Mr Baldwin ? '

' What do I think of Mr Baldwin, my dear ? ' repeated

Mr Carteret slowly   ' I think very highly of him indeed : a
most accomplished young man I consider him, and excessively obliging, I'm sure.   I don't flatter myself, you know,
Margaret, with any notion that I am a particularly delightful companion for any one; indeed, since our great loss, I
am best alone I think, or with you—-with you, my dear,' and
her father patted Margaret's head just as he had been used
to pat it when she was a little child ; ' and still, he seems to
like being with me, and takes the greatest interest in my
collection   Excessively liberal he is, too, and I can assure
you very few collectors, however rich they may be, are *that*.
He has shared his magnificent specimens of lepidoptera with
me, and I have not another friend in the world who would
do that.   Think of him ? ' said Mr Carteret again, returning to Margaret's question.   ' I think most highly of him.
But why do you ask me ?   Don't you think well of him
yourself ? '

Margaret looked up hastily, dropped her eyes again, and
said :

' Oh yes, papa ; I—I do, indeed ; but I wanted to ask you,
because——' A quick tapping at the window interrupted
her.   Haldane stood outside, and his sister left her seat and
went to him.

' Come out for a walk, Madge,' he said.   ' James is queer
this evening, and says he will just give the governor half-an-
hour, and then go to bed.   You don't want them both, do
you, sir ? '   Haldane asked the question with his head inside
and his body outside the window.   ' I thought not.   Here's
James now.'   At that moment Mr Dugdale entered the
room.   ' Come on ; you can get your bonnet and shawl ;
the door is open.'

Margaret had not turned her face from the window, and
she now stepped out into the verandah.   She had not seen

the expression on James Dugdale's face. Instinct caused her to avoid him. She had not yet faced the subject in her own mind, she had not yet reckoned with herself about it.

'Has she written to him? Is he coming here? How is it?'

These were the questions which repeated themselves in James's brain as he tried to talk to Mr Carteret, and tried *not* to follow the footsteps of the woman whose way was daily deviating more and more widely from his.

The brother and sister walked down the terrace and into the pleasaunce together.

Haldane had been exposed to the fascinations of the eldest Miss Crofton for the last ten days or so, and, being rather defenceless under such circumstances, though not, as he said of himself, 'a lady's man,' he was very likely to capitulate, unless some providential occurrence furnished him with a change of occupation, and thus diverted his mind.

At present the eldest Miss Crofton—her papa, her mamma, her little brother, a wonderfully clever child, and particularly fond of being 'taken round the lawn' on Haldane's horse, with only Haldane on one side and his sister on the other to hold him on—her housekeeping science, and her equestrian feats, afforded Haldane topics of conversation of which Margaret showed no weariness. Her attention certainly did wander a little, but Haldane did not perceive it.

They had passed through the gate into the fields which bordered on Davyntry, and Haldane had just pleaded for a little more time out, the evening was so beautiful—adding his conviction that every woman in the world was greedy about her tea, and that Margaret would not be half so pale if she drank less of that pernicious decoction—when she started so violently that he could not fail to perceive it.

'What's the matter?' he asked, in surprise.

'Nothing,' said Margaret. 'There's—there's some one coming.'

'So there is,' said Haldane, looking at a figure advancing quickly towards them from the direction of Davyntry; 'and it is Baldwin.'

The blood rushed violently into Margaret's cheeks, her feet were rooted to the ground for a moment, as she felt the whole scene around her grow indistinct; the next, she was meeting Mr Baldwin with composure which far surpassed his own, and in the first glance of her candid eyes, which looked up at him shyly, but entirely with their owner's will, he read the answer to his letter.

'If you will take Margaret home to this important and ever-recurring tea, Baldwin,' said Haldane Carteret, 'I will go on a little farther, and smoke my cigar.'

He went away from them quickly, and saying to himself, 'It is to be, I think.'

CHAPTER XIV

FULL COMPENSATION.

It did not fall to Margaret Hungerford's lot to resume the topic of her interrupted conversation with her father. Mr Baldwin took that upon himself, and so sped in his mission, that the old gentleman declared himself happier than he had ever been in his life before; and then, suddenly and remorsefully reminiscent of his late domestic affliction, he added, 'If only poor Sibylla were here with us to share all this good fortune!' An aspiration which Mr Baldwin could have found it in his heart to echo, so full was that heart of joy.

In the love of this man for Margaret there was so much of generous kindness, such an intense desire to fill her life with a full and compensating happiness, to efface the past utterly, and give her in the present all that the heart of the most exacting woman could covet, that he regarded his success with more than the natural and customary exultation of a lover to whom 'yes' has been said or rather implied. That Margaret realized, or indeed understood, even in its broad outlines, the alteration in the external circumstances of her life which her becoming his wife would effect, he did not imagine; and he exulted to an extent which he would hitherto have believed impossible in the knowledge that he could give her wealth and position only inferior to his love.

Beyond a vague understanding that Mr Baldwin was a very rich man for a commoner, and that, as the property was entailed on heirs general, Lady Davyntry would have it in the event of his dying childless, Mr Carteret had no clear notions about the position in which his daughter's second marriage would place her, and Mr Baldwin's explanations rather puzzled and confounded the worthy gentleman. He had shrunk as much as possible from realizing to himself the circumstances of Margaret's life in Australia, the disastrous experiences of her first marriage, and he now showed his dread of them chiefly by the complacency, the delight with which he dwelt upon the happiness which he anticipated for her in the society of Mr Baldwin, so accomplished a man, so perfect a gentleman, and withal such a lover of natural history. He was not disposed to take other matters deeply into consideration, and it was chiefly Haldane with whom the preliminaries of the marriage, which was to take place soon, and with as little stir or parade as possible, were discussed. The young man's exultation was extreme. He expressed his feelings pretty freely, after his usual fashion, to everybody; but he reserved the full flow of his delight for James Dugdale's special edification.

'It isn't the correct thing to talk to Baldwin about, of course,' he said one day; 'but I find it very hard to hold my tongue, when I think of that ruffian Hungerford, and that it was through me she first saw him, and got the chance of bringing misery on herself. I long to tell Baldwin all about him. But it wouldn't do. I wonder if he knows much concerning him.'

'Nothing, I should say,' returned James shortly,—he never could be induced to say much when the topic of Margaret and her lover was in any way under discussion,— but the unsuspecting Haldane, in whose eyes James Dugdale, though a more interesting companion, was a contemporary of his father, and in the 'fogey' category, did not notice this reluctance.

'Well, I suppose not,' said Haldane musingly. 'It's a pity; for he would understand what we all think about *him*, if he did; and I don't see how he is to realize that otherwise.'

'Margaret will teach him how he is estimated,' said James sadly.

'I hope so,' was Haldane's hearty and emphatic reply. 'By Jove! it's a wonderful thing, when you come to think of it, that anybody should have things made up to them so completely as Madge is going to have them made up. I don't mean only his money, you know. I wonder how she will get on in Scotland, how she will play her part among the people there. I dare say Baldwin's neighbours will not like her much; I suppose the mothers in that part of the world looked upon him as their natural prey.'

'I don't know about that,' said James, 'but I fancy Margaret will be quite able to hold her own wherever she may go; she is the sort of woman who may be safely trusted with wealth and station.'

This was by no means the only conversation which took place between the ex-tutor and the ex-pupil on the subject then engrossing the attention of the families at Davyntry and Chayleigh; Haldane's exuberant delight was apt to communicate itself after a similar fashion very frequently, and altogether he subjected his friend just then to a not inconsiderable amount of pain.

During the few weeks which intervened before the period named, very shortly after their engagement, for the marriage of Margaret Hungerford and Fitzwilliam Baldwin, there was no approach on Margaret's part to any confidential intercourse with James Dugdale. By tacit mutual consent they avoided each other, and yet she never so wronged in her thoughts the man who loved her with so disinterested a love, as to believe him alienated from her, jealous of the good fortune of another, or grudging to her of the happiness which was to be hers.

In the experience of her own feelings, in the engrossment of her own heart and thoughts in the new and roseate prospects which had opened suddenly before her, after her long wandering in dreary ways, she had learned to comprehend James Dugdale. She knew now how patiently and constantly he had loved and still loved her; she knew now what had given him a prescient knowledge of her former self-sought doom; she knew what had inspired the efforts he had made to avert it from her. Inexpressible kindness and pity for him, painful gratitude towards this man whom she never could have loved, filled Margaret's heart; but she kept aloof from him. Explanation between them there could not be— it would be equally bad for both. He who had so striven to avert her misery would be consoled by her perfect happiness; in the time to come, the blessed peaceful time, he should share it.

So she and James lived in the usual close relation, and Mr Carteret and Haldane talked freely of the coming event, of the splendid prospects opening before Margaret; but never a word was spoken directly between the two.

A strongly appreciative friendship had sprung up between Mr Baldwin and James Dugdale. The elder man regarded the younger without one feeling of envy of the good looks, the good health, the physical activity,—in all which he was himself deficient,—but with a thorough comprehension of the difference between them which they constituted, and an almost womanish admiration of one so richly dowered by nature.

Since Mr Baldwin's engagement to Margaret,—though James had loyally forced himself to utter the congratulations of whose truth and meaning none could form a truer estimate than he,—there had been little intercourse between them. Mr Baldwin now claimed Margaret as his chief companion during his daily and lengthy visits to Chayleigh; and she, with all a woman's tact and instinctive delicacy, quietly aided the unobserved severance between himself and James, of which her lover was wholly unconscious.

So the time—a time of such exceeding and incredible happiness to Margaret, that not all her previous experience of the delusions of life could avail to check the avidity with which she enjoyed every hour of it, and listened with greedy ears to every promise and protestation for the future— went on.

On one point only she found she was not to have her own wishes carried out, wishes shared to the utmost by Mr Baldwin. Her father did not take kindly to the idea of leaving Chayleigh. His reasons were amusingly characteristic.

'You see, my dear,' he said, when the matter had been urged upon him, with every kind of plea and prayer by Margaret, and with respectful earnestness by Mr Baldwin, 'I should never feel quite myself, I should never feel quite comfortable away from my collection. You, my dear Margaret, never had any great taste in that way, and of course you don't understand it; but there's Baldwin, now. You wouldn't like to part with your collection, would you? You have a great many other reasons for liking the Deane, of course, besides that; but considering only that, you would not like it?'

'Good heavens, sir!' exclaimed Mr Baldwin, 'how could you imagine such a thing as that we ever dreamed of parting you and your collection? Why, we should as soon have thought of asking you to leave your arms or legs after you. Of course you'll move your collection to the Deane; there's room for a dozen of the size.'

Mr Carteret was a little put out, not exactly annoyed, but *gêné;* and Margaret, who understood him perfectly, stopped her lover's flow of protestation and proposal by a look, and they soon left him to himself; whereupon Mr Carteret immediately summoned James, and imparted to him the nature of the conversation which had just taken place.

'Baldwin is the very best fellow in the world, James,' said the old gentleman in a confidential tone; 'but, between you and me, we collectors and lovers of natural history are rather odd in our ways; we have our little peculiarities, and our little jealousies, and our little envies. You know I would not deny Baldwin's good qualities; and he has been very generous too in giving me specimens; but I have a kind of notion, for all that, that he would have no objection to my collection finding its way to the Deane.'

Here Mr Carteret looked at James Dugdale, as if he

had made a surprisingly deep discovery; and James Dugdale had considerable difficulty in concealing his amusement.

'Now you can, I am sure, quite understand that, however I may appreciate Baldwin, I have no fancy for seeing my collection, after working at it all these years, merged in another—merged, my dear James!'

And Mr Carteret's tone grew positively irate while he tapped Dugdale's arm impatiently with his long fingers.

'But, sir,' said James, 'I quite understand all that; but how about parting with Margaret? If she is to be at the Deane, hadn't you better be there also? She is of more importance to you than even your collection, is she not?'

'Well, yes, in a certain sense,' said the old gentleman, rather dubiously and reluctantly; 'in a certain sense, of course she is; but, then, I can go to the Deane when I like, and she can come here when she likes; and so long as I know she is happy (and she cannot fail to be *happy* this time), I don't so much mind. But I really could not part with my collection; and if it were moved and merged, I should feel I had parted with it. No, no, Margery and Baldwin will be great companions for each other, and they will do very well without us, James; we will just stay quietly here in the old place, and I am sure Haldane will undertake not to move my collection when I am gone.'

Immediately after this conversation, Mr Carteret applied himself with great assiduity to the precious pursuit which, in the great interest of the domestic discussions then pending, he had somewhat neglected, and showed his jealous zeal for his beloved specimens by a thousand little indications which Margaret perceived, and which she interpreted to Mr Baldwin, very much to his amusement.

'Haldane,' said James Dugdale to Captain Carteret, 'I think you had better give Margaret a hint that she had better not urge her father's leaving Chayleigh; depend upon it, he will never consent, except it be very much against his will; and if she presses him, she will only run the risk of making him like Baldwin very much less than he does at present.

'You are quite right,' said Haldane, who was busily engaged in mending the eldest Miss Crofton's riding-whip; 'but why don't you tell her so yourself?'

James was rather embarrassed by the question; but he said, 'It would come better from you.'

'Would it? I don't see it. However, I don't mind. I'll speak to her. All right.'

Haldane did speak to Margaret; and she acquiesced in James's opinion, and conformed to his advice. The subject dropped, and Mr Carteret entirely recovered his spirits. Haldane had another little matter to negotiate with his sister, in which he was not so successful. He knew the wedding was to be very quiet indeed; but everybody either then knew, or soon would know, that such an event was in contemplation; and he could not see that it could make any difference to Margaret just to have the eldest Miss Crofton for her bridesmaid. He could assure his sister the eldest, 'Lucy, you know,' was 'an extremely nice girl,' and her admiration of Margaret quite enthusiastic.

Margaret was quite sure Lucy Crofton was a very nice girl indeed; and she would have her for her bridesmaid, had she any intention of indulging in such an accessory, but she had none; and Haldane (of course men did not understand such matters) had not reflected that to invite Miss Lucy in such a capacity must imply inviting all her family as spectators, and entail the undying enmity of the 'neighbourhood' at their exclusion.

'Oh, hang it, Madge,' said Haldane in impatient disdain

of this reasoning, 'we are not people of such importance that the neighbourhood need kick up a row because we are married or buried without their assistance.'

'We are not,' said Margaret gently, 'but Fitzwilliam is; and don't you suppose, you dear stupid boy, that there are plenty of people to envy me my good fortune, of which they only know the flimsy surface, and to find me guilty of all sorts of insolences that I never dreamt of, if they only get the chance?'

'I never thought of that. You're quite right, after all, Madge,' said Haldane ruefully.

'There's a good deal you have never thought of, and which my life has made plain to me,' said Margaret; and then she added in a lower tone, 'Can you not understand, Hal, how terribly trying my wedding will be to me, how many painful thoughts it must bring me? Can you not see that I must wish to get through it as quietly as possible?'

This was the first word of reference, however distant, to the past which her brother had heard from Margaret's lips; this was the first time he had ever seen the hard, lowering, stern, self-despising look upon her face, which had been familiar to all the other dwellers at Chayleigh before his return, and before she had accepted her new life and hope.

She looked gloomily out over the prospect as she spoke. She and Haldane were walking together, and were just then opposite to the beeches. She caught Haldane's arm, and turned him sharply round, then walked rapidly away from the spot.

'What's the matter?' said her brother. He felt what she had just said deeply, notwithstanding his *insouciance*. 'What are you walking so fast for? You look as if you saw a ghost!'

'What, in the daylight, Hal?' said Margaret with a forced laugh. 'No, we are rather late; let us go in.'

The pleasure of Lady Davyntry in the perfect success of all her most cherished wishes would have been delightful to witness to any observer of a philosophic tendency. It is so rarely that any one is happy and grateful in proportion to one's anxiety and effort. Such purely disinterested pleasure as was hers is not frequently desired or enjoyed.

'If anybody had told me I could ever feel so happy again in a world which my Richard has left, I certainly would not have believed them,' said Eleanor, as Margaret strove to thank her for the welcome she gave her to the proud and happy position soon to be hers; 'and you would hardly believe me, Madge, if I were to tell you how short a time after the day I tried to make Fitz spy you through the glass there, and he was much too proper and genteel to do anything of the kind, I began to look forward to this happy event.'

To do Lady Davyntry justice, it was some time before she admitted minor considerations in support of her vast and intense satisfaction; it was actually twenty-four hours after her brother had informed her that Margaret had accepted him, when she found herself saying aloud, in the gladness of her heart and the privacy of her own room, 'How delightful it is to think that now there is no danger of his marrying a Scotchwoman! How savage Jessie Mac Alpine will be!'

The dew was shining on the grass and the flowers, the birds had hardly begun their morning hymn, on a morning in the gorgeous month of June, when Margaret Hungerford, wrapped in a white dressing-gown, and leaning out of the passion-flower-framed window of her room, looked out towards the woods of Davyntry. The tall, fantastic, twisted chimneys and turrets, rich with the deep red of the old brick-work, showed through the leaf-laden trees. Margaret's pale, clear, spiritual face was turned towards them, her hands were clasped upon the window-sill ; she leaned more forward still, and her long hair was stirred by the light wind.

'The one only thing he asks me for his sake,' she mur-mured ; 'but oh, how difficult, how impossible, never to look back, never voluntarily to look back upon the past again ! To live for the present and the future, to live only in his life, as he lives only in mine. Ah, that is easy for him, or at least easier; and it may be so—but for me, for me.' She swayed her slight figure to and fro, and wrung her hands. It was long since the gesture had ceased to be habitual now. ' I will try, I will keep my word to you, in all honest intention at least, my darling, my love, my husband ! ' She slightly waved one hand towards the woods, and a beautiful flush spread itself over her face. ' I will turn all my heart for ever from the past, if any effort of my will can do it, and live in your life only.'

A few hours later, the quietest wedding that had ever been known in that part of the country took place in the parish church of Chayleigh, very much to the dissatisfaction of the few spectators who had had sufficient good fortune to be correctly informed of the early hour appointed for the ceremony.

' Gray silk, my dear, and a chip bonnet, as plain as you please,' said Miss Laughton, the village dressmaker, to Miss Harland, the village milliner. ' I should like to know what poor Mrs Carteret, that's dead and gone, but had as genteel a taste in dress as ever I knew, would say to such a set-out as that.'

' I expect, Jemima,' replied Miss Harland, who had a

strong dash of spite in her composition, and felt herself aggrieved at the loss of Mrs Hungerford's modest custom in the article of widow's caps—'I expect madam would not have caught Mr Baldwin easy, if Mrs Carteret was alive; and gray silk and chip is good enough for her. I wonder what she wore at her wedding, when she ran away with Mr Hungerford—which he was a gay chap, whatever they had to say against him.'

In these days, the avoidance of festive proceedings on the occasion of a marriage is not unusual; but when Margaret was married, that the bride and bridegroom should drive away from the church-door was an almost unheard-of proceeding. Nevertheless, Mr Baldwin and Margaret departed after that fashion; and Lady Davyntry only returned to Chayleigh to console Mr Carteret, who really did not seem to need consolation.

A few days later, as Margaret and her husband were strolling arm-in-arm in the evening along the sea-shore of a then almost unknown village in South Wales,—now a prosperous and consequently intolerable 'watering-place,'— Mr Baldwin said to her—they had been talking of some letters he had had from his steward:

'I wonder if you have any doubts in your mind about liking the Deane, Margaret. I am longing to see you there to watch you making acquaintance with the place, taking your throne in your own kingdom.'

'And I, she said with a smile and a wistful look in her gray eyes, 'sometimes think that when I am there I shall feel like Lady Burleigh.'

CHAPTER XV

THREE LETTERS.

EIGHTEEN months had elapsed since the marriage of Fitzwilliam Baldwin and Margaret Hungerford,—a period which had brought about few changes at Chayleigh, beyond the departure, at an early stage of its duration, of Haldane Carteret to join his regiment, and which had been productive of only one event of importance. The eldest Miss Crofton had terminated at her leisure, after Margaret's departure, the capture of the young captain, as he was called by a courteous anticipation of the natural course of events, and there was every reason to suppose that the ensuing year would witness a second wedding from Chayleigh, in the parish church, which should be by no means obnoxious to public sentiment, on the score of quiet, if the eldest Miss Crofton should have her own way, which, indeed, the fair Lucy generally contrived to procure in every affair in which she was interested.

Her parents entirely approved of the engagement. She had no fortune, and Haldane's prospective independence was certain. It was a very nice thing for her to be wife to the future Mr Carteret of Chayleigh, and almost a nicer thing for her to be sister-in-law to Mrs Meriton Baldwin of the Deane.

Margaret had become a wonderfully important personage in the neighbourhood she had left. Every particular of her household, every item of her expenditure, and—when she stayed a month at her father's house after her little daughter's birth, prior to going abroad for an indefinite period now more than six months ago--every article of her dress, was a subject of discussion and interest to people who had taken no particular notice of her in her previous stages of existence. The eldest Miss Crofton had a little ovation when she returned from a visit to the Deane, and simple Mr Carteret was surprised to find how many friends he was possessed of, how many inquirers were unwearyingly anxious to learn the latest news of ' dear Mrs Baldwin.'

The quiet household at Chayleigh pursued its usual routine course, and little change had come to the two men, the one old, the other now elderly, who were its chief members. Of that little, the greater portion had fallen to the share of James Dugdale. His always bent and twisted figure was now more bent and twisted, his hair was grayer and scantier, his eyes were more hollow, his face was more worn, his quiet manner quieter, his rare smile more seldom seen. Any one familiar with his appearance eighteen months before, who had seen him enter the cheerful breakfast-room at Chayleigh one bright winter's morning, when Christmas-day was but a week off, would have found it difficult to believe that the interval had been so short.

James Dugdale stood by the fire for a few minutes, then glancing round at the breakfast-table, he muttered, 'The post is not in—behind time—the snow, I suppose,' and went to the large window, against which he leaned, idly watching the birds as they hopped about on the snow-laden ground, and extracted bits of leaves and dry morsels of twig from its niggard breast. He was still standing there when Mr Carteret came in, closely followed by a servant with a small tray laden with letters, which he duly sorted and placed before their respective claimants.

There was a large foreign letter among those addressed to James Dugdale, but he let it lie beside his plate unnoticed;

all his attention was for the letter which Mr Carteret was deciphering with laborious difficulty.

'From Margaret,' said the old gentleman at length, taking off his double glasses with an air of relief, and laying them on the table. 'She *does* write such a scratchy hand, it quite makes my head ache to read it.'

'Where are they now?' asked James.

'At Sorrento. Margaret writes in great delight about the place and the climate, and the people they meet there, and the beauty and health of little Gerty. And Baldwin adds a postscript about the *cicale*, which is just what I wanted to know; he considers there's no doubt about their chirp being much stronger and more prolonged than our grasshopper's, and he has carefully examined the articulations.'

'Does Margaret say anything about her own health?' interrupted James, so impatiently that he felt ashamed of himself the next minute, although Mr Carteret took the sudden suppression of his favourite topic with perfect meekness, as he made answer:

'Yes, a good deal. Here it is, read the letter for yourself, James,'—and he handed over the document to his companion, and betook himself to the perusal of a scientific review,—a production rarer in those days than now,—and for whose appearance Mr Carteret was apt to look with eagerness.

James Dugdale read the letter which Margaret Baldwin had written to her father from end to end, and then he turned back to the beginning, and read it through again. No document which could come from any human hand could have such a charm and value for him as one of her letters.

His feelings had undergone no change as regarded her, though, as regarded himself, they had become purified from the little dross of selfishness and vain regret that had hung

about them for a little after she had left Chayleigh. He
could now rejoice, with a pure and true heart, in her exceeding, her perfect happiness; he could think of her husband,
whom she loved with an intense and passionate devotion
which had transformed her character, as it seemed at times
to transfigure her face, illumining it with a heavenly light
—with ardent friendship and gratitude as the giver of such
happiness, and with sincere and ungrudging admiration as
the being who was capable of inspiring such a love. He
could thank God now, from his inmost heart, for the change
which had been wrought in, and for, the woman he loved
with a love which angels might have seen with approval. All
he had longed and prayed and striven for, was her good—and
it had come—it had been sent in the utmost abundance; and
he never murmured now, ever so lightly, that *he* had not
been suffered to count for anything in the fulfilment of his
hope, in the answer to his prayer.

He read, with keen delight, the simple but strong words
in which Margaret described to her father the peace, happiness, companionship, and luxury of her life. Only the light-
est cloud had cast a shade over the brightness of Margaret's
life since her marriage. She had been rather delicate in
health after the birth of her child, and a warmer climate than
that of Scotland had been recommended for her. Mr Baldwin had not been sorry for the opportunity thus afforded
him of indulging Margaret and himself by visiting the countries so well known to him, but which his wife had never
seen. Her experience of travel had been one of wretchedness; in this respect, also, he would make the present contrast with and efface the past. The 'Lady Burleigh' feeling which Margaret had anticipated had come upon her
sometimes, in the stately and well-ordered luxury of her new
home; she had sometimes experienced a startling sense of

the discrepancy between the things she had seen and suffered, and her surroundings at the Deane ; but these fitful feelings had not recurred often or remained with her long, and she had become deeply attached to her beautiful home. Nevertheless, she, too, had welcomed the prospect of a foreign tour ; and during her visit, *en route*, to Chayleigh, she had spoken so freely and frequently to James of her anticipations of pleasure, of the delight she took in her husband's cultivated taste, and in his manifold learning, that James perceived how rapidly and variously her intellect had developed in the sunshine of happiness and domestic love.

'Though she has always been the first of women in my mind,' James Dugdale had said to himself then, ' I would not have said she was either decidedly clever or decidedly handsome formerly, and now she is both beautiful and brilliant.'

And so she was. It was not the praise of prejudice which pronounced her so. There were many who would, if they could, have denied such attributes to Mrs Baldwin of the Deane, but they might as well have attempted to deny light to the sunshine.

In this letter, which James Dugdale read with such pleasure, Margaret said she was stronger, ' much stronger,' and that every one thought her looking very well. ' Fitzwilliam is so much of that opinion,' she wrote, ' that he thinks this is a favourable opportunity of having a life-size portrait taken of me, especially as a first-rate artist has just been introduced to us,—if the picture be successful, a replica shall be made for you. The long windows of our sitting-rooms open on a terrace overhanging the sea, and the walls are overrun with passion-flower—just like those at home, which James used to take such care of. I mean to have my picture taken standing in the centre window, with my little Gertrude in my arms. If you don't like this, or prefer any other pose, say so when you write. Eleanor is delighted with the notion.'

The tone of the whole letter was that of happiness, full, heartfelt, not wanting in anything. James Dugdale held it still in his hands, when he had read it through for the second time, and fell into one of the reveries which were habitual to him. It showed him Margaret, as he had seen her on the day of her unexpected return, pale, stern, defiant of the bitterness of her fate,—her slight form, clad in its heavy mourning robes, framed by the passion-flower tendrils, the woman in whose face he read more than confirmation of all he had ever feared or prophesied of evil for her, and in whose letter there was such a story of happiness as it falls but rarely to the lot of any mortal to have to tell. He had never felt so entirely, purely, unselfishly happy about Margaret as he felt at that moment.

'You have no letter from Haldane, have you?' asked Mr Carteret, as he relinquished his review for his coffee-cup. 'I have not, and Margery complains that he has not written.'

The question reminded James of his hitherto disregarded letters. He turned to the table and took them up:

'No, sir, there's no letter from Haldane.'

Mr Carteret uttered a feeble sound of dissatisfaction, but made no further remark, and James opened the foreign letter, which was, as he expected, from Hayes Meredith. It announced the writer's intended departure from Melbourne by the first ship after that which should carry the present letter, and named the period at which the writer hoped to reach England.

'The Yarra is a quick sailer,' wrote Hayes Meredith, and we expect to be in Liverpool a few weeks later than the

Emu. My former letters will have explained how all difficulties subsided, but up to the last I have not felt quite confident of being able to get away, and thought it was well to write only one ship in advance.'

There was a good deal of expression of pleasure at the prospect of seeing his old friend again, and introducing his son to him, on Hayes Meredith's part, some anxiety about his son's future, and warm thanks to James for certain propositions he had made concerning him.

'My friend Meredith and his son have sailed at last, sir,' said James, addressing Mr Carteret. 'He will be here soon, I fancy, if they have had fine weather.'

'Indeed,' said Mr Carteret. 'I hope he is bringing the opossum and wombat skins, and the treeworm and boomerang you asked him for. I should like to have them really brought from the spot, you know. One can buy such things from the dealers, of course, but they are never so interesting, and often not genuine.'

'I have no doubt, sir, they will all arrive quite safely.'

'You have asked Mr Meredith and his son to come here direct, I hope, James?'

'Yes, I obeyed your kind instructions in that.'

'What a pity Margery is not here,' said Mr Carteret, with a placid little sigh, 'to see her kind friend!'

'Never mind, sir; Margaret will have plenty of opportunity for seeing Meredith. He will not remain less than six months in England.'

In the pleasure and the excitement caused by the prospect of his friend's arrival (it was not customary or possible then for people to drop in from Melbourne for a week or two, and be heard of next at Salt Lake), James did not immediately remember what Margaret had said when Hayes Meredith's coming had first been talked of—that if he or any one came from the place which had witnessed her suffering and degradation, to her father's house, she would feel it to be an evil omen to her. When at length he did recall her expression of feeling about it, he smiled.

'How she would laugh at herself if I were to remind her now that she once said that! What could be an ill omen to her now? What could bring evil near her now?—God bless her!'

Some weeks later the Yarra, having encountered boisterous weather in the Channel, arrived at Liverpool. On the day but one following its arrival, James Dugdale received a short note from Hayes Meredith, which contained these words:

'*Liverpool, Jan.* 24.

'MY DEAR DUGDALE,—We have arrived, and Robert and I hope to get to Chayleigh by Thursday. Should Mrs Baldwin be in Scotland, endeavour to induce her to see me, at her father's house, in preference to any other place, as soon as possible. Do this, if you can, without alarming her, but at all events, and under all risks, *do it*. Circumstances which occurred immediately before my departure make it indispensable that I should see her *at once* on important and, I regret to add, unpleasant business. I am too tired and dizzy to write more.—Yours, HAYES MEREDITH.'

CHAPTER XVI.

HAYES MEREDITH'S REVELATION.

IT had seldom fallen to the lot of James Dugdale to experience more painful mental disquietude than that in which he passed the interval between the receipt of Hayes Meredith's letter and the arrival of his friend, accompanied by his son, at Chayleigh. Mr Carteret, always unobservant, did not notice the preoccupation of James's manner, and James had decided, within a few minutes after he had read the communication which had so disturbed him, that he would not mention the matter to the old gentleman at all, if concealment were practicable—certainly not before it should become indispensable, if it should ever prove to be so.

An unpleasant communication to be made to Margaret! What could it be? The vain question whose solution was so near, and yet appeared to him so distant, in his impatience repeated itself perpetually in every waking hour, and he would frequently start from his sleep, roused by a terrible sense of undefined trouble impending over the woman who never ceased to occupy the chief place in his thoughts. The problem took every imaginable shape in his mind. The little knowledge he had of the circumstances of Margaret's life in Australia left him scope for all kinds of conjectures and did not impose superior probability on any. Was there a secret reason beyond, more pressing than her natural, easily explicable shrinking from the revival of pain and humiliation, which kept Margaret so absolutely and resolutely silent concerning the years of her suffering and exile? Was there something which she knew and dreaded, which might come to light at any time, which was soon to come to light now, in the background of her memory? Was there some transaction of Hungerford's, involving disgraceful consequences, which had been dragged into publicity, in which she, too, must be involved, as well as the dead man's worthless memory? This might be the case; it might be debts, swindling, anything; and the brilliant and happy marriage she had made, might be destined to be clouded over by the shadow of her former life.

James Dugdale suffered very keenly during the few days in which he pondered upon these things. He tortured himself with apprehension, and knew that, to a certain extent, it must be groundless. The only real, serious injury which could come out of the dark storehouse of the past, into the present life of Fitzwilliam Baldwin's wife, must be one of a nature to interfere with her relations towards her husband. She could afford to defy every other kind of harm. She was raised far above the influence of all material evil, and removed from the sphere in which the doings of people like Hungerford and his associates were ever heard of. Her marriage bucklered her no less against present than past evil; on all sides but one. When James weighed calmly the matter of which he never ceased to think, he called in the 'succours of thought' to the discomfiture of 'fear,' which in its vague has greater torment than in its most defined shape, and drew upon their resources largely. Margaret had indeed been reticent with him, with her father, with Haldane, even, he felt persuaded, with her sister-in-law Lady Davyntry; but had she been equally reticent with Baldwin? He thought she had not; he hoped, he believed she had not; that the confidence existing between her and her husband was as perfect as their mutual love, and that, however strictly she might have maintained a silence, which Baldwin would have been the last man in the world to induce or wish her to break, up to the period of her marriage, he did not doubt that Margaret's husband was now in possession of all the facts of her past life, so that no painful intelligence could find him more or less unprepared than his wife to meet it.

It needed the frequent repetition of this belief to himself, the frequent repetition of the grounds on which it was founded, to enable James Dugdale to subdue the apprehensions inspired by Hayes Meredith's letter. His delicate health, his nervous susceptibility, the almost feminine sensitiveness of his temperament, made suspense, anxiety, and apprehension peculiarly trying to him ; and the servants at Chayleigh, keener observers than their master, quickly found out that something was wrong with Mr Dugdale, and that the arrival of the two gentlemen from foreign parts, for whose reception preparations were being duly made, would not be a cause of unalloyed pleasure to him.

The urgency of Meredith's request, that there might be no delay in a meeting between himself and Margaret, gave James much uneasiness, because, in addition to the general vagueness of the matter, he did not in this particular instance know what to do. Hayes Meredith did not wish her to be alarmed (which looked as if he believed her to be ignorant of the unpleasant intelligence to which he alluded, as if he contemplated the necessity of its being broken to her with caution), but he laid stress on the necessity of an immediate meeting. How was this to be accomplished ? Meredith had not thought of such a contingency as that which actually existed. He had supposed it probable Mr and Mrs Baldwin would be in Scotland when his letter should reach James Dugdale, which must create a delay of a few days indeed, but he had not contemplated their absence at such a distance as must imply the postponement of a meeting for weeks.

James did not know what to do. To summon Margaret and Mr Baldwin to return at once, without any clue to the meaning of the communication awaiting them, would be to alarm them to an extent, which, under any circumstances within the reach of his imagination, must be unnecessary ; and from the possible responsibility involved in not procuring their return he naturally shrank. He could not communicate with Meredith, whose letters bore no address but

'Liverpool;' there was nothing for it but the painful process of patience.

Mr Carteret talked of Margaret more than usual in the interval between the arrival of Meredith's letter and the day on which he was expected at Chayleigh; the association of ideas made him garrulous, and he expatiated largely to James upon the pleasure which Mr Meredith would feel on seeing his *protégée* of the bad old times so differently circumstanced, and the splendid hospitality with which he would certainly be entertained at the Deane. Baldwin would return sooner than he had intended, no doubt, in consequence of Mr Meredith's visit to England.

When Mr Carteret expressed his opinion, apparently oblivious of the fact that the state of Margaret's health rendered her remaining abroad peculiarly desirable, James heard him with a sense of partial relief. It would be much gained, let the unpleasant business before them be what it might, if Mr Carteret could be kept from alarm or pain in connection with it. If he could be brought to regard the sudden return of Margaret as a natural event, considering his placid nature and secluded habits, it might be readily practicable to secure him from all knowledge of what had occurred.

There was strong ·anticipative consolation for James Dugdale in this reflection. Reason with himself as he would, strive against it as he might, there was a presentiment of evil upon James's heart, a thrill of dread of the interruption of that happiness in which he found such pure and disinterested delight, and he dared not think of such a dread extending itself to the old man, who had built such an edifice of pride and contentment on his daughter's fortunes, and would have so little strength to bear, not alone its crumbling, but any shock to its stability.

'Let it be what it may, I think it can be hidden from him,' said James Dugdale, as he bade Mr Carteret good-night for the last time before all his suspense should be resolved into certainty.

That particular aspect of nature, to which the complacent epithets 'good old English' have been most frequently applied by poets and novelists, presented itself at Chayleigh, in perfection, on the day of Hayes Meredith's arrival. 'Our English summer' has become rather mythical in this generation, and the most bearable kind of cold weather, keen, bright, frosty, kindly (to those who can afford ubiquitous fires and double windows), occurs in miserably small proportion to the dull, damp, despairing winter of fogs and rain. It was not so between twenty and thirty years ago, however, and the eyes of the long-expatriated Englishman were refreshed, and those of his colonial-born son astonished, by the beauty and novelty of the scenery through which they passed on their journey southwards.

Chayleigh was one of those places which look particularly beautiful in winter. It boasted splendid evergreens, and grassy slopes carefully kept, and the holly trees, freshly glistening after a fall of snow, which had just disappeared, were grouped about the low picturesque house like ideal trees in a fancy sketch of the proper home of Christmas. It was difficult to realize that the only dwellers in the pleasant house, from whose long low windows innumerable lights twinkled brightly, were two men, the one old in years, and older still in his quiet ways, in his deadness of sympathy with the outer world, the other declining also in years, and carrying, in a frail and suffering body, a heart quite purged of self, but heavy-laden with trouble for one far dearer than self had ever been to him.

11

Fair women and bright children should have tenanted such a home as that to which Mr Carteret, a little later than the hour at which they were expected, bade Hayes Meredith and his son a hearty if somewhat old-fashioned welcome.

When the post-chaise which brought the travellers stopped, James Dugdale met his old friend as he stepped out, and the two looked at each other with the contending feelings of pain and pleasure which such a meeting was calculated to produce. Time had so altered each that the other would not have recognized him had their meeting been a chance one ; but when, a little later, they regarded each other more closely, many familiar looks and expressions, turns of feature and of phrase, made themselves observed in both, which restored the old feeling of familiarity.

Then James Dugdale saw the strong, frank, hopeful young man, with his vivacious black eyes, and his strong limbs, his cheery laugh, and his jovial self-reliant temper, once more, and found all those qualities again in the world-taught, and the world-sobered, but not world-worn, man whose gray hair was the only physical mark of time set upon him.

Then Hayes Meredith saw the pale, stooped student, with form awry and spiritual sensitive face, bearing upon it the inexplicable painful expression which malformation gives,—the keen intelligence, the sadly strong faculty of suffering, the equally keen affections and firm will. Time had set many a mark upon James. He had had rich brown curls, the only gift of youth dealt lavishly to him by nature, but they were gone now, and his hair was thin and gray, and the lines in his face were more numerous and deeper than might have been fitting at twenty additional years. But Hayes Meredith saw that same face under the lines, and in a wonderfully short time he found himself saying to himself—' I should feel as if we were boys together again, only that Dugdale, poor fellow, never was a boy.'

'Is Mrs Baldwin here?' was Meredith's first question to his friend, after the undemonstrative English greeting, which said so little and meant so much.

'No, she is abroad.'

'How unfortunate!'

'What is the matter? Is anything very wrong?'

'No, no, we'll put it right—but we cannot talk of it now. When can I have some time with you quite alone?'

'To-night, if you are not too tired,' returned James, who was intensely impatient to hear what had to be told, but to whose sensitive nerves the strong, steady, almost unconcerned manner of his friend conveyed some little assurance.

'To-night, then.'

There was no farther private conversation between the two. Hayes Meredith devoted himself to Mr Carteret, whose placid character afforded him considerable amusement, in its contrast with those of the bustling and energetic companions of his ordinary life. To Mr Carteret, Hayes Meredith was an altogether new and delightful *trouvaille*. That he came from a new world, of infinite interest and importance to England; that he could tell of his own personal experience, particulars of the great events, political, commercial, and social, to which colonial enterprise had given rise; that, as a member of a strange community, with all the interest of a foreign land, and all the sympathy of fellowship of race attaching to them, Mr Carteret knew, if he had cared to think about it, and he might perhaps, merely as an intellectual exercise, have comprehended, that there was something remarkable about his guest in that aspect. But he did not care about it in the least. The political, social, and commercial life of either this half of the world or the other half was a matter of entire indifference to him. He was eminently desirous to ascertain, as soon as politeness warranted the inquiry, whether Mr Meredith had brought to England the 'specimens' which James Dugdale had bespoken, and that point satisfactorily disposed of, and an early hour on the following day appointed for their disinterment from the general mass of luggage, he turned the conversation without delay on the cranial peculiarities of 'black fellows,' the number of species into which the marsupial genus may be divided, and the properties of the turpentine tree. On all these matters Hayes Meredith sustained a very credible examination, and during its course rapidly arrived at a very kindly feeling towards his gentle and eccentric but eminently kind-hearted entertainer. There was a curious occult sympathy between the minds of James Dugdale and Hayes Meredith, as the latter thought:

'If it could be hidden from the poor old gentleman, and I really see no reason why he should ever know it, what a good thing it will be!'

Mr Carteret had taken an early opportunity of expressing, not ungracefully, his sense of the kindness which his daughter had received at the hands of Mr Meredith and his family, and his regret that she was not then at Chayleigh to welcome him. The embarrassment with which his guest received his courteous observations, and the little allusion which he afterwards made to Margaret, though it would have been natural that she should have been the prevailing subject of their conversation, did not strike Mr Carteret in the least, though James Dugdale perceived it plainly and painfully, and it rendered the task which he had set himself—that of entertaining Robert Meredith—anything but easy. The mere notion of such a possibility as taking any notice of a

boy, after having once shaken hands with him, and told him
he was very happy to see him, and hoped he would make
himself quite at home at Chayleigh, would never have occurred to Mr Carteret.   About boys, as boys, he knew very
little indeed; but if the word aversion could ever be used
with propriety in describing a sentiment entertained by Mr
Carteret, he might be said to regard them with aversion.
They made noises, they opened doors unnecessarily often,
and they never shut them; they trod on people's feet, and
tore people's dresses; they did not wash their hands with
decent frequency; and once a terrible specimen of the genus,
having been admitted to a view of his precious case of Cape
butterflies, thrust his plebeian and intrusive elbow through
the glass.   This was final.

'I don't like boys,' said Mr Carteret; 'I don't understand
them.   Keep them away from me, please.'

He had listened with a mild shudder to Haldane's
praises of that 'wonderfully clever child,' the eldest Miss
Crofton's 'little brother;' and had turned a desperately deaf
ear to all hints that an invitation for the urchin to inspect
the wonders of the 'collection' might be regarded by the
Crofton family as an attention.

'Wonderfully clever, is he?' said Mr Carteret musingly; 'what a nuisance he must be!'

Haldane did not mention the talented creature again,
and no boy had ever troubled Mr Carteret from that hour
until now.   He had the satisfaction of knowing, when his
prompt invitation was extended to James Dugdale's friends,
that Robert Meredith was a big boy—not an objectionable
child, with precocious ideas, prying eyes, and fingers addicted
to mischief—had it been otherwise, his patience and hospitality would have been sorely tried.

'You will see to the young gentleman, Foster,' he had

said to his confidential servant ; 'I dare say he will like a good deal to eat and drink, and you can see that he does not wear strong boots in the house, and—ah—hem, Foster, you can make him understand—politely, you know—that people in general don't go into my rooms. You understand, Foster ? '

'Oh yes, sir ; I understand,' said Foster, in a tone which to Mr Carteret's sensitive ears implied an almost unfeeling indifference, but Foster acted on the hint for all that, and the result was remarkable.

Mr Carteret never once had reason to complain of Robert Meredith. The boy never vexed or worried him ; he seemed to have an intuitive comprehension of his feelings and prejudices, of his harmless little oddities, and in a silent distant kind of way—for though a wonderful exception, Robert was still a boy, and therefore to be avoided—Mr Carteret actually came to like him. In which particular he formed an exception to the entire household as then assembled at Chayleigh, and even when it received the accession of Mr Baldwin, Margaret, and their little daughter. No one else in the house liked Robert Meredith.

The preoccupation of James Dugdale's mind, the anxiety and suspense of some days, which grew stronger and less endurable now when a few hours only divided him from learning, with absolute certainty, the evil tidings which Hayes Meredith had to communicate, rendered his friend's son and his affairs objects of very secondary interest to him. When he thought of the business which had induced Meredith to undertake such a voyage to England, such an absence from home, he roused himself to remember the keen interest he had taken in the father's projects for, and on account of, the son. But he could only remember it ; he could not feel it again. When he should know the worst, when he and

Meredith should have had their private talk that night, then things would resume their proper proportion, then he should be able to fulfil all his friend's behests, with the aid of his hand and his heart alike. But now, only the face of Margaret, pale, wan, stern, with the youth and bloom gone from it, as he had seen her when she first came home; only the face of Margaret, transfigured in the light of love and joy, of pride and pleasure, as he had seen her last, held his attention. Her form seemed to flit before him in the air. The sound of her voice mingled, to his fancy, with all other sounds. The effort to control his feelings, and bide his time, almost surpassed his strength. Afterwards, when he recalled that day, and tried to remember his impressions of Robert Meredith, James recollected him as a quiet, gentlemanly, self-possessed boy, with a handsome face, a good figure, and an intelligent expression—a little shy, perhaps, but James did not see that until afterwards. A boy without the objectionable habits of boys, but also without the frankness which beseems boyhood. A boy who watched Mr Carteret's conversation with his father, and rapidly perceived that gentleman's harmless eccentricities, and who, when he found that a total absence of observation was one of them, marked each fresh exhibition of them with a contemptuous sneer, which would not have been out of place on the countenance of a full-grown demon. He had a good deal of the early-reached decision in opinion and in manner which is a feature in most young colonials, but he was not unpleasantly 'bumptious;' and James Dugdale, had his mind been free to permit him to find pleasure in anything, would have enjoyed making the acquaintance of his old friend's son.

At length the two men found themselves alone in James Dugdale's room.

'Our consultation is likely to be a long one, Dugdale,'

said Meredith, as he seated himself close by the fire. 'Is there any danger of our being interrupted or overheard ? '

'None whatever,' James answered. He felt unable to speak, to ask a question, now that the time had come.

Meredith looked at him compassionately, but shrugged his shoulders at the same time, imperceptibly. He understood his friend's sensitiveness ; his weakness he could not understand. 'I may as well tell you at once,' he said, 'about this bad business.' He took a paper from a pocket-book as he spoke. 'Tell me the exact date of Mr Baldwin's marriage.'

James named it without adding a word. Then Meredith handed him the paper he held, and James, having read it hastily, looked up at him with a pale horrified face.

CHAPTER XVII.

CONSULTATION.

THE paper which caused James Dugdale such painful emotion was a certificate of the identification and burial of the body of Godfrey Hungerford, and was dated rather more than a year after the marriage of his supposed widow with Fitzwilliam Meriton Baldwin, and two years and five months later than the period at which his death in the bush had been reported to Margaret.

In reply to the eager questions which James asked him, when he had somewhat recovered his composure, Hayes Meredith told his companion that he had the best of all confirmation of the truth of the statement which that document set forth—that of his own eyes. There was not the faintest hope of error, not the slightest chance that in this matter any trick, any design to extort money was concerned. That such might be the case had been Hayes Meredith's first idea, when, as he told James Dugdale, he had received a mysterious communication from a 'pal' of Hungerford's, who was anything but favourably known to the Melbourne police, to the effect that the supposed murdered man was alive, and might be found, under an assumed name, in a wretched hovel in one of the poorest and least reputable quarters of the town.

' It was necessary to satisfy myself about the thing without delay,' said Meredith; 'and I did not lose an hour. I met the messenger at the place appointed in the note, and told him, if any one had formed the goodly scheme of deceiving me by personating Hungerford, it would signally fail. I could not be deceived on such a point, and should simply expose the fraud at once. On the other hand, if this man, who appeared, from the other fellow's report, to be in a rapidly dying state, should really prove to be Hungerford, I could not understand his applying to me, on whom he had no claim whatever, and should certainly not get the chance of establishing one. The man, a seedy gambler, whom I remembered having seen with Hungerford,—his name was Oakley,—said he had no intention to deceive me. They were 'pals' in misfortune and misery, Hungerford and himself, and wanted nothing but a little help from me. Hungerford had been saved from murder by a black woman, and had wandered for months, enduring an amazing amount of suffering. How so self-indulgent a dog as he was ever bore it, I can't understand; but he had a love of life in him I have never seen equalled; he clung to life, and fought for it madly, when his agonies in the hospital were perfectly unbearable to see. After some time, they struck the trail of such civilization as is going in the remoter districts of our part of the world; and Hungerford got away, and one of the first persons he fell in with was this Oakley. He did not give me a very clear account of what they did, and, as you may suppose, I was not very anxious to know; it was very likely all the harm in their power, at all events; they both made cause for themselves to be chary of recognition, and afraid of the strong arm of the law.'

'Did this Oakley mention Margaret?'

'Only cursorily. He said they had been forced to venture into Melbourne, and he had 'asked about' and discovered that Mrs Hungerford had lived quietly and respectably, presumably by my assistance, after her husband left her, and had sailed for England when the news of his death was spread in Melbourne. He said Hungerford was glad when he found his wife had got away safely; he could never hope to rise in this world any more, and he did not wish her to suffer any farther.'

'The ruffian acknowledged his wickedness, then?' said James.

'Well, yes, he did; I must say he did. I went on to the hospital with Oakley, and saw in a moment there was no mistake about it. The man lying there, in the last stage of destitution, and of that peculiar depth of loathsome disease which only comes from drink, was certainly Godfrey Hungerford. I need not tell you what I felt, as I looked at him and thought of his unconscious wife. I had your letter, telling me about her being at Chayleigh, in my pocket-book at the time.'

'No, you need not tell me,' said James; 'it must have been most horrible.'

'It was just that,' said Meredith, with a rueful look and a shake of the head; 'such a miserable creature as he was to see, I hope I never may have to look at again. I said very little to him—nothing about Margaret. He did thank me in a rough kind of way, and said he knew if he could get me communicated with I would help him.',

'Did he not ask you if you knew anything of Margaret after she left Melbourne? Did he show no anxiety for her fate?'

'No; I think in addition to his natural heartlessness and selfishness his mind was much enfeebled by disease at this time, and he was sinking fast. He had no friend, no acquaintance, he told me, but Oakley; and I was careful to ask him whether Oakley was the only person who knew that he was still alive, and then in Melbourne. He declared to me that such was the case. I told him I asked in case he should recover, when, if he knew any other persons, I might try to interest them in his case. But I am certain that in this instance he told the truth. He was entered on the books of the hospital as John Perry, and had not borne his own name during all the months of his wandering life. He went off into a short slumber while I sat by him, and strange thoughts came into my mind as I looked at his wretched, vice-worn, poverty-stricken face, and thought of what he must have been when he first came across that fine young creature's path, and even what he was when I went to see them at your request. I assure you he had even then good looks and a pleasant manner, and scoundrel as I knew him to be, greater scoundrel as I afterwards found him, I could not altogether wonder that that woman had cared for him once.'

'Poor girl, poor girl,' said James. His elbows were on the table, and his face rested on his clasped hands. His hollow eyes looked out eagerly at Hayes Meredith, whose strength and composure formed a touching contrast to his nervous weakness.

'To go on with my story,' Meredith continued: 'I told

Hungerford I should see him again, and left money for his use; Oakley was to let me know how he was; and when I left him I took a long walk, as my way is when I am puzzled, so as to get time to think it out. My first impulse was to write to you at once, but I discarded the suggestion on more mature consideration. Everything must, of course, depend on whether the man lived or died. The one was almost too bad to fear, the other was almost too good to hope for. Among your letters there was one in which I recollected you had told me all the particulars of Margaret's marriage, and the peculiar circumstances of Mr Baldwin's property. I went home, after a long and anxious cogitation, during which I made up my mind, at all events, not to write; and read this letter. Here are the memoranda I made from it.'

He laid a long slip of paper on the table before James, who glanced anxiously at it, but did not take it up.

'You see, Dugdale,' continued Meredith, after he had mended the fire, and thrown himself back in his chair, with his hands extended, and the finger tips joined in an attitude of demonstration, 'this matter has more than one side to it; more than the side I can see you are dwelling on, very painfully, and very naturally—Margaret's feelings. As for that part of it, it is dreadful, of course; but then she need never know any of the particulars.'

'I hope not—I trust not,' said Dugdale in a low constrained voice. 'If I know anything of her, the idea of the scene you describe taking place while she was in the midst of happiness and luxury would make her wretched for many a day. Think of her having to endure that, after having already lived through the horror of believing that the man she had loved, and sacrificed herself for, was murdered.'

Meredith looked at James, closely and inquiringly, for a moment. This intense comprehension, this almost painful truth and excess of sympathy, puzzled him. While the external consequences of the discovery which had been made, the results to Mrs Baldwin herself, her husband, and her child pressed upon his own attention, James was lost in the sentimental bearing of the matter, in the retrospective personal grief which it must cause to Margaret, estimating her feelings at a high degree of refinement and intensity. Meredith could not make this out very clearly, but thinking 'it is just like him; he always was a strange dreamy creature, who never looked at anything like other people,' he went on to discuss the subject from his own point of view.

'That is all very true, Dugdale,' he continued, 'and, as I said before, I really do not see that she need ever know more than the fact stated in that paper. But what you and I have got to consider, without unnecessary delay, and to act upon with all possible promptitude, is this fact: at the present moment Margaret is not Mr Baldwin's wife, and her daughter, who, if I understand your statement aright, is heiress to all her father's property, is illegitimate.'

'The child would inherit all if there were no son,' said James.

'Precisely so. Now, you see, Dugdale, this is the great question. If we can contrive to inform Mr Baldwin of what has happened, and get him to break it as gently as possible to Margaret, and then have them married privately, of course there need not be any difficulty about that; and without an hour's unnecessary delay things may be all right, and no one in the world but ourselves and themselves a bit the wiser. If the first child had been a son, it would indeed have been a bad, a hopeless business; but the little girl will be no worse off if her mother has a son, and I dare say she will have half-a-dozen. Cheer up, Dugdale; you see it is not so black as it looked at first; there is some unpleasantness to be gone through, and then you will see all will come right.'

'Perhaps,' said Dugdale dubiously. The expression of pain and foreboding deepened in his face with every moment. 'But it is a dreadful misfortune. Margaret lives for that child; she loves it wonderfully; she will break her heart over the knowledge that little Gerty is illegitimate, though no one in the world but herself should ever know it

'Nonsense,' said Meredith, 'she will do nothing of the kind; or, if she does, she must be a very different woman from the Mrs Hungerford I knew; she must be much softer both of head and of heart.'

'She *is* a very different woman,' said James, 'and her heart is softer. I never saw anything like the influence happiness has had upon her, and I dread, more than I can express, the change which such a blow as this falling upon her in the midst of her joy, and when her health is delicate too, may produce.'

'Her health delicate, is it?' said Meredith. 'Ah, by-the-by, you said so when you mentioned her being abroad. Another child expected?'

'I believe so.'

'By Jove, that's good news! Why, don't you see, Dugdale, that sets it all right. Ten chances to one this will be a boy, and there's the rightful heir to the Deane for you! Look here '—he took the memorandum from the table—'all landed property entailed—just so—provision for younger children to be made out of funded property, and the very large savings of Baldwin's minority and also the savings from their income, which are likely to be considerable, as the estates are rising rapidly in value—a coal-mine having been discovered on the Deane'—he laid the paper down, rose, and walked briskly about the room. 'The little girl's position will not be in the least altered. Baldwin must settle the money upon her in some special way; whatever her share of the provision made for younger children may be, the boy would naturally succeed, and all the difficulty be thus gotten over.'

'How would it be if there were no other child?' said James.

'Ah! that would, indeed, be difficult,' replied Meredith; 'I don't know what could be done then. Mr Baldwin is not the sort of man to do a thing which certainly would be wrong in the abstract, though I cannot see the practical injustice of it; in the case of there being no other child, of course the rightful heir is the individual who would inherit in case Baldwin should die without heirs.'

'Lady Davyntry then,' said James.

'Baldwin's sister? Yes—then she is the heir. She is not likely to marry, is she?'

'Quite certain not to do so, I should say.'

'I fancy she would consent to anything that should be proposed in her brother's interests—if any proposal on the subject should ever become necessary. And after her?'

'I don't know. It must be some very distant relative, for I never heard the name mentioned, or the contingency alluded to.'

'Well, well, we need not think about it. In fact, we are wandering away altogether from the only subjects we have to discuss: the best means of getting the Baldwins home without alarming them, and the most expeditious way of having them married privately, but with all legal security, so that if ever any clue to this unfortunate occurrence should be obtained by any one interested, the rights of the heir may be secured beyond the possibility of injury.'

'Yes; we must be careful of that,' said James; but his

tone was absent, and he was evidently unable to take any comfort from Meredith's cheerful view of the circumstances. Then, after a short pause, he said, 'I am very ignorant of law, but I have a kind of notion that we may be tormenting ourselves unnecessarily. I have heard that in Scotland the marriage of parents subsequent to the birth of children renders them legitimate. Would not this marriage legitimatize little Gerty?'

'Certainly not,' said Meredith, and he almost smiled; 'this is a very different case. The truth is, Margaret has unconsciously committed bigamy, and when Gertrude Baldwin was born, not only was Margaret not Mr Baldwin's wife, but she actually was Godfrey Hungerford's.'

James Dugdale shrunk from the words as though they had been blows. What was this but the truth which he had known from the moment he cast his eyes upon the paper which Meredith had put into his hands? and yet, set thus broadly before him, it seemed far more awful. What had become of all the arguments he had addressed to himself now? Where was the assurance he had felt that fate could not harm Margaret? that evil or calumny, or the dead and gone disgraces of her dark days, could not touch Mrs Baldwin, in her pride of place, and in her perfect happiness? Where were the plausibilities with which he had striven to lull his fears to rest? All gone, vanished, as dead as the exultant pleasure with which he had read Margaret's letter on that bright morning, which might have been a hundred years ago, so distant, so out of his sight, did it now appear. He covered his face with his hands, and kept silence for some time.

During the interval Meredith paced the room thoughtfully. When at length James spoke, it was not in continuation of the last subject.

'How long did he—Hungerford, I mean—live after you saw him ? '

'Only a few days. Oakley came to me one morning, and told me he was dying, and wished to see me. I went, but he was not sensible, and he never rallied again. Then I had him buried, rather more decently than in hospital style, under his assumed name. Oakley signed this paper, as you see. He had no notion I attached any specific value or interest to its contents—I believe he thought it an oddity of mine, one of my business-like ways, to have everything in black and white. But I considered that I might not live to tell you this by word of mouth, and in that case I should have forwarded the evidence to you; or you might not live to hear from me, and in that case I must have proof to put before Mr Baldwin.'

'You did quite right,' said James. 'Where is Oakley ? '

'I gave him a trifle to get up a decent appearance, and he was trying to get employment as a clerk or bookkeeper in some of the third-rate places of business, when I left,' said Meredith; ' he was rather a clever fellow, though a great scamp. Perhaps poverty had steadied him, and he may get on. At all events, I have seen too much of successful blackguardism, I suppose—one sees a deal of it in colonial life, to be sure—to condemn unsuccessful blackguardism to starving.'

'He is positively the only person in possession of this lamentable secret on your side of the world ? '

'Positively the only person, and as he knows nothing whatever concerning Margaret—not whether she is still alive, indeed—and, I presume, never heard her maiden name or her father's place of abode, I should not think the slightest danger is ever to be, at any time, apprehended from him. And now, Dugdale, let us be practical. I am getting tired,

12

and yet I don't want to leave you to-night until we have
finally arranged what is to be done.   Mrs Baldwin would
have good reason to complain of us, if we left her in her
present position an hour longer than we can possibly avoid.'

At this most true observation James winced.   His heart
and his fancy were alike busy, realizing every element of
pain in Margaret's position.

After some more discussion, it was arranged between the
friends that a letter should be written to Mr Baldwin of a
strictly confidential nature, in which he should be urged to
bring his wife to England without delay—the pretext being
left to him to assign—and that James and Meredith should
meet Mr and Mrs Baldwin in London.   No explanation of
their movements would be required by Mr Carteret, and the
whole affair of the revelation and the marriage could then
be quietly managed without exciting suspicion in any quarter.

'Well, that's settled, old fellow,' said Meredith as he
shook Dugdale's hand heartily, 'and we will bring Margaret
back here as surely Baldwin's wife as she now believes herself to be, and nothing more will ever come out of this business.   It looked much uglier at a distance than it does near,
I assure you.'

But James made no reply to his friend's cheery speech.
He went sadly to his room, and sat before the fire pondering.
The flames flickered and danced, and sent odd reflections
over his face, but the thoughtful, painful gaze never relaxed,
the abstraction of the hollow eyes never lessened, and the
slow-coming dawn of the wintry day found him still there,
and still thinking, sadly and painfully.

CHAPTER XVIII.

THE RETURN.

No time was lost by James Dugdale in acting upon the resolution which had been arrived at by him and his friend. The task of writing to Mr Baldwin was one of the most painful which it had ever been his lot to fulfil, and as his pen traced the lines destined to carry such dismay, to cause such irremediable grief to his friend, and to the woman whom he had loved so well and so patiently, he thought somewhat bitterly of the strangeness of his fate. Twice he had been destined to traverse Margaret's path in the bright hours of her existence, twice he had been appointed to convey to her words of disappointment, of bitterness, of doom. Life had given him little, he thought, in proportion to that which he had been called upon to suffer. Only one human creature was very precious to him, and he was so little to her that she would never even comprehend the misery he had to suffer, and must still suffer, through her. A general sort of sympathy she would expect from him and recognize, but she would never know that he would cheerfully have borne anything in the shape of suffering that could have been devised, to save her from the knowledge of the facts which his hand was then recording on the paper so soon to meet and blast Fitzwilliam Baldwin's eyes. He had sometimes thought, just before her marriage, that Margaret had divined and partly penetrated his secret ; but she did not think of it now, he felt assured, even if she had. All the fulness and beauty of life, all its best and brightest possibilities, had been opened to her, had been given to her in such lavish abundance, that her mind had no room for anything outside its own felicity.

Thus James thought; but in thus thinking he did not rightly understand Margaret. Her mind was more capacious, her nature was more steadfast, than he knew, and she had measured the depth and the strength of his love for her more accurately than he guessed, and held it in more dear, grateful, and compassionate remembrance than he would have dared to hope. At the very time when he was writing to her, Margaret, in her sunny Italian home, was thinking and talking of James to her husband and to Lady Davyntry, who had always entertained much regard for Mr Dugdale of an unintelligible nature, for she admitted readily that she did not understand him.

'Nothing could be more acceptable to Gerty's godfather,' Margaret was saying, 'than a portrait of Gerty—and of me. He shall have the small one we have ordered; and the large one for papa must be begun as soon as we get his answer to my last letter.

'You ought to have heard from him before this about it, Madge, should you not?' asked Lady Davyntry, looking up from her work; 'it is time for a letter.'

'Not quite, according to papa's measurement, Nelly. He generally takes a fortnight to make up his mind about any question he is asked, and then another fortnight to put the result on paper. I had a letter from James, you know, but he said nothing about the picture.'

'We'll have it begun at once, Margaret,' said Mr Baldwin, who was standing by the verandah, looking out upon the shining, blue, foam-flecked sea. 'I don't like a thing of that kind being put off. I wonder Dugdale does not answer for your father. And, by-the-by,' he continued, crossing the room, and taking a seat beside his wife, 'they are tolerably

busy just now at Chayleigh; it must be about the time of
Mr Meredith's arrival. What date did Dugdale mention?'

'He thought about the 25th,' said Margaret.

As she spoke the colour in her cheek waned, and there
was a slight change in the expression of her face, which was
a bright face now, but always mobile and a sure index to her
feelings; a change which indicated to her husband, on whom
no look of hers was ever lost, that the mention of Hayes
Meredith's name had a disturbing effect upon her. He saw
it, and understood it, and it vexed him, for, not with, her.

This was the one weakness in Margaret which troubled
her perfect peace and happiness, and through them his. Not
all the unequalled contentment of her lot had power to ob-
literate the past for her so completely as to deprive association of its power to wound.

There was one evil which all her husband's love and care
could not keep quite away from her—the dark shadow of the
bad bygone days when he as yet had no place in her life.
She tried hard to fulfil her promise to her husband; she
lived for him as truly and completely as ever any woman
lived for any man, and she was a wonderfully happy human
being.

But this one weakness clung to her still. The feeling of
dread, misgiving, reluctance with which she had heard at
first of Hayes Meredith's intention of coming to England,
had never changed or lessened. She tried to escape from it,
to forget it; she condemned her own weakness much more
severely than Mr Baldwin condemned it, but there it remained all the same, as present as if she had not condemned it
at all. She had felt that she escaped much by being abroad
when Mr Meredith should arrive, she had blushed for her
ingratitude in feeling it, she had persuaded herself that
when he should have arrived, and she should know that he

was in England, this strange, for the present unconquerable, feeling might wear off. It must be in a great measure nervous, she thought; it had come upon her so often and oppressively before her child's birth—surely it would vanish then. Time had brought her such immeasurably rich compensation, 'good measure, pressed down, and running over,' she had but this one thing more to ask of time, and that would come.

It was on a glorious day, even for Naples, that Fitzwilliam Baldwin, happily alone when it arrived, received James Dugdale's letter. Margaret, her child, and Lady Davyntry had gone out, intending to remain away for some hours, to the villa of friends of Eleanor's, who rejoiced immensely in the society of the English family. Mr Baldwin was to join them in the afternoon, a sociable arrangement tending to rescue the ladies from boredom, without subjecting the gentleman to the same.

The writing of the letter which came to the beautiful villa by the sea, that glorious day, had been attended with difficulties which are not easily described. Partly from his knowledge of the man, and partly from the gift of insight and sympathy which he possessed in a rare degree, James Dugdale could enter into the perplexity and intricacy of the trouble of which he was the harbinger, and could follow the inevitable workings of Mr Baldwin's mind under the circumstances. Meredith had at first proposed that the truth should not be told to Baldwin, that he should only be prepared for important news of an unpleasant character, and urged to return as speedily as possible. But James would not agree to this.

'No,' he said, 'the truth must be told, and borne somehow; and a plain simple statement of it to a man like Baldwin is the best thing to be done, and will enable him to bear it best. If he is kept in suspense, he will be unable to keep her from suspicion, and that is the great point for him to secure.'

That Mr Baldwin would exert himself to the utmost to conceal his feelings until they reached England, James did not doubt; and that he would acquiesce in their view of the case he felt assured. With this view, and in this spirit, the terrible letter was written; how it was read, how the full knowledge of the meaning of its contents was endured, no human being ever knew.

In the midst of the great bewilderment which fell upon Fitzwilliam Baldwin, while he sat with his eyes fixed upon Dugdale's letter, in the midst of the rush of wildly-varying but all-painful feeling which took possession of him, two things were uppermost in his mind: the one that the news which had reached him might be hidden until their arrival in England from Margaret, the other that the birth of a son would set this dreadful matter right, as far as it was capable of rectification.

As the hours during which he was absorbed in deep and agonizing reverie wore away, he saw these two points more and more clearly, and began to take comfort from them. Dugdale had laid so much stress in his letter upon the certainty of the truth being known to no one but Meredith and himself, upon the feasibility of such prompt and ready action, that it would be necessary only to let Margaret learn the need of the second marriage ceremony just before the time of its performance, and upon the fortunate circumstance that the little one so unintentionally wronged would be placed beyond the reach of injury when the expected event should have taken place, that the heart-stricken reader could not but see the force of his arguments.

He thought very little of himself in all this. A swift

sharp pang of regret when he felt that he had failed in the great task he had set himself, the high privilege he had striven for—that the woman whom he loved with such love as his experience told him men very rarely had to bestow, was not placed by that love, and all the defences with which it had surrounded her, beyond the reach of the stings of fortune—a piercing, agonizing sense of defeat, of failure,—and all he suffered in his own person, on his own account, was finished and over. But for *her*, for Margaret—she who, in the midst of her happiness, in the summertide of her pride, and the security of her good fortune, dreaded the slightest, most passing reference to the past, whose sensitiveness and delicacy was tortured even now with a sense of degradation in the clinging of the old associations of the past—for her, he suffered as much as it was in his nature—which had largely the faculty of pain—to suffer.

When the time drew near at which he must prepare to meet Margaret, to find himself under her calm, but, where he was concerned, keen observation, forced to deceive her in fact, and to feign a state of spirits utterly foreign to the truth, he started up with a sudden fear that the havoc which had been at work within him might have made its mark upon his face. He knew that his wife—and when the dear familiar word came into his thoughts, he shuddered at the sudden realization it forced upon him of the awful truth, she was not his wife—that Margaret would detect trouble in his face with unerring keenness and certainty.

He must devise a pretext for their sudden return, Dugdale had said in the letter. Of course, and it must be found, must be decided upon, at once. He stood still before a mirror and looked at his face. It was pale and haggard, as though he had gone through a long illness, and had grown suddenly older in it. The pretext which would account to

Margaret for this face of his must needs be a serious one. And if it must, why not make it the true pretext? Could he devise to tell her any trouble, loss, or calamity affecting him which she would not share to the full? Were they not, indeed, and in the holiest truth of that mysterious tie of love, one? Would she not grieve as much for an imaginary evil, if it could thus affect him, as for the real cross which she would have to carry? At first, his wondering gaze upon his own changed face in the glass, Fitzwilliam Baldwin thought —'Yes, I may as well tell her the truth; she cannot take it worse than she will take anything affecting me only!'

But, again, a little reflection stopped him. If the truth were revealed to Margaret now, it would be so far different from any trouble that could come to them in the ordinary course of their united life, that it must sever them. From the instant that Margaret should know that she was not his wife there would be no more liberty for her, but restraint between them, and the action of a feeling which would take strong root in her delicate and sensitive mind. No, he must guard her, as her warm-hearted but cool-judging friends had decided, against the discovery—he should win her forgiveness afterwards for a small deception involving so much to be gained in this terrible crisis of their fate.

He roamed from room to room of the beautiful villa overhanging the sea, and looked drearily around him on all the familiar objects associated with their everyday life. They were all familiar, true, and yet they were so strange. On them all there was the impress of the dreariness and the desolation which sweeps in the wake of a great shock, of a sudden event after which life can never again be the same, over all the soulless things in the midst of which we live. These were Margaret's rooms, and she was flitting about them when he saw her and them last, and they could never look the same again—neither they nor Margaret. Could it be true? Was it real, or a dream?

He stopped and pulled out James's letter, and read it again; and once more the full terrible reality struck him as with a palpable physical blow. This, then, was the fulfilment of that vague dread which Margaret confessed to having felt, that 'superstitious terror' which had pursued her often when her life was fullest of blessings and happiness. James Dugdale had not erroneously estimated the confidence which he believed to exist between Fitzwilliam Baldwin and Margaret. It was thorough, perfect, absolute. There had not been a thought of her heart hidden from her husband, and therefore he was fully able to comprehend all the depth and bearing, the full weight and severity, of the calamity which had come upon them.

What a mockery was the beauty of the scene on which he looked! What warmth or light was there in the sunshine now—what music was there in the play of the bright waves upon the curving coast? Then he took himself to task for weakness. He ought to have stood the shock of even such intelligence better than this. Where were the strength and manliness which never before had failed him? In other straits and trials of his life he had always manifested and been proud, after a fashion, of manifesting strength and composure; but in this they failed him. Strength had forsaken his limbs, and there was no composure in the ashen face he looked at in the glass; for the chief weight of this crushing sorrow must fall, not on himself, but on one much dearer—on her whose happiness he had set before him as the chief aim and effort of his life.

There was a common-sense practical point of view in which he ought to look at it—the point of view in which Dugdale's letter had placed it, the point of view which was

so much more clearly perceptible to Hayes Meredith than to
James. After all, the evil was transient, if irreparable; and
the proposed precautions, taken with good will and good
sense, could not fail. But Fitzwilliam Baldwin was not
quite master of himself in this crisis; a touch of the same
presentiment which had haunted Margaret came now to him,
and made him tremble before an undefined dread dimly
looming behind the clear and ascertained truth.

When he set himself seriously to decide upon the pretext by which he should account to Margaret for the sudden
change of all their plans, Mr Baldwin was not slow about
finding one.

Margaret knew little in detail of the management and
circumstances of the large property of which she was the
mistress. This ignorance arose neither from incapacity nor
from lack of interest, but came solely from a little of the
' Lady Burleigh' feeling, combined with the full occupation
of her mind in the delights of her home and her household,
and the idea that she always had time before her for the
acquisition of a knowledge of what she called ' Fitzwilliam's
office business.' Lady Davyntry was not much wiser; indeed, she rather trusted to her brother's knowing all about
her affairs, and transacting all business relating to Davyntry,
than troubled herself with inquiring into matters regarding
the Deane.

The pretext, then, should be a letter from the factor at
the Deane, and urgent interests of the property at stake,
requiring the master's presence. Lady Davyntry, he knew,
would immediately propose that she and Margaret should
remain at Naples until Mr Baldwin should have transacted
his business, to which he must be careful to lend a sufficiently unpleasant aspect, and be able to rejoin them. But Mr
Baldwin knew he might make his mind easy on that score.

Certain as he was that his sister would make this proposition—which, under the circumstances, and especially in
consideration of Margaret's situation, would be eminently
and palpably reasonable—he was at least as certain that Margaret would not consent to remaining at Naples if he had
to leave her. He might safely trust to the gently-maintain-
ed but perfectly-assured self-will of Margaret under such
circumstances ; and this confidence reduced the difficulties of
his task very considerably.

His plan was all arranged, and the first rush of the sea
of his troubles had subsided, when he mounted his horse
(Mr Baldwin's horses were famous in Naples) and rode
slowly away from the home in which he had been so happy,
—so marvellously happy it seemed to him, now that the
disturbing element had come in,—to meet Margaret, feeling
like a man in a dream.

'Something has happened! What is it ? ' said Margaret
in a whisper to her husband, as soon as he had gone through
the formalities of the occasion, and she could approach him
without being remarked. ' Is there any bad news from
home ? Is anything wrong with papa ? '

'Nothing, my darling. I have been upset by some unpleasant intelligence from Curtis. It is only a matter of
business ; you shall hear all about it when we get home.'

' Only a matter of business. Thank God ! But you look
very ill, Fitzwilliam. Is it anything very wrong ? '

' Yes; it may involve me in much annoyance. But I cannot say more now. Don't look so anxiously at me ; I am
not ill, only worried over the affair. Can you get away
soon ? '

' Yes, immediately. I have only to gather up Eleanor
and baby.'

She smiled faintly as she spoke, and he returned the smile more faintly still.

'Gather them up, then, and let us go.'

The few minutes consumed in leave-taking were very tedious to Fitzwilliam Baldwin, and his pale face and uncontrollably absent manner did not pass unnoticed by the lady of the house.

'I am sure there is something the matter with Mr Baldwin,' said Mrs Sinclair to her husband, when the visitors had departed, a strange sort of gloom accompanying their leave-taking. 'Did you notice, William, how ill he looked?—just like a man who had seen a ghost.'

'Nonsense,' was the uncompromising reply of Mr Sinclair; 'I dare say he is not well. You should not say such things before the children, Minnie; you'll see now we shall have them gravely demanding to be informed what is a ghost. What shall you do then?'

'Refer them to you, sir, as the source and dispenser of universal knowledge. And it's all very well for you to say "nonsense;" but I am certain something is very wrong with Mr Baldwin. However, if there is, we shall soon know it. I am sure I hope not, for his sister's sake.'

'And his wife's, surely; she is a very sweet creature.'

'I prefer Lady Davyntry,' said Mrs Sinclair shortly; and the conversation dropped.

Mr Baldwin was perfectly right in his anticipation of the manner in which the communication he had to make to his 'womankind' would be received by them. Lady Davyntry was very voluble, Margaret was very silent and closely observant of her husband.

'What a horrid nuisance, my dear Fitz!' said Lady Davyntry; 'and I must say I think it is extremely stupid of Curtis. Of course I don't pretend to understand mining business, and rights and royalties, and all the rest of it; but I do wonder he needs must bother you about it just now, when we are all so comfortable here, and Madge getting ever so much better. I suppose writing to these odious people would not do?'

'No, Eleanor, certainly not,' replied her brother; 'I must go to them, there's nothing else for it; I saw that at once.'

'Dear, how tiresome! And how long shall you be away, Fitz?'

'It is impossible to tell, Nelly; and I must start as soon as possible.—How soon can you be ready, Margaret?'

There was an extraordinary tenderness in his tone, something beyond the customary unfailing sweetness with which he invariably addressed her; a compassionate unconscious deference in his manner which thrilled her sensitive nerves. She had not removed her gaze from her husband's face since he had made the communication which he had promised; but she had not spoken a word. Now she said simply, still looking at him:

'I can be ready to start to-morrow, if you are.'

'To start to-morrow, Madge!' exclaimed Lady Davyntry in half-angry, half-incredulous astonishment. 'You cannot mean it. There was never such an idea entertained by Fitz, I am certain, as your going.—Of course you don't mean it?' And she turned anxiously to her brother.

'I certainly did think Margaret would come with me,' returned Mr Baldwin.

'I assure you, Nelly,' said Margaret, 'nothing could induce me to remain here without him.'

Lady Davyntry was very good-humoured, as she always was, but very voluble and eager in her remonstrances. The discussion was somewhat of a relief to Mr Baldwin, and it ended as he had foreseen it would end. Margaret and her little daughter would accompany him to England, and his sister would remain at Naples. The servants, with the exception of the child's nurse, were to be left at the villa. Mr Baldwin had remembered that the absence of attendants on Margaret and himself would materially contribute to the maintenance of that secrecy which was so necessary. The simplicity of the personal habits of both rendered their travelling without servants a matter of surprise to no one.

'You are quite sure you will be back in a month, Fitz?' Lady Davyntry said at the close of the discussion, when she had accepted the inevitable with her usual unfailing cheerfulness, and was actually almost ready to think the plan a very pleasant variety. 'You must, you know, for I don't believe it would be safe for Margaret to travel after a longer time; and you know what Cooper said about March in England for her chest. And a month will give you time to settle all this bothering business. I really think I should get rid of Curtis, if I were you, and give Madge plenty of time to see Mr Carteret. I have some lovely lava to send him; and, Madge, I will let you have the flat knife Signor Lanzi gave me, you know—the one they found in Pompeii. They say it belonged to Sallust's cook, and he used to slap it on the dresser when dinner was ready to be served. Mr Carteret would be delighted to have it; don't you think so?'

'I am sure he would,' Margaret answered absently.

Lady Davyntry went on: 'You mustn't worry about this business, Fitz; it is not like you to bother so about any mere matter of money.'

'It is more than a mere matter of money, Nelly,' said Mr Baldwin hastily. 'But there, don't let us talk of it any more.—You will get ready to start on Wednesday, Margaret; and, please God, we shall all be here together again before long.'

He left the women together, and went away, pleading letters to be written for the mail in the morning. As he closed the door, Margaret's quick ear caught the sound of a heavy sigh. In her turn she thought what Eleanor had said, 'It is not like him to think so much of a mere matter of money;' for his explanation had not made it clear to her that anything more than money was concerned.

Her sister-in-law talked on and on to her, growing more excited by and better pleased with the occurrences of the day as she did so, until she finally persuaded herself that no real harm, or even permanent unpleasantness, could come out of them to her brother. Margaret hardly heard her. Her heart was heavy and troubled; and that night, as she and her husband stood by the bed where their child was sleeping, watching the infant's happy slumber, as was their invariable custom, she gathered confirmation of her shapeless misgiving from the expression of his face, from the infinite tenderness of his tone to her, and the deep melancholy of the look he turned upon the child.

'Is there a shadow, a dread, a skeleton in *his* past too?' Margaret mused, when she was alone; 'and am I about to find it out? I thought there was nothing in all his noble history which needed an hour's concealment, or could bring a cloud to his face. But I must, as surely I can, trust him. If there be more to tell than he has told,—and I think there must be, for what is a money risk to him and me?—it is my part to wait patiently until the time comes for me to know it. When he thinks it right, he will tell me; until then I ought to be satisfied, and I *will*. He said the chief part of his business would be in London; I shall hear all about it there.'

Calling to her aid her former habit of self-control,—a little fallen into disuse in the new and perfect happiness of her life, in which it was seldom needed,—Margaret did not embarrass Mr Baldwin by a question, by the slightest betrayal that she suspected any concealment on his part; but she said to herself very frequently, in the brief interval before the commencement of their journey, 'I shall learn the truth in London.'

The old presentiment which had once haunted her so constantly, which had been so readily awakened by the merest chimerical cause, of which she had felt guilty, ashamed, combating its influence by reasoning upon its ingratitude, its weakness, its unworthiness, had left her, it seemed, at this time. No shadow from the brooding wings of the terrific truth swept across her soul.

The journey was commenced at the appointed time, and safely accomplished, with as much celerity as was possible nearly thirty years ago.

On their arrival in London, the travellers went to a hotel in Bond-street, and Margaret, much tired by the journey, fell almost immediately into a sound sleep. They had reached London at noon, and it was quite dark when she awoke. The glimmering firelight showed her Mr Baldwin's figure seated beside her bed, and she awoke to the consciousness that he was looking at her with terrible intentness.

'Are you quite rested, my darling?' he said.

'Quite.'

She answered only one word. The time had come, and she was afraid, though still no shadow from the brooding wings of the terrific truth swept across her soul. He kissed her on the forehead, and rose. Then he said,

13

'Come down as quickly as you can. I asked Dugdal
and Mr Meredith to meet us in London, and they are here

CHAPTER XIX.

THE MARRIAGE.

A SILENT party was assembled in the large old-fashione
room in which Margaret's presence was awaited. On the high
mantel clusters of tall wax-candles were grouped, which
failed to light the dusky apartment half-way along its lengt
or across its breadth, but threw their lustre around the
hearth, covered with a Turkey rug.

Hayes Meredith leaned moodily against the fluted side
of the grim black-marble chimneypiece, with one foot on
the brass fender, and his keen dark glance turned towards
the glowing red fire. James Dugdale sat in a heavy arm-
chair, his head leaning back against the red-leather cushion
his long thin fingers grasping the sides of the chair, his face
always pale, now of an ashen-gray colour, and the nervous
tremor which pervaded his entire frame painfully evident to
the two stronger men. Mr Baldwin paced the room with
folded arms. All three were silent. They had said all that
was to be said in the absence of her whom their consultation concerned so deeply.

A light tread in the passage outside the door caught Mr
Baldwin's strained ear. James Dugdale heard it too, but he
did not move; he only closed his eyes, and passed his hand
across his brow. In another moment Margaret was in the
room, was within the luminous circle made by the light, and
had advanced towards Meredith. Her face was deadly pale,
but her eyes were bright, and the old look of resolution

which he had so often remarked and admired struck him
once more, with his first glance at her. Her figure was as
slight and girlish as when he had seen her last, the principal
change was in the rich dress, now become habitual to her.

Hayes Meredith tried hard to make his earnest greeting
as gladsome as it might have been; to say, 'I told you we
should meet again—you see I was a true prophet;' but
there was something in her face which made it quite
impossible. She shook hands with him, and then she turned
to James, who had now stood up, and laid her hand upon
his shoulder. Fitzwilliam Baldwin made no sign. The
worst had come now, and he had very little strength to
face it.

'James,' she said, 'is my father dead?'

'Good God, Margaret,' he made answer, catching her
hands in his, 'no! What can have put such an idea, such a
fear, into your mind? He is quite well.'

She kissed him on the cheek, and sat down, keeping her
hand on his arm still, and, slightly turning her head towards
Baldwin, said in a quiet voice,

'I know there is something wrong. My husband is
concealing something from me; he is right in having concealed it so far, for he is always right—' she paused for a
moment to smile at him, and then Meredith did not know
the face—he had never seen *that* look in it—'and he has
asked you to meet us here and tell me what it is, because he
cannot bear to tell me himself. Well, I will hear anything
you have to tell me, if it is his wish '—again she paused and
smiled at him—'but he is here, and well; my father, and
my child, and you '—she pressed James's arm with the
hand that lay upon it—'are well; what can there be for me
to fear so very much that my husband should dread to tell
it to me himself?'

She turned an earnest, imploring gaze on James, and saw the look he directed at Meredith. Baldwin stepped hastily towards her, but she stretched her hand out, and shrank away from him. The terrible truth was fast swooping down upon her now.

'It does not come from him,' she said breathlessly; 'it is the resurrection of the past—it is my old dread—it is bad news that *you* have brought '—her white face addressed itself to Meredith—'tell me what it is quickly, for God's sake! I can bear to know it—I cannot bear the suspense.'

'I will tell you, my dear,' said Meredith; and he left his place, and put his strong arm round her—the other two stood side by side at a little distance. 'It is bad news, but not very bad; the trouble it brings will soon be over, and no ill can ever come of it. Do you remember when we heard, one night when you were at my house, that Hunger-ford had been murdered?'

She started and said, 'Yes, yes.'

'You recollect the date?'

'Perfectly.' Her voice was hardly audible.

'He did not meet that dreadful fate, Margaret. He did not die thus, or then.'

'Thank God!' she said. And then, in a bewildered way she thought for a moment, and cried out, 'He is not dead He is not dead! That is your news—your dreadful news!

'No, my darling, no,' said Mr Baldwin, coming to her side. 'It is not so bad as that. Thank God, your fears are so far beyond the truth. He is dead. We are not parted No, no.'

'No, no,' continued Meredith, still holding her; 'it is no so bad as that. Hungerford is dead; I saw his body, and I gave it decent burial; but he did not die until long after the time when you believed him dead.'

'When did he die?' she asked. The relief was immense; but if the news she was to hear was only *that*, it was rather good than bad. 'When *did* he die?'

Meredith hesitated. Baldwin turned away.

'Tell me,' she insisted.

'He died only a short time ago,' said Meredith slowly. 'He died only a few days before I left Melbourne.'

She was still standing, upheld by his arm, but she lost consciousness for a little as she stood. He placed her gently in a chair, and they kept aloof from her, until her eyes opened, and she drew a long breath. Then she lifted her hand to her forehead, and slowly pushed the hair away from it.

'You are better now?' said James.

'I am quite well,' she said. 'Let me understand this. I don't quite take it in.'

'It is better that she should understand all about it at once, Baldwin,' said Meredith. 'The shock is over now, and time must not be lost. The only difference this unfortunate affair will make to you, my dear, is that you must be married over again.'

He spoke the words with extreme reluctance, and Margaret's face crimsoned.

'What,' she exclaimed, 'do you mean?' And then she said gently, 'Ah—yes—I see—I understand,' and covering her face with her hands she burst into tears.

Mr Baldwin knelt down by her chair, and gently drew one hand from before her eyes.

'I think you had better leave her with me now for a little while,' he said

The two men went silently away.

All through the hours of the wintry night, Margaret

strove with the anguish that had come on her as bravely as she had striven against that which had turned her youth to bitterness. But she strove now with a different kind of strength, and she had consolation then denied to her. Yet even in that consolation there was more sorrow. In the past she had stood alone, her grief was hers only, her misery troubled no one's peace, or she did not realize that it had any outside influence; she had to fight the battle all alone, in patience, in endurance, in defiance, no softening influence, no gentle thoughts and blessed hopes to hamper or to aid her. The hard material conflict of life had been hers, and in her heart the sting of cruel mortification, of bitter disappointment, disgust, and scorn.

But she had borne this all alone, and had been able to bear it, had come through it somehow, and, if severely wounded, had hidden her wounds, now healed by the balm of love and happiness. But in this sorrow she did not stand alone; she had the additional misery that it had brought grief upon the man who had changed her whole life into gladness, him to whom she owed all, and more than realized every dim misgiving she had ever felt when the idea of a second marriage presented itself.

She had seen Meredith and Dugdale again, after her long interview with Mr Baldwin had come to an end—an interview full of exquisite pain to both, and yet stored among the most precious memories of their lives—and had learned all the particulars of the plan of action upon which they had decided. Then she had requested that she might be left quite alone, until her presence should be necessary in the morning. During this trying time Margaret had successfully maintained her composure, and when she left them the three men remained silent for several minutes, under the impression produced by her calmness, good sense, and self-control. Meredith was the first to break the silence.

'How wonderfully she has borne it!' he said. 'I never hoped she would have taken it like that, though I have seen her in great trouble before, and ought to have known what she could do and bear when the screw was put on her.'

'I have never seen her in any trouble until now,' said Mr Baldwin—there was a strange kind of pain to him in this first association with the man who had seen and helped Margaret in the time now again linked so mysteriously to the present—' she does, indeed, bear this wonderfully.'

'I doubt whether any of us—whether even *you*—can tell what it is to her,' said James, and there was a little impatience in his tone.

Who could really know what she suffered but he—he, dowered with the power of feeling and understanding grief as these two men, so different, and yet in some qualities of their organization so alike, were not dowered?

The exceptional circumstances had broken down the ordinary barriers which would have shut out the subject, and the three talked over the history of Margaret's life in Australia fully and freely Hayes Meredith told the others all he knew, and from his narrative Mr Baldwin learnt how tolerantly, how mercifully, Margaret had dealt with the wretched man who had made her youth so miserable, and how, while telling him the simple terrible truth as she saw it, there was much she had not seen, had failed to understand. And, as he listened to the story, and thought how the ghost of the horrid past had risen up again to blight her, he felt as if all the love with which he had loved her were nothing in comparison with that which filled his heart now; and he grieved purely, unselfishly, for her, as she was then grieving for him.

Margaret had taken her child into her room. The nurse, weary of the journey, was nothing loth to be rid of her charge, and being an honest, stupid, bovine sort of person, and therefore admirably suited to her functions, she did not trouble her mind about her mistress's movements or remark her appearance. The little girl, already strikingly like her mother, now slept tranquilly in Margaret's arms, and now, when in the restlessness of mental suffering she could not sit still, but walked about the room, in a deep chair before the fire.

As the night wore on, Margaret would kneel beside the chair, and look at the child by the fire-light, and then stand up again, and resume her wandering up and down. Surely the dawn was very long in coming. She lived through those hours as probably every one in every kind of suffering lives through certain supreme hours of that experience ; in alternate paroxysms of acute anguish, spells of quiet concentrated thought, and lapses of dull pain, in which there is a kind of confused forgetfulness, wanting little of being quite a blank. When the latter came, she would rock the child upon her knees before the fire, or stand idly at the window, the curtain held back in her hand, and her face pressed against the cold damp panes.

Memory formed a rack on which she was stretched, until her powers of endurance were almost exhausted, and when the release came, it was accompanied by the stupor which follows terrible physical pain. Every circumstance of her past life, every pain in it, from the fiercest pang to the most ignominious little insult, came up to her, and gave her a deliberate wrench, and above all, the sense of loneliness in all this, contradictory though such a feeling was to the general tenor of her thoughts, oppressed her. No one could share that trouble with her which came from the past—therein she must suffer alone.

Then she would force herself to think of the dead man,
and what he had suffered; to realize that he had actually
been living, and her husband, while she was on her voyage
to England, while she was living her peaceful life at Chayleigh, while—and at this point in her thoughts she shuddered,
and a deadly coldness laid hold upon her—while she had
loved and married another man, had filled a high position,
and enjoyed all that wealth, station, and consideration could
give her. The full horror of her position swept over her
then, and afterwards came the deadness, the confusion, the
vain helpless weeping over her child, the natural shrinking
from what the morrow was to bring, the strange wondering
sense of a totally false position, of an utterly new and disturbing element in her life, making all that had gone before
seem unreal.

The hardest of all was to know, to make herself believe
practically, that she, bearing Fitzwilliam Baldwin's name—
she, the mother of his child—was not his wife. She knew
how innocently, how unconsciously, she had done this wrong;
they had made it plain to her how small its importance
really was; but she was oppressed with a sense of shame
and anguish in reference to it, almost intolerable, even when
she did not turn her thoughts towards her child.

When she did not! That was seldom, indeed; for, underlying all the rest, there was the agony of the wrong her
child had sustained, never to be assuaged, and many times
during that dreadful night she uttered aloud to the unconscious infant some of the burden of her soul. The injury to
her child, the possible touch of disgrace on the stainless
story of Baldwin's life; he who, as she said to herself over
and over again, had lived in unblemished honour before the
world, he who never needed, never wished to hide thought,

or word, or deed of his, he who so loved her—these constituted the almost unbearable agony of the grief which had
come upon her.

They had told her whence the remedy for all this evil was
to be looked for. If the child to be born three months
hence should prove to be a son, the wrong would be righted;
little Gerty would be no worse than if this had never happened, for it was not in any reason to be feared that the
secret should ever transpire.

'And if my child should not be a son?' she had asked
them simply.

'Then there would be two to share Baldwin's savings,
and the unentailed property,' Hayes Meredith had answered
her, 'and you would have to wait till the son and heir really
did arrive.'

She had said no more then, and now, as she mused over
all that had been said, a passionate prayer arose in her heart,
that the child for whose birth she now hoped, with feelings
so widely, so sadly different from what they had been, might
be a son. If it were so, Baldwin would be satisfied; the
sting would be taken out of this calamity for him, though
for her it never could be.

James Dugdale was right in the estimate he had formed
of her feelings, little as she supposed that they were within
any human ken. She did love little Gertrude wonderfully;
and to know her to be illegitimate, to know that she must
owe her name and place in the world to a concealment, a
false pretence, was a wound in the mother's heart never to
be healed, and whose aching was never to be allayed.

So the hours wore away, and with their wearing there
came to Margaret an increased sense of unreality. The
ground she had trodden so securely was mined and shaken
beneath her feet, and with the stability all the sweetness of

her life had also passed away. In her thoughts she tried to avoid the keen remembrance of that beautiful, pure summertime of love and joy, over which this shadow had fallen, but she could not keep away from it; its twilight had too newly come. With keen intolerable swiftness and clearness a thousand memories of her beautiful, stately home came to haunt her, like forms of the dead, and it was all in vain that she strove to believe, with the friends who had endeavoured to cheer and console her, that the black shadow which had fallen between that home and her could ever be lifted more.

When the wintry dawn had fully come, she lay down on her bed, with her child in her arms, and slept. One tiny infant hand was doubled up against the mother's neck and her tear-stained cheek rested on the soft brown curls of the baby's hair.

Margaret's slumber did not last long. She awoke long before the time at which she had told Baldwin she would be ready. When she drew back the curtains and let in the cold gleaming light, there was as yet but little stir or noise in the street, and the shops opposite the hotel were but slowly struggling into their full-dressed and business-like appearance. She turned from the window, and looked at her face in the glass. Was that face the same that had looked out at her only this time yesterday? She could hardly believe it was, so ghastly, so worn, so old it showed now. She turned away abruptly, and took off her dress, which she replaced by a dressing-gown, and shook down her rich hair about her neck and shoulders. Presently the child awoke and cried, and Margaret carried her to her nurse. She did not kiss the child, or look at her, after she had placed her in the woman's arms, but went away at once, with her teeth set.

How horrible, how unnatural, how shameful it seemed to Margaret, as she dressed herself in the plainest garments

her'travelling trunks supplied, that this should be her wedding-day, and she was dressing for her marriage! All the
painful feelings which she had experienced were concentrated and expressed in those terrible, almost incredible words.
She went through her unaided task steadily, only avoiding
seeing her face in the glass; and when it was quite done,
when her shawl, and bonnet, and gloves were on, she knelt
down by her bed, with her face upon the coverlet, and her
clasped hands outstretched, and there she prayed and waited.

At nine o'clock James Dugdale knocked at the door of
Margaret's room. She opened the door at his summons
and silently gave him her hand.

'Baldwin is in the sitting-room,' he said. 'I see you
are quite ready. Are you feeling strong?'

'I am perfectly well,' she replied.

They went down-stairs, and into the room which the party
had occupied on the preceding evening. Preparations for
breakfast were in active progress, and two waiters were con-
ducting them with as much fuss and display of alacrity as
possible.

Hayes Meredith greeted Margaret with a cheeful aspect.
Mr Baldwin merely set a chair for her. Their 'good-mor-
row' was but a look, and what a pang this caused Margaret!
The servants were not to know they had not met till then.

To the practical, business-like mind of Hayes Meredith
the painful matter on hand had not, indeed, ceased to be
painful, but had advanced so far towards a happy termination, which should end its embarrassment positively, and in
all human probability its danger, that he felt able to be
cheerful without much effort or affectation, and took upon
himself the task of keeping up appearances, to which his
companions were much less equal. He really ate his breakfast, while the other three made the poorest pretence of do-

ing so, and he did the talking about an early shopping expedition which had been proposed over-night.

At length this portion of the trial came to an end in its turn, and Margaret, accompanied by James, and followed by Meredith and Baldwin, left the hotel on foot. The two waiters witnessed the departure of the party.

'A precious glum lot for a party wot is wisitin' the metrop'lis, eh, William?' said one to the other.

'Ain't they just, Jim! They are swells, though, from wot I hear.'

When they reached Piccadilly Meredith procured a hackney-coach, and the silent little company were driven to the City. Margaret sat back, leaning her head in the corner with closed eyes. The three men hardly spoke. The way seemed very long, and yet when the coach stopped, in obedience to Meredith's directions to the driver, in a crooked, narrow, dirty little street, which she had a confused notion was near the great river, Margaret started, and her heart, which had lain like a lump of lead in her breast, began to beat violently.

'A few minutes' walking, but by a tortuous way, brought them to a shabby little old church, damp, mouldy, and of disused aspect, and into the presence of a clergyman whose appearance matched admirably with that of the building, for he, too, was shabby, little, and old, and looked as if he were mouldered by time and seclusion. An ancient clerk, who apparently combined the clerkly office with those of the pew-opener and the verger, was the only other person present. Not even a stray boy, not even a servant-girl out on an errand, or a nursemaid airing her charges in the damp, had been tempted, by the rare spectacle of an open church-door, to enter the building.

A little whispered conversation with the shabby little old

clergyman, a paper shown by Meredith, and a ghost-like beckoning by the clerk, with intent to marshal the wedding-party to their places, and all was ready. The words of the solemn marriage-service, which it was so dreadful to those two to repeat, which they had spoken once with such joyful hearts, were said for the second time, and nothing but the signing of the register remained to be done.

As Mr Baldwin with his wife followed the shabby little old clergyman into the vestry, he whispered to Margaret,

'It is all over now, dearest; nothing can ever trouble or part us more but death.'

She pressed the arm on which she was leaning very close to her breast, but she answered him never a word.

'Sign your name here, if you please, madam,' said the clerk, putting a dirty withered old finger on the blank space in the large book which held in such trite record so many first chapters of human histories.

Mr Baldwin had already signed, and was looking at his wife with eager attention. He saw the spasm of agony which crossed her face as she wrote 'Margaret Hungerford.' James Dugdale saw it too.

When Meredith and Dugdale in their turn had signed the register, and Mr Baldwin had astonished the clergyman, to a degree unprecedented in his mild and mouldy existence, by the magnificence of the sum with which he rewarded his services, all was done, and the wedding-party left the church. Mr Baldwin and Margaret got into the coach, and were driven to a shop in Piccadilly. There the driver, who was rather surprised at the novelty of a bridal pair being 'dropped' at a shop instead of being taken home in orthodox style to breakfast, was dismissed. Mr and Mrs Baldwin returned to the hotel, as they had left it, on foot.

'Let me see—what's the name of the church and the parson?' said Hayes Meredith to James Dugdale, as they stood in the street when the coach had taken Baldwin and Margaret away, and the church-door was shut upon them.

He had an old-fashioned red morocco-leather pocket-book, with a complicated clasp, composed of brass wire, open in his hand, and he carefully noted down James's reply, heading the memorandum with the initials,

F. M. B.

M. H.

'What do you write that down for?' James asked him.

'Partly from habit, old fellow, and partly because I never was concerned in so strange an affair before, and I have a fancy for reminding myself of it.'

He had put up the pocket-book as he spoke, and they were walking slowly away.

'I remember well,' said Meredith, 'when I said good-bye to her on board the Boomerang, I wondered what sort of fate awaited her in England. It is a very enviable one on the whole, in spite of this little cloud, which I look upon as quite blown over. It might have been an ugly business if that poor wretch had pulled through in the hospital. What a comfort that it has all been so capitally managed, isn't it?'

'Yes,' said James absently; 'how very, very miserable she looked!'

'Never mind that—it was natural—it was all so awkward, you know. Why, now that it is over, I can hardly believe it. But she will be all right to-morrow—the journey had something to do with her looks, you must remember.'

When they reached the hotel they found Mr Baldwin alone in the sitting-room. Hayes Meredith had recovered his spirits much more than any of the party. He was quite chatty, and inclined to enjoy himself, now that it was possible, in the delightful novelty of London. Besides, he judged wisely that the less difference the event of the morning should be allowed to make in the disposition of the day the better.

Mr Baldwin was ready to devote himself to his guest's pleasure, and a pleasant programme was soon made out. On reference being made to Margaret she said she would remain at home all day, with the child. James, too, pleaded fatigue, and did not leave the house. And when the other two were gone he thought, ' No one, not even *he*, knows what this is to her so well as I know it.'

CHAPTER XX.

SHADOWS.

ON the third day after the quiet marriage ceremony had been performed in the City church, Margaret Baldwin, her husband, and their child left London for Chayleigh. She had been told that her father knew nothing of the revelation which it had been Hayes Meredith's difficult task to impart to her, and she felt that she owed much to the wise consideration which had concealed it. In the first place, to have enlightened her father would only have been to inflict unnecessary pain upon him, and in the second, it would have embarrassed her extremely.

To keep her feelings in this supreme hour of her fate as much to herself as possible was her great desire, and especially as regarded her father. His pride and delight in the good fortune which had befallen her were so great, his absolute oblivion of the past was so complete and so satisfactory, that she would not, if even it could have made things better rather than worse for her, have had the one feeling disturbed, or the other altered. He had never mentioned her first husband's name to her, and she would not, to spare herself any suffering, have had an occasion arise in which it must needs be mentioned. So, as they travelled towards her old home, there was nothing in the prospect of her meeting with her father to disturb her, and the events of the week she had just gone through began to seem already distant.

After the day of the marriage, Baldwin had not spoken of the grief that had befallen them. If it had been possible for him to love her better, more tenderly, more entirely, more deferentially than before, he would have done so ; but it was not possible. In all conceivable respects their union was perfect ; not even sorrow could draw them more closely together. Neither could sorrow part them, as sometimes it does part, almost imperceptibly, but yet surely, those whose mutual affection is not solidified by perfect similarity of temperament.

The gravity of Margaret's character, which had been increased by the experiences of her life, by the deadly influences which had tarnished her youth, had been much tempered of late by the cordial cheerfulness, the unfailing sweetness of disposition, which characterized Baldwin, and which, being entirely free from the least tinge of levity, harmonized perfectly with her sensitiveness. So, in this grief, they felt alike, and while he comprehended, in its innermost depths and intricacy of feeling, the distress she suffered, he comprehended also that she needed no assurance of his appreciation and sympathy.

The details of business and the arrangements for the future which the terrible discovery had made necessary were

14

imparted to her by Hayes Meredith, and never discussed
between her and Baldwin. She understood that in the
wildly improbable—indeed, as far as human ken could penetrate, impossible—contingency that the truth should ever
become known, the little Gertrude's future was to be made
secure, by special precautions taken with that intent by her
father. Thus no material anxiety oppressed her for the
sake of the child, over whom, nevertheless, she grieved with
a persistent intensity which would have seemed ominous
and alarming to any one aware of it. But that no one
knew; the infant was the sole and unconscious witness of
the mother's suffering.

What intense shame and misery, what incoherent passionate tenderness, what vague but haunting dread, what
foreshadowing of possible evil, had possession of her soul, as,
her head bent down over the little girl sleeping in her arms,
Margaret approached her father's house!

Mr Carteret was standing at the entrance, and behind
him, in the shade of the portico, was a figure whom Margaret did not recognize, and whom she was about to pass,
having received her father's affectionate greeting, when Mr
Baldwin said, 'This is Mr Meredith's son, Margaret,' and
Robert held out his hand. Then she spoke to the boy, but
hastily, being anxious to get her child and her father out of
the cold air.

When the whole party had entered the house, and Mr
Baldwin and Mr Carteret were talking by the fire in the
study, Robert Meredith stood still in the hall watching the
light snow flakes which had begun to fall sparingly, and
which had the charm of novelty to him, and thinking not
over-pleasantly of Margaret.

'A proud, stuck-up fine lady,' the boy muttered, and the
expression of scorn which made his face so evil at times

came over it. ' I suppose she thinks I don't remember her
in her shabby old clothes, and with her hauds all rough. I
suppose she faucies I was too much of a child to know all
about her when she used to do our needlework, and my
mother used to puzzle her head to make out jobs for her,
because she was too proud to take the money as a present.
I saw it all, though they didn't tell me; and I wonder how
she would like me to tell her fine husband or her old fool of
a father all about it ! I remember how they talked about
her at home when the black fellows killed Mr Hungerford,
and my father said they might venture to take her into the
house now, until she could be sent to England. And my
lady's too fine to look at one now, is she, with her precious
self and her precious brat wrapped up in velvet and fur.' And
the boy pulled off a chair in the hall a mantle of Margaret's
which had been thrown there, and kicked it into a corner.

It would be difficult to do justice to the vile expression
of his handsome face, as, having given vent to this ebullition
of senseless rage, he again stood, looking through the side
windows of the hall door for the approach of the carriage
which was to bring his father and James Dugdale to Chayleigh. The boy's chief characteristic was an extreme and
besetting egotism, which Margaret had unconsciously offended. She would not have thought much or perhaps at
all of the fact had she known it, but from the moment when,
with a polite but careless greeting to Robert Meredith, she
had passed on into the house, she had an enemy in the son
of her old friend.

'I thought Margaret would be in a hurry home,' said
the unconscious Mr Carteret, in a sagacious tone to his son-
in-law, ' when Meredith came. She received much kinduess
from him, and I knew she would like to acknowledge it as
soon as possible.'

'And I too, sir,' said Baldwin. 'What a good fellow he is, and a fine hearty fellow! What do you think of the boy?'

'A very fair kind of boy indeed,' said Mr Carteret, with unusual alacrity; 'never requires to be told anything twice, and is never in the way. If he is noisy at all, he keeps it all for out-of-doors, I assure you. And not ignorant, by any means: gave me a very intelligible account of the habits of the wombat and the opossum. Really a very tolerable boy, Baldwin; I fancy you won't mind him much.'

This was warm praise, and quite an enthusiastic supposition, for Mr Carteret. Baldwin was much reassured by it; he and Margaret had been rather alarmed at the contemplation of his possible sufferings at finding himself alone with a real live boy. Baldwin was glad too of the excuse for talking about something apart from himself and Margaret. The most natural thing for him to say under the circumstances would have been, 'Well, sir, and how do you think Margaret is looking?' but he hesitated about saying it, and was relieved when Mr Carteret volunteered the opinion that she was looking very well, and began to question him about their doings in foreign parts.

Thus the time was whiled away until Meredith and Dugdale arrived, and Margaret, announcing that the child was asleep, came to sit with her father. A look from her husband showed her that all was well, and a look in return from her released him.

The evening passed away quietly. No incident of any moment occurred. Mr Carteret displayed no curiosity about Meredith's business in London, though he was very congratulatory concerning the fortunate coincidence of the return of Mr and Mrs Baldwin, and very solicitous about the danger of James Dugdale's being made ill by the journey and the excitement of London, which presented itself to Mr Carteret in most alarming colours. He had not been in 'town' since Mrs Carteret's death, and if, contrary to his usual placid habit, he speculated about his own future at all, it certainly was to the effect that he hoped he never should be there again.

The old gentleman was in a state of supreme mental content just now. He was very happy in all respects, and the return of Margaret and Mr Baldwin completed his felicity. His daughter's account of her health was very satisfactory, and perhaps she need not go abroad again. They spoke of going on to the Deane if the weather should not prove very severe, and for his part he hoped they would do so. He had no great liking for foreign countries, and no strong faith in the remedial properties of their climate; and though he was very glad that Margaret had tried Italy and profited by it, he should be still more glad that she should decide on staying at home. With a splendid home, every conceivable comfort, and improved health, she need not gad about any more, especially under present circumstances.

On the whole, Mr Carteret's state of mind was one of enviable contentment on the evening of his daughter's return, and as she and her husband commented on it when they were alone, they felt that his entire unconsciousness was most fortunate. They had nothing to fear from suspicion or inquisitiveness on his part—he was incapable of the one, except in the case of a traveller reporting on newly-discovered natural objects, or of the latter, except in the case of birds, beasts, and creeping things.

There was one dissatisfied person among the little party at Chayleigh on the night of the return. It was Robert Meredith. He had not succeeded in discovering the object of his father's visit to London. ' I am going to London with

Mr Dugdale, for a few days, on particular business,' his father had said to him before they went away. But he had not explained the nature of the business, and the boy was vexed by this reticence. He had quick, subtle perceptions, and he had detected some trouble in his father's mind before they left home, and during the voyage. He had a secret conviction that this visit to London, whose object Meredith, an open-mannered, unreserved man with every one, and always frank and hearty in his dealings with his children, had not explained, had reference to this undiscovered source of trouble.

Robert listened to all the conversation which took place during the evening, and closely watched the countenances of every one present, but nothing transpired which shed the least light on the matter which excited his curiosity. He had not failed to remark that, though his father had told him all about his correspondence with Dugdale, and how he looked to him for advice and assistance in forwarding Robert's wishes, as to his education in England and his future career, the subject had not yet been discussed, and he had been left to amuse himself, and become familiar with the house and the surroundings, as best he might. A less shrewd and more amiable person than Robert Meredith would have imputed this to the pleasure of old friends in meeting after a separation of many years, and to the number and interest of the subjects they had to discuss. But Robert Meredith was not likely to entertain an hypothesis in which sentiment claimed a part, and was likely to resent anything which looked like a postponement of his claims to those of any subject or interest whatsoever.

To baffle this youth's curiosity was to excite his anger and animosity—to make him determined that he *would* get to the bottom of the mystery sought to be concealed from him—to fill him with the belief that it must be evil in its

nature, and its discovery profitable. It was to call out into active display all that was as yet worst in a nature whose
capacity for evil Margaret had early detected, and concerning
which his father had conceived many unspoken misgivings.

'It is almost as if he had come to England about these
people's affairs, and not about mine,' said Robert Meredith
to himself. 'I wonder how many more days are to be lost
before I hear what is to be done about me.'

Margaret happened to glance towards him as this thought
passed through his mind, and the expression of his face
struck her painfully. 'He was a bad child as I remember
him—a bad, sly, deceitful, heartless child—and he is a bad
boy. He will be a bad man, I fear.' She allowed these sentiments to influence her manner to Robert Meredith more
than she was conscious of—it was polite indeed, but cold
and distant.

It would have been depressing to a shy or sensitive person, but Robert Meredith was neither. He felt her manner
indeed, and thought with a sneer, that considering the friendship she professed for his father, she might at least have
feigned some interest in him. But he did not care. This
rich woman, of high station and social importance, which his
colonial notions rather magnified, must befriend him in
material concerns, and, therefore, how she felt towards him
was a thing of no consequence whatever. She could not
dislike him more than he disliked her, for he hated her and
her fine husband. He remembered her poor, and almost at
the mercy of his parents for daily bread, and now she was
rich and independent of every one, and he hated her. How
had she gained all the world had to give, all he had longed
for, since in his childhood he had read and heard of the great
world, and all its prizes and luxuries? Only by her beauty,
only by a man's foolish love for her.

The boy's precocious mind dwelt upon this thought with peculiar bitterness and a kind of rage. He hated Baldwin, too, though with less of personal dislike than Margaret. He was the first man whom Robert Meredith had ever seen with whose wealth no idea of effort, of labour, of speculation, of uncertainty was associated, and the boy's ambition and his avarice alike revolted against the contemplation of a position which he coveted with all the strength of his heart, and which he knew could never be his. This man, who passed him over as a mere boy—this man, who had given wealth and station to a woman whom Robert disliked and despised—was born to all these good things; he had not to long for them vainly, or to strive for them through long and weary toilsome years, with only the chance of winning them at last, which was to be his own lot in life. He might live as he listed, and the money he should have to spend would still be there.

Then there was a strife in the boy's mind between the burning desire for wealth, and the pleasures which wealth procures, and distaste to, revolt against, the toil by which it must be earned. In the evil soil of his nature such plants were ripe of growth, and he rebelled blindly against the inevitable lot which awaited him. Only in the presence of Baldwin and Margaret, only in the innumerable trifling occurrences and allusions—all strange and striking to the colonial-bred boy—which mark the presence and the daily habits of persons to whom wealth is familiar, had Robert Meredith been brought to understand the distinction between his own position in life and that of persons of assured fortune. As he learned the lesson, he also learned to hate the unconscious teachers.

He learned, by the discussion of plans which he heard in the course of the evening, that his father intended to visit Mr Baldwin at the Deane, and that he was to be of the party. The prospect gave him no pleasure. He should see this fine lady, then, in her grand home. If he dared, how he should like to say a few things, in seeming innocent unconsciousness, which should remind her of the time when he had seen her in his father's house, and known far more about her than she or any one would have believed possible! The impulse to say something which should offend Mrs Baldwin grew upon him; but he dared not yield to it, and his animosity increased towards the unconscious individual on whose account he was forced to impose restraint upon his spiteful and vicious nature.

Margaret retired early, and as she extended her hand to him with a kind 'good-night!' the diamonds which sparkled upon it caught his attention. Once more she marked the sinister look—half smile, half sneer—which came into his face. He was thinking, 'I wonder whether you would like Mr Baldwin to know about the trumpery ring my mother sold for you, and how you cried when you had to come to her afterwards, and tell her you had nothing left to sell.'

On the following day the weather was bright, dry, and cheerful; Meredith, Baldwin, and Robert went out early, bent on a long walk. During the forenoon Margaret did not come down-stairs, but in the afternoon she went to her father's study in search of James. She found him there, a large folio was on a reading-desk before him, but it was long since he had turned a page.

'Put this with the letters for post,' she said, handing him a packet directed to Lady Davyntry, 'and come out with me for a while.'

James looked at her anxiously. She had a wearied, exhausted expression in her face, and her cheeks were deeply flushed.

'You are very tired, Margaret?'

'Yes, I am. I am easily tired now, and I have been writing for hours.'

They went out together, and walked along the terrace into the flower-garden, which looked dreary in its desolate wintry condition.   At first they talked vaguely of trifles, but after a while they fell into deep and earnest conversation, and Margaret leaned closely on James's arm as they walked, now quickly, now slowly, and sometimes she held him standing still, as she impressed upon him something that she was saying with emphasis.

The walk and the conference lasted long, and when at length the warning chill of sunset came, and James reminded Margaret of the danger of cold and fatigue, and she yielded to his counsel, and turned towards the house, traces of deep emotion were visible upon the faces of both.

'I will not speak thus to you again,' said Margaret, as they reached the portico ; 'but I have implicit faith in your remembrance of what I have said, and in your promise.'

'You may trust both,' James answered her in an earnest but broken voice ; 'I will remember, and I will send for Rose Moore.'

'I am delighted you have made up your mind not to re-turn to Italy,' said Mr Carteret a day or two later. 'So much travelling would be very unfit for you, and your son and heir ought certainly to be born at the Deane.'

CHAPTER XXI.

FAMILY AFFAIRS.

THE eldest Miss Crofton was enthusiastically delighted when the intelligence of Mrs Baldwin's unexpected return to Chayleigh reached her, which was on the morning after the event. It was very natural that she should like the importance which she acquired in the small but almost distressingly respectable circle of society in which she 'moved,' as the unaccountable phrase in use goes, from her position in regard to Mrs Baldwin. To her the Willises, &c., looked for the latest intelligence concerning Margaret; to her the excellent, if rather too inexorably managing, wife of the rector of the parish—a lady known to the population as 'the Reverend Mrs Carroll'—intrusted the task of procuring donations from Mr Baldwin for a startling number of 'charitable purposes,' and through the discursive medium of her letters Haldane conducted his correspondence by proxy with his sister.

The eldest Miss Crofton entertained one supreme ambition. It was that she might become Margaret's 'particular friend,' confidante, and, eventually, favourite sister-in-law. She had not as yet attained any of the degrees of the position to which she aspired, but that slight impediment by no means interfered with her assumption, for the edification of her friends and the general public, of the completed character.

She entertained considerable jealousy of Lady Davyntry, who was, she argued, in her frequent cogitations on this subject, much older than Margaret, and 'not a bit more' her sister-in-law than she (Lucy Crofton) was destined to be at no distant time. She was particularly well pleased to learn that Lady Davyntry had not accompanied her brother and his wife on their return to England, and promised herself, within five minutes of her having learned that Margaret was at Chayleigh, that she would make the most of the opportunity now open to her.

It was not altogether, it was indeed not much, from self-interest, or any mean variety of that pervading meanness, that the eldest Miss Crofton proposed to herself to be 'great friends' with Mrs Baldwin; there was a good deal of real girlish enthusiasm about her, and it found a natural outlet in the direction of vehement admiration for the sister of her future husband,—admiration not disturbed by any perception or suspicion of her own inferiority. Such a suspicion was by no means likely to suggest itself to Lucy Crofton in connection with any one, especially at the present interesting and important epoch of her life—for she knew, as well as any young lady in England, how to *exploiter* the great fact of being 'engaged.'

As for Margaret, she liked the pretty, lively, passably well-bred girl well enough for her own, and was resolved to like her better, and to befriend her in every possible way, for her brother's, sake; but a missish intimacy of the kind which Lucy longed for was completely foreign to her tastes and habits. While Lucy Crofton pleased herself by commenting on the similarity between them in point of age, Margaret was trying to realize that such was actually the case, trying to realize that she had ever been young, putting a strong constraint upon herself to turn her mind into the same groove as that in which the girl's mind ran. Between herself and all the thoughts, plans, hopes, and pleasures of girlhood lay a deep and wide gulf, not formed

alone of the privileges and duties of her present position, not
fashioned by her unusual gravity and strength of character,
but the work of the past—an enduring monument of the
terrible truths which had sent her of late a terrible me-
mento.

Thus it happened that when Margaret received a note
profusely underlined, and crowded with interjections, superlatives, all kinds of epistolary explosives from the eldest Miss
Crofton, announcing her intention of coming a little later to
pass a ' delightful long afternoon ' with her darling friend,
she experienced a sudden accession of weariness of spirit
which communicated itself to her aspect, and attracted the
attention of her father, who immediately asked her if anything ailed her.

' Nothing whatever, papa,' replied Margaret ; and informed him after a minute or so that Lucy was coming to
see her.

Provided Lucy did not come to Chayleigh accompanied
by her wonderfully clever little brother, and did not pester
him with questions intended to evince her lively interest in
his collection, which, however, manifested much more clearly
her profound ignorance of all its components, Mr Carteret
was perfectly indifferent to her movements. She did not
interest him, but she was perfectly respectable, eligible, and,
he understood, amiable ; and if she interested Haldane, that
was quite enough for him. A simple sincerity, which never
degenerated into rudeness, characterized Mr Carteret ; and
he perfectly understood the distinction between saying what
he did not think and leaving much that he did think unsaid
—a useful branch of practical science, social and domestic.
So he made no comment on Margaret's reply.

But Hayes Meredith, who had not yet seen Captain
Carteret's future bride, was rather curious about her, and

addressed a question concerning her to Margaret, which she, being in an absent mood, did not hear. Mr Baldwin answered promptly and expansively, giving Lucy Crofton praise for good looks, good manners, good abilities, and good temper. The three men went on to talk of Haldane, his promotion, his general prospects, and the time fixed for his marriage, which was not to take place until the autumn. During this conversation Margaret rose from the breakfast-table, and stood thoughtfully beside the fire, and Robert Meredith employed himself in listening to the talkers and watching her face.

'Amiable creature!' he thought—and the sneer which was strangely habitual to so young a face settled upon his lips as he thus mentally apostrophized her—' you don't care a pin for the girl; you are bored by her coming here, and she's a long way prettier than ever you were, fine lady as you think yourself.'

Then, as Margaret looked up, with a bright flush on her face, with the air of one who suddenly remembers, or has something painful or embarrassing suggested by a passing remark, the boy thought—

'I shouldn't wonder if she's jealous of this pretty girl, who has always been a lady, and knows nothing about the low life and ruffianism she could tell her of.'

Wide of the mark as were the speculations of the boy, in whose mind a dislike of Margaret, strong in proportion to its causelessness, had taken root, he was not wrong in assigning the change in Margaret's expression from reverie to active painful thought to something in which Lucy Crofton was concerned.

She had been informed of her brother's plans; but in the strangely combined distraction and concentration of her mind since her trouble had fallen upon her—trouble which

each day was lightening for removing from her husband—
she had almost forgotten them, she had never taken them
into consideration as among the circumstances which she
must influence, or which might influence her. The words
which had roused her from her reverie reminded her she had
something to do in this matter.

'Why is Haldane's marriage put off till the summer?'
she said.

'It is not put off,' said James. 'There never was any
idea of its taking place sooner, that I know of;—was there,
sir?'

'No,' said Mr Carteret, 'I think not.—Indeed, Margery,
I fancy it was so settled with a view to your being at home
then. We did not think you would come home so soon,
you know.'

'When is Haldane coming here, papa?'

'Very soon. Early next month he hopes to get leave.'

Margaret said no more, and the party shortly afterwards
dispersed for their several morning avocations.

James Dugdale's attention had been caught by Margaret's look and manner when she spoke of her brother's
marriage. He discerned something painful in her mind in
reference to it, but he could not trace its nature, and he
could not question her just then.

Margaret went to her room, and seated in her old place
by the window—its floral framework bore no blossom now—
thought out the subject which had come into her mind.

Miss Crofton arrived punctually, and found the drawing-room into which she was shown—very much against her
will, for she would have preferred a tumultuous rush up-
stairs, and the entrée to the nursery region—occupied only
by Robert Meredith. They had met during Hayes Meredith's

expedition to London, and Lucy, though an engaged young
lady, and therefore, of course, impervious to the temptations
of coquetry, had perceived with quite sufficient distinctness
that this 'remarkably nice boy,' as she afterwards called
him, thought her very pretty, and found her rattling, rapid,
girlish talk—which had the delightful effect of setting him
quite at his ease—very attractive.

Nothing could be more ridiculous, of course; but then
nothing was more common than for very young persons of
the male sex (somehow, Miss Lucy avoided calling him a
'boy' in her thoughts) to 'take a fancy' to girls or women
much older than themselves; and in some not clearly-ex-
plained or distinctly-understood way, it was supposed to be
very 'safe' for them to do so. She had no objection to the
admiration even of so young an admirer as Robert Meredith,
and she was pleased as well as amused by the candid and
unequivocal pleasure which Robert manifested on seeing
her. The youthful colonial did not suffer in the least from
the disease of shyness, and was pleasantly unembarrassed in
the presence of the eldest Miss Crofton.

The two had had time to talk over the unexpected return
of Mr and Mrs Baldwin; and Miss Crofton, who was by no
means deficient in perception, had had an opportunity of
observing that her young admirer did not share her enthusiasm for Margaret, but was, on the contrary, distinctly
cold and disdainful in the few remarks which he permitted
himself to make concerning her, before Margaret made her
appearance. When she did so, and Miss Crofton had started
up and rapturously embraced her, that young lady and
Robert Meredith alike remarked simultaneously that she
was startlingly pale.

After a great many questions had been asked by Lucy
and answered by Margaret, in whose manner there was an

indefinable change which her friend felt very soon, and
which puzzled her, Margaret took Miss Crofton up-stairs
for an inspection of little 'Gertrude and the 'thoroughly
confidential' talk for which Lucy declared herself irre-
pressibly eager.

'If she knew—if she only knew—this pure, harmless
creature,' Margaret thought, with a pang of fierce pain as
Lucy Crofton hugged the child and talked to her, and appealed to the nurse in support of her admiration, for which
Gerty was poutingly ungrateful,—'if she did but know
how it has been with me since we last met, and how it is
with my child!'

'You are shivering, Margaret. You seem very cold.
Let me poke the fire up before we settle ourselves. And
now tell me all about yourself, how you really are; of
course one could not ask before that young Meredith. I
want to see his father so much. By-the-by, Haldane told
me you knew him so well in Australia. You don't look
very well, I think, but you are much stronger than when
you went abroad.'

'I am much stronger,' said Margaret. 'But before I
talk about myself, and I have a deal to tell you,'—Miss
Crofton was delighted,—'I want to talk to you about yourself and Haldane.'

Miss Crofton was perfectly willing to enter on so congenial a subject, and she told Margaret all about the arrangements, which included many festive proceedings, to
which the girl naturally attached pleasurable anticipations.
When she had reached that portion of the programme which
included the names and dresses of the bridesmaids, she
stopped abruptly, and said with some embarrassment:

'Why do you look so grave, Margaret?—is anything
wrong?' Then she added, before Margaret could speak,

15

'Ah, I know, you don't like a gay wedding; I remember how quiet your own was; but, you see, it would seem so odd if mine wasn't gay, and besides, I like it; it's not the same, you know.'

'I know, dear,' Margaret said very gently, 'it is not at all the same thing, and I can quite understand your wishing to have a gay wedding. But I want you to listen to me, and to do what I am going to ask you. It is something in which you can do me a great service.'

This was delightful, this was being the 'great friend,' indeed this was very like being the favourite sister-in-law. So Lucy promptly knelt down by Margaret's chair, and putting her arm round her, assured her, with much emphasis, of her readiness to do anything she could for her pleasure.

There was a short pause, during which Margaret looked at the girl with a grave sweet smile, and took her disengaged hand; then she spoke:

'Haldane is coming here very soon, my father tells me. What leave has he got?'

'A month.'

'Now, Lucy, don't be astonished, and don't say no at once. I want you to be married during his leave, instead of waiting until the autumn.'

'Margaret! Why?' asked Lucy, in a tone which fully expressed all the surprise she had been requested not to feel.

'I will tell you, Lucy. In a short time I am likely to have another baby. You did not know that, at least you did not know it was to be so soon; and I am very, very anxious—so anxious, that if I cannot have my own way in this it will be very bad for me—that your marriage should be over before a time comes when I may be very ill—you know I was very ill indeed after Gerty's birth.'

'I know,' said Lucy, still with the surprised look.

'And I feel sure, dear Lucy, that if you are not married until the summer I shall not be here.'

'Not be here, Margaret! You surely do not mean—'

'I mean nothing to frighten you, Lucy, but I do mean this. I have not been well lately, and I have been sent away as you know ; I ought not to be here now, the doctors would say—but it cannot be helped; we were obliged to come to England, and I may be sent away again, and not be able to go to your wedding. In short, Lucy,' and here Mrs Baldwin lost her composure, 'I have set my heart on this. Will you make the sacrifice for me ? will you put up with a much quieter wedding, and go and spend your honeymoon at our villa at Naples ? '

'I don't know what to think,' said Lucy ; 'I would do anything you liked, but it does not quite depend upon me ; there's papa and mamma, and Haldane, you know.'

'I fancy Haldane will not object to your marriage being hurried a little,' said Margaret, with a smile; 'and I have generally understood that Miss Lucy Crofton contrives to get her own way with papa and mamma.'

Margaret was very unlikely to remember her own importance out of season ; but it was not unseasonable that she should think of it now, and feel comforted by the assurance that Mr and Mrs Crofton would probably yield to any very strongly urged wish of hers.

Lucy laughed a little—the imputation of power over anybody was not unpleasing to this young lady, who, after a fashion which had not hitherto developed into unamiability, dearly loved her own way.

'But Lady Davyntry is at Naples,' she said in a tone which was very reassuring to Margaret, who felt that the chief question was virtually disposed of, and details only now remained to be mastered.

' She is ; but I am going to ask her to come home, since
I find I cannot return.   We must go to the Deane soon, if
you will only be good, and let things be arranged as I wish.
I need not go until after your wedding ; but my husband
and I wish that the child should be born at the Deane.'

' Of course,' assented Lucy, ' and you want it to be a boy,
don't you, Margaret ? '

' Yes, we hope it may be a boy.'

' Well, whether it is a boy or a girl, I must be its god-
mother.   You will let that be a promise, won't you ? '

A long conversation ensued, and Lucy bade Margaret
farewell until the morrow, with a delightful consciousness
that she had achieved the position she had so much desired.

Margaret told Mr Baldwin her wish with regard to
Haldane's marriage, and the steps she had taken towards
its fulfilment.   He found no fault with it, but failed to comprehend her reasons.

' I can understand your dislike of the kind of wedding
the Croftons would have been likely to institute,' he said ;
' but you might have escaped it on the plea of your health.'

' No,' she replied, ' I could not do that—I could not hurt
the feelings of all these good people, and I could not endure
the wedding.   Even as it will be now, think how painful it
must be to me.'

Her husband understood all those simple words implied,
but he passed them over unnoticed.   It grieved him inexpressibly to observe that Margaret had not shaken off the
impression of the occurrence from which his own happy,
hopeful nature had rallied so much more quickly.

' I know, my darling, I know—and, indeed, I ought not
to have asked you for a reason, because you are the least
fanciful of women—it would be true masculine logic to refuse
to aid you in one fancy, but I am not going to be logical

after that fashion. I will write to Haldane, and get everything settled.'

Accordingly, everything was settled. Mr Carteret was
acquiescent as usual, and with his customary politeness congratulated himself on the presence of Mr Meredith and his son
on so interesting an occasion. The Croftons were benignant.
Dear Mrs Baldwin had made such a point of their daughter's
profiting by her villa at Naples, and had set her heart so
completely on the matter, and, of course, dear Mrs Baldwin
must just now be considered in everything. Haldane was
delighted, and all went well.

'Margaret,' said James Dugdale, when all had been
arranged, 'why is this fixed idea always present with you?
Can you not shake it off? Ever since you came home I
have been watching you, and hoping that you were yielding
to the influence of time; but I see now, since you have set
yourself to arrange Haldane's marriage, that this is a vain
hope. Why is it, Margaret?'

'You ask me why it is?' she replied. 'You—can you
say it is not in your own mind also? Can you say that you
ever really believed that I could get over the thing that has
befallen me? You may call it superstition, and no doubt it
is so. I fancy such a youth as mine is fruitful ground for
the sowing and the nurture of superstition, if such be the
sense of doom, of an inevitable fate hanging over me; but
it is stronger than I, and you know I am not generally weak,
James. It is always there,—always before me,—I can see
nothing else, think of nothing else.'

'I know, dear, I know; but when your health is stronger—believe me, Margaret, I do not wish to mock you with an
assurance that you can ever quite get over what has happened—when your child, the son and heir, is born, you will be
better; you will wonder at yourself that you allowed such

sway to these dark forebodings. Think of all you have to
make you happy, Margaret, and don't, don't yield to the
presentiment which is due to your health alone.'

She laid her hand on his arm with a smile.

'Supposing it be so, James; supposing all I think and
feel—all the horrors which come to me in the night-watches,
all the memories perfectly distinct in their pain, whereas I
could not recall an hour of the brief happiness I ever knew
in my days of delusion—supposing all this to be a mere
groundless state of suffering, and *you* know better'—here
her clear gray eyes looked at him with an expression of in-
effable trust and compassion—'what harm have I done? *If
I live*, this marriage may as well be over; and *if I die*, I
have spared my husband and my father one sharp pang, at
any rate. Haldane would be very sorry, but he would
want to be married all the same, and it would be hard upon
Fitzwilliam and my father.'

'And me?' he asked her, as if the question were wrung
from him by an irresistible impulse of suffering.

Her hand still lay upon his shoulder, and her clear gray
eyes, which deepened and darkened as she slowly spoke,
still looked steadily into his.

'And *you*, James. No, I have no power to save you a
pang more or less; it would not make any difference *to you*.'

There was a strange cruel satisfaction to him in her
words. It was something, nay, it was very much, that she
should know and acknowledge that with her all that had
vital interest for him began and ended, that the gift of his
heart, pure, generous, disinterested, was understood and accepted. There was silence between them for some time,
and then they talked of more general subjects, and just before their interview came to an end their talk turned upon
little Gertrude.

'You will always love her best, James; both my children will be dear to you,' said Margaret, 'but you will always love her whom her mother unconsciously wronged best.'

Lady Davyntry made her appearance at Davyntry in due season, and the set of Neapolitan coral, which she brought as her contribution to the worldly goods of the bride, was so magnificent, that Lucy could not find it in her heart to cherish any such unpleasant sentiment as jealousy against Eleanor, and determined that the 'great friend's' scheme should extend to her also.

The return of her sister-in-law was a great pleasure, but also a great trial for Margaret. Her presence renewed painfully the scene of secret humiliation, of severance from those who had nothing to hide, from which she had already suffered so much ; and the phantoms of the past came forth and swarmed about her, as Eleanor overwhelmed her with caresses, and declared her delight at being once more with her, and her vivid perception of the improvement in 'baby.'

The most unsuspicious and unexacting of women, Eleanor Davyntry had been so perfectly satisfied with the reasons assigned by her brother for his return to England, that it never occurred to her to ask him a question on the subject. She was very eloquent concerning the beauty of the season at Naples, assured Haldane that she had left everything in perfect order for the reception of his bride, and wound up a long and animated monologue by informing Margaret that she had brought with her the unfinished portraits.

'What a pity!' interrupted Baldwin ; 'they may be injured, and surely you knew we intended to return.'

'Yes, I did,' said Eleanor, 'but I thought Mr Carteret would like to see them as they are, and I never reflected that they might be injured.'

The few days which followed the arrival of Lady Davyntry were full of the confusion and discomfort which ordinarily precede a wedding, even on the quietest scale. The
Merediths, father and son, had gone to Oxford, where
Hayes Meredith had one or two old friends among the
University authorities. They were not to return until the
day before the wedding. *Mr Carteret was rather 'put out'
by the inevitable atmosphere of fuss and preparation, and
Margaret devoted herself as much as possible to him, passing
in his study all the time she could subtract from the demands of the bride-elect and her brother. Mr Baldwin was
much with Lady Davyntry, and James Dugdale kept himself,
after his fashion, as much as possible to himself.

On the day before that fixed for Haldane's marriage all
the inmates of Chayleigh were assembled, and Lady Davyntry was of the party. They had been talking cheerfully of
the event anticipated on the morrow, and Eleanor had been
expressing her fears that Mr Carteret would feel very lonely
after his son's departure—fears which that placid gentleman
did by no means entertain on his own account—when Hayes
Meredith and Robert arrived. The evening passed away
rapidly, and the little party broke up early. Meredith
joined Dugdale in his sitting-room, and the friends proceeded
to the discussion of the business on which Hayes Meredith
had come to England. With two exceptions they adhered
strictly to this one matter. The first was of a trifling nature.

'Did you happen to see my pocket-book anywhere
about?' Meredith asked.

'No,' said Dugdale; 'you mean your red-leather one, I
suppose?'

'Yes.'

'I have not seen it, or heard of its being found in the
house.'

'I must have lost it on our journey to Oxford, I suppose,' said Meredith. 'It's of no consequence; there was no money in it, and nobody but myself could understand the memoranda.'

The second exception was of a graver kind; it, too, arose on Meredith's part.

'I am sorry to see Margaret looking so ill,' he said. 'I was very much struck by her looks this evening. Has she been looking so ill as this since I saw her last?'

'No,' replied James; 'she has over-exerted herself lately, I fancy, and she has never gotten over the shock.'

'Has she not?' said Meredith quickly. 'That's a very bad job; very likely to tell against her, I should think. Isn't it rather weak of her, though, to dwell so much as to injure her health on a thing that is of so little real consequence, after all?'

'I suppose it is,' said James; and he seemed unwilling to say more.

But the matter had evidently made an impression on Meredith, for he said again,

'I thought her looking very ill, feverish, and nervous, and quite unlike herself. Do you think Baldwin perceives it?'

'No,' said James shortly, 'I don't think he does. Margaret never complains.'

'Well, well, it will all be right when the heir to the Deane comes to put an end to uncertainty and fear, if she has any.'

And then he led the conversation to his own affairs.

'I like your friend so much, Madge,' said Lady Davyntry to Mrs Baldwin, as the sisters-in-law were enjoying the customary dressing-room confabulation. 'He is such a frank, hearty, good, fellow, and not the least rough, or what

we think of as "colonial," in his manners.   What a pleasure
it must have been to you to see him again!'

'Yes,' said Margaret absently.

'How tired your voice sounds, darling! you are quite
knocked up, I am afraid.   You must go to bed at once, and
try to be all right by to-morrow.   I delight in the idea of a
wedding; it is ages since I have been at one, except yours.
What sort of a boy is Mr Meredith's son?' she continued,
in a discursive way to which she was rather prone; 'he
looks clever.'

'He looks knowing,' said Margaret, 'more than clever, I
think.   I don't like him.'

'If she knew—if she, too, only knew,' ran the changeless
refrain of Margaret's thoughts when she was again alone,
'if she could but know what I have lived through since she
saw me last!   What a change has fallen on everything—
what a deadly blight!   How hard, and how utterly in vain, I
strive against this phantom which haunts me!   If I had but
listened to the warning which came to me when I found out
first that he loved me, the warning which her words and the
yearning of my own weak heart dispelled!   If I had but
heeded the secret inspiration which told me my past should
never be taken into any honest, unsullied life!   And yet, O
my God, how happy, how wonderfully, fearfully happy I
was for a while—for happiness is a fearful thing in this per-
ishing world.   Would I have heeded any warning that bade
me renounce it?   Could I have given him up, even for his
own sake?'

She rose and paced the room in one of those keen but
transient paroxysms of distress which, all unknown by any
human being, were of frequent occurrence, and which had
not quite subsided when her husband came into her dressing-
room.

'Margaret,' he said to her gravely, when he had elicited from her an avowal of some of her feelings, 'you are bringing this dead past into our life yourself, as no other power on earth could bring it. Do you remember when you promised to live for me only? Can you not keep your word? This is the trial of that faith you pledged to me. Is it failing you!'

'No,' she said, 'no, it is not failing, and I can keep my word. But'—and she clasped her arms around his neck and burst into sudden tears—'my child, my child!'

CHAPTER XXII.

MARGARET'S PRESENTIMENT.

THAT noun of multitude, 'the neighbourhood,' was at first disposed to take it very ill that the wedding of the eldest Miss Crofton should be despoiled of any of its contemplated gaiety and display, by what it was pleased to call the 'airs which Mrs Baldwin gave herself.' It bethought itself of Margaret's marriage, and arrived at the very probable conclusion that she was disposed to be a little jealous of her sister-in-law elect, and not disposed to allow her to ' have a fuss made about her' if she could help it.

Poor Mrs Crofton found her explanations and apologies coldly received; which distressed her, for she was a slave to conventional observances, and visited and received visits with exasperating regularity, and Mrs Baldwin's popularity declined. But not permanently; when it was understood that her return to the Deane was desirable for a reason which every one understood, and whose force all recognized, opinions were modified, and general good-humour was restored.

The preparations for the wedding went on, and nothing

was wanting to the cheerfulness and content of all concerned, except less inquietude regarding Margaret. They remembered afterwards that it happened so frequently that, when they came to think of it, they were amazed that the circumstance had not impressed them more deeply at the time : that when any two of the small party at Chayleigh met, one would say to the other, ' How ill Margaret looks to-day ! ' or, ' She is looking better to-day ; ' or, ' She seems hardly so well, I think ; ' the phrases varying widely, but each conveying the fact that Margaret's looks and health, Margaret's spirits and general demeanour, were in some form or other the objects of general attention, and were altered from their ordinary condition.

Mr Carteret's solicitude about her was fitful, and easily tranquillized. He would question her anxiously enough when she came down to breakfast in the morning, and be so uneasy and unhappy if she did not come down, that, perceiving that circumstance, she was rarely absent from the breakfast-table. But when the day advanced, and Margaret began to look brighter, he would remark that she ' had got some colour now, and looked quite herself again,' and, with the inconsequence which is frequently observable among persons who are constantly in the presence of even the most beloved objects, he failed to notice how often she required to ' look quite herself again,' in order to remove his transient uneasiness.

She looked very handsome at this time ; handsomer than she had ever looked, even at the period when people had first found out that there was no great exaggeration in calling Mrs Baldwin ' a beauty.' The broad brow, the sweet serious lips, which kept all their firmness, but had less severity than in the old time, the large sensible gray eyes, the delicate face, which had never had much colour, and now had permanently less, wore a spiritualized expression which made itself felt by those who never thought of analyzing it.

Among the number were the Croftons, Hayes Meredith, and Lady Davyntry. Mr Baldwin was not so blind. He saw that a change, which impressed him painfully, had come over the face and the spirit of the woman whom he loved more and more with every day of the union which had hitherto surpassed the hopes he had built upon it in happiness, and the only mistake he made was in believing that he quite understood that change, its origin, its nature, and its extent. He knew Margaret too well, had been too completely the confidant of her misgivings and hesitations previous to their marriage, and of the relief, the peace, the rehabilitation which had come to her since, to under-estimate the severity of the blow which had fallen upon her; but there was one aspect of her trouble in which he had never regarded it, in which it was her earnest desire, her constant effort, that he should never see it.

He had no knowledge of the presentiment under which Margaret laboured; he had never suspected her of such a weakness; and if it had been revealed to him, he would have unhesitatingly referred it to the condition of her health, have pronounced it a passing nervous affection, and dismissed it from his thoughts. He had never heard her express any of the vague, formless, but unconquerable apprehension with which she had learned the probability of Hayes Meredith's coming to England; he had no idea that a foregone conclusion in her mind lent the truth which had been revealed to her an additional power to wound and torture her, which was doing its work, unrecognized, before his eyes.

One of the most sympathetic, generous, unselfish of men, Fitzwilliam Baldwin united cheerfulness of disposition with good sense to a degree not so frequently attained as would be desirable in the interests of human nature ; and while he comprehended to the utmost the realities of the misfortune which had befallen Margaret, himself, and their child, he would have been 'slow to appreciate, had he been aware of its existence, the imaginary evil with which Margaret's morbid fancy had invested it.   When this wedding, with all its painful associations—so painful for them both that they never spoke of the subject when they were alone—should be over, Margaret would be quite herself again ; and she would find so much to occupy and interest her at the Deane, she would be able to throw off the impressions of the past, and to welcome the new interest which was so soon to be lent to her life with nearly all the gladness it would have commanded had the incident they had to deplore never occurred.

He had a keen perception, though he did not care to examine its origin very closely, that Margaret would find it a relief to be rid of the presence of Meredith and his son. They were associated with all that had been most painful, most humiliating, in the old life ; they had brought the evil tidings which had cast a heavy gloom over the calm sunny happiness of the new, and she could not be happy or oblivious in their presence—could not, that is to say, at present, in her abnormal state of sensitiveness and nervousness.

Fitzwilliam Baldwin did not cordially like Robert Meredith.   He felt that he did not understand the boy, and his frank nature involuntarily recoiled, with an unexplained antipathy, from contact with a disposition so *voilée*, so little open, so calculating, as his observation convinced him that of Robert Meredith was.   Quite unselfish, and very simple in his habits and ideas, Mr Baldwin was none the less apt to discover the absence or the opposite of those qualities, and it was very shortly after their return to Chayleigh that he said to his wife,

'Meredith intends to make a lawyer of his son, he tells me.'

'Yes,' said Margaret, 'it is quite decided, I understand. I dare say he will do well, he has plenty of ability.'

'He has, and a few other qualifications, such as cunning and coolness, and a grand faculty for taking care of himself, which people say are calculated to insure success in that line of life.'

'You don't like lawyers,' said Margaret.

'I don't like Robert Meredith; do you?' said her husband.

'No,' she replied promptly, 'I do not; more than that, I ought to be ashamed of myself, I suppose, and yet I can't contrive to be; but I dislike the boy extremely, more than I could venture to tell; the feeling I have about him troubles me—it is difficult for me to hide it.'

'I don't think you do hide it, Margaret,' said Baldwin; 'I only know you did not hide it from me. I never saw you laboriously polite and attentive to any one before; your kindness to every one is genuine, as everything else about you, darling; but to this youngster you are not spontaneous by any means.'

'You are right,' she said, 'I am not. There is something hateful to me about him. I suppose I am afflicted with one of those feminine follies which I have always despised, and have taken an antipathy to the boy. Very wrong, and very ungrateful of me,' she added sorrowfully.

'Neither wrong nor ungrateful,' her husband answered in a tone of remonstrance. 'You are ready to do him all the substantial benefit in your power, as I am for his father's sake. There is no ingratitude in that; and as for your not liking him being wrong—'

'Ah, but I don't stop at *not* liking him,' said Margaret;

'if I did, my conscience would not reproach me as it does. I hope his father does not perceive anything in my manner.'

'Nothing more unlikely. Meredith does not observe you so closely or understand you so well as I do; and I don't think any one but myself could find out that you dislike the boy; and I was assisted, I must acknowledge, by a lively fellow-feeling. I should not wonder if Robert was perfectly aware that he is not a favourite with you.'

'I am sure there is nothing in my manner or that of any one else,' said Margaret, 'which in any way touches himself, that he fails to perceive.'

'Fortunately it does not matter. He loses nothing material by our not happening to take a fancy to him, and I don't think he is a person to suffer from any sentimental regrets. More than that, Margaret—and enough to have made me dislike him—I don't think he likes you.'

'Like me! He hates me,' she said vehemently. 'I catch his eye sometimes when he looks at me, and wonder how so young a face can express so much bad feeling. I have seen such a diabolical sneer upon his face sometimes, particularly when either my father or his father spoke affectionately to me, as almost startled me—for my own sake, I mean.'

'For your own sake?' said Mr Baldwin in a tone of some annoyance. 'How can you say such a foolish thing? Why on earth should you give such a thing a moment's thought? What can it possibly matter to you that you are the object of an impertinent dislike to a boy like young Meredith?'

'Nothing, indeed,' answered Margaret, 'and I will never think of it again. You are all in a conspiracy to spoil me, I think, and thus I am foolish enough to be surprised and uncomfortable when any one dislikes me without a reason.'

No more was said then on this subject, and Mr Baldwin dismissed it from his mind. The conversation he had had with his wife had just so much effect upon him and no more, that he took very little notice of Robert, and displayed no more interest than politeness demanded in the discussions concerning him and his future, which just then shared the attention of the family party at Chayleigh with Captain Carteret's rapidly approaching marriage.

This circumstance the young gentleman was not slow to notice, and it had the effect of intensifying the feeling with which he regarded Margaret.

'She has put her fine husband up to snubbing me, has she?' he said to himself one day, when Mr Baldwin had taken less notice of him than usual. 'Now I wonder what *that's* for. Perhaps she's afraid of the goodness of my memory. I dare say she has told him a whole pack of lies about the time she was in Melbourne, and she's afraid, if I walked or rode out with him, I might get upon the subject. And I only wish he would give me a chance, that's all.'

But nothing was more unlikely than that Mr Baldwin should give Robert Meredith such a 'chance,' and that the boy's natural quickness soon made him understand. The only person with whom he associated at this time, who afforded him any opportunity for his spiteful confidences, was the bride-elect.

Lucy was still pleased by the unrepressed admiration of the only male creature within the sphere of Mrs Baldwin's influence who was wholly unimpressed by her attractions. The 'great friend's' project, though, according to Miss Lucy Crofton's somewhat shallow perceptions, triumphantly successful, did not in the least interfere with so thoroughly legitimate a development of feminine proclivities.

To be sure, the subject of Margaret's first marriage, and

16

her disastrous life in Melbourne, was one which Lucy had never heard touched upon, even in the most intimate conversations among the family at Chayleigh. Her affianced Haldane had never spoken to her, except in the briefest and most general terms, of that painful episode in the family history. But that did not constitute, according to Lucy's not very scrupulous or refined code of delicacy, any barrier to her talking and hearing as much about it in any other available manner as she could.

She even persuaded herself that it was her 'place' and a kind of 'duty' to learn as much about her future sister-in-law as possible; people would talk, and it was only proper and right, when certain subjects were introduced, that she, in her future capacity of Mrs Haldane Carteret (the cards were printed, and very new, and shiny, and important they looked), should know exactly 'how things stood,' and what she should have to say. Which was a reflection full of foresight on the part of the eldest Miss Crofton, and partaking somewhat of the nature of prophecy, as, from the hour of Mrs Baldwin's marriage, the subject of her colonial life had never been revived in the coteries of 'the neighbourhood.'

Robert Meredith had method in his mischief. He did not offend the *amour propre* of Lucy by speaking contemptuously of Mrs Baldwin, or betraying the dislike which he entertained towards her; he dexterously mingled in the revelations which he made to Lucy an affected compassion for Margaret's past sorrows, and a congratulatory compassion of her present enviable position, with artful insinuations of the incongruity between the Mrs Baldwin of the present and the Mrs Hungerford of the past, and a kind of bashful wonder, which he modestly imputed to his colonial ignorance of the ways of society, how any person could pos-

sibly consider Miss Lucy Crofton other than in every
respect superior to Mrs Baldwin.

The boyish flattery pleased Lucy's vanity, the boyish admiration pleased her, and she entirely deprecated the idea
that Robert's manners and ideas were not on a par with
those of other people born on this side of the ocean.

'You must remember,' she said with much coquetry, and
a smile which she intended to be immensely knowing, 'that
Mrs Baldwin is a great lady in her way, and I am not of
anything like so much importance. I fancy that would
make as much difference in your part of the world as here.'

And then they talked a great deal of his part of the
world; and Robert acknowledged that his most earnest
desire was that he might never see Australia again. And
Lucy Crofton confessed that she was very glad Haldane
could not be sent *there*, at least on that odious 'foreign service,' which she thought a detestable and absurd injustice,
devised for the purpose of making the wives and families of
military men miserable. She was quite alive to the fact that
they were highly ornamental, but could not see that soldiers
were of the slightest use at home—and as to abroad, they
never did anything there, since war had ceased, but die of
fevers and all sorts of horrors. So the pair pursued an animated and congenial conversation, of which it is only necessary to record two sentences.

'I suppose you have no one belonging to you in Australia?' Robert Meredith asked Miss Crofton, in a tone which
implied that to so exceptionally delightful a being nothing
so objectionable as a colonial connection could possibly
belong.

'No one that I know anything about; there is a cousin
of papa's—much younger than papa, he is—who got into
trouble, and they sent him out there; but none of us ever

saw him, and I don't know what has become of him. I don't even know his name rightly; it is something like Oldham, or Otway, or Oakley.'

'How do you feel, Madge? are you sure you are equal to this business?' said Lady Davyntry to Margaret, as she came into her sister-in-law's room on the morning of Haldane's marriage. 'Haldane is walking about the hall in the most horrid temper, your father is lingering over the last importation of bats, as if he were bidding them an eternal farewell, and the carriage is just coming round, so I thought I would come and look after you two. I felt sure you would be with the child. What a shame not to bring her to the wedding!—Isn't it, Gerty?' and Lady Davyntry, looking very handsome and stately in her brave attire, took the little girl out of her mother's arms, and paused for a reply.

Margaret was quite ready. She was very well, she said, and felt quite equal to the wedding festivities.

'That's right; I like weddings, when one isn't a principal; they are very pleasant. How pale you are, Margaret! Are you really quite well?

'She is really quite well,' said Mr Baldwin; 'don't worry her, Eleanor.'

The slightest look of surprise came into Eleanor's sweet-tempered face, but it passed away in a moment, and they all went down to the hall, where Margaret received many compliments from her father on her dress and appearance, and where Haldane on seeing them first assumed a foolish expression of countenance, which he wore permanently for the rest of the day.

The carriages were announced. Margaret and her husband, Lady Davyntry and Mr Carteret, were to occupy one;

the other was to convey Haldane, Hayes Meredith and his son, and James Dugdale.

'Where is James?' asked Mr Carteret. 'I have not seen him this morning.'

Nobody had seen him but Haldane, who explained that he had preferred walking on to the church.

'Just like him,' said Haldane, 'he is such an odd fellow; only fancy his asking me to get him off appearing at breakfast. Could not stand it, he said, and was sure he would never be missed. Of course I said he must have his own way, though I couldn't make him out. He could stand Margaret's wedding well enough.'

The last day of Margaret's stay at Chayleigh had arrived. All arrangements had been made for the departure of Mr and Mrs Baldwin and Mr Carteret. An extraordinary event was about to take place in the life of the tranquil old gentleman. He was about to be separated from the collection for an indefinite period, and taken to the Deane, a place whose much-talked-of splendours he had never even experienced a desire to behold, having been perfectly comfortable in the knowledge that they existed and were enjoyed by his daughter.

That her father should be induced to accompany her to Scotland, that she should not be parted from him, had been so urgent a desire on Margaret's part, that her husband and James Dugdale had set themselves resolutely to obtain its realization, and they had succeeded, with some difficulty. The collection was a great obstacle, but then Mr Baldwin's collection—whose treasures the old gentleman politely and sincerely declared his eagerness to inspect, while he secretly cherished a pleasing conviction that he should find them very inferior to those of his own—was a great inducement:

besides, he had corresponded formerly with a certain Professor Bayly, of Glasgow, who had some brilliant theories connected with *Bos primus*, and this would be a favourable opportunity for seeing the Professor, who rarely 'came South,' as he called visiting England.

He was not at all disturbed by Margaret's eager desire that he should accompany her; he did not perceive in it the contradiction to her usual unselfish consideration for others, which James Dugdale saw and thoroughly understood, and which Mr Baldwin saw and did not understand, but set down to the general account of her 'nervousness.' He had been rather unhappy at first about the journey and the change; but James's cheerful prognostications, and the unexpected discovery that Foster, his inseparable servant, whose displeasure was a calamity not to be lightly incurred, so far from objecting to the tremendous undertaking, ' took to ' the notion of a visit to the Deane very kindly, was a relief which no false shame interfered to prevent; Mr Carteret candidly admitting, and the whole family thankfully recognizing.

'I don't know how I should have got through this day,' Margaret said to James, as they stood together on the terrace under the verandah, and she plucked a few of the tender young leaves which had begun to unfold, under the persuasion of the spring time—'I don't know how I should have got through this day, if papa had not agreed to come with us. It is bad enough as it is; a last day '—she was folding the tiny leaves now, and putting them between the covers of her pocket-book—'is always dreadful—dreadful to *me*, I mean. It sounds stupid and commonplace to talk of the uncertainty of life, but I don't think other people live always under the presence of the remembrance, the conviction of it, as I do. It is always over me, and it makes everything

which has anything of finality about it peculiarly impressive
to me.'

Her hand was resting on his arm now, and they turned
away from the house-front and walked down the grassy
slope.

'Do you—do you mean that this sense of uncertainty relates to yourself?' he asked her, speaking
with evident effort and holding her arm more closely to
him.

'Yes,' she replied calmly; 'I am never tortured by any
fears about those I love now; the time was when I was first
very, very happy; when the wonderful, glorious sense of
the life that had opened to me came upon me fully; when I
hardly dared to recognize it, because of the shadow of death.
Then it hung over my husband and my child; over my
father—and—you.'

He shook his head with an involuntary deprecatory
movement, and a momentary flicker of pain disturbed his
grave thoughtful eyes.

'And it lent an intensity which sometimes I could hardly
bear to every hour of my life—my wonderfully happy life,'
she repeated, and looked all around her in a loving solemn
way which struck the listener to the heart. 'But then the
thing I had dreaded, though I had never divined its form,
though it had gradually faded from my mind, came upon me
—you know how, James, and how rebellious I was under
my trial; no one knows but God and you—and then, then
the shadow was lightened. It never has fallen again over
them or you; it hangs only over me, and—James, look at
me, don't turn away—I want to remember every look in
your face to-day; it is not a shadow at all, but only a veil
before the light whose glory I could not bear yet awhile.
That is all, indeed.'

He did not speak, and she felt that a sharp thrill of pain ran through his spare form.

'Don't be angry with me,' she went on in soft pleading tones, 'don't think I distress you needlessly, I do so want you to hear me—to leave what I am saying to you in your mind. When I first told you that I had a presentiment that I had suffered my last sorrow, that all was to be peace for me henceforth, except in thinking of my child, you were not persuaded; you imputed it to the shock my nerves had received, and you think so still. It is not so indeed, even with respect to my child. I am tranquil and happy now; I don't know why, I cannot account for it. Nothing in the circumstances is susceptible of change, and I see those circumstances as clearly as I saw them when they first existed; but I am changed. I feel as if my vision had been enlarged; I feel as if the horizon had widened before me, and with the great space has come great calm—calm of mind—like what travellers tell us comes with the immense mountain solitudes, when all the world beneath looks little, and yet the great loneliness lifts one up nearer to heaven, and has no fear or trembling in it. I am not unquiet now, James, not even for the child. The wrong that I have done her God will right.'

James Dugdale said hastily, 'You have done her no conscious wrong, and all will be righted.'

'Yes, I know; I am saying so; but not in our way, James, not as we—' she paused a very little, almost imperceptibly—'not as you would have it. But that it will be righted I have not the smallest doubt, not the least fear. You will remember, James, that I said to you the wrong I did my child will be righted.'

'Remember!' he said in keen distress. 'What do you mean, Margaret? Have you still the same presentiment? Is this your former talk with me over again?'

'Yes,' she replied, 'and no. When I talked with you before I was troubled, sad, and afraid. Now I am neither sad, troubled, nor afraid.'

'You are ill. There is something which you know and are hiding from us which makes you think and speak thus.'

'No, indeed.'

There was conviction in her tone, and he could but look at her and wait until she should speak again. She did not speak for a few moments, and then she resumed in a firm voice:

'I want to say to you all that is in my mind—at least as far as it can be said. I am not ill in any serious way, and I am not hiding anything which ought to be made known; and yet I do believe that I am not to live much longer in this world, and I acknowledge with a full heart that the richest portion of happiness ever given to a woman has been, is mine. When this trouble, the only one I have had in my new life, came to me, it changed me, and changed everything to me for a time; but the first effect is quite past, and the wound my pride received is healed. I don't think about that now; but I do think of the wonderful compensation, if I may dare to use a word which sounds like bringing God to a reckoning for His dealings with one of His creatures, which has been made to me, and I feel that I have lived all my days. The old presentiment that I had of evil to come to me from Australia, and its fulfilment, and the suffering and struggle, all are alike gone now, quieted down, and the peace has come which I do not believe anything is ever to disturb more.'

'Margaret, Margaret!' he said, 'I cannot bear this; you must not speak thus; if you persist in doing so, there *must* be some reason for it. It is not like you to have such morbid fancies.'

'And it is not like you to misunderstand me,' she interrupted gently. 'Can you not see that I am telling you what is in my mind on what I believe will be my *last* day in my old home, because, if I am right, it will make you happy in the time to come to remember it?'

'Happy!' he repeated with impatience.

'Yes, happy! and if I am not right, and this is indeed but a morbid fancy, it will have done you no harm to hear it. You have listened to many a fancy of mine, dear old friend.'

Tears gathered in her eyes now, and two large drops fell from the dark eyelashes unheeded.

'I have, I have,' he said, 'but to what fancies! How can you speak thus, Margaret? How can you think so calmly of leaving those who love you so much, those in whose love you confess you have found so much happiness? Your husband, your child, your father!'

'I cannot tell you,' she said; 'I cannot explain it, and because I cannot I am forced to believe it, to feel that it is so. The world seems far away from me somehow, even my own small precious world. You remember, when I spoke to you before, I told you how much I dreaded the effect of what had happened on myself, on my own feelings—how strangely the sense I have always had of being so much older than my husband, the dread of losing the power of enjoying the great happiness of my life, had seized hold of me?'

'I remember.'

'Well,' she continued, 'all this fear has left me now—indeed, all fear of every kind, and the power of suffering, I think. When I think of the grief of those I shall have to leave, if my presentiment is realized, I don't shrink from it as I did when the first thought of the possible future came to me. After all, it is for such a little, little time.'

Her eyes were raised upwards to the light, and a smile which the listener could not bear to see, and yet looked at —thinking, with the vain tenderness so fruitful in pangs of every kind and degree of intensity, that at least he never, never should be able to recall *that* look—came brightly over her face, and slowly faded.

'Oh no, Margaret; life is awfully long—hopelessly long.'

'It seems so sometimes, but it has ceased to seem so to me. You must not grieve for what I am saying to you. If all is what you will think right with me, and we are here together again, you will be glad to think, to remember how I told you all that was in my heart; if it is otherwise, you will be far more than glad, James.'

In his heart there arose at that moment a desperately strong, an almost irresistible longing to tell her now, for the first time and the last, how he had loved her all his life. But he resisted the longing—he was used to self-restraint— and said not a word which could trouble her peace.

They returned to the house shortly after, and went in by the drawing-room window. At the foot of the green slope Margaret paused for a minute, and looked with a smile at the open window of her room. A white curtain fluttered about it; there was a stir as of life in the room, but there was no one there.

'You will take care of the passion-flower, James?' she said. 'I think the blossoms will be splendid this year.'

A few hours later, and the house was deserted by all but James Dugdale. Hayes Meredith and his son had escorted Lady Davyntry to her own house, and gone on from thence to dine with the Croftons.

The first letter which James Dugdale received was from

Margaret. She wrote in good spirits, and gave an amusing account of her father's delight with the Deane, and admiration—a little qualified by the difficulty of acknowledging at least its equality with his own—of Mr Baldwin's collection, and his frequent expressions of surprise at finding the journey by no means so disagreeable or portentous an undertaking as he had expected. She was very well, except that she had taken cold.

A day or two later Lady Davyntry heard from her brother. Margaret was not so well; the cold was obstinate and exhausting; he deeply regretted her return to Scotland; only for the risk of travelling, he should take her away immediately. The next letter was not more reassuring, and Lady Davyntry made up her mind to go to Scotland without delay. In this resolution James Dugdale, with a sick and sinking heart, confirmed her. Not a word of actual danger was said in the letters which reached Davyntry daily, but the alarm which James felt was not slow to communicate itself to Eleanor.

'She has been delicate for a long time,' said Lady Davyntry to James, 'and very much more so latterly than she ever acknowledged.'

In reply to her proposal to go at once to the Deane, Eleanor had an urgent letter of thanks from her brother. Margaret was not better—strangely weak indeed. Lady Davyntry was to start on the next day but one after the receipt of this letter, and James went over to Davyntry on the intervening day. He had a long interview with Eleanor, and, having left her, was walking wearily towards home, when he saw Hayes Meredith and Robert rapidly advancing to meet him. He quickened his pace, and they met where the footpath wound by the clump of beech-trees, once so distasteful in Margaret's sight. There was not a gleam of

colour in Meredith's face, and as James came up the boy
shrunk back behind his father

'What's the matter?' said James, coming to a dead stop
in front of Meredith.

'My dear fellow, you will need courage. Baldwin's valet
has come from the Deane.'

'Yes!' said James in a gasping voice.

'Margaret was much worse after Baldwin wrote, and the
child—a girl—was born that afternoon. The child—'

'Is dead?' James tore his coat open as he asked the
question, as if choking.

'No, my dear fellow'—his friend took his arm firmly
within his own—'the poor child is alive, but Margaret is
gone.'

<hr />

CHAPTER XXIII.

AFTER A YEAR.

Lady Davyntry to James Dugdale.

'THE DEANE, MARCH 17, 18—.

'MY DEAR MR DUGDALE,—Your last letter, imposing
upon me the task of advising my brother, in the sense of the
conclusions arrived at by yourself and Mr Meredith, gave
me a great deal to think about. I could not answer it fully
before, and I am sure the result which I have now to state
to you will not, in reality, be displeasing to you, but I cannot uphold its soundness of wisdom, in a worldly sense,
even to my own judgment—though it carries with it all my
sympathies; and I am confident Mr Meredith will entirely
disapprove of it.

' I was obliged to be careful in selecting an opportunity for entering upon the discussion prescribed by your letter with Fitzwilliam. Since his great affliction fell upon him, he is not so gentle, so easy of access, as he used to be ; and though he will sometimes talk freely to me of the past, the occasions must be of his own choosing. Hence the delay. I took the best means, as I thought, of making him understand the gravity and earnestness of the matter it was necessary he should consider—I read your letter to him. The mere hearing of it distressed him very much. He said, what I also felt, that he had not thought it could be possible to make him feel the loss of Margaret more deeply, but that the statement of his present position, so clear, so true, so indisputable, has made him feel it. He listened while I read the letter again, at his request, and then left me suddenly, saying he would tell me what to answer as soon as he could.

' Some days elapsed, and we saw very little of him—I perceived that one of his dark moods was upon him—and yesterday he came to me, to tell me to answer your letter. He took me to the sitting-room which was Margaret's, and where everything remains just as she left it on the last day that she came down-stairs at the Deane. I suppose he felt that I could understand his decision more clearly, and be less inclined to listen to all the reasons which render it unwise, when everything around should speak of her whose undimmed memory dictated it.

' The sum of what he said to me—with many strayings from the matter, and so much revival of the past in all its first bitterness, that I was astonished, such a faculty of grief being rarely seen in a man—was this. He cannot bring himself to contemplate, as you and Mr Meredith are agreed he ought, a second marriage. As nearly as possible, this was what he said :

' " When we found out the wrong which had been innocently done to Gertrude, we hoped, indeed we were so persuaded, that the child we were expecting would be a boy, and the wrong be thus righted, that we never looked beyond the birth of the child, or discussed the future in any way with reference to a disappointment in that particular. The child would be the heir, and Gertrude's future would be safe, rich, and prosperous. Such were our dreams—and when the fearful awakening came, it was some time before I understood all it meant. It was weeks before I remembered that the wrong done to the child my Margaret had loved so much, that she broke her heart because that wrong had been done, could never be righted now. It was very long before the thought occurred to me that those to whom this dreadful truth was known would perceive that a second marriage, by giving me the chance of a male heir, and thus putting the two children on an equal footing in the eyes of the world, would afford me the only means of avoiding injustice to Eleanor."

' Here he stopped, and said he suffered equally about both children, for the youngest had also sustained the greatest loss of all. Then he continued:

' " I did think of this sometimes, but with horror, and a full knowledge that though it would be a just and wise thing in one sense for the interests of my children, it would be unjust and unwise towards them and myself, and any woman whom I might induce to marry me, in another. I dare say you will think I am talking nonsense, forgetting the influence, which, however slow, is always sure, of the lapse of time— forgetting that others have been heavily bereaved and yet have found consolation, and even come to know much happiness again—when I tell you that I never could take the slightest interest in any woman any more. Well, supposing I am wrong there—I don't think I can be; there is something in my inmost heart which tells me I am right—we are dealing now not with the future, but with the present. James is right in pointing out that I must make up my mind to some course, and I am glad Meredith is still interested in me and in the children's future. Time may alter my state of mind, but if it does, no arrangements made now will be irrevocable.

' " But, as my life is uncertain, I am not justified in allowing any more time to go by, without providing, as well as I can, for the contingencies which may arise. Tell James I am deeply impressed with the truth of this, and the strong necessity of acting on all he and Meredith have set before me, though I cannot act upon it in the way in which they prescribe. For the present—and you will not need to be assured that I am not regardless of what Margaret would wish—I must only make all the reparation which money can make to Eleanor."

' Then Fitzwilliam entered into a full explanation of the position of the estate, and gave me the enclosed memorandum, which he wishes you and Mr Meredith to see, and showed me how the ready money he can leave to Eleanor, and the income, apart from the entailed estate, which he can settle on her, in reality amount to within two thousand a year of the income which must come to Gertrude as heir of entail. To this purpose he intends to devote all this money, his great object being to render the position of his children as nearly equal as possible, and so reduce the unintentional injustice done to Eleanor, and the wrong, now past atonement, inflicted on Gertrude, to such small dimensions as may relieve him from any suffering on the subject,

' He has requested that no portion of Mr Carteret's property should be left to either of the children. They will be rich enough, and he considers, very justly, that Haldane's children will have a superior claim on Mr Carteret, who was feverishly anxious, Fitzwilliam tells me, to have all his affairs settled ; when he spoke to him, he did not like this idea at all, he is so much attached to little Gertrude ; but when my brother told him he knew it would have been Margaret's wish that her brother should have all it was in their father's power to give, he was satisfied, and promised that it should be so.

' In telling you this, I dare say I am repeating what is already known to you ; but I give it its place in the conversation between us, as bearing upon the point that the only way in which the past can now be repaired, is by securing to the children as much equality in money matters as possible.

' As a branch of this subject, I may tell you that the future disposition of my property has been discussed between us. In Davyntry I have, as I dare say you know, only a life-interest, and the money of which I have to dispose comes to me from my father. It is six hundred a year, and I shall at once make my will in favour of Eleanor. Thus the inequality in the fortunes of the girls will be decreased, and Fitzwilliam is much less likely than ever to live up to his income. The girls will both be very rich heiresses, no doubt, and I do not think any of us who are in the secret need feel that the advantage to Gerty of appearing as the heiress of the Deane is very material.

' Her father feels very deeply the condition of the entail which prescribed that she must bear her own name, her husband being obliged to assume it. There is a sting in that which you will thoroughly comprehend. He asked me if I thought that remembrance had contributed to the pain

17

which Margaret had suffered about this calamity, but I could assure him conscientiously that I did not think it had ever occurred to her. The child was so mere an infant, and the strong hope and expectation, disappointed by Eleanor's birth, possessed them so completely, that money matters, in connection with the future, were never discussed between them. He confirmed me in this. They never were; and now it is a keen source of regret to him, because, he says, he should be fortified by the knowledge of how she would have desired he should act, under the present circumstances.

' Poor fellow ! I listened to him, seriously of course ; but, sad as it was, I could hardly keep from smiling at the way in which he confounds the present with the past, forgetting that he had no fear, no misgivings, no presentiment, and therefore that no reason existed for such a discussion. All this will appear impracticable to Mr Meredith, but he will have patience with my brother; he saw enough of what their life together was, to understand, in some degree, the immeasurable loss. My ignorance of all that had occurred, at the time of Margaret's death, is, perhaps, regretable on this score, that I might have gotten at more of her mind than, for his sake, she would have betrayed to him ; but it is too late now to repair that ignorance, and we must only do the best we can in the children's interests.

' Keeping in view the change time may produce—that my brother is still a young man, and that a second marriage may not always be so repugnant to him as it is at present—I think we may rest satisfied in having induced him to contemplate, and, no doubt as soon as possible to make, a proper disposition of his property. As for the children, they are as happy as little unconscious creatures like them can be, and I do not think their father's making a second marriage would be an undivided blessing for them. Where is there a second Margaret to be found?

'Fitzwilliam spoke to me very freely on this point. He could not pretend to any woman that he loved her; and as, in that case, his second wife must necessarily marry him for mercenary motives, could he regard any woman who would do so as a fitting representative of their mother to his children—could he make her even tolerably happy, thus entering upon a life in which there could be no mutual respect? Such arguments are all-powerful with a woman, especially with me; for I know how pure, how disinterested, our lost Margaret's feelings and motives in her marriage were, and remember only too well seeing how they were realized—the doubt and dread she expressed when she first recognized the prospect for the future which lay before her. How wonderful and dreadful it seems to speak of her thus in the past, to refer to that which seemed so completely all in all to us then, and is now gone for ever!

'My brother is content with the care the children have from me, and, far more effectually, from Rose. Time teaches me her value more and more forcibly, and I am more and more thankful that, in the blackest and worst time of our distress, you suggested her being sent for. How strange and fortunate that Margaret had given you a clue to what her wishes would have been! Neither Fitzwilliam nor I would have thought of her; indeed, I had entirely forgotten the "Irish-Australian importation of Margaret's," as I once heard poor Mrs Carteret speak of her. She is a comfort to us all past describing.

'I do not know whether Fitzwilliam has told you that Terence Doran, Rose's husband, is coming to him in a month as factor. He is a very clever young man, we understand, and, though well placed in Ireland, willing to come here, for his wife's sake, to enable her to remain with the children. I have no intention of leaving the Deane for the present. Fitzwilliam seems restless; he does not say so, but I fancy he wishes to go abroad again. I should not be surprised if he started off soon on some prolonged tour.

'You ask me about the children. Before I reply to your questions, let me tell you how sorry we all are that there is no chance of our seeing you here. We understand, of course, that the state of your own health, and the duty you feel imposed upon you with regard to poor Mr Carteret, to whom it would be naturally most distasteful to come here, furnish indisputable reasons for your absence, but we do not the less regret it. I infer from the news that Mr Meredith means to leave England next month, that he has satisfactorily brought all his business to a conclusion. His return will be a great boon to his family. An absence which, by the time he reaches Melbourne, will have been prolonged to nearly two years, is a terrible slice out of this short mortal life. I suppose all the arrangements made for his son have succeeded to his satisfaction, and that you, with your invariable kindness, have undertaken the supervision of the boy.

'And now, about the children. Gertrude is a fine child, very like Margaret in face, and, so far as one can judge of so young a child, of a nice disposition, rather grave and sensitive. Her father idolizes her; he is never weary of the little girl's company, and I can see that he is always tracing the likeness to the face hidden from him for a while. Little Eleanor is delicate and peevish; indeed, if it be not foolish to say so of an infant, I should say she is of a passionate nature; she is not so pretty as Gertrude, but has large brown eyes, quite unlike either her sister or her poor mother. She is Rose Doran's favourite, and I can trace sometimes, in her candid Irish face, some surprise and displeasure when she notices my brother's intense affection for the elder girl. She has no knowledge of anything which makes the child an object of compassionate love to the father.'

'MARCH 18.

'When I had written so far, I was interrupted by Fitzwilliam. He brought me a letter which he has written to Mr Janvrin, of Lincoln's Inn, his solicitor, and which contains instructions for the drawing up of a will according to the plan I have mentioned. He wishes me to recapitulate to you what would be the children's positions in the event of his death, unmarried, and not having revoked his will.

'Gertrude would succeed to all the entailed property, chargeable, as in Fitzwilliam's case, with a provision for her younger children.

'Eleanor would have all the savings from the general income up to the time of her father's death, and all such property as is not included in the entail.

'Haldane Carteret and I are named as the guardians and trustees, and my brother signifies his wish that his children should reside alternately with either Mrs Carteret or me, according to the general convenience.

'Will you kindly communicate this to Mr Meredith, together with my personal acknowledgment of the kind interest he has taken in us all during the sorrowful period of his stay in England?

'Always, my dear Mr Dugdale, most faithfully yours,
ELEANOR DAVYNTRY.'

James Dugdale to Lady Davyntry.

'CHAYLEIGH, MARCH 20.

'MY DEAR LADY DAVYNTRY,—I have to thank you for your kind and explanatory letter. I never expected Baldwin to take the view of the matter on which I wrote to you which Meredith takes. Meredith is so much more a man of the world than I am, has so much longer a head, and so much sounder judgment, that I could not hesitate to transmit to you and Baldwin his views, in which the world, could it know what we are so unfortunate as to know, would no doubt recognize reason and force. Well, we too recognize them, but that is all.

'All the dispositions which you tell me Baldwin has made are admirable under the circumstances, and considering his determination, which I do not think is likely to yield to the influence of time, which cannot restore her who was lost, and will, I am convinced, but increase his appreciation of the extent and severity of that loss. Gertrude gains only in name and appearance, and does her sister no real injury. I have often thought how terrible Baldwin's position would have been had not Eleanor lived. Then he must either have married again, or done an injury to the heir of entail by permitting Gertrude to succeed. Meredith was asking me about the succession, but I could not tell him. I fancy I heard, but I don't remember where, when, or how, that the next heir is a distant relative, with whom Baldwin is not acquainted.

'Mr Carteret had told me, before I received your letter, Baldwin's wishes about his will, and that he intended to comply with them. The only legacy Gertrude will inherit from her grandfather is the unfinished portrait which you brought from Naples. He never mentioned it, or seemed to notice that I had had it unpacked and placed in the study, until the day on which he mentioned Baldwin's request, and then he looked at it, quite a fond, quiet smile. The calm, the impassibility of old age is coming over him, fortunately for him.

'But while I perfectly understand the force and approve the object of the representation which Baldwin has made to Mr Carteret, and while I heartily approve the reason and the generosity of the disposition you intend making of such portion of your property as is within your power, I do not think I am bound by similar restrictions. Partly because the little I possess is so small, so utterly trivial and unimportant, in comparison with the handsome fortune which the measures Baldwin is taking will secure, with your assistance, to Eleanor ; and partly because I feel towards the elder child in a peculiar way, almost inexplicable to myself—I intend to bequeath to Gertrude the small sum I possess the power of bequeathing.

'She shall have it when I am gone, and it shall be left at her free and uncontrolled disposition ; it will add a little yearly sum to her pleasures, or, if she be as like her mother in her nature as in her face, to her charities. It will be a great pleasure to me to know that Gertrude, whose splendid inheritance will come to her by a real though guiltless error, will at least have that small heritage in her own real undisputable right—not as the heiress of anything or any one, only as Margaret's child.

'I am so glad to know what you tell me concerning Rose Doran. She was always a good, genuine creature, and it is almost as rare as it is pleasant to anticipate excellence and not to be disappointed. Baldwin should be careful, however, of annoying her by displaying too marked a preference for Gerty. Rose is a very shrewd person, and in her impulsive Irish mind the process, which should make her suspicious of a reason for this preference, and jealous for the child whose life cost that of her mother, would not be a difficult one.

'Meredith's plans are unchanged. He has every reason

to be satisfied with the arrangements made for Robert. I have no doubt the boy will do well. He wants neither ability nor application; I wish he had as much heart and as much frankness. Davyntry is looking very well, lonely, of course, but well taken care of; I ramble about there almost every day. Haldane and his wife are expected next week at the Croftons.

'Yours, dear Lady Davyntry, always truly,

'JAMES DUGDALE.'

Kayes Meredith to Fitzwilliam Meriton Baldwin.

'CHAYLEIGH, APRIL 2.

MY DEAR BALDWIN,—I am off in a short time now, and this is to say good-bye—most likely for ever. At my time of life I am not likely to get back to England again, unless, indeed, I should make a fortune by some very unlikely hazard, of which not the faintest indication appears at present.

' I am very much obliged to you for letting me know all the arrangements you have made. I am sure you know my feeling in the matter was interest, not curiosity, and though not only the safest, surest, speediest, but also the most natural and agreeable way of putting an end to your difficulties appeared to me to be a second marriage, I am not going to blame you because you don't think so. I know the difficulties of the position, but, after all, you inflict a mere technical wrong on one sister, while you make up for it by endowing her with a much larger fortune than she would have had, had her real position been what her apparent one is—that of a younger child.

' From what you say of the amount of the savings which you expect to leave to Eleanor, I should think she would be little less rich than Gertrude, and without the burden of a large landed estate and establishment to keep up—also enjoying the immense advantage of being able to dispose of her property as she chooses, an advantage which Gertrude will not enjoy, and which, with my colonial ideas, I am disposed to estimate very highly indeed.

'I have so many kindnesses and attentions to thank you for, that I must put all my acknowledgments into this one, and beg you to believe that I feel them deeply. The most welcome of all the acts of friendship I have received from you is your promise not to lose sight of Robert. He will get on well, I think. If he does not, his heart will be more in fault than his head, in my belief.

'As to O——, I hardly know what to think of your proposal. I doubt its being altogether safe to open communications voluntarily with a man of his sort. He is so very likely, after his kind, to impute some bad, or at least suspicious, motive to an act of charity which I should not be disposed to give him credit for understanding or believing in. The least danger we should have to fear would be his establishing himself as a regular pensioner in consideration of your aid extended to him in so inexplicable a fashion.

'But, beyond this, there is more to apprehend. I think I told you he knew nothing of M——, not even her former name, nor her destination in England. If he receives a sum of money from you, he will naturally make inquiries about you, and there will be no means of keeping the required information from him. Once supply him with a clue to any connection between you and his worthy comrade deceased, and O—— must be very unlike the man I believe him to be, and must have profited very insufficiently by such companionship, if he does not see his way to a profitable secret, and the chance of *chantage*, in a very short time. This is the risk I foresee, and which I should not like to run.

'At the same time, I understand the feeling which has dictated the proposition you make to me, and I can quite believe, remembering her noble nature so well as I do remember it, that M—— would, as you suppose, have been glad to rescue from want the man to whom H—— owed, after all, relief in his last days, if to him she also owed the knowledge of her sorrow. I propose therefore (subject to your approval), when I arrive at Melbourne, to inquire, with judicious caution, into what has become of O——, and if I find him living and in distress, to assist him to a limited extent, provided he is not quite so incorrigible a scoundrel as that assisting him would be enabling him to prey on society on a larger and more successful scale.

'I would suggest, however, that under no circumstances should he be told that the money comes from you. I shall be credited, if I find him a proper object, or anything short of an entirely unjustifiable object, for your bounty, with a charitable action, which it certainly never would have come into my head to perform; but I am quite willing, if it gives you any pleasure or consolation, to carry the burden of undeserved praise and such gratitude as is to be expected from O——, not a very oppressive quantity, I fancy.

'I am glad to hear good news of you all from Dugdale. And now, my dear Baldwin, nothing remains for me to say, except that which cannot be written. Farewell. We shall hear how the world wags for each of us through Dugdale.

'Yours faithfully,
'HAYES MEREDITH.'

Mrs Haldane Carteret to Miss Crofton.

'CHAYLEIGH, APRIL 18.

'MY DEAR MINNIE,—I promised to write to you as soon
as I arrived here, but I have been so busy, finding myself in
a manner at home, and *tant soit peu* mistress of the house,
that I could not manage it. No doubt you find it desperately
dull at school, but then you are coming out after a while,
and the vacation is not far off—and I can assure you I am
almost as dull here as you are. I have my own way in
everything, to be sure; but then that is not of much use,
unless one has something in view which it is worth while
to be persistent about. And really the old gentleman,
though he is a dear nice old thing and sweet-tempered to a
degree, is very tiresome.

'You know, of course, from mamma's letter, that Haldane is not coming for a week or two. He has to remain in
London to meet Mr Baldwin on some *very important* business. I believe it is simply that Haldane is to be made
trustee and guardian to our little nieces, if their father dies,
and that cannot be anything very particular; but then, you
know, there never were such children. (I am sure I shall
not wish mine to be made such a fuss with, not that it is in
the least likely.) Everything that concerns them must be
fussed and bothered about in the most intolerable way.

'A great deal of this is Lady Davyntry's fault; I must
say, though she and I are the greatest friends—as such near
relations ought to be—she does worry me sometimes. However, she is not here to worry me now; she is at the Deane,
and writes to Mr Carteret almost every day, of course about
nothing but the children. If they are made so much of now
when they are infants, what will it be when they are grown
up enough to understand, and be utterly spoiled by it, as of

course they must be? It would not be easy to imagine worse training for the heiresses ; however, you don't want me to moralize about them, but to tell you some news. And so I would, my dear Minnie, if I had any to tell, but I have not.

'Mr Dugdale is, if possible, less amusing than ever : but I see very little of him. He has installed himself in poor Margaret's room—fortunately for me it is not the best room, as I suspect I should have had some difficulty in making him decamp, for he is excessively pertinacious in a quiet way, and as for Mr Carteret interfering, one might as well expect one of his pinned butterflies to stand up for one's rights ; so there he generally is, except at meal-times, or when he is wandering about at Davyntry. The fact is, the house, and every one in it, is be-Baldwinized to an intolerable extent.

'Of course I was dreadfully sorry for poor dear Margaret. I must have been, considering she was my sister-in-law, if even she had not been my greatest friend ; but there is reason in everything, and I should not be doing my duty to Haldane if I went on fretting for ever ; there's nothing men dislike so much in women as moping, or an over-exhibition of feeling. I assure you if she had died only last week—and after all, the melancholy event took place at the Deane, you know, and not here at all—the house could not be more mopey.

'I don't think it is quite fair to me, considering the state of my health, and that my spirits naturally require a little rousing ; and really sometimes, when I can get nothing out of Mr Carteret but " Yes, my dear," or " No, my dear," and when I know he is thinking rather of Margaret or of the collection—such a lot of trash as it is, and it takes up such a quantity of room—I am quite provoked. And as for Mr Dugdale, it is worse ; for though he is very polite, I declare

I don't think he ever really sees me, and I am sure, if he was asked suddenly, on oath, he could not tell whether my hair is red, black, or gray. And *it is* a nuisance when there are only two men in the house with one that they should be men of that sort.

'I don't suppose it will be much better when Haldane comes, for I fancy there is not the faintest chance of any company; nothing but Carteret and Crofton, Crofton and Carteret,—after a whole year, too, it is a little too bad. I have slipped out of mourning, though, that's a comfort. You know I never look well in black, and it is not *the dress* after all, is it? Haldane thought I might go on with the grays and lilacs, but mourning, however slight, is not considered lucky, and though I am not at all superstitious myself, it would never do to offend other people's prejudices, would it?

'There is really nothing to look forward to until you come home, except, perhaps, a visit from Robert Meredith; and he is only a boy; but he is very clever and amusing, and greatly inclined to make a fool of himself about me. Of course it would not do to encourage him if he were older; but it does me no harm, and keeps him out of mischief. His father has sailed for Melbourne. I really have no more to say, as of course you get all the home news from mamma.—Your affectionate sister,

'LUCY CARTERET.

'P.S. I have just heard from Haldane. It is almost settled that he is to leave the army. Mr Baldwin is going in a few days to the East, and intends to be away for three years at the least.'

CHAPTER XXIV.

An unusually beautiful day, in an exceptionally beautiful summer, and a grand old mansion, in all its bravery, wearing its best air of preparation and festivity. Even in the merest outline such a picture has its charms ; and that which the sunshine lighted up on one particular occasion, about to be described, merited close attention, and the study of its every detail.

Sheltered by a fine plantation, which, in any other than the land of flood and fell, might have been called a forest, and situated on the incline of a conical hill, the low park land, picturesquely planted, stretching away from it, until lost in the boundary of trees beneath,—a large, imposing house, built of gray, cut stone, presented its wide and lofty façade to the light. The architecture was irregular, picturesque, and effective ; and now, with its numerous windows, some sparkling in the sunshine, others thrown wide open to admit the sweet air, the Deane had an almost palatial appearance. Along the front ran a wide stone terrace, from which three flights of steps, one in the centre, and one at either end, led down to an Italian garden, intersected by the wide avenue.

Large French windows opened on this stone expanse, and now, in the lazy summer day, the silken curtains were faintly stirring, and the sound of voices, and of occasional low laughter, came softly to the hearing of two persons, a man and a woman, who were seated on a garden bench, in an angle of the terrace. The countless sounds of Nature,

which make a music all their own, were around them, and
the scene had in it every element of beauty and joy; but
these two persons seemed to be but little moved by it, to
have little in common with all that surrounded them and
with the feelings it was calculated to suggest.

They were for the most part silent, and when they spoke
it was sadly and slowly, as they speak upon whom the
memory of the past is strong, and who habitually live in it
more than in the present. There was a deference in the
tone and manner of the woman, which would have made an
observer aware that though the utmost kindliness and un-
restraint existed in her relations with her companion, she
was not his equal in station; and her manner of speaking,
though quite free from all that ordinarily constitutes vul-
garity, would have betrayed that difference still more plainly.

She was a tall woman, apparently about forty years old,
and handsome, in a peculiar style. Her face was not refined,
and yet far from common; the features well formed, and the
expression eminently candid and sensible. Health and
content were plainly to be read in the still bright complexion
and clear gray Irish eyes. She wore a handsome silk dress,
and a lace cap covered her still abundant dark hair, and in
her dress and air were unmistakable indications of her
position in life. She looked what she was, the responsible
head of a household, authoritative and respected.

We have seen her before, many years ago, on board the
ship which brought Margaret Hungerford to England; Margaret Hungerford, who has slept for nearly twenty years
under the shade of the great yew in the churchyard, which
is not so far from the Deane but that sharp eyes can mark
where the darker line of its solemn trees crosses the woods
of the lower park land. The years have set their mark upon
the handsome Irish girl, who had won such trust and affec-

tion from the forlorn young widow, who had done with it all now, all love and fear, all sorrow and forlornness, and need of help, for ever. Not only for ever, but so long ago, that her name and memory were mere traditions, while the trees she had planted were still but youngsters among trees, and the path cut through the Fir Field by her directions was still known as the 'new' road.

'There, on the spot where she had often sat with Baldwin and talked of the future, which they were never to see, Margaret's friend, humble indeed, but rightly judged and worthily trusted, sat, this beautiful summer's day, in the untouched prime of her health and strength and comeliness, and talked of the dear dead woman ; but vaguely, timidly, as the long dead are spoken of when they are mentioned at all to one from whom the years had not obscured her, though they had gathered the dimness which age brings around every other image of the past and of the future.

He with whom Rose Doran talked was an old man, but older in mind and in health than in years, of which he had not yet seen the allotted number. Of a slight, spare figure always, and now so bowed that the malformation of the shoulders was merged in the general bending weakness of the frame, and the stooped head was habitually held downwards, the old man might have been of any age to which infirmity like his could attain. Even on this warm day he was wrapped in a cloak lined with fur, and his white transparent face looked as if warm blood had never coloured the fine closely-wrinkled skin, on which the innumerable lines were marked as though they had been cunningly drawn by needles. He wore a low-crowned, wide-leaved soft hat, and scanty silver locks showed under the brim; but if the hat had been removed it would have been seen that the head which it had covered was almost entirely bald, and of the same transparent ivory texture as the face.

It would be difficult to imagine anything more fragile-looking than the old man, as he sat, wrapped in his cloak, his bowed shoulders supported by the angle of the terrace, and his hands, long, white, and skeleton-like, placidly folded on his knees. The only trace of vigour remaining in him was to be found in the eyes, and here expression, feeling, memory yet lingered, and sometimes gave forth such gleams of light and purpose as seemed to tell of the youth of the soul within him still.

A crutch stood against the wall by his side, and a thick stick, with a strong ivory handle, lay upon the bench. These were unmistakable signs of the feebleness and decay which had come to the old man, but they would not have told a close observer more than might have been learned by a glance at his feet. They were not distorted, none of the ugly shapelessness of age and disease was to be seen there. They were slim, and shapely, and neatly attired, in the old-fashioned silk stocking and buckled shoe of a more polite and formal period, but they were totally inexpressive. No one could have looked at the old man's feet set comfortably upon a soft lambskin rug, but remaining there quite motionless, without seeing that they had almost ceased to do their work. With much difficulty, and very slowly, by the aid of the crutch and the stick, they would still carry him a little way from the sunny sitting-room on the ground floor to the sunny corner of the terrace, for the most part—but that was all.

He was not discontented that it should be all, for he suffered little now in his old age—perhaps he had suffered as much as he could before that time came; and was no more irritable or peevish. A little tired, a little wondering betimes that he had so long to wait, while so many whose day had promised to be prolonged and bright in its morning had

18

passed on, out of sight, before him : but a happy old man,
for all that, in a quiet, musing way, and 'very little trouble
to any one.'

Yes, that was the general opinion of Mr Dugdale, old
Mr Dugdale, as the household, for some unexplained reason,
called him, and few things vexed the spirit of Gertrude
Baldwin so nearly beyond bearing, as the assurances to that
effect which her aunt, Mrs Carteret, was in the habit of pro-
mulgating to an inquisitive and sympathizing neighbourhood.
For Mrs Carteret (she had been the eldest Miss Crofton a
great many years ago) was not of a very refined nature, and
it is just possible that when she commented on Mr Dugdale's
reduced and sometimes almost deathlike appearance, to the
effect that any one 'to see him would think he could die off
quite easily,' she rather resented his not availing himself of
that apparent facility without delay.   He did not, however ;
and Mrs Carteret was the only person who ever found the
gentle, kindly man in the way, and she never dared to hint
to her husband that she did so.

Her niece inherited from her dead mother all the quick-
sightedness which made her keen to see and to suffer, where
her affections were concerned, and the first seeds of dissension had been sown some years before, between the aunt and
the niece, by the girl's perceiving that 'old' Mr Dugdale
was not considered by Mrs Carteret as such an acquisition
to the family party at the Deane as its fair and gentle, but
high-spirited, young mistress held him to be.   It was on
that occasion that Gertrude had contrived, very mildly and
very skilfully, but still after a decided and unmistakable
fashion, to remind her aunt of the fact that she, and not Mrs
Carteret, was the lady of the house in which the old man
had been found *de trop ;* and thence had originated a state
of things destined to produce most unforeseen consequences.

The immediate result, however, had been an increased observance in manner, and an additional dislike in reality, to Mr Dugdale, on the part of Mrs Carteret, which the old man perceived—as indeed he perceived everything, for his powers of observation were by no means enfeebled—but which it never occurred to him to resent. What could it possibly signify to him that Mrs Carteret did not like him, and wished it might be in her power to get rid of him? It was not in her power; it was not within the compass of any earthly will to separate him from Margaret's child; and as for Mrs Carteret herself, it is to be feared that old Mr Dugdale, after the saturnine fashion of his earlier years, cherished a quiet contempt for that lady, while he readily acknowledged that she was a good sort of woman in her way. It was not in his way, that was all.

Mrs Doran was especially devoted to Mr Dugdale, to whom she owed the prosperous position which she had held in the household at the Deane for so many years now, that she was as much a part of the place to the inhabitants as the forest trees or the family portraits. Consequently she was not particularly attached to Mrs Carteret, and presumed occasionally to criticise that lady's proceedings after a fashion which, had she been aware of it, would have gone far to fortify her in one of her favourite and most frequently-expressed opinions, that it was a great mistake to keep servants too long. 'They always presume upon it, and become impertinent and troublesome.'

But Mrs Carteret would never have ventured to include Mrs Doran among the 'servants' otherwise than in her most private cogitations. Rose was a privileged person there, by a more sacred if not a stronger right than that of Mrs Carteret herself.

But on this bright, beautiful day, when the old man had

come out upon the terrace to bask awhile in the genial sunshine, why was Rose Doran with him ? Ordinarily he had
younger, fairer companions, in whose faces and voices there
were many happy, sad memories for him, and whose love and
care brightened the days fast going down to the last setting
of the sun of his life. They were absent to-day, and the two
to whom, of all the numerous household at the Deane, the
day had most of retrospective meaning were alone together.

'It's wonderful how well I remember her, sir,' Rose was
saying ; 'sometimes that is. There's many a day I disremember her entirely, but when I do think about her—as to-
day—I can see her plain. And I'm glad, somehow, I never
saw her in her grandeur ; for if I did, an' all the years that
have gone by since then, I couldn't but think no one else
had a right to it.'

'I understand what you mean, Rose, and when I remember her, sometimes, as you say, it isn't in her grandeur, but
as she was when you and she came home first.'

'Yes, sir, and you saw us goin' in at the door of the little
inn—who'd ever think there'd be a hotel as big as Morrison's,
and a deal cleaner, in the very same place now ?—and you
not knowin' us, and she seein' you in a minute. Isn't it
strange, Mr Dugdale, to remember it after twenty, ay, more
than twenty years ? How long is it then, sir, rightly ? '

'Twenty-three years and some months, Rose.'

'True for you, sir. And now Miss Gerty's to be her own
mistress, and no one to say by your leave or with your leave
to her, the darling ! The master would have been a proud
man, rest his soul ! this day.'

The old man did not notice her remark. But after a
little while, as if he had been thinking over it, he bowed the
bent head still lower, and moved the thin white hands, and
sighed.

'Are you chilly at all, sir?' asked his quickly-observant companion. 'The sun is shifting a little; would you like to go in?'

'No,' he replied; and then asked, after a pause, 'How are they getting on?'

'Beautifully,' Rose answered. 'The house is a picture; and as to the ball-room, nothing could be more beautiful. Miss Eleanor has it all done out with flowers, and I'm only afraid she'll be tired before the time comes for the dancing. Do you think you'll be able to sit up to see it, sir?'

'I don't know, Rose; but I will try. Gerty seems to wish it so much, foolish child; as if it could make any difference to her that an old man like me should be there to see her happy and admired.'

'An' why shouldn't she?' remonstrated Rose in a tone almost of vexation. 'Do you think the children oughtn't to have some nature in them? If Miss Gerty was no better nor a baby when the mistress—the Lord be good to her!—was taken, and Miss Eleanor never saw the smile of her mother's face at all, sure they know about her all the same, and it's more and not less they think about her, the older they grow, and the better they know the want of a mother, through seeing other people with mothers and fathers and friends of all kinds, and no one to dare to deny them—not that I'm sayin' or thinkin' there's any one would harm innocent lambs like them, nor try to put between them—but the world's a quare world, Mr Dugdale, and they're beginnin' to find it out, and the more they know of it, the more they miss the mother they never knew at all, and the father they did not know much about—and the more they cling to them that did know, and can tell them. Many's the time, Mr Dugdale, that Miss Gerty has said to me, "Isn't it odd that Uncle James remembers mamma much better than Uncle Carteret or Aunt Lucy remember her, and can tell us much more about our father ?—and yet they were all young people together, and near relations, and he wasn't." And it was only the other day, when you told Miss Gerty she was to have the poor mistress's picture for her comin' of age, she says to me, "There's Uncle and Aunt Carteret couldn't tell me whether it's like her or not; and there's Uncle James knows all about it, and can tell when I'm like her and when Nelly is, and yet they say old people forget everything." Beggin' your pardon, sir, for saying you're old, but the dear child said the very words. An' so, if she didn't want you to-night to see her in her glory, and to be like the smile of the father and mother that's in heaven upon her, I wouldn't think much of her, Mr Dugdale, 'deed I wouldn't then.'

'Well, well, Rose, it seems the children are of your opinion, for they have made me promise to sit up as late as possible; and I have heard as much about their dresses as either their maids or yourself, I'll be bound.'

'An' beautiful they'll look in them, Mr Dugdale, particularly Miss Gerty. Don't you think she grows wonderfully like her mother? Not that I ever saw her look bright and happy like Miss Gerty; but I think she must have been just like her, after she was married to the poor master. You know I went away before that, sir; but perhaps you disremember.'

'No, no, Rose, I remember. I remember it all very well, because she told me if she wanted you and could not send for you herself I was to do so, because Mr Baldwin did not know you. No, no; it is a long time ago, a very long time, but I don't forget, I don't forget.'

'An' you see the likeness, sir ?'

'Yes, I see the likeness, I see it very plainly; as we

grow old, time seems so much shorter that it does not appear at all strange to me that I should remember her so well. There were many years during which I could hardly recall her face even when I was looking at the picture, but all that dimness seems to have cleared away now, and all my memory come back. Gerty is wonderfully like her, only more placid; her manner is more like her father's.'

They were silent for a time, during which Rose Doran knitted diligently,—her fingers were never idle, and her subordinates in the household said the same of her eyes and ears,—and then she began to talk again.

'It'll be a fine ball, sir. They say the beautifulest, except the Duke's, that ever was in this part of the country. And sure, so it ought, for where's there the like of Miss Baldwin of the Deane for beauty or for fortune either? An' what could be too good in the way of a ball for *her*?'

There was a note of challenge in the Irishwoman's voice. Mr Dugdale observed it with amusement, and replied,

'I dare say it will go off very well. Mrs Carteret is a good hand at this kind of thing.'

'She is,' said Rose shortly; 'and as it's Miss Gerty's money it's all to come out of, she'll have no notion of saving anything.'

This was the nearest approach to a frank expression of her not-particularly-exalted opinion of Mrs Carteret on which Rose had ever ventured, and Mr Dugdale did not encourage her to pursue it by any remark; but, observing that the girls had said they would come out to him, and were after their time, and that he would go and look for them, he began to make slow preparations for a change of place.

Rose's steady arm aided him, and he was soon proceeding slowly along the terrace, his crutch under his left arm and his stick in his right hand, while Rose walked by his side.

As he slowly and apparently painfully dragged himself along
—only apparently, for he rarely suffered pain now — Mr
Dugdale presented a picture of decrepitude which contrasted
strangely with a picture which any observer, had there
chanced to be one upon the terrace that day, might have
seen, and which he and Rose stood still to look at with intense pleasure.

Through the open windows of a large room upon the terrace the interior was to be seen. The apartment was of
splendid dimensions, and the richly-decorated walls and ceil-
ing were ornamented with classical designs appropriate to
the festive purposes of a ball-room. A bank of flowers was
constructed to enclose a space designed for an orchestra, and
several musical instruments were already arranged in their
places.

A grand piano was in the middle, and a lady was seated
before it, whose nimble fingers were flying over the keys,
producing the strains of a brilliantly provocative and inspiriting valse. The lady was not 'alone. In the centre of the
room, whose polished floor was almost as bright and slippery
as glass, stood two young girls, the arms of each around the
waist of the other, their heads thrown back, their eyes
beaming with laughter, and their hearts beating with the exertion of the wild dance they had just concluded.

As Mr Dugdale and Rose drew near the window, the
pause for breath came to a conclusion, the music gush-
ed forth, more than ever inviting, and the dancers were
off again, spinning round and round in their girlish glee in
a boisterous exaggeration of the figure of the dance, irre-
sistibly merry and attractive. They flew down the length
of the room, crossed to its extremity, and came whirling up
to the central window. There stood Mr Dugdale with up-
lifted threatening stick, and Rose, with her knitting dropped,

fascinated with admiration. Then they checked their head-
long career, and, with some difficulty, came to a stop opposite the pair on the terrace, laughingly shaking their heads
in imitation of the pretended rebuke they were conveying.

'A rational way to rehearse for your ball, Gerty,' said
Mr Dugdale, as he stepped, with the assistance of the young
girl's ready hand, into the room, followed by Rose. 'And a
capital plan for you, Nelly, who are so easily tired. You
silly children, don't you think you will have enough dancing
to-night ? '

'Not half enough,' replied one of the girls, 'not quarter;
none of the people will stay after five or six at the latest.'

'I should hope not, indeed,' said Mr Dugdale. 'And you
are resolved to begin punctually at ten ; you *are* unconscion-
able.'

'And then you know, Uncle James,' said the girl whom
he had called Gerty, 'we cannot dance together to-night;
we are grown up, you know, hopelessly grown up ; it's awful,
isn't it ? and besides—besides, Aunt Lucy tempted us with
her beautiful playing—and the floor is so delightful; and
now don't you really, really think it will be a delightful
ball ? '

'I have not the smallest misgiving about it, Gerty,
though I don't know much of balls. But I am sure Mrs
Carteret will join me in urging you not to tire yourselves
any more just now.'

Mrs Carteret left the piano, and joined the girls, who
immediately entered on a discussion of the measures already
taken for the beautification of the ball-room, and the possibility of still farther adorning it, which was finally pronounced hopeless, everything being already quite perfect,
and the party adjourned to luncheon.

So the years had sped away, and all the fears, and hopes, and sorrows they had given birth to had also come to their death, according to the wonderful law of immutability, and were no more. The mother in her marble tomb beneath the yew-tree, the father in his unmarked grave in the desert, but united in the country too far off for mortal ken or comprehension, were well-nigh forgotten here; and their children were women now.

The little party assembled at the Deane on this occasion —the twenty-first anniversary of Gertrude Baldwin's birth —had but little sadness among them, and were visited with but slight recollections of the far distant past. Twenty years is a long time. No saying can be more trite and more true; yet there are persons and circumstances, and, more than all, there are feelings, which are not forgotten, ignored, killed in twenty years.

There were two unseen guests that day at the table—at whose head Mrs Carteret, who was in a gracious, not to say gushing mood, insisted on Gertrude's taking her place for the first time—whose presence Mr Dugdale felt, though he was an old man now, and his fancy was no longer active. He had his place opposite to Gertrude, and from it he could see, hanging on the wall behind her chair, her father's portrait. It was a fine picture, the work of a first-rate artist, and the face was full of harmony and expression. The graceful lines, the rich colouring of youthful manhood, were there, and the sunny blue eyes smiled as if they could see the gay girls, the handsome, self-conscious, self-important woman, the wan and feeble old man. From the portrait Mr Dugdale's glance wandered to the girlish face and figure before him and just under it; and a pang of exceeding keen and bitter remembrance smote him—ay, after twenty years.

Gertrude Meriton Baldwin was a handsomer girl than

her mother had been, but wonderfully like her. No trouble, no care, no touch of degradation, humiliation, concealment, bitterness of any kind, had ever lighted on the daughter's well-cared-for girlhood, which had been permitted all its natural expansion, all its legitimate enjoyment and careless gladness. No passion, unwise and ungoverned, had come into her life to trouble and disturb it too soon—to fill it with vain illusions, and the sure heritage of disappointment. A happy childhood had grown into a happy girlhood, and now that happy girlhood had ripened into a womanhood, with every promise of happiness for the future.

She was taller than her mother, and had more colour; but the features were almost the same. The brow was a little less broad, the lips were fuller, but the eyes were in no way different, so far as they had been called upon for expression up to the present time; they had looked like Margaret's, and no doubt would so look in every farther development of life, circumstance, and character.

Eleanor, who amused herself during the luncheon,—at which Mr Dugdale was unusually silent, and Mrs Carteret occupied herself rather emphatically, on the plea that dinner was a doubtful good when a ball was in preparation,—was not in the least like her father, her mother, or her sister. She was very small, delicately formed, and fragile in appearance, with a clear dark complexion, large black eyes, and a profusion of glossy black hair, which, especially when in close contrast with the clear gray eyes and soft brown hair of her sister, gave her a foreign appearance, of which she was quite conscious and rather proud.

Hitherto there had been no difference in the lot of the sisters. The childish joys and sorrows of the one had been those of the other, and girlhood had brought to them no separate fortune. Nor were things materially altered now.

The independence of action which Gertrude attained upon this day would be Eleanor's in a very short time, and in point of wealth they were nearly equal. For each there had been a long minority. Eleanor Davyntry had not long survived her brother, and all her disposable fortune was her younger niece's. Apart from their orphanhood, no girls could have had a more enviable lot than the two who were in such wild spirits on that summer's day, which invested one of them with all the dignity of legal womanhood, and all the responsibility of a great heiress.

Eleanor was of a different temperament from that of Gertrude, more vehement, more passionate, less self-reliant, less sustained. Hitherto the difference had shown itself but seldom and slightly, and there had been little or nothing to develop it. But a shrewd observer would have noticed it, even in the manner in which each regarded the promised pleasure of the evening, in the easy joyousness of the one, and the passionate eagerness of the other.

When luncheon had nearly reached a conclusion, the sound of wheels upon the drive sent Eleanor rushing to the window. A stylish dog-cart, in which were seated a tall, fine-looking, rather heavy middle-aged man and an irreproachable groom, was rapidly approaching the house.

'It is uncle,' said Eleanor; 'now we shall know for certain who's coming from Edinburgh. What a good thing you thought of the telegraph, aunt!'

'Yes,' said Mrs Carteret. 'When one has to put people up for the night, it is better to know exactly how many to expect.'

In a few minutes Haldane Carteret was in the room, and had handed an open telegraphic despatch to Gertrude.

'They're all coming, you see,' he said good-humouredly; 'and *you'll* be glad to hear, Lucy, there's no doubt about

Meredith. He has got that troublesome business settled, as he always does get everything settled he puts his mind to, and he will be down by the mail, and here by eleven.'

'That *is* delightful,' said Gertrude, with frank outspoken pleasure. 'You have brought nothing but good news, uncle.'

'And the programmes—isn't that what you call them ? I hope they're all right.'

'I'm sure they are.—Aunt, what room are you going to give Mr Meredith ?'

Then ensued a domestic discussion, in which Gertrude and Mrs Carteret took an active share ; but Eleanor stood looking out of the window, and did not utter a word.

CHAPTER XXV

ROBERT MEREDITH.

THE twenty years which had rolled over the head of Robert Meredith, the anxiously expected guest, since last we saw him, may be thus briefly recapitulated. The school selected by James Dugdale for his protégé's education was the now celebrated, but then little heard-of, Grammar-school of Lowebarre. Not that the *alumni*, as they delight to call themselves, recognize their old place of education by any such familiar name. To them it is and always will be the Fairfax-school ; they are 'Fairfaxians,' and the word Lowebarre is altogether ignored.

The *fons et origo* of these academic groves, pleasantly situate in the immediate vicinity of the metropolis, was one Sir Anthony Fairfax, a worthy knight of the time of Queen Elizabeth, who, having lived his life merrily, according to the fashion of the old English gentlemen of those days, more especially in the matter of the consumption of sack and the carrying out of the *droits de seigneurie,* thought it better towards his latter days to endeavour to get up a few entries on the other side of the ledger of his life, and found the easiest method in the doing a deed of beneficence on a large scale. This was nothing less than the foundation of a school at Lowebarre, where a portion of his property was situate, for the education of forty boys, who were to be gratuitously instructed in the learned languages, and morally and religiously brought up. How the scheme worked in those dark ages it is, of course, impossible to say.

But ten years before Robert Meredith was inducted into the *arcana* of the classics the Fairfax school was in a very low state indeed, and the Fairfaxians themselves were no better than a set of roughs. The head-master, an old gentleman who had been classically educated, indeed, but over whose head the rust of many years of farming had accumulated, took little heed of his scholars, whose numbers consequently dwindled half-year by half-year, and who, as they neglected not only the arts but everything else but stone-throwing and orchard-robbing, had no manners to soften, and became brutal.

This state of affairs could not last. One of the governors or trustees acting under the founder's will saw that not merely was the muster-roll of the school diminishing, but its social *status* was almost gone. He called a meeting of his coadjutors, impressed upon them the necessity of taking vigorous steps for getting rid of the then head-master, and of at once procuring the services of a man ready to go with the times. Advertisements judiciously worded were sent to all the newspapers, inviting candidates for the head-mastership of the Fairfax school, and dilating in glowing terms on the advantages of that position; but time passed, and the post yet remained open. Those who presented themselves were too much of the stamp of the existing holder of the situation to suit the enlarged views of the trustees, and it was not until Mr Warwick, the governor who had first suggested the reform, busied himself personally in the matter, that the fitting individual was secured.

The Rev. Charles Crampton, who, having taken a first-class in classics and a second in mathematics, having been Fellow of his college and tutor of some of the best men of their years, had finally succumbed to the power of love, and subsided into a curacy of seventy-five pounds a year, was Mr Warwick's selection. He brought with him testimonials of the highest character; but what weighed most with Mr Warwick was the earnest recommendation of James Dugdale, who had been Mr Crampton's college friend.

Poor Charles Crampton, when he sacrificed his fellowship for love, had little notion that he would have to pass the remainder of his life in grinding in a mill of boys. To study the Fathers, to prepare two or three editions of his favourite classic authors, to play in a more modern and refined manner the part of the parson in the 'Deserted Village,' had been his hope. But though the old adage was not followed, though when Poverty came in at the door (and she did come speedily enough, not in her harshest, fiercest aspect it is true, but looking quite grimly enough to frighten an educated and refined gentleman), Love did not fly out of the window, yet Charles Crampton had suffered sufficiently from *turpis egestas* to induce him at once to accept the offer.

The salary of the Fairfax head-mastership, though not large, quintupled his then income; the position held out to him was that of a gentleman, and though he had not any wild ideas of the dignity and responsibility of a school-mastership, the notion of having to battle in aid of a failing cause

pleased and invigorated him, more especially when he reflected that, should he succeed, the *kudos* of that success
would be all his own.

So the Reverend Charles Crampton was installed at
Lowebarre, and the wisdom of Mr Warwick's selection was
speedily proved. Men of position and influence in the
world, who had been Mr Crampton's friends at college;
others, a little younger, to whom he had been tutor; and
the neighbouring gentry, when they found they had resident
among them one who was not merely a scholar and a man of
parts, but by birth and breeding one of themselves,—sent
their sons to the Fairfax school, and received Mr and Mrs
Crampton with all politeness and attention.

By the time that Robert Meredith arrived at Lowebarre
the school was thoroughly well known; its scholars num-
bered nearly two hundred; its ' speech-days ' were attended,
as the local journals happily expressed it, ' by lords spiritual
and temporal, the dignitaries of the Bar, the Bench, and the
Senate, and the flower of the aristocracy;' while, source of
Mr Crampton's greatest pride, there stood on either side of
the Gothic window in the great school-hall, on a chocolate
ground, in gold letters, a list of the exhibitioners of the
school, and of the honours gained by Fairfaxians, at the
two universities.

To a boy brought up amidst the incongruities of colonial
life the order and regularity of the Fairfax school possessed
all the elements of bewildering novelty But with his
habitual quietude and secret observation Robert Meredith
set himself to work to acquire an insight into the characters
both of his masters and his school-fellows, and determined,
according to his wont, to turn the result of his studies to
his own benefit.

The forty boys provided for by the beneficence of good

old Sir Anthony Fairfax—'foundation-boys,' as they were called—were now, of course, in a considerable minority in the school. They were for the most part sons of residents in the immediate neighbourhood ; but for the benefit of those young gentlemen who came from afar, the head-master received boarders at his own house, and at another under his immediate control, while certain of the under-masters enjoyed similar privileges.

The number of young gentlemen received under Mr Crampton's own roof was rigidly limited to three ; for Mrs Crampton was a nervous little woman, who shrunk from the sound of cantering bluchers, and whose housekeeping talent was not of an extensive order. The triumvirate paid highly, more highly than James Dugdale thought necessary ; and Hayes Meredith was of his opinion. The boy would have to rough it in after-life, he said,—'roughing it' was a traditional idea with him,—and it would be useless to bring the lad up on velvet. So that Robert found his quarters in Mr Crampton's second boarding-house, where forty or fifty lads, all the sons of gentlemen of modern fortune, dwelt in more or less harmony out of school-hours, and were presided over by Mr Boldero, the mathematical master.

On his first entry into this herd of boys, Robert Meredith felt that he could scarcely congratulate himself on his lines having fallen in pleasant places. He had sufficient acuteness to foresee what the lively youths amongst whom he was about to dwell would reckon as his deficiencies, and consequently would select and enter upon at once to his immediate opprobrium. That he was colonial, and not English born, would be, he was aware, immediately resented with scorn by his companions, and regarded as a reason for overwhelming him with obloquy. It was, therefore, a fact to be kept most secret ; but after the lapse of a few days it was inadvertently revealed by the 'chum' to whom alone Robert had mentioned the circumstance. When once known it afforded subject for the keenest sarcasm; 'bushranger,' 'kangaroo,' 'ticket-of-leave,' were among the choice epithets bestowed upon him.

It would not be either pleasant or profitable to linger over the story of Robert Meredith's school-days. They have no interest for us beyond this, that they developed his disposition, and insensibly influenced all his after-life. He regarded his schoolmates with scorn as unbounded as it was studiously concealed, and he cultivated their unsuspecting good-will with a success which rendered him in a short time, in all points essential to his comfort, their master. He made rapid progress in his studies, and kept before his mind with steadiness which was certainly wonderful at his age—and, had it been induced by a more elevated actuating motive, would have been most admirable—the purpose with which he had come to England.

When the end of his schoolboy life drew near, and the much longed-for University career was about to begin, Robert Meredith took leave of Mr Crampton with mutual assurances of good-will. If the conscientious and reverend gentleman had been closely questioned with regard to his sentiments concerning his clever colonial pupil, he must have acknowledged that he admired rather than liked him. But there was no one to dive into the secrets of his soul, and in the letter which Mr Crampton addressed to Mr Dugdale on the occasion, he gave him, with perfect truth, a highly favourable account of Robert Meredith, of which one sentence really contained the pith. 'He is conspicuous for talent,' wrote the reverend gentleman; 'but I think even his abilities are less marked than his tact, in which he surpasses any young man whose character has come under my observation.'

'So in argument, and so in life—tact is a great matter.'

Behold the guiding spirit of Robert Meredith's career, even in its present fledgling days. It was tact that made him eschew anything that might look like 'sapping,' or rigidity of morals, as much as he eschewed dissipation and actual fast life while at college. It was tact that made his wine-parties, though the numbers invited were small, and the liquids by no means so expensive as those furnished by many of his acquaintances, the pleasantest in the University. It was tact that took him now and then into the hunting-field, that made him a constant attendant at Bullingdon and Cowley Marsh, where his bowling and batting rendered him a welcome ally and a formidable opponent; and it was tact which allotted him just that amount of work necessary for a fair start in his future career.

Robert Meredith knew perfectly that in that future career at the bar the honours gained at college would have little weight—that the position to be gained would depend materially upon the talent and industry brought to bear upon the dry study of the law itself, upon the mastery of technical details; above all, upon the reading of that greatest of problems, the human heart, and the motives influencing it. To hold his own was all he aimed at while at college, and he did so; but some of his friends, who knew what really lay in him, were grievously disappointed when the lists were published, and it was found that Robert Meredith had only gained a double second. George Ritherdon grieved openly, and refused to be comforted even by his own success, and by the acclamations which rang round the steady reading set of Bodhamites when it was known that George Ritherdon's name stood at the head of the first class.

The two friends were not to be separated—that was Ritherdon's greatest consolation. Mr Plowden, the great conveyancer of the Middle Temple, had made arrangements

to receive both of them to read with him; and in the very
dingy chambers occupied by that great professor of the law
they speedily found themselves installed. A man overgrown
with legal rust, and prematurely drowsy with a life-long
residence within the 'dusty purlieus of the law,' was Mr
Plowden; but his name was well known, his fame was
thoroughly established; many of his pupils were leading
men at the bar; and the dry tomes which bore his name as
author were recognized text-books of the profession.

Moreover, James Dugdale had heard, from certain old
college chums, that underneath Mr Plowden's legal crust
there was to be found a keen knowledge of human nature,
and a certain power of will, which, properly exercised, would
be of the greatest assistance in moulding and forming such
a character as Robert Meredith's. It was, therefore, with
a comfortable sense of duty done that James Dugdale saw
the young man established in Mr Plowden's chambers, and,
from all he had heard, he was by no means sorry that Robert
was to have George Ritherdon as his companion.

There are certain persons who seem to be specially designed and cut out by nature for prosperity, and with
whom, on the whole, it does not seem to disagree. They
bear the test well, they are not arrogant, insolent, or apparently unfeeling, and they make more friends than enemies.
Such people find many true believers in them, to surround
them with a sincere and heartfelt worship, to regard all
their good fortune as their indisputable right, and resent
any cross, crook, or turning in it as an injustice on the part
of Providence, or 'some one.' We all know one person at
least of this class, for whose 'luck' it is difficult to account,
except as 'luck,' and of whom no one has anything unfa-
vourable to say, or the disposition to say it.

Robert Meredith was one of this favoured class of

persons. He had the good fortune to possess certain external gifts which go far towards making a man popular, and under which it is always difficult, especially to women, to believe that a cold heart is concealed. The handsome lad had grown up into a handsomer man, and one chiefly remarkable for his easy and graceful manners, which harmonized with an elegant figure and a voice which had a very deceptive depth, sweetness, and impressiveness of intonation about it.

The ardent admirer, the unswerving true believer, in Meredith's case was, as we have seen, George Ritherdon; and it would have been curious and interesting to investigate the extent and importance of the influence of this early contracted and steadily maintained friendship on the lives of both men, and on the estimation in which Meredith was held by the world outside that companionship.

He would have been very loth to believe that any particle of his importance, a shade of warmth in the manner of his welcome anywhere, an impulse of confidence in his ability, leading to his being employed in cases above his apparent mark and standing, were the result of an unexpressed belief in George Ritherdon, a tacit but very general respect and admiration for the earnest, honest, irreproachable integrity of the man, who was clever, indeed, as well as good, but so much more exceptionally good than exceptionally clever, that the latter quality was almost overlooked by his friends, who were numerous and influential. Wherever George's influence could reach, wherever his efforts could be made available, Meredith's interests were safe, Meredith's ambition was aided.

Naturally of a frank and communicative disposition, liking sympathy and the expression of it, fond of his home and his family, and ever ready to be actively interested in all that concerned them, there was not an incident in his history, direct or indirect, with which he would not have made his ' chum ' acquainted on the least hint of the ' chum's ' desiring to know it; and, in fact, Robert Meredith, who had too much tact to permit his friend to perceive that his communicativeness occasionally bored him, was in thorough possession of his friend's history past and present.

But this was not reciprocal, except in a very superficial scale. Robert Meredith was perhaps not intentionally reticent with George Ritherdon, and it occurred very seldom to the latter to think his friend reticent at all, but he was habitually cautious. The same quality which had made him a taciturn observer in the house at Chayleigh, able to conceal his dislike of Mr Baldwin, and to appreciate thoroughly without appearing to observe the tie which bound James Dugdale to his old friend's daughter, now in his manhood enabled him to win the regard of others, and to learn all about them, without letting them either find out much about him, or offending them, or inspiring them with distrust by cold and calculated reserve.

As a matter of fact, George Ritherdon knew very much less of his friend than his friend knew of him, and of one portion of his life he was in absolute ignorance. It was that which included his residence at Chayleigh, and his subsequent relations with the families of Carteret and Baldwin. George had heard the names in casual mention, and he knew that when Meredith went for a fortnight or so to Scotland in the ' long ' he went to a place called the Deane, where a retired officer of artillery, named Haldane Carteret, lived, who kept a very good house, and gave ' men ' some very capital shooting.

But George did not shoot; and had he been devoted to

that manly pursuit, he would never have thought it in the
least unkind or negligent in Meredith to have omitted to
share his opportunities in that way with him; he would
never have thought about it at all indeed; so the Deane
was quite unknown territory, even speculatively, to this
good fellow. He knew nothing of the young heiress and
her sister. No stray photograph or missish letter, left
about in the careless disarray of bachelor's chambers, had
ever excited George's curiosity, or led to 'chaff' on his part
upon Meredith's predilection for travelling north, whenever
he could spare the time to travel at all, upon his indifference
to 'the palms and temples of the south.' George was not
an adept in the polite modern art of 'chaff,' and few men
could have been found to offer less occasion for its exercise
than Robert Meredith.

It had sometimes occurred to George to wonder why a
man so popular with women, so 'rising' as Robert Meredith,
a man who had undoubtedly, in default of some untoward
accident, a brilliant professional career and all its concomi-
tant social advantages before him, had not married; but this
was a matter on which he would not have considered that
even their close friendship would have justified him in putting any questions to Meredith.

The *tu quoque* which might have been Meredith's reply
was of easy explanation. George Ritherdon had had a disappointment in his youth, and had never thought seriously
about marriage since. The disappointment had taken place
in his early imprudent days, when no connection, even distantly collateral, existed in his mind between money and
marriage, and he had long since arrived at the conviction
that, even if it did come into his head or heart to fall in
love again, he could not afford to marry, and therefore must,
acting upon the gentlemanly precepts which had always

governed him, resist any such inclination as dishonourable to himself and ungenerous towards its object.

The world had 'marched' to a very quick step indeed since the days of George's almost boyhood, when the beautiful but penniless Camilla Jackson had fascinated him 'into fits' at a carpet dance in the neighbourhood of his father's house, and he had forthwith set to work, in the fervent realms of his imagination, to fit up, furnish, and start a most desirable and charming little establishment, to be presided over by that young lady in the delightful capacity of wife. Of course the beautiful Camilla was always to be attired in the choicest French millinery and the clearest white muslins. Laundresses' bills had no place, nor had those of the *modiste*, in the unsophisticated imagination of the young man, and breakages were as far from his thoughts as babies.

George had lived and learned since then, and he dreamed no more dreams now; he knew better. Unless some tremendous, wholly unexpected, and extravagantly unlikely piece of good luck should come in his way—something about as probable as the adventures of Sindbad or Prince Camaralzaman, in which case he would immediately look about for an eligible young lady to take the larger share of it off his unaccustomed hands—George would now never marry.

Camilla had disdained the white muslin and the millinery regardless of the washing bill, of which indeed she had early been taught by an exemplary and fearfully managing mother to be ceaselessly reminiscent; and George not unfrequently saw her now in a carriage, the mere varnish whereof told of wealth of perfectly aggressive amount, in a carriage crammed with healthy, clean, rich-looking children, and gorgeously arrayed in velvets and furs of great price.

That Meredith was not a marrying man was the conclusion at which George Ritherdon arrived, when he discussed with himself the oddity of the coincidence which threw them together, and speculated upon how long the engagement would last.

In one respect the friends were very differently circumstanced. George Ritherdon had 'no end' of relations, cousins by the score, aunts and uncles in liberal proportions. But Robert Meredith was a lonely man. His colonial origin explained that. He had never sought to renew any of the ties of family connection broken by his father when he left England; he had found friends steady and serviceable, and he wisely preferred contenting himself with them to cultivating dubiously disposed relatives. Boy though he was, he made a correct hit in this.

'If they were likely to be any use to me, my father would have put me in some kind of communication with them; he certainly would have looked them up when he came home, which he never did.'

Therefore Robert never troubled himself more about any of the family connections on this side of the world, and, indeed, troubled himself very little about those on the other. As time went by he was accustomed to say to himself that he knew they were all getting on well, and that was enough for him. Sometimes he wondered whether he should ever see them again; whether, if he did not 'see his way' here, he might not go in for colonial practice; whether one or more of his brothers, children when he saw them last, might not take the same fancy which he had taken for seeing the old world. But nothing of all this happened.

Robert Meredith had neared the end of his college career when intelligence of his father's death reached him, and caused him genuine, if temporary, suffering. His thoughts went back then to the old home and the old times, and he did feel for a time a disinterested wish that he had been with his mother—how she had loved him, how she loved him still, through all those years of separation!—when this calamity came upon her. The necessity for a large correspondence with his brothers, and the feeling, always a terrible one in cases where a long distance lies between persons affected by the same event, that his father's death had taken place while he was quite unconscious of it, and was already long past when he heard of it, touched chords dulled if not silenced.

The account which he received of family affairs was prosperous : one of his sisters was already married, the other would follow her example after a due and decorous lapse of time. His brothers were to carry on Hayes Meredith's business, in whose profits his father left him a small share. Altogether, apart from feeling — and it was unusual for Robert Meredith to find it difficult to keep any matter of consideration apart from feeling—the position of affairs was eminently satisfactory, and the young man, ambitious, industrious, and self-reliant, felt that he and his were well treated by fate.

He felt the blank which his father's death created a good deal. He had corresponded with him· very regularly, and the freshness and vigour, the plain practical sense and shrewdness of the older man's mind had been pleasant and useful to the younger. He had not expected the event, either. Hayes Meredith was a strong, hale, athletic man, and his son had always thought of him as he had last seen him. No bad accounts of his health had ever reached Robert, and he had never thought of his father's death as a probable occurrence.

On the whole this was the most remarkable event, and by many degrees the most impressive, which had befallen in Meredith's life, and its influence upon him was decidedly injurious. He had always been hard, and from that time he became harder—not in appearance, nothing was more characteristic of the young man than his easy and sympathetic manner, but in reality he felt more solitary now that the one bond of intellectual companionship between him and his home was broken, and this solitude was not good for him. As for his mother, he was apt to think of her as a very good woman in her way—an excellent woman indeed. A man must be much worse than Robert Meredith before he ceases to believe this of his own mother; but she knew nothing whatever of the world—of the old world particularly—and could not be made to understand it. He wrote to her—he never neglected doing so; but there was more expression than truth of feeling in his letters, and the mail day was not a pleasant epoch.

CHAPTER XXVI.

TIME AND CHANGE.

WHILE Mr Carteret lived, Robert Meredith had been a frequent visitor at Chayleigh. The quiet, eccentric old gentleman had remained in the old house, and had faithfully guarded his beloved collection to the last. But that emporium of curiosities had not received many additions after Mrs Baldwin's death. The old man had taken, after a time, a little feeble pleasure in it, it is true; but only because those about him had acted on the hint which Margaret herself had given them, after the death of Mrs Carteret, and persuaded him to resume his care of the collection because his daughter had been so fond of it.

Always quiet, uncomplaining, and kind to every one, the

old man would have had rather a snubbed and subdued kind of life of it, under the rule of Haldane's bouncing Lucy, but for the vigilance of James Dugdale. That silent and unsuspected sufferer sedulously watched and cared for the old man, and Mrs Haldane, who by no means liked him, so far respected and feared him that she never ventured to dispute any of his arrangements for Mr Carteret's welfare.

He continued to like Lucy ' pretty well,' and to regard Robert Meredith with special favour, though he lived long enough to see Robert pass quite out of the category of exceptional boys. Indeed, so much did he like him, that at one time he entertained an idea of bequeathing to him the famous collection, after the demise of James Dugdale, who was to have a life interest in its delights and treasures ; but on the old gentleman's broaching the subject to him one day, Robert Meredith put the objections to the scheme so very strongly to him, that he acknowledged the superior wisdom of his young friend, bowed to his decision, and liked him more than ever for his disinterestedness.

Robert represented to him that, though the possession of the collection must afford to any happy mortal capable of appreciating it the purest and most lasting gratification, not so much the pleasure of the individual as the preservation, the dignity, and the safe-keeping of the collection itself ought to be considered. Unhappily, he, Robert Meredith, was not likely to possess a house in which the treasure might be conveniently and suitably lodged, and it was a melancholy fact that neither Haldane nor his wife appreciated the collection; and, when the present owner of Chayleigh should be no more, and his bequest should have come into operation, there would arise the grievous necessity of dislodging the collection.

Under these circumstances—stated very carefully by Robert Meredith, who knew that his particular friend Mrs Haldane would bundle both James and the collection out

of doors with the smallest possible delay on the commencement of her absolute reign, unless indeed some very valuable
consideration should attach itself to her not doing so—he
suggested that Mr Carteret would do well to conquer his
objection to the 'merging' of the collection.   That it should
be ' merged ' after his death was a less painful contingency
to contemplate than that it should be destroyed or materially injured.   The best, the most effectual plan would be,
that Mr Carteret should bequeath the collection, on James
Dugdale's death, to his granddaughter, the heiress of the
Deane, with the request that it might be transferred thither,
there to remain as an heirloom for ever.   The old gentleman submitted with a sigh ; and this testamentary arrangement was actually made.

The friendship between Robert and Mrs Haldane, which
had commenced in his boyish admiration of her, and her
keen appreciation of the sentiment, remained unabated,
which, considering that the pretty and vivacious Lucy was
not conspicuous for steadiness of feeling, was not a little
remarkable.   Perhaps the lady believed in her secret soul,
as the years wore on, that she could have explained Robert's
not being a marrying man.

A strictly proper and virtuous British matron was Mrs
Haldane Carteret—a very dragon of propriety indeed, and a
lady who would not have received her own sister, if she had
been so unlucky as to ' get talked of '—and therefore this
insinuation must be fully explained, in order to prevent the
slightest misapprehension on the subject.   Lucy would have
been unspeakably shocked had it ever been said or thought
by any one that Robert Meredith entertained any feeling
warmer than the most strictly regulated friendship for her ;
but she did not object to a secret sentiment on her own part,
which sometimes found expression in reverie, and in a murmured ' poor boy,' in a little genial sense of satisfaction as
the time went by and Robert did not marry, and was not

talked of as likely to marry—when his polite attention to her underwent no alteration, and she still felt she enjoyed his confidence. Mrs Haldane was a little mistaken in the latter particular. She did *not* enjoy the confidence of Robert Meredith ; but neither was any other person in possession of that privilege, though it was one of the charms, or rather the achievements, of his manner, that he could convey the flattering impression to any one he pleased.

When Haldane and his wife were put, by the death of Mr Carteret, in possession of Chayleigh—an event which occurred seven years after Margaret's decease, and four years later than that of Mr Baldwin—James Dugdale continued to reside in the old house, which had been his home for so many years, only until the return of Lady Davyntry and her orphan nieces to England. Haldane Carteret, a ' good fellow ' in all the popular acceptation of the word, was rather a weak fellow also, especially where his pretty wife's whims or feelings were concerned ; and not all his sincere and grateful regard for his old friend could prevent his feeling relieved, when James told him he could not resist Lady Davyntry's pressing entreaty that he should take up his abode with her and ' the children.' Every one spoke of the orphan girls as ' the children,' and their fatherless and motherless estate was wonderfully tempered to them.

The Deane had been let by Mr Baldwin's executors for a long term of years ; but James Dugdale applied to the tenant in possession for permission to have the collection transferred thither, and received it. Thus Mrs Haldane was disembarrassed within a very short period of her father-in-law and his incomprehensible curiosities and of James Dugdale. To do her justice, Mrs Haldane was sorry for the gentle, quiet old man ; and it certainly was not with reference to him that she expressed her satisfaction, when all the flittings had been accomplished, in ' being at last the mistress of her own house.' There must have been a good deal of the imaginative faculty about Mrs Haldane Carteret when she rejoiced in her freedom from trammels; for it never could have occurred to anybody that she had not been thoroughly and indisputably the mistress of Chayleigh from the day of her arrival there. But there is a great deal in imagination, and Mrs Haldane knew her own business best.

When James Dugdale left Chayleigh, as a residence, for ever, the passion-flower which embowered the window of the room which had once been Margaret's, and had ever since been his, was in the full beauty and richness of its bloom. He cut a few twigs and leaves, and one or two of the grand solemn flowers, and took his leave of the room and the window and the tree. It was very painful, even after all those years—more painful than those to whom life is full of activity and change could conceive or would believe. But so thoroughly was this a final parting, and so truly did James Dugdale feel it so, that when, some time afterwards, Mrs Haldane, having read in some new medical treatise that 'green things'—as she generally termed everything that grew, from the cedar of Lebanon to the parsley of private life—were unwholesome on the walls of a house, had the passion-flower and the trellis cleared away, and the wall above the verandah neatly whitewashed, it hardly gave him a pang.

In all the changes which befell the family at Chayleigh, Robert Meredith had a certain share. Mr Carteret never ceased to like him, to look for his coming, to enjoy, in his quiet way, the adaptive young man's society. James never permitted the interest he had taken in him for his old friend's sake—his old friend dead and gone now, like all the rest—to flag or falter. Perhaps he held by that feeling all the more conscientiously that he had never been much drawn towards Robert Meredith individually. The feeling towards him which he and Margaret had shared at the first had remained with him always, like all his feelings; for it was part of the constitution of his mind, a part powerful for suffering, that he did not change.

When Lady Davyntry went abroad with 'the children' James Dugdale's life had become more than ever solitary; and, though conscious that he derived very little pleasure from Robert's presence, he encouraged the visits which Mrs Haldane was ever ready to invite.

But a day of still greater change came—a sad and heavy day to James Dugdale, and of tremendous loss and evil to the orphan girls. Lady Davyntry died—not suddenly, but unexpectedly—and the full responsibility of the guardianship of Gertrude and Eleanor Baldwin was thrown upon Haldane Carteret and James Dugdale. Davyntry, in which Mr Baldwin's sister had only a life interest, passed into the possession of the young man who had succeeded to the title on the death of Sir Richard Davyntry; and the choice of the guardians to the young girls, as to the future home of their wards, lay between Chayleigh and the Deane, of which it became possible for them to resume possession shortly after Lady Davyntry's death.

When the decision which assigned the Deane to the young heiresses as their future abode had been reached and acted upon, Robert Meredith naturally ceased to have much intercourse with the Carterets and with James Dugdale.

Haldane was very much pleased with the kind of life he led at the Deane. He made a first-rate 'country gentleman,' an ardent sportsman, a pleasant companion, hospitable, kind-hearted, *insouciant*, fond of the place and of everything in it, devoted to his wife—'absurdly so,' as the spinsters of the neighbourhood, a remarkably numerous class even for Scotland, declared—and most indulgent and affectionate to his nieces. This latter quality the aforesaid spinsters accounted for satisfactorily on the double grounds, that it was not likely he would be anything but indulgent to such rich girls—of course he expected to be well recompensed when they came into 'all their property'—and that, as he had no children of his own, he might very well care for his 'poor dear sister's fatherless girls.'

The worthy ex-captain of artillery knew little and cared less how people accounted for the strange phenomena of his fulfilling carefully and conscientiously a sacred duty. He was a good, happy, unsuspicious man, and 'the children' loved him better than any one in the world, except James Dugdale and Rose Doran.

Mrs Carteret was in the habit of 'going south' much more frequently than Haldane did so; she liked a few weeks in London in the season, and she scrupulously visited her own family, by whom she was regarded with much affection and admiration, not quite unmingled with awe.

The eldest Miss Crofton's 'match' had 'turned out' much better than the family had expected, and Lucy Carteret shone very brilliantly indeed in the reflected light shed upon her by the wealth and station of her husband's nieces and wards. On the occasion of her visits to England she always saw a good deal of Robert Meredith; and so—owing to the convenience of modern locomotion, Mrs Carteret's former home had been brought within easy reach of London —Robert was a not unfrequent guest of old Mr Crofton's when his daughter was sojourning there. Chayleigh had been advantageously let by Haldane for some years beyond the term of his nieces' minority.

On the last occasion of her 'going south' Mrs Carteret had been accompanied by Eleanor Baldwin, whose health, always delicate, had recently occasioned her uncle and aunt some anxiety. She had enjoyed her trip, and Robert had been very much with both ladies. Never had Mrs Carteret been more thoroughly convinced that he was one of the most charming of men; never had the secret suspicion, that she could, if she chose, explain the reason of his having re-

20

mained up to his present age unmarried, presented itself so frequently and so strongly to her mind.

Robert Meredith had been told by Mrs Carteret that Haldane intended to celebrate the attainment of her majority by the heiress of the Deane in splendid style, and he had received from her a pressing invitation to be present on the occasion. The time of year made it difficult for him to feel sure of being able to leave town ; but he promised that he would go to the Deane on that auspicious and delightful occasion, then six months in perspective, if he could possibly manage it.

It was during this visit of Mrs Carteret to London that George Ritherdon made her acquaintance, and saw for the first time one of 'the Baldwin children,' of whom he had heard occasional casual mention. Robert Meredith's ' chum ' pleased Mrs Carteret much, especially when he did the honours of the Temple Church to her and Eleanor ; and while explaining all the objects of interest and their associations, did so with a happy and successful assumption of merely refreshing their memory, which was indicative of the nicest tact. The general result was that, when Robert Meredith received a formal reminder of his promise to come to the Deane for Gertrude's birthday, the letter enclosed a pressing invitation to George Ritherdon to accompany his friend.

' Of course you'll come. There's much less to keep you in town than there is to keep me, for that matter, so you can't pretend to object,' said Meredith, as the friends were discussing their letters and their breakfast simultaneously.

'I should like it very much indeed,' said Ritherdon ; ' but—'

' Very well, of course you'll do it,' interrupted Meredith ; and was about to say something more, when the entrance of their ' mutual ' servant suspended the conversation.

The man addressed himself to Robert, with the information that a person was then waiting in the passage, who urgently requested to be admitted to see him ; that the person was an old man, not of remarkably prosperous appearance ; and that he had replied to the servant's remonstrance, on his presenting himself at such an unseemly hour, that he was sure Mr Meredith would see him, for he came from Australia, and from his own ' people ' there.

-Surprised, but by no means discomposed, Robert Meredith made no reply to the servant, but said to George Ritherdon,

' It sounds odd.   I suppose I ought to see him.'

' I think so, old fellow ; and I'll clear off; ' which he did.

' Show the old person from Australia in, William,' said Meredith to the servant, and added to himself, ' I wonder what he has got to say to me—nothing I need mind.   I should have had bad news by post, if there was any to send.

CHAPTER XXVII.

THE HEIRESS OF THE DEANE.

' ARE you nearly ready, girls ? ' asked Mrs Haldane Carteret of her nieces, as she entered the large dressing-room which divided the bed-rooms occupied by Gertrude and Eleanor Baldwin, and was joint territory, common of them both.

This apartment was very handsomely proportioned, and furnished in a sumptuous style.   It abounded in light and looking-glasses, and the two young girls then under the hands of their respective maids had the advantage of seeing themselves reflected many times in mirrors fixed and mirrors movable.   Their ball-room toilette was almost complete, and the smaller supplementary articles of their paraphernalia of adornment were strewn about the room in pretty profusion.

'We are very nearly ready, Aunt Lucy,' replied Eleanor;
'are there any people come yet?'

'Yes, the Congreves, and Rennies, and Comrie of Largs;
they always make a point of being the first arrivals and the
last departures everywhere,' said Mrs Carteret, as she profited
by the long mirror which formed the reverse of the door
by which she had entered to rearrange the folds of her remarkably becoming dress of blue satin and silver. 'Pray
make haste, Gerty. It does not so much matter about Nelly,
but you really must be in the reception-room before any
more people come. Just imagine your not being there
when Lord and Lady Gelston arrive, or even Sir Maitland
and Lady Cardeness.'

Mrs Haldane Carteret was a woman of 'perfectly well-
proportioned mind. She knew how to define the distinctions
of rank as accurately as a king-at-arms, and could balance
the comparative turpitude of a slight to a baron with that
of a slight to a baronet with quite a mathematical nicety of
precision.

'Almost ready, Aunt Lucy. Only my gloves and brace-
lets to put on, and then I am ready. But I certainly shall
not go down without Nelly; she would get on much better
without me than I should without her' (here the girl smiled
as her mother had smiled in the brief days of her happy and
contented love). 'We should have been ready sooner, but
that we took a final scamper off to the guests' rooms to see
how Rose had disposed of Mr Meredith and Mr Ritherdon.'

'Ah, by-the-by, I suppose they have arrived,' said Mrs
Carteret; 'I must go and see them. I will come back again,
and I hope you will both be ready.'

In a few minutes the preparations were complete, and
the two young girls were receiving the unequivocal compliments of their maids and their mirrors. Happy, joyous,
hopeful, handsome creatures they looked, as they stood,
their arms entwined, surveying their lithe, graceful, white-

robed figures with natural pride and very pardonable vanity.
The glance of the elder girl dwelt only passingly upon herself; it turned then to dwell upon her sister with delight,
with exultation.

'How beautiful you look, my darling Nelly! I am sure
no one in the room will be able to compare with you to-
night.'

'Not you, Gertrude? Are you not the queen of the ball
in every sense? Depend upon it, no one will have eyes to-
night for any one except the heiress of the Deane.'

'Then every one will be blind and foolish,' returned Gertrude, as she gave the speaker a sisterly push; 'and there
are a few whom I don't think that of, Nelly. Don't you
dread the idea of the speech-making at supper? I do, and
Uncle Haldane does, because he will have to return thanks
for me; and I'm sure everybody else does, because Lord
Gelston is so frightfully longwinded and historical, and so
tremendously well up in the history of all the Meritons and
all the Baldwins, and who married, and whom, and when
they did it, and there's no stopping him when he starts;
however, we must think of the dancing and the fun, and not
remember the dreadful speeches until they come to be made.'

'I dare say you won't mind them so much when the time
comes,' said Nelly, with the least touch of something unpleasant in her voice; 'at all events, I need not—they will
not make any speeches about *me*, that's a comfort!'

'My darling Nelly! as if I thought about it for *myself*. If
you must listen and look pleased at tiresomeness, what does
it matter of what is *apropos?* and where is the difference
between you and me?'

'Very present, very perceptible, after this day,' said
Nelly; 'no one will fail to keep it in mind. Did you not
notice what Aunt Lucy said? My being ready or not did
not matter, but the presence of "the heiress of the Deane"
was indispensable.

'I did hear it,' said Gertrude, turning a flushed cheek and a deprecatory glance upon her sister; 'and did you not hear what I said? But here come Aunt Lucy and Rose.'

The entry of Rose Doran was the signal for enthusiastic comments on the appearance of the two young girls, and the little cloud which had threatened for a moment to gather over the sisters was joyously dissipated. Mr Dugdale wished to see them in his sitting-room, Rose said, before they went down-stairs, and she had come to bring them to him.

'You'll have time enough to let the old gentleman have a peep at you, my darlings,' said the good woman, whose eyes were moist with the rising tears produced by many associations which almost overpowered the admiration and delight with which she regarded the girls; 'though there's a dale o' quality come, they're all in the study, makin' sure of their cloaks and things, or drinkin' coffee and chattin' to one another. So go to the old man, my girls; he won't keep ye a minute.'

'He surely won't disappoint us,' exclaimed Gertrude; 'he promised to come down, and he *must!*'

'So he will, alanna,' said Rose, using the same term of endearment, and in the same soothing tone, with which she had been wont to assuage Gertrude's griefs in her childhood —'never you fear, so he will, when the room is full, and he can get round behind the people to his own chair in the corner; only he wants a look at you all to himself first.'

'Then I will go on,' said Mrs Haldane in rather a vexed tone. 'You will find me in the morning-room; and pray, Gerty, make no delay.'

Then Mrs Haldane walked majestically away, her blue and silver train rustling superbly over the crimson-velvet carpet of the long, wide corridor, which, like the grand staircase, was of polished oak.

Mr Dugdale's rooms at the Deane were in a quiet and secluded part of the spacious house, attainable by a small staircase which was approached by a curtained archway opening off the corridor into which the girls' rooms opened. The rooms were handsome, though not large, and were luxuriously furnished, but they were chiefly remarkable for the numerous evidences of feminine care, taste, and industry in their arrangement. The comfortable and the ornamental were dexterously united in these rooms, in which needlework abounded, and whose most prized decorations were the work of the pencils of the two girls.

The apartments consisted of three rooms—bed-room, dressing-room, and sitting-room, the latter lined with books, and bearing many indications that the studies, tastes, and habits which had occupied James Dugdale's youth and manhood had lightened the burden of his infirmities, and taken the deadly sting out of his sorrows, were not abandoned now in his old age. And in truth this was the case; the feebleness which had invaded the delicate and sensitive frame more and more surely with each succeeding year, had not touched the mind. That was strong, active, bright, full of vitality still, promising extinction or even dimness only with the dissolution of the frame.

In his frequent fits of thinking about himself, and yet out of himself—as though he were contemplating the problems presented by the existence, and pondering the future, of another—James Dugdale was wont to wonder at his own tenacity of life. Ever since his youth he had been a sufferer in body, and had sustained great trials of mind; he had been always more or less feeble, and of the nervous febrile temperament which is said (erroneously) to wear itself out rapidly. But he had lived on and on, and the young, the strong, the prosperous, the happy, had passed before him, and been lost in the dimness of the separation of death.

He had been carefully dressed by his servant for the festivities of the evening, and had lain down upon the couch beside the windows of his sitting-room, from which a beau-

tiful view was to be had in the day-time, through which the
summer moonlight was streaming now, and had fallen into a
reverie.   His mind was singularly placid, his memory was
singularly clearly to-night, as he lay still, listening to the
stir in the house, his face turned from the light of the can-
dles which burned on the tables and the mantelpiece ; and
passing in mental review the persons and the events of long
years ago.

How perfectly distinct and vivid they were to-night—
his parents, his boyhood, the time when it was first discovered that he must never expect to be a healthy, vigorous man
—his student days and their associations, the friends of that
period of his life ! Hayes Meredith was a young man—how
curiously his memory reproduced him ; and then his cousin
Sibylla, his sole kinswoman and his steady friend—the old
man who had loved him so well, and the sad dark episode of
Margaret's marriage.   How plainly he could see Godfrey
Hungerford, and how distinctly he could recall the instinctive dislike, suspicion, repulsion he had caused him, and
which he early learnt to know was bitter jealousy ! Baldwin
and Lady Davyntry, that kind, sympathizing friend of later
days—she whom he still mourned with a poignancy which
time had blunted in the case of the others ;—it was hard to
understand, very wonderful to realize, that they were dead
and he alive—he went on with his ordinary life betimes, and
did not think about it much, but to-night it seemed impossible.

The wonderful incompleteness, the unmeaningness of
life, the phantasmagoria of fragmentary existences occupied
him, while all around him were preparations for a festival.
Lastly came the image of Margaret, back in all the freshness
of her youth, beauty, and happiness, as she had been twenty
years ago, and the old man wondered at the strange distinctness of his memory.

Twenty years ! a long, long time even at an earlier period

of life, a wonderfully long time at his, to keep the memory green. He had had and lost many friends, but only one love; yes, that was the explanation; that was why she, who had died young long ago, never to grow old, never to have any withering touch of time laid upon her beauty, she who was to be remembered as a radiant creature always, had never had a predecessor, a successor, or a rival in his heart; so there was no other image to trouble or confuse hers. The circumstances which had killed her, as he felt, as surely as disease had ever killed,—they, too, returned freshly to his memory; he seemed to live through those old, old days again, and in some degree to realize once more their keen anxiety and distress.

How it had all passed away—how little it had really mattered—how little anything really mattered, after all, except the other world, and the reunion there, without which life, the most renowned as much as the meanest, would indeed be 'a tale told by an idiot,' and, in the multitude of the ages, and the spanlike brevity of its own duration, 'signifying nothing'! It seemed like a dream, and yet it was all real: she had lived and suffered, feared, foreseen, and died under this very roof, beneath which he dwelt, and from which its master went forth a patient, but none the less a broken-hearted man, to die afar off, to lie in the solemn dust of the grand old world.

Were they, the two whom he remembered so well in their youth and love and happiness, any nearer to him than the most ancient of the ancient dead? Was there any difference or degree in all that inconceivable separation? Who could tell him that? Who could still the pang, which time can never lessen, which comes with the immeasurable change? We are in time and space, and they, the dead, are, as we say, beyond their bounds, set free from them. What, then, is their share with us?

He was thinking of these things, which indeed were

wont to occupy his mind when he was very peaceful and alone, and thinking also how very brief all our uncertainty is—how short a time the Creator keeps His creatures in ignorance and suspense, and that he was very near to the lifting of the curtain—when Gertrude and Eleanor Baldwin came into the room, and gaily challenged his admiration of their ball-dresses, their wreaths, their bouquets, and their general appearance.

With the keenly strong remembrance of Margaret which he had been dwelling upon freshly before him, James Dugdale was struck by the likeness which Gertrude presented to her mother. Her face was more strictly handsome, her figure promised to be fuller and grander, but the resemblance in feature, in gesture, in voice, in all the subtler affinities which constitute the truth of such resemblance, was complete. Had she stood thus, in her white dress, flower-crowned, by his couch, alone, James Dugdale might have thought the spirit world had unbarred its portals for a little to give him a glimpse of Margaret in her eternal youth; but her arm was linked in that of her sister, and the old man's gaze included them both.

'Do I like you, you witches?' said Mr Dugdale; 'what a question! I think you are both incomparably perfect, and among all the compliments you will hear to-night, I don't think you will have a more satisfactory one than that. I see you are wearing your pearls, Nelly.—Where are your diamonds, Miss Baldwin?'

Gertrude blushed, and looked a little uncomfortable.

'I would rather not wear them,' she said; 'pearls don't matter much, but diamonds would make too much difference between Nelly and me. I asked Uncle Haldane, and he said I certainly need not wear them unless I liked; indeed, ho said it is better taste for an unmarried woman, while she is very young, not to wear diamonds; so they are undisturbed in all their grandeur.'

'Isn't she ridiculous?' said Eleanor. 'I am sure if I were in her place I should wear my diamonds, especially to-night.'

'I am quite sure you would do no such thing, Nelly,' said Miss Baldwin; 'and we must go now, or Aunt Lucy will be put out.—Mind you come down soon; I shall be looking out for you.'

Then the two girls kissed the old man affectionately and left him. There was some trouble in James Dugdale's mind when the light forms disappeared, and he listened to the murmur of their voices for a few moments, before it died away when they reached the grand staircase.

'If Eleanor were in Gertrude's place!' The girl's words had struck a chord of painful remembrance in the old man's mind. The time had come now when the wrong done to the younger by the elder, the wrong done to the children by the parents in all unconsciousness, was to bear its first fruits. As the years had gone by, and especially since Lady Davyntry's death had left James Dugdale sole possessor of the knowledge of the truth, he had remembered it but seldom.

When the news of Mr Baldwin's death had reached England, he and Lady Davyntry had spoken together much and solemnly of the mysterious dealings of Providence with the family. They had silently accepted his resolution—never to give Margaret a successor in his heart and house—and, in view of that determination, they had regarded the arrangement which he had made of his property as in every respect wise and commendable. But they had secretly hoped that time, whose unfailing influence, however disliked or even struggled against, they both had too much experience of life to doubt or dispute, would modify and finally upset Mr Baldwin's resolution on that point, and that the girls might eventually be removed from what they wisely regarded as a perilous and undesirable position.

Wealth and station would always be theirs, even if a second marriage should give a male heir to the Deane.

But these hopes were not destined to be realized. Mr Baldwin never returned from his journey to the East, and the heavy weight of heiress-ship fell upon his daughters in their childhood. Of late years the secret of which he alone was in possession had begun to appear dreamlike and mythical to James Dugdale. It had been a terrible thing in its time, but that time was past and its terror with it, and it was only an old memory now—an old memory which Nelly's words had awakened, just when he did not care to have it evoked, just when it was as painful as it ever could be any more.

The old man rose from his couch and went to a bookcase with glass doors, which faced the mantelpiece in his sitting-room. On one of the lower shelves, within easy reach of his hand, lay a large blue-velvet casket. He took it out, set it on the table, and opened it. It contained a picture—the portrait of Margaret with her infant in her arms, which she had had painted for him at Naples twenty years before. The portrait was surrounded by a frame of peculiar design. It consisted of a wreath of passion-flowers, the stems and leaves in gold, the flowers in white enamel, with every detail of form and colouring accurately carried out. This was the only jeweller's work which had ever been done by James Dugdale's order; this was the most valuable article in every sense in his possession. He placed the picture on the table, and sat down before it and looked at it intently, studying in every line the likeness which had impressed him so deeply to-night; and then he replaced it in the casket, which he re-consigned to the bookcase. This done, he rang for his servant and went down to the ball-room, whence delightful strains of brilliant music were issuing, blended with the sound of voices and the tread of dancing feet.

The scene was a beautiful one. All that money, taste,

and goodwill could accomplish to render the fête given in celebration of Gertrude's birthday successfully charming, had been done, and the result was eminently satisfactory. Many of the guests had come from distances which in England would have been regarded as invincible obstacles—would indeed have rendered the sending of invitations a meaningless, or according to our amiable insular phrase a 'French,' compliment—but which in Scotland were regarded as mere matters of course. An unusual number of pretty girls adorned the ball-room, and they danced with pleasure and animation also peculiarly Scotch.

Gertrude had gone through the ordeal of congratulation very well; and now, very much relieved that that part of the business had come to a conclusion, was dancing a surprisingly animated quadrille with Lord Gelston, while Lady Gelston was talking superlatives to Haldane Carteret, who had wisely decided, some years before, on coming to live in Scotland, that there was more to be gained than lost by being understood at once to be excluded from the category of dancing men.

The room, much longer than its width, and beautifully decorated and lighted, was amply occupied without being over-filled; and the splendid many-coloured dresses, the moving figures, the soft sound of speech and laughter, the indescribable joyous rustle which pervades an assemblage where youth and beauty are in the majority, made up a scene to whose attraction James Dugdale's nerves vibrated strangely. He had been present on few similar occasions in his life, and he looked about him with the pleased curiosity of a child. The military contingent had duly arrived from Edinburgh, Leith, and Hamilton, and were enjoying their accustomed popularity.

Of the many faces in the room there were few known to James Dugdale, with the exception of those of the near neighbours to the Deane. Before he had time to become

familiar with the movement and the glitter of the unaccustomed scene, a pause occurred in the dancing, and the group
nearest to him broke up and moved away. Then he saw
Eleanor Baldwin talking to a gentleman whose figure
seemed very familiar to him, though he could not see his
face. Eleanor was looking up at the gentleman, her face
full of light and animation, a rich colour in her cheeks, her
dark eyes sparkling with pleasure. Almost as soon as he
saw her, she saw him, and said :

'Oh, there's Uncle James ; let us go and speak to him.'

She walked quickly across the room, followed by her
companion, who was, as James Dugdale then perceived,
Robert Meredith. The old man and the man no longer
young indeed, but still and ever a boy to him, greeted each
other warmly.

'When did you come, Robert ? Why have I not seen
you before ? '

'We came down by the mail, sir, and found the ladies
gone to dress ; and Mrs Doran said you were resting, in
preparation for the fatigue of the evening, so we would not
disturb you. I am glad to see you looking so well, sir.'

'Thank you, Robert—where's Ritherdon ? '

'He has gone in chase of Gerty, Uncle James,' said
Eleanor; 'he wants to know what dances she can spare
him, I believe ; but I fancy he has not much chance—*even
I* could only promise positively for one.'

Robert Meredith looked at her narrowly as he said :

'Ritherdon has pluck, I must say. I never dreamed of
such a privilege as dancing to-night with the lady of the
Deane. But I did calculate upon a *raccroc de noces* for to-
morrow—I suppose that's safe ? '

'I suppose so,' said Eleanor.

'*You* kept a few dances for me, didn't you ? ' he asked.

'Yes, I did, but I am nobody, you know.'

'This is one of them,' said Meredith, and then, as he led

her away into the throng, again set in motion by the music, he said meaningly, 'and I do not know,—at least, *I do*.'

His arm was round her now, and he had whirled her into the circle of waltzers, and the girl felt that the bright scene was brighter, the music sweeter and more inspiriting, the dance more delightful, because of the words and the tone in which he had spoken them.

George Ritherdon had been quite as unsuccessful in his quest as Eleanor had foreseen, and as soon as Gertrude had convinced him of his ill-fortune, by permitting him to read the record of the pretty little ivory and silver *carnet* which hung at her waist, he, in his turn, made his way to Mr Dugdale's chair. There he remained until Nelly's one dance should be 'due,' talking with the old man, who was wonderfully bright and unwearied of things in general, and of the young ladies in particular.

It was an unfashionable peculiarity of George Ritherdon's that he was always deferential towards age, even when age was much less venerable and less intelligent, much more *arrière* than in the case of Mr Dugdale. Therefore, let the subjects on which the old gentleman had chosen to talk with him have been as dull and uninteresting to him as possible, he would have exerted himself to converse about them pleasantly, and with the air of attention and interest which is the truest conversational politeness.

But in the present instance no effort was required. Ritherdon felt a sincere and growing interest in 'the children,' as Mr Dugdale soon began to call them in talking to him, and found something which appealed to his heart— strangely soft, pure, and upright in its impulses, considering the length of time it had pulsated amid the world,—in the long-enduring, constant family friendship which bound the old man's life up with that of these young people, who were no kin of his. The ball was the gayest, the most success-ful, in George Ritherdon's opinion, at which he had ever

' assisted,' the night a happy and memorable one in his life ;
but no part of it was more thoroughly enjoyable to him than
the time he passed seated by the old man's side, their conversation interrupted only by the people who came up to
speak to Mr Dugdale, and by the girls, who paid him flying
visits.

Robert Meredith and his friend saw little of each other
during the night, until after James Dugdale had retired,
which he did when supper was announced. That sumptuous entertainment was as terrible an ordeal as Gertrude
had expected. Lord Gelston was as inexorably long-winded,
as overwhelmingly genealogical as usual ; and if anything
could have made her more uncomfortable than the ponder-
ous congratulations of the noble lord, and the marked attentions of Lady Gelston and the Honourable Mr Dort, the
eldest son of the distinguished but by no means wealthy
pair, it would have been the kindly but inartistic efforts of
her Uncle Haldane, who was neither a ready thinker nor
an adept at speaking, to express how far short of her personal qualities fell the gifts of wealth and station allotted
to her.

A very decent amount of general attention was bestowed
upon Lord Gelston and Haldane Carteret, and the speeches
of both were received with all proper enthusiasm ; but there
was one listener who heard them with more than the attention of politeness, and with a smile on his lips which, if ' the
children's ' dead mother saw it, must have reminded her of
one she had known and disliked in earthly days long ago.
But even the speeches were over at last, and the younger
guests left the banquet and returned to the ball-room, and
dancing recommenced. Nothing equals in vigour and per-
severance Scotch dancing, no entertainment is capable of
such preternatural prolongation as a Scotch ball. The in-
stitution might be the modern successor of the feasts of the
Norsemen in the Bersekyr days.

'Do these people ever intend to leave off, do you think ?' George Ritherdon asked of Robert Meredith, when the external light had become difficult of exclusion, and all the dowagers had given over talking and taking refreshment, except that of slumber.

'I don't know indeed; doesn't look like it; but there's no reason why we shouldn't,' returned Meredith; 'let us say good-morning to Mrs Carteret, and decamp.'

A masterly manœuvre, which they put into instant execution, unobserved by any one but Eleanor Baldwin. She had danced several times with Meredith during the night, and had contrived to give Ritherdon 'one more' in addition to the promised valse; she had been very gay, happy, and animated; much admired and fully conscious of it; but now she grew tired, and began to wish the ball were over. People were unreasonable to keep it up so late; this was making a toil of a pleasure; no, she really could not join in this interminable cotillon. She wondered whether Aunt Lucy would mind her leaving the room; she would find her and ask her. So she did find Mrs Haldane Carteret, who was looking rather yellow and elderly in the mixed intrusive light, and Mrs Haldane answered her rather snappishly.

'Yes, yes, of course you may go. It is really absurdly late; no wonder you're tired; I am sure I am. Gerty must remain of course, but you may go.'

Eleanor had got the permission she desired, and she left the room, but not gladly. The manner of that permission did not please her; many little things of the same kind had hurt her lately; and as she slowly mounted the stairs her face was dark, and she muttered to herself,

'Gerty must of course remain, but you may go.'

An hour later, when the morning had fairly asserted its sway, when the latest lingering of the guests not staying in

the house had departed, fortified by hot strong coffee against
the fatigue of their homeward route, when to those staying
in the house welcome announcement had been made that
breakfast was to be served at twelve, and continued for an
indefinite time,—Gertrude Baldwin entered her dressing-
room.   She had desired that her maid should not remain
up, and having glanced into Eleanor's bed-room, and seen
that she was asleep, she took off her ball-dress, set the windows wide open, and sat down in her dressing-gown, letting
the sweet morning air play upon her face to calm the hurry
of her spirits and to think.

This had been an eventful day for that young girl; indeed, the whole preceding week, during which her guardians,
Haldane Carteret and James Dugdale, had explained to her
in resigning their trust all the particulars of her position,
had been of great moment in her life.   Previously she had
known, vaguely, that she was very rich, and she had had a
tolerably clear notion of the origin and ordering of her
wealth, but she fully understood it now.   Her uncle had
wished her to give her attention to the accounts of the
estate, as he explained them to her, and she had complied
with his wish.   In the course of these transactions she had
been shown her father's will, and had been made acquainted
as minutely with her sister Eleanor's position as with her
own.

The time up to that day had been so full of business, and
all the hours of the day and night just gone had been so full
of pleasure, that she felt strongly the need of a little leisure
and solitude now.   She was glad Nelly was asleep, glad she
had not been obliged to talk over the ball with her—glad to
put the ball itself out of her thoughts for a little, although
she had enjoyed it with all the unaffected zest of her age.

Gertrude was not tired; she had danced incessantly,
and the emotions of the day had been many and various
but she was strong and very happy, in all the unruffled

peace of her girlhood, which had only progressed hitherto
in prosperity, and she rarely felt fatigue. The fresh morning air, the calm, the solitude, were better for her than
sleep. Presently a delicious stillness fell on everything;
no more doors were shut or opened, no desultory footsteps
loitered about; the birds' music only filled the air with the
most beautiful of the sounds of morning.

There came with the day to Gertrude a sense of change.
She realized her womanhood now—she realized her position,
and it appeared to her a very solemn and responsible one.
Her uncle had told her, in answer to her request, that he
would continue to exercise the functions from which the
attainment of her majority formally discharged him—that
he would do so provided she would take an active part in
the conduct of the estate, urging the necessity which existed
for her duly qualifying herself for the independent adminis-
tration of her affairs in the future. He reminded her that
she could only hold the property in trust for her children,
if she were destined to become a wife and mother, and must
therefore learn how to save from her large income.

'You see, my dear,' Haldane had said to her, 'everything
not included in the entail is left absolutely to Nelly, and in
this respect she is better off than you are. She is not indeed so rich, but she can dispose of her property, by settlement and by will, just as she pleases, whereas you cannot
dispose of a shilling. Your eldest son, or your eldest daughter, if you have no son, must inherit all. The estate is
chargeable for the benefit of younger children to a very
small extent. I will show you how and how much presently.
The fortune your grandfather gave to your aunt, Lady
Davyntry, and which Eleanor inherits from her, was almost
entirely derived from accumulations and other extraneous
property. So, you see, Nelly's money is more absolutely
hers than yours is yours; but though you have not so much
freedom, there is one advantage in your position. If you

fall into bad hands, which God forbid, and we will take all possible care to prevent—yes, Gerty, don't look so horrified, my child, all the men in the world are not good, as your poor mother could have told you—your money will be safe; no man can beggar *you ;* whereas Eleanor would be quite helpless in such a case. There is nothing to protect her; her husband, if he could only persuade her to marry without a strict settlement, could make ducks and drakes of her money, if he chose.'

' But surely she never would be persuaded to do anything so foolish and so unprincipled,' said Gertrude, with a pretty air of dignity, woman-of-the-worldishness, and landed proprietor combined, and feeling already as if she had the deepest appreciation of the rights, privileges, and duties of property.

' I don't know that, my dear,' said Haldane; ' women are easily persuaded to folly, and there are men who have a knack of persuading you that imprudence is generosity, and self-sacrifice proved by endangering other people's peace and prosperity—as your poor mother could also have told you. However, we need not make ourselves prematurely uncomfortable about Nelly. Let us hope her choice may be wise and happy, and that she may use the freedom her father and her aunt left her with discretion.'

The discussion then turned upon other matters of business, and this part of the subject was abandoned.

It returned to Gertrude Baldwin's thoughts as she looked pensively abroad on her wide domains in the early morning, and it troubled her.

' We were both so little when he left us,' she thought, ' that I don't think my father could have preferred Nelly very much to me, and my mother only saw her for a minute before she died. Rose told me she had scarcely strength to hold the baby to her breast, and not strength enough to speak a word to it, so she cannot have loved her more than me; I was with her for a little time—it is very strange. What care has been taken to give her all he could give; and nothing left to me for my own self, on account of my own self! And how strange Uncle James looked when I said so! I am sure he understands that I feel it and wonder at it.

'How little I know of my mother, and I so like her, he says! Perhaps I am old enough now for them to tell me more about her and that first marriage of hers, which I am sure must have been something dreadful. I will ask Uncle James some day when he is very well. Aunt Lucy has never told us anything but that she and mamma were great friends, and mamma was "a dear thing." Somehow I don't like to hear our dear dead mother spoken of as "a dear thing"—absurd, I dare say, but I do not; and dear Aunt Eleanor never talked of her as anything but papa's wife—his idolized wife.

'How well I remember when I first began to understand that he died of her loss in reality, though it took time to kill him, because he was good and patient and tried to be resigned! But he could not live longer without her, and God knew it and did not ask him. I remember so well when Aunt Eleanor told me that, and seemed to know it so well, that she could better bear to know that he was dead than to know that he was still wandering about, because there was no home for him here. I wonder was he very fond of us—or perhaps he was not able to be. I am sure he tried. Ah, well! this we can never, never know until we are orphan children no longer; and any doubt dishonours him.

'To think that I am so important a personage, the owner of a great estate, the employer of so many of my fellow-creatures,—with so much power in my weak woman's hands for good or for evil,—and that I am all this solely because of great misfortune—solely because I am an orphan! If they were living, there might indeed have been rejoicing here to-day, for our pleasure and our parents' pride; but no more. It is wonderful to think of that,—wonderful to think of what might have been. Shall I be a good woman, I wonder? Shall I be a faithful steward? I don't know—I am so ignorant; but for Uncle James, I am so lonely. At least I will try—for my father's sake, and mamma's, and his, and for my own sake and for God's; but oh, I wish, I wish I could have found in my father's will anything, however trifling, which he desired to come to me from him, for my own sake.'

Tears were standing in the dark, clear gray eyes of the young lady of the Deane, and she had forgotten all about the birthday ball.

CHAPTER XXVIII.

THE 'RACCROC DE NOCES.'

THE breakfast-table at the Deane was but scantily furnished with guests at noon on the day after the ball, and only among the younger portion of that restricted number did the spirit of 'talking it over' prevail. The gentlemen, with the exception of George Ritherdon, discussed their breakfast and their newspapers, and the matrons were decidedly sleepy and a little cross. George was in high spirits. He had very thorough notions on the subject of enjoying a holiday, and he included among them the delight of escaping from the obligation of reading newspapers.

'Look at your friend, Mr What's-his-name, of some queer place, like Sir Walter Scott's novels,' he whispered to Gertrude. 'The idea of coming on a brief visit to Paradise, and troubling your head about foreign politics and the money-market! There he goes—Prussia, indeed! What a combination of ideas—Bochum Dollfs and the Deane!'

Gertrude laughed. The pleasant unaffected gaiety of

his manner pleased her. She had not been prepared to find George Ritherdon so light of heart, so ready to be amused, and to acknowledge it. She knew that he was younger than his chum Robert Meredith ; but she had fancied there would be some resemblance between them, when she should come to know them better, in a few days' close association with them. But there was no resemblance ; the friendship between them, the daily companionship had brought about no assimilation, and there was one circumstance which set Gerty thinking and puzzling to find out why it should be so. She had known Robert Meredith for years; her acquaintance with George Ritherdon was of the slightest; and yet, when the day after the ball came in its turn to a conclusion, and she once again set her mind to the task of 'thinking it over,' she felt that she knew more of George Ritherdon, had seen more certain indications of his disposition, and could divine more of his life, than she knew, had seen, or could divine in the case of Robert Meredith. The girl was of a thoughtful speculative turn of mind, an observer of character, and imaginative. She pondered a good deal upon the subject, and constantly recurred to her first thought. 'How odd it is that I should feel as if I could tell at once how Mr Ritherdon would act in any given case, and I don't feel that in the least about Robert Meredith !'

'I was horribly ill-treated last night,' George said, after he and Gertrude had exchanged ideas on the subject of newspapers in vacation time. 'You ask me to a ball, Miss Baldwin, and then don't give me a dance. I call it treacherous and inhospitable.'

'I couldn't help it,' said Gerty earnestly, with perfect simplicity. 'I had to "dance down the set," as they say in the country dances—to begin at the beginning of the table of precedence, and go on to the end.'

'A very unfair advantage for the fogeys,' said George

Ritherdon, not without having made sure that none of Gertrude's partners of last night were at the table.

'The Honourable Dort would be grateful if he heard
you, Ritherdon,' observed Meredith.

'I suppose one couldn't reasonably call *him* a fogey,' returned George.

Gertrude laughed ; but Eleanor said sharply,

'No, he is only a fool.'

Meredith was seated next her, and while the others went
on talking, he said to her in a low tone,

'Do you think him a fool ? I don't. He knows the
value of first impressions, and being early in the field, or I
am much mistaken.'

If Robert Meredith had made a similar remark to Gertrude, she would simply have looked at him with her grave
gray eyes, in utter ignorance of his meaning ; but Nelly
understood him perfectly.

'He *is* an admirer of Gerty's,' she said.

'And a more ardent admirer of the Deane,' said Meredith. 'Do you like him ?'

'Not at all. Not that it matters whether I do or not ;
but Gerty does not either. I dare say Lord and Lady Gelston think it would be a very good thing.'

'No doubt they do. Nothing more suitable could be
devised ; and as people of their class usually believe that
human affairs are strictly regulated according to their convenience, and look upon Providence as a kind of confidential
and trustworthy agent, more or less adroit, but entirely in
their interests, no doubt they have it all settled comfortably.
There was the complacent ring of such a plan in that pomp-
ous old donkey's bray last night, and a kind of protecting
mother-in-law-like air about the old woman, which I should
not have liked had I been in your sister's place.'

Eleanor's cheek flushed ; the tone, even more than the
words, told upon her.

'What detestable impertinence!' she said. 'The idea of people who are held to be nobler than others making such calculations, and condescending to such meanness for money!'

'Not in the least surprising; as you will find when you know the world a little better. That the wind should be tempered to the shorn lambs of the aristocracy by the intervention of commoner people's money, they regard as a natural law; and as they are the most irresponsible, they are the most shameless class in society. As to their condescending to meanness for money, you don't reflect—as, indeed, how should you?—that money is the object which best repays such condescension.'

There was a dubious look in Nelly's face. The young girl was flattered and pleased that this handsome accomplished man of the world—who was so much more *her* friend, in consequence of their association in London, than her sister's—should talk to her thus, giving her the benefit of his experience; and yet there might be something to be said, if not for Mr Dort's parents, for Mr Dort himself. Her colour deepened, as she said timidly,

'How well *you* must know the world, to be able to discern people's motives and see through their schemes so readily! But perhaps Mr Dort really cares for Gertrude.'

'Perhaps he does. She is a nice girl; and if her fortune and position don't spoil her, any man might well "care for her," as you call it, for herself. But the disinterestedness of Mr Dort is not affected, to my mind, by the fact that the appendage to the fortune he is hunting does not happen to be disagreeable. Supposing she had not the fortune, or supposing she lost it, would Mr Dort care for—that is, marry —your sister then?'

'I don't suppose he would,' said Eleanor thoughtfully.

'And I am sure he would not,' said Meredith. Then, as there was a general rising and dispersion of the company, he added in a whisper, and with a glance beneath which the girl's eyes fell, 'The privilege of being loved for herself is the proudest any woman can boast, and cannot be included in an entail.'

'Mr M'Ilwaine wants to see you for half-an-hour, Gertrude, before he returns to Glasgow,' said Haldane Carteret to his niece as she was leaving the breakfast-room, accompanied by Nelly and two young ladies who formed part of the 'staying company' at the Deane.

'Does he?' said Gertrude. 'What for? It won't take me half-an-hour to bid him good-bye.'

'Business, my dear, business,' said her uncle. 'You are a woman of business now, you know, and must attend to it.'

'I wonder how often I have had notice of *that* fact,' said Gerty. 'I will go to Mr M'Ilwaine now, uncle; but you must come too, please.—And, Nelly, will you take all the people to the croquet-ground? I will come as soon as I can.'

Gertrude went away with her uncle, and Nelly led the way to an ante-room, in which garden-hats and other articles of casual equipment were to be found.

'It is to be hoped Captain Carteret will not keep on reminding Miss Baldwin of her duties and dignities,' whispered Meredith to Eleanor, as the party assembled on the terrace. 'It will be embarrassing if he does, though she carries it off well, with her pretty air of unconsciousness.'

Eleanor said nothing in answer, but her face darkened, and the first sentence she spoke afterwards had a harsh tone in it.

The day was very fine, the summer heat was tempered by a cool breeze, and the glare of the sun was softened by flitting fleecy clouds. The group collected on the beautifully-kept croquet-ground of the Deane was as pretty and as picturesque as any which was to be seen under the summer sky that day. Mrs Haldane Carteret, who was by no means ' a frisky matron,' but who enjoyed unbroken animal spirits and much better health than she could have been induced to acknowledge, was particularly fond of croquet, which, as her feet and ankles were irreproachable, was not to be wondered at. She was an indefatigable, a perfectly good-humoured player, and owed not a little of her popularity in the neighbourhood to her ever-ready willingness to get up croquet-parties at home, or to go out to them.

Haldane too was not a bad or a reluctant player; and, on the whole, the Deane held a creditable place in the long list of country houses much devoted to this popular science.

Miss Congreve and her sister ' perfectly doated on' croquet, and all the young men were enthusiasts in the art, except George Ritherdon, who played too badly to like it, and had never gotten over the painful remembrance of having once caused a young lady, whose face was fairer than her temper, to weep tears of spite and wrathfulness by his blunders in a ' match.'

'How long is this going to last ? ' George asked Meredith, when the game was fairly inaugurated, and the animation of the party proved how much to their taste their proceedings were.

Meredith did not answer until he had watched with narrow and critical interest the stroke which Nelly was then about to make. When the ball had rolled through the hoop, and it was somebody else's turn, he said,

'Until such time as, having breakfasted at twelve with the prospect of dining at seven, we can contrive to fancy that we want something to eat, I suppose.'

'Well, then, as I don't play, and cannot flatter myself I shall be missed, I shall go in, write some letters, and have a stroll. You will tell Miss Baldwin I don't play croquet, if she should do me the honour to remark my absence ? '

'Certainly,' said Meredith ; and as George turned away, he said to Eleanor,

'I will tell your sister, if she likes, that George does not play croquet or any other game.'

She looked up inquiringly.

'No,' he said ; 'he is the most thoroughly honest—indeed, I might say the only thoroughly honest—man, who has not any brains, of my acquaintance. *He* won't lay siege to the heiress, and have no eyes for anybody else, no matter how superior ; and yet a little or a good deal of money would be as valuable to George as to most men, I believe.'

'I thought Mr Ritherdon seemed very much taken with Gertrude,' said Nelly, who had ceased for the moment to perform the mystic evolutions of the noble game, in a confidential tone, into which she had unconsciously dropped when speaking to Meredith.

'No doubt, so he is ; but if she imagines he is going to be an easy conquest—to propose and be rejected—she will be mistaken.'

A little while ago, and who would have dared to speak in such a tone of her sister to Eleanor Baldwin ? Whom would she have believed, who should have told her that she could have heard unmoved insinuations almost amounting to accusations of that sister's vanity, pride, and coquetry ? The sweet poison of flattery was taking effect, the deadly plant of jealousy was taking ready root.

'I suppose,' she said, 'every man who comes to the house will be set down as a *prétendant* of Gertrude's—that is to be expected. If any man of our acquaintance has real self-respect, he will keep away.'

'Indeed !' said Meredith. 'Would you make no exceptions to so harsh a rule ?—not in favour of those to whom Miss Baldwin would be nothing, except your sister?'

'Nelly, Nelly, what are you about ? You are moonstruck, I think !' exclaimed Mrs Haldane Carteret, whose superabundant alertness could not brook an interval in the game ; and Eleanor was absolved by this direct appeal from any necessity to take notice of the words spoken by Meredith.

No immediate opportunity of again addressing Eleanor arose, so Meredith divided his attentions, in claiming her due share of which Mrs Carteret was very exacting, among the party in general, which was shortly reinforced by the arrival of a number of visitors from the 'contagious countries,' and, conspicuous among them, Mr Dort. This honourable young gentleman, though all his parents and friends could possibly desire, in point of fashion, was perhaps a little less than people in general might have desired in point of brains. Indeed, he possessed as little of that important ingredient in the composition of humanity as was at all consistent with his keeping up his animal life and keeping himself out of an idiot asylum.

In appearance he was rather prepossessing; for he had a well-bred not-too-pretty face, 'nice' hair (and a capital valet, who rarely received his wages), a tolerably good figure, and better taste in dress than is usually combined with fatuity. He never talked much, which was a good thing for himself and his friends. He had a dim kind of notion that he did not get at his ideas, or at any rate did not put them in words, with quite so much facility as other people did, and so, actuated by a feeble gleam of common sense, he remained tolerably silent in general. As he naturally enjoyed the aristocratic privilege of not being required to exert himself for anybody's good or convenience, he experienced no sort of awkwardness or misgiving when, on making a call, after the ordinary greeting of civilized life (with all the r's eliminated, and all the words jumbled together), he remained perfectly silent, in contemplation of the chimneypiece, except when a dog was present, then he pulled its ears, until the conclusion of his visit. He was very harmless, except to tradespeople, and not unamiable—rather cheerful and happy indeed than otherwise, though his habitual expression was one of vapid discontent. He would have made it sar-

donic if he could, but he couldn't; he had too little nose
and not enough moustache for that, and his strong-minded
mamma had advised him to give it up.

'I know your Cousin Adolphus does it,' Lady Gelston
said indulgently; 'but just consider his natural advantages.
Don't do it, Matthew; you *can't* sneer with an upper lip
like yours; and, besides, why *should* you sneer?'

'There's something in that, ma'am, certainly,' returned
her admiring son, with his usual deliberation. 'I really
don't see why I should; because, you see, I ain't clever
enough for people to expect it:' which was the cleverest
thing the Honourable Matthew had ever said, up to that
period of his existence.

The young ladies in the neighbourhood rather liked Mr
Dort.   He was a good deal in Scotland, chiefly because he
found an alarming scarcity of ready money was apt to set in,
after he had made a comparatively short sojourn in London,
and each time this happened he would remark to his friends,
in the tone and with the manner of a discoverer,

'And there are things one *must* have money for, don't
you know? one can't tick for everything—cabs, and waiters,
and so on, don't you know?'

This unhappy perversity of circumstances brought the
Honourable Matthew home to his ancestral castle earlier,
and caused him to remain there longer, than was customary
with the territorial magnates; and Lord and Lady Gelston
were, also for sound pecuniary reasons, all-the-year-rounders,
and very good neighbours with every family entitled to that
distinction.   The young ladies, then, liked Mr Dort.   He
was useful, agreeable, and 'safe.'   Now this peculiar-sound-
ing qualification was one which, however puzzling to the uninitiated, was thoroughly understood in the neighbourhood,
and its general acceptation made things very pleasant.

The young ladies might like Mr Dort, and Mr Dort
might and did like the young ladies, without any risk of un-

due expectations being excited, or female jealousies and rivalries being aroused. Every one knew that Mr Dort's parents intended their son to marry an heiress, and that Mr Dort himself was quite of their opinion. When the appointed time and the selected heiress should come, the young ladies were prepared to give up Mr Dort with cheerfulness. Perhaps they hoped the chosen heiress might be ugly, and certainly they hoped she would 'behave properly to the neighbourhood,' but there their single-minded cogitations stopped. A good deal of the feudal spirit lingered about the Gelston precincts, and if the son of the Lord and the Lady, the heir of the undeniably grand, if rather out-at-elbows, castle, had been a monk, or a married man, he could hardly have been more secure from a design on the part of any young lady to convert herself into the Honourable Mrs Dort.

The pleasantest unanimity of feeling prevailed in the community respecting him, and all the married ladies declared they 'quite felt for dear Lady Gelston,' in her natural anxiety to 'have her son settled.' Her son was not particularly anxious about it himself, but then it was not his way to be particularly anxious about anything but the 'sit' of his garments, and the punctuality of his meals, and this indifference was normal. Local heiresses were not plentiful in the vicinity of Gelston, but Lady Gelston did not trust to the home supply. She had long ago enlisted the sympathies and the services of such of her friends as enjoyed favourable opportunities for 'knowing about that sort of thing,' and who either had no sons, or such as were happily disposed of. She was a practically-minded woman, and fully alive to the advantage of securing as many resources as possible.

Lady Gelston would have been perfectly capable of the insolence of considering her son's success in the case of the local heiresses—*par excellence,* Miss Baldwin—perfectly indubitable, but of the folly she was not capable. He would have a very good chance, she felt convinced, and she was determined he should try it as soon as it would be decently possible for him to do so.

'Matt is not the only young man of rank she will meet, even here,' said the lady, when she condescended to explain her views to her acquiescent lord.

Who, be it observed, was quite as well convinced of the advantages of the alliance, and quite as anxious it should take place, as his wife; but who preferred repose to action, gave her ladyship credit for practical ability and a contrary taste, and entertained a general idea that scheming in all its departments had better be left to a woman.

'Matt's chance will be before she goes to London,' continued her ladyship; 'and I really think it is a good one. She likes him, and that goes a great way with a girl'—said as if she were gently compassionating a weakness—'and I think the Carterets are sensible people, likely to see their own advantage in her marrying into a family who are on good terms with them, and can make it worth their while to behave nicely. Then there's the advantage *to her* of the connection. Our son, my dear, living *here*, is a better match for her than Lord Anybody's son, living elsewhere, and unconnected with her people. Really, nothing could be more —more providential, I really consider it, for her.' And Lady Gelston nodded approvingly, as if the power alluded to had been present, and could have appreciated the polite encouragement.

'Well, my dear, you seem to have taken everything into consideration, and I have no doubt you are right. I hope *they* will see it in the same light.'

'I hope so; but if they don't—and that's why I am anxious Matt should not lose time'—Lady Gelston had a trick of parenthesis—'I shall see about that Treherne girl—Mrs Peile's niece, you know. Lady John Tarbett sent me a very satisfactory account of her the other day. And, by-the-by, that reminds me I must go and answer her letter.'

Had Lady Gelston been conscious that all her acquaintances were thoroughly aware of the projects which she cherished in reference to Gertrude Baldwin, she would not have been in the least annoyed. The matter presented itself to her mind in a practical common-sense aspect, much as his designs with regard to the 'middle-aged lady' presented themselves to the mind of Mr Peter Magnus. 'Husband on one side, wife on the other;' fortune on one side, rank on the other; mutual accommodation, excellent arrangement for all parties—a little condescending on the part of the Honourable Matthew perhaps, but then the girl was really very rich, and that was all about it. Any one ordinarily clear-sighted, and with any knowledge of the world at all, *must* recognize the advantages to all parties. If the Carterets and Miss Baldwin were insensible to them—well, it would be provoking, but there were other heiresses, and certain conditions of heiress-ship were tolerably frequent, in which an Honourable Matthew would be a greater prize than to Miss Meriton Baldwin of the Deane.

When Mr Dort made his appearance on the Deane croquet-ground, there was not an individual present who did not know that he was there with a definite purpose, and in obedience to the orders of Lady Gelston, and they all watched his proceedings with curiosity. The fates were not propitious to the Honourable Matthew, who had been preparing, on his way, certain pretty speeches, which he flattered himself would be effective, and would help towards 'getting it over,' which was his periphrastic manner of alluding, in his self-communings, to the proposal appointed to be made to Miss Baldwin. Gertrude was not present, and everybody was intent upon croquet.

'Where is your sister?' he asked Eleanor, after they

22

had exchanged good-morrows, and agreed that the ball of the previous night had been a successful festivity.

The droll directness of the question was too much for Nelly; she laughed outright.

'I really cannot tell you,' she replied; 'she ought to have been here long ago; but no doubt she will come now.'

'I hope so,' said Mr Dort with fervent seriousness. 'I should think she would soon come.'

And then he retired modestly to a garden-seat and softly repeated the phrases, which he began to find it desperately difficult to retain in his memory.

Robert Meredith had adhered with some tenacity to the croquet-party, and had been a witness to this little scene. The amusement, just a little dashed with pique, which Eleanor displayed did not escape him.

He is an original, certainly,' said Meredith, 'which, for the sake of humanity, it is to be hoped will not be extensively copied. I fancy he will propose to-day.'

'Very likely,' said Nelly; 'every one knows he, or his mother, has intended it for a long time. In fact, Gerty rather wants to have it over, as Mr Dort is not a bad creature, and the sooner he understands that, though she has no notion of marrying him, he may come here all the same, the pleasanter it will be for all parties.'

'Of course she *has* no notion of marrying him?'

'Mr Meredith, you are insulting! Gerty marry Matt Dort—an idiot like that!'

'An idiot with an old title and a castle to match, in not distant perspective, combination of county influence, &c. &c. &c.,' said Meredith, smiling; 'not so very improbable, after all.'

'So Lady Gelston thinks,' replied Nelly; 'and won't it be a sell—the slang is delightfully expressive—when she finds it is not he.'

'And wouldn't it be a sell for her ladyship if it were ? ' thought Meredith.

'I suppose it will, indeed,' was his reply. 'Though all this is very amusing, I fancy I should consider it very humiliating if I were a woman. I cannot see anything enviable in a position which exposes one to such barefaced speculation.'

'Nonsense!' returned Eleanor, with a forced smile; 'depend on it, if you were a woman, you would like very well to be in Gertrude's position, and have every one making much of you.'

As she spoke she threw down her mallet, and declared herself tired of croquet.

'Here is Gertrude at last,' said Mrs Haldane Carteret, and all the party looked in the direction of the house. There was Gertrude, coming along the terrace, and with her George Ritherdon, supporting on his arm Mr Dugdale.

'Let us go and meet them,' said Eleanor, 'and tell Gerty to put the Honourable Matthew out of pain as soon as possible.'

'He is to be here this evening, I suppose,' said Meredith, as they moved off the croquet-ground.

'Yes,' answered Eleanor; 'Lady Gelston carefully provided for that last night—not that it was necessary, for he would have invited himself, and come under any circumstances.'

When Eleanor and Meredith joined Miss Baldwin and her escort, George Ritherdon said to his friend :

'I will ask you to take my place. I find the post-hour here is horribly early, and I must really let my mother know where I am.'

'What on earth have you been doing ? ' said Meredith, as he offered his arm to Mr Dugdale. 'You went away two hours ago to write letters, you said.'

'I think we are to blame,' said Gerty. 'Mr Ritherdon

found us in the morning-room—found Uncle James and me, I mean—and we got talking, as Miss Congreve says, and—'

'And I had an opportunity of finding out how much Ritherdon is to be liked,' interposed Mr Dugdale, George being now out of hearing. 'I congratulate you on your companion, Robert.'

Meredith replied cordially, and the party advanced towards the lawn. The two girls preceded Mr Dugdale and Meredith, and as the sound of their voices reached the latter, he correctly divined that they were amusing themselves at the expense of Mr Dort. On the approach of Miss Baldwin, the Honourable Matthew promptly abandoned the garden bench, from which no blandishments had previously availed to entice him, and repeated the phrases which had occasioned him so much trouble, with very suspicious glibness, to the undisguised amusement of the two girls. Mr Dort was not in the least abashed. He had no sense of humour and not a particle of bashfulness, and, if he had reasoned on the subject at all, would have imputed their hilarity to the natural propensity of women to giggle, rather than have entertained any suspicion that he had made himself ridiculous. But he never reasoned, and he was always perfectly comfortable.

The afternoon passed merrily away, and a pleasant dinner-party succeeded. George Ritherdon had become quite a popular person before the promised dance—not at all splendid, in comparison with the ball of the preceding evening—began, and he confided to Meredith his surprise at finding himself 'getting on so well,' he who was such a bad hand at 'society business.'

Gertrude gave him several dances that evening,—Miss Congreve thought rather too many,—and she gave Mr Dort one, and a tolerably prolonged audience in the ante-room, after which it was generally observed that the expression of discontent habitual to his features was more marked than usual. He left the Deane long before the party broke up, and found his lady mother still up, and ready to receive his report of proceedings.

'Well, Matt, how have you got on?' was her ladyship's terse question.

'I haven't got on at all,' replied the Honourable Matthew. 'She said "No" almost before I'd asked her, and was so infernally pleasant about it, that, hang it! I couldn't get up anything like the proper thing under the circumstances,—you know, mother,—the "may not time—can you not give me a hope?" business.'

'Excessively provoking,' said Lady Gelston, turning very red in the face, and speaking in a tone which was the peculiar aversion of her son : 'she is a stupid perverse girl, and I'm certain you mismanaged the affair.'

'No, I didn't,' said the Honourable Matt; 'there ain't much management about it, that I can see. I said, "Will you marry me?"—that's flat, I think,—and she said, "Certainly not;" *that's* flat, I think;—a perfect flounder, in my opinion.'

'Well, well, it can't be helped,' said Lady Gelston, with a glance at her son which might have meant that she had arrived at a comprehension of what a fool he really was. 'There, go away, and let me get to bed. It's too bad; but there's no help for it. We must only try elsewhere,' she continued, as if speaking to herself.

'Stop a bit, mother,' interposed the Honourable Matt, without the least impatience or any change of expression, 'I want to consult you about something. Don't you think what I particularly want is ready money—money that isn't tied up, I mean—not the entail business, don't you know, but the other thing?'

'I think you want money in any way and in any quantity in which it can be had,' returned Lady Gelston impatiently. 'How can you ask such foolish questions?'

'I'm not. I heard all about Nelly Baldwin's money to-night. Captain Carteret was talking about it to old Largs, and he's so deaf that the Captain had to roar all the particulars; and I'll tell you what, mother,—by Jove, I'll go in for Nelly.'

Robert Meredith and George Ritherdon were to remain a week at the Deane. The three days which succeeded their arrival were passed in the ordinary pleasurable pursuits of a luxurious and hospitable country-house, and were unmarked by any events which made themselves at all conspicuous. Nevertheless they were days with a meaning, an epoch with a history, and their course included two incidents. The sisters had a quarrel, which they kept strictly to themselves; and George Ritherdon received a long letter, which he read with profound amazement, which he promptly destroyed, and concerning whose contents he said not a word to any one.

CHAPTER XXIX.

THE FIRST MOVES IN THE GAME.

SOME time passed away, after the memorable fête which had celebrated the majority of Miss Meriton Baldwin of the Deane, during which, to an uninitiated observer, the aspect of affairs in that splendid and well-regulated mansion remained unchanged. County festivities took place; and the importance of the young ladies at the Deane was not a better established fact than their popularity.

With the comic seriousness which distinguished him, the Honourable Matthew Dort had 'gone in for Nelly.' He visited at the Deane with tranquil regularity, he played croquet imperturbably; only that he now watched Eleanor's balls, and was as confident she would 'croquet' everybody as he had formerly been free from doubt about Gertrude's prowess ; he rehearsed his speeches, and uttered them with entire self-possession. In due time he proposed to Eleanor, in the exact terms in which he had already done Gertrude that honour ; and he was refused by her quite as definitively, but less politely than he had been refused by her sister. On this occasion also he went home to his mother, and related to her his defeat with a happy absence of embarrassment.

Lady Gelston was very angry. She really did not know what the world—and especially the young women who were in it—was coming to ; she wondered who the Baldwin girls expected to get. But of one thing she was convinced—Matthew must have made a fool of himself somehow, or he could not have failed in both instances. The accused Matthew did not defend himself. Very likely he had made a fool of himself, but it could not be helped. Neither Gertrude nor Eleanor would marry him, and it was quite clear he could not make either of them do so. His mother had much better not worry herself about them ; and when the shooting was over, or he was tired of it, he would 'look-up that girl of Lady Jane Tarbert's.'

With this prospect, and with the intention of snubbing the Baldwins, Lady Gelston was forced to be content. But the snubbing, though her ladyship was an adept in the practice, did not succeed. The Baldwins declined to perceive that they were snubbed, and the neighbourhood declined to follow Lady Gelston's lead in this particular. The Deane was the most popular house in the country, and the Baldwins were the happiest and most enviable people.

This fair surface was but a deceitful seeming ; at least, so far as the sisters were concerned. An estrangement, which had had its commencement on Gertrude's birthday, and had since increased by insensible degrees, had grown up between them ; an estrangement which not all their efforts

—made in the case of Eleanor from pride, in that of Gertrude from wounded feeling—could hide from the notice of their uncle and aunt, from James Dugdale and Rose Doran; an estrangement which made each eagerly court external associations, and find relief, in the frequent presence of others, from the constant sense of their changed relation. James Dugdale saw this change with keen sorrow; but when he attempted to investigate it, he was met by Gertrude with an earnest assurance that she was entirely ignorant of its origin, and an equally earnest entreaty that he would not speak to Eleanor about it. It would be useless, Gertrude said, and she must put her faith in time and her sister's truer interpretation of her.

Appeal to Eleanor was met with flat denial, and an angry refusal to submit to interference, which in itself betrayed the evil root of all this dissension. Gertrude was supreme, the angry sister said; *she* was nothing. Gertrude of course could not err; all the good things of this world were for Gertrude, including the absolute subservience of her sister. But she might not, indeed she should not, find it quite so easy to command *that*. A good deal of harm was done by Mrs Carteret, not intentionally, but yet after her characteristic fashion. She much preferred Eleanor to Gertrude, and she made herself a partisan of the former, by pitying her, because *she* only could know how little she was really to blame. Haldane treated the matter very lightly. He regarded it as a girlish squabble, which would resolve itself into nothing in a very short time, and at the worst would be dissipated by a stronger feeling. So soon as a lover should appear on the scene, their good-humoured uncle believed it would be all right,—provided indeed they did not happen to fall in love with the same man, and quarrel desperately about him.

Rose Doran regarded the state of things with anger and horror.

' It's just the devil's work, sir,' she said to Mr Dugdale ;
' puttin' jealousy and bitterness between them two, fatherless and motherless as they are, and no one to show them
the only kind of love in which there's no room for more or
less. It's just the devil's work, and he's doing it bravely ;
and Miss Nelly's to his hand, for that jealousy was always
in her ; not but there's somebody behindhand, I'm sure of
it, puttin' coals on the fire.'

Rose was at first disposed to suspect Mrs Carteret of
this supererogatory work, but she did not continue to suspect her. She knew the girls so thoroughly, she was in no
doubt respecting the amount of influence their aunt could
exert over them, and in Nelly's case she was aware this was
much less than in that of Gertrude. Besides, Mrs Doran's
practical wisdom controlled her feminine suspicion; she
could not discern an adequate motive, and she therefore ex-
onerated Aunt Lucy. But she was no less convinced that,
in this unhappy matter, Eleanor was not left alone to the
unassisted promptings of her disposition, in which Rose had
early perceived the terrible taint of jealousy. And her acute
observation guided her aright before long; it guided her to
an individual whom she had instinctively distrusted in his
boyhood—to Robert Meredith.

Though she had hardly seen him for many years past,
and though, in her position in the household at the Deane,
she had not come into any contact with him of late, Rose
Doran had never got over the dislike of Robert Meredith
which she had conceived at the terrible time of her beloved
mistress's death. On that occasion James Dugdale had
obeyed Margaret's instructions so faithfully and promptly,
that Rose Moore had reached the Deane in time to kneel
beside her unclosed coffin, and whisper, on her cold lips, the
promise on which she had instinctively relied,—the promise
that her children should be henceforth Rose's sacred charge
and care. Among the mourners at the funeral of Mrs

Baldwin were Hayes Meredith and his son; the former
entirely absorbed in grief for the event, and in thoughts of
the future, as his secret knowledge forced him to contemplate it; the latter, with ample leisure of mind to look about
him, to observe and admire, and with the pleasant conviction
that every one was too much occupied to take any notice of
him. He conducted himself with propriety at the funeral,
and afterwards, while he was in sight of the family; and he
was far from supposing that Rose Moore was watching his
looks and his manner, on other occasions, with mingled disgust and curiosity, and that she said to herself, 'The Lord
be good to us! but I believe, upon my soul and faith, *the
boy is glad she's taken.*'

Rose had never deliberately recalled this impression
during all the years which had witnessed her faithful fulfilment of her vow, but she had never lost it; and the conviction which now came to her, during Robert Meredith's
stay at the Deane, and which gained strength with every
day which ensued on his departure, had its origin in it.
Had it needed confirmation, it would have obtained it from
the utter and peremptory rejection of her good offices, on
Nelly's part, and the burst of angry disdain with which the
infatuated girl met her suggestion, that Mr Meredith was
no friend of Gertrude's. Eleanor Baldwin had travelled no
small distance on the thorny road of evil, when she rewarded
Rose's suggestion with a haughty request, which fired Rose's
Irish blood, but with a flame quickly quenched in healing
waters of love and pity,—that she would in future remember,
and keep, *her place.*

'It's because I never forget my place, the place your
mother put me in, Miss Nelly, that I warn you,' said her
faithful friend.

Then Eleanor felt ashamed of herself; but pride and
anger and deadly jealousy carried the day over the whole-
some sentiment, and she turned away hastily, leaving Rose
without a word.

In much more than its external meaning was that festival time of deep importance to Gertrude and Eleanor Meriton Baldwin. It was fraught with the fate of both. While Robert Meredith and his friend remained at the Deane, the relation of the sisters ·was unchanged in appearance. It seemed as if their mysterious quarrel had had no lasting effect. The after estrangement was, however, its legitimate fruit, as well as the consequence of the pernicious ideas which Robert Meredith had set himself assiduously to culti- vate in the mind of Nelly. An explanation of the state of mind of Robert Meredith, at the termination of his visit to the Deane, will sufficiently elucidate the quarrel of the sisters, and its distressing results.

Robert Meredith had arrived at the Deane full of one purpose, which had been vaguely present to his mind for some years, but to which certain circumstances had of late lent consistency, fixedness, and urgency. This purpose was to make himself acceptable in the eyes of Miss Baldwin. He had hitherto troubled himself but little about the young lady. When she should have reached her majority, his time should have come. It had arrived ; and not Mr M'Ilwaine himself—who had gone to the Deane, accompanied by the huge mass of papers to which Haldane Carteret had found it difficult to induce his niece to give reasonable attention— had proceeded thither with a more strictly business-like purpose in view than that which actuated the handsome barrister. Robert would have despised himself as sincerely, and almost as much, as he was in the habit of despising his neighbours, if he had been capable of permitting sentiment to influence him in so grave an affair as that of securing his fortune for life,—which was precisely his purpose ; and he had formed his plans totally irrespective of Gertrude's at- tractions, or their possible influence upon himself. He had two schemes in his mind, both, in his belief, equally practic- able ; and he determined to be guided by circumstances as to which of the two he should adopt. If the second should

present itself as the more advisable, an indispensable preliminary to the secure playing of the long game it would
involve was the alienation of the sisters. It could do no
harm, in any case, to make an immediate move in that direction ; and therefore Robert Meredith made it.

When Eleanor Baldwin made her escape from the ball-
room on that memorable night, leaving her sister to the
cares which her superior importance devolved upon her,
Robert Meredith's eager words of admiration, and still more
expressive looks, had filled the girl's heart—already danger-
ously trembling towards him—-with a strange tumultuous
joy, contending with the jealous bitterness he had contrived
to implant in it. But when he and George Ritherdon bade
one another good-night at the door of George's room, after
a brief commentary upon the beauty of the morning, he had
enough that was ever in his thoughts to keep him from
sleep. The comparative advantages of the first of his plans
over the second had immensely increased in his estimation.

The beauty, the simplicity, the tender pathetic grace of
Gertrude, had struck with a strange attractive freshness
upon his palled sense, and he had awakened, with a delicious
consciousness, to the conviction that he might combine the
utmost gratification of two passions by the successful prosecution of his scheme. To make that delicate, refined, lovely
girl love him as passionately, as foolishly, as the dark beauty,
her sister, would love him, if it suited his purpose to encourage the dawning feeling he had seen in her eyes, and
felt in every movement and word of hers during the evening, would indeed be triumph, adding a delicious flavour to
the wealth and station which should be his. He understood
now what the charm was which Gertrude's mother, whom
he had hated, had had for men—the charm of a pure and
refined intellectuality, with underlying possibilities of intense and exalted feeling,—these were to be divined in the
depths of the clear gray, unabashed eyes, and in the sensitive

curves of a mouth as delicate as her mother's, but less ascetic.

Had he made a favourable impression on Gertrude? Had she learned from her sister's report to regard him with favour, and had he confirmed that report? He did not feel comfortably certain on this point. Gertrude had not given him any indication beyond the additional attention which he claimed as Mr Dugdale's particular friend. But Robert Meredith did not trouble himself much on this point; he had time before him, and he knew perfectly well how to use it. But it was characteristic of the man that, though he dwelt, to his last waking moment, upon Gertrude's beauty and charm, he thought, just as he fell asleep, 'If she thwarts me, it will all add zest to the revenge which Miss Eleanor's eyes tell me is secure in any case.'

The story of the remainder of Robert Meredith's visit may be briefly told. Gertrude did thwart him. Not intentionally; for she, being the most candid of girls, was wholly incapable of understanding his double-dealing policy. She frankly regarded him as her sister's admirer, and she unreservedly regretted that he should be so. She did not like Robert Meredith; between him and her there was an absolute absence of sympathy, and she shrank with an inexplicable repugnance and fear from his looks—covert and yet bold—and from the admiration which he insinuated, the understanding which he attempted to imply, whenever he could take or contrive an opportunity of doing so, unobserved and unheard by Eleanor. She avoided him whenever it was possible, and she never remained alone with him.

Robert Meredith was a vain man—but vanity was not his ruling passion, one or two others had precedence of it—therefore he did not fail to see, or hesitate to confess to himself, that Gertrude had thwarted him, that there would not be room, in the accomplishment of his scheme, for the delicious gratification of two passions at once, and that he would do well to fall back upon the second game, for playing which he had the cards in his hand. It was not without intense mortification he made this avowal to himself. He was a man to whom failure was indeed bitter; but he speedily found consolation in musing upon the perfection of a certain revenge which he meditated.

'If she would marry me, in ignorance,' he said to himself, 'I should be the Deane's master and hers; but, if she would not marry me under any circumstances, to escape any penalty—and I begin to think that is certain now—I have her in my power, and *all, all, all* will be mine.'

These reflections, made by Robert Meredith during the week which was to conclude his stay at the Deane, led him to take a certain resolution, whose execution was fraught with immediate results to the sisters.

A small but very animated dancing-party had taken place at the Deane; and Robert had closely studied the demeanour of Gertrude and Eleanor to him and to each other. The estrangement of the sisters had not then become manifest; but he detected and exulted in it. On Gertrude's part there was a nervous anxiety to put Eleanor forward, to consult her, to defer to her in everything; on Eleanor's there was an affectation of indifference, an assumption of deference, a giving of herself the appearance of being a guest, which was in extremely bad taste, but thoroughly delightful to Robert Meredith. If a servant asked Eleanor a question, she pointedly referred him to her sister; she professed an entire ignorance of Miss Baldwin's plans for the evening; she divided herself from her in innumerable little expressive ways, which Gertrude noted with a sick heart and a manner which betrayed painful nervousness; and she abandoned herself to the influence of the flattery and the insidious suggestions of the tempter to a degree which justified him in believing that he might be entirely sure of her, whether the pursuit of his purpose should lead him to break her heart by marrying her sister, or crown her hopes by marrying herself.

It was Gertrude's custom to resort to the library every morning after breakfast, and there to occupy herself with her drawing, at a table beside a large window which opened on the lawn. She was usually undisturbed, as Mr Dugdale remained in his own rooms all the morning, her uncle frequented the stable and farmyard, Eleanor devoted the morning hours to music, and Mrs Carteret had no attraction towards the library. George Ritherdon had sometimes found his way thither; and Gertrude had, on those occasions, found it not unpleasant to lay aside her pencil, and discuss with her guest some of the contents of her amply-stored bookshelves. But George was engaged in writing letters on the morning which followed the before-mentioned dancing-party; and Robert Meredith found Miss Baldwin, as he expected, alone. Gertrude tried hard to receive him in the most ordinary way, but her embarrassment was distressingly apparent; and he coolly showed her that he perceived it. After a few words—she could hardly have told what words —she collected her drawing-materials, and said something confusedly about being waited for by Mrs Carteret, as she rose to leave the room. But Robert Meredith, with a bold fixed look, which, in spite of herself, she saw and felt in every nerve, detained her; and gravely informing her that he had purposely selected that opportunity of finding her alone, in order to make a communication of importance to her, requested her to listen to him. His manner was not loverlike, it was even, under all the formality of his address, slightly contemptuous; but she knew instantly what it was she had to listen to, and a prayer arose in her heart by a sudden inexplicable impulse. She resumed her seat, and leaning her arm on the table which divided her from Robert Meredith, she shaded her eyes with her hand, and prepared to listen to him.

It was as her instinctive dread had told her. In set phrase, and with his bold covetous eyes fixed upon her, Meredith told her his errand,—told her he loved her, and asked her to marry him—made mention too of her wealth, and the risk he ran of being misinterpreted by the world, of having base motives imparted to him—a risk more than counterbalanced by his love, and his faith in his ability to make her understand and believe that she was sought by him for herself alone.

Robert Meredith spoke well, and with fire and energy; but, as Gertrude listened to him, her distress and embarrassment subsided, and she removed the sheltering hand from her eyes. When he urgently entreated her to reply, she said very gently:

'I should feel more pain, Mr Meredith, in telling you that I cannot return the preference with which you honour me, if I did not feel so convinced that your love for me is only imaginary. Had it been real, you would not have remembered my wealth, or cared about the opinion of the world.'

This answer staggered the man to whom it was addressed more than any indignation could have done. He burst out into renewed protestations; but Gertrude, with grave dignity, begged him to desist, and again asserting that as her guardian's friend he should ever be esteemed hers, assured him it was useless to pursue his suit. Then she rose, and moved towards the door.

'Is this a final answer, Miss Baldwin?' asked Meredith.

'Quite final, Mr Meredith.'

'Stay a moment. May I hope you will not add to the mortification of this refusal the injury of making it known to Mr Dugdale or Mrs Carteret, indeed to any one? I confess I could hardly endure the ridicule or the compassion which must attend a rejected suitor of the heiress of the Deane.'

There was a devil's sneer in his voice and on his face; but Gerty took no heed of it, as she replied, with quiet dignity,

'We have a code of honour also, we women, Mr Meredith; and you may be quite sure I shall never so far offend against it as to mention this matter to *any one*.' Then she added, with a sweet smile, in which her perfect incredulity regarding his professions was fully though unconsciously expressed:

'I will leave you now; and I hope you will forget all this as soon and as completely as I shall.'

Robert Meredith followed her with his eyes as she left the room, and passing along the terrace, went down into her flower-garden, and lingered there, utterly oblivious of him; and a deadly feeling of hatred, such hatred as springs most profusely from baffled passion, arose in his heart, and blossomed into sudden strength and purpose.

'Yes,' he muttered; 'you have taken up the thread of your mother's story, and you shall spin it out to some purpose. A little while, and Eleanor will be of age; and then, my fine heiress of the Deane, then we shall see who has won to-day. A little while, and if I can only keep Oakley quiet till then, I am safe. Safe! more than safe,—triumphant, victorious!'

It was on the next day that Nelly, intoxicated by the artful flatteries of Robert Meredith, and tortured by the jealousy which he had fostered, taunted her sister with the powerlessness of money to purchase love. The taunt fell harmlessly on Gertrude's pure and upright heart; but it startled her, uttered by her sister. How had Nelly come by such knowledge, and why did she apply it to her? She hastily asked her why; and to her astonishment was answered, that in one treasure at least Nelly was richer than she was—the treasure of a brave and true man's love! The reply shook Gertrude like a reed. There was indeed one man who answered to this description; there was one man to win whose love would be the most blissful lot which Heaven could bestow. There was one man, who never, by word or deed or look, had implied to Gertrude Baldwin that such a

23

lot might be hers—had her sister won *him?* Well indeed might she exult, if she were so supremely blest, and hold not Gertrude only, but all womankind her inferiors. Pale and breathless, she awaited the complete elucidation to be expected from Eleanor's taunting wrath, and it came. It came, not as her fearful shrinking heart had foreboden, but in the avowal that Eleanor spoke of Robert Meredith.

With the passing away of the great pang of terror that had clutched at her heart, Gertrude was again calm and clear-sighted; but she was deeply grieved. She felt how unworthy was the man her sister loved, how baseless her belief that she possessed his affections. She was far from being able to comprehend such a nature as that of Robert Meredith; but she had a vague consciousness that, in his binding her to secrecy respecting his proposal to her, there had been a treacherous intent; and though she would not break her promise, she appealed to her sister on grounds and terms which a little more knowledge of human nature would have taught her must be in vain. Then came the inevitable result, a bitter and lasting quarrel, and an ineradicable belief on Eleanor's part that Gertrude's refusal to credit Meredith's love for her sister arose from the most despicable motives—pride, envy, and jealousy. Where was the sisterly love, where was the unbroken confidence of years, now? Blasted by the fierce breath of passion, poisoned by the insidious art of the tempter.

So a treacherous appearance of calm and happiness existed at the Deane during the months which succeeded the departure of the friends, and none but those concerned were aware of two circumstances which had entirely changed the lives of the bright and beautiful sisters. One was the fact that Eleanor Baldwin was secretly betrothed to Robert Meredith, with the understanding that on her coming of age she would marry him, with or without the consent of her relatives. The other was that the plodding industrious

barrister George Ritherdon, who carried back to his chambers
in the Temple more than one unaccustomed sensation, had
taken with him, unconsciously, the unasked heart of the
young mistress of the Deane.

CHAPTER XXX.

DRIFTING.

With the commencement of the season, Major and Mrs
Carteret and their nieces followed the multitude to London.
This proceeding was but little in accordance with the wishes
of Gertrude Baldwin, who loved her home and her de-
pendents, the pleasant routine of her country duties and
recreations; but she could not oppose herself to the general
opinion that it was the right thing to do, in which even Mr
Dugdale, her great support and ally, agreed with the others.
In her capacity of woman of fashion, Mrs Carteret was
quite shocked that Gertrude should have passed her twenty-
first year without coming out in proper style in London;
but in that of chaperone, or, as she called it, maternal friend
to a great heiress, she had recognized the wisdom and propriety of permitting her to attain to years of discretion before
she should be formally delivered over to the wiles of the
fortune-hunters and the perils of the ' great world.'   Not
but that there were fortune-hunters in Scotland, witness the
Honourable Matthew Dort; but Gertrude was not likely to
be bewildered by their devices in the sober atmosphere of
her home.

Miss Baldwin's mind had not changed on the subject of
the superiority of her Scottish home to anything which a
London residence could offer, and which would certainly
wear an air of triumph for her, however false that air might
be.   Gertrude was by no means worldly wise.   She had

none of the cynical foresight leading her to see in every one who approached her a covetous idolater of her wealth. She would have regarded herself with horror if she had lost her faith in love or friendship; and indeed she had been so accustomed to the presence of wealth all her life, that she did not understand its effects on others, and had no mental standard by which to estimate its value, either material or moral. It was not, therefore, from any unwomanly disdain of the motives of those whom she was to sojourn amongst in London that Gertrude took the prospect coolly, showing none of the excitement and exultation to which Eleanor gave unrestrained expression, and which made her amiable to Gertrude to an extent unparalleled for many months past. The truth was that there was a secret in Gertrude's heart, a preoccupation of Gertrude's mind, to which everything beside, so far as she was individually concerned, had to yield. This pervading sentiment did not render her selfish, she was as ready with her sympathies for others as ever, but it did make her absent and indifferent.

Robert Meredith and his friend had passed a fortnight at Christmas at the Deane, and there the plans of the family for the coming season had been discussed. Gertrude had learned with surprise and discomfiture that her living in London, where he lived, would not imply her seeing very much of George Ritherdon. She fancied he had been at some pains to make her understand this, and the consciousness rendered her uneasy. Why had he dwelt upon the busy nature of his life, the diversity between his occupations and hers? Why had he drawn a merry sketch for her of the wide difference between the society, such as it was, in which alone he had a footing, and the gilded saloons which were to throw their doors open for her? He had not offended her by cynicism, which was as far from his happy and loyal nature as from hers; but he had made her thoughtful and uncomfortable by an insistence upon this point, which she

could but refer to a wish to make her understand that she
must not expect him to contribute to the anticipated pleasures of her sojourn in London. And with this conviction
vanished all such anticipations from Gertrude's fancy.

That was an enchanted fortnight. The hours had flown,
and a beautiful new world had opened itself to the girl's
perception. She had been too happy to be afraid of Robert
Meredith, or ungracious to him. She had utterly forgotten
the rule of action she had laid down for herself, in consideration of her sister's perverse jealousy and alienation.
She had determined to treat Meredith with cold politeness,
to show him and Eleanor that she imputed to his sinister
influence the state of things which occasioned her so much
pain. But she forgot the pain ; she was happy, and the
sunshine of her content spread all around her.

Robert Meredith had a difficult game to play at this
time, but he played it with skill and success. It is not a
light test of skill when an elderly coquette is persuaded by
a *ci-devant* admirer to abandon the conquering for the confidential *rôle*, and this was precisely the test which Robert
Meredith applied to his *savoir faire*. The secret betrothal
between himself and Eleanor placed them on so secure a
footing, that he was able, without annoying Eleanor, notwithstanding her exacting disposition, to devote much of his
time to Mrs Carteret, towards whom his tone modified itself
from the slightly vulgar, somewhat obtrusive gallantry which
had been wont to characterize it, to the very perfection of
deferential observance and highly-prized intimacy. He had
appealed to some of Eleanor's best feelings in order to
induce her to consent to the secrecy of their engagement—
to her disinclination to produce family discord, to her duty
of avoiding the rendering of her aunt's position as between
her and Gertrude difficult, and to her noble confidence in
his judgment and fidelity, which it should be his loftiest
aim in life to justify and reward.

He had not only poisoned Eleanor's mind against her sister, but he had succeeded in undermining the grateful affection which the misguided girl had once entertained for Mr Dugdale. He had made her remark the preference which, in many small ways, the old man showed for Gertrude—a preference of whose origin and justification Eleanor had no knowledge to enable her to understand it aright—and assured her that in him too, in deference to that universal baseness which dictated subservience to her sister's wealth, Eleanor would find a bitter opponent to her love, a ruthless adversary of her happiness. His wicked counsels prevailed. Something romantic in the girl's disposition responded to the idea of a persecuted passion; and the demon of jealousy, now thoroughly awakened in her, wrought unrestrained all the mischief her human evil genius desired. Meredith counselled Eleanor to soften her manner towards Gertrude, for the better security of their secret against the danger of her awakened suspicions; and she obeyed him. He forbade her to tell Mrs Carteret all the truth, lest it might hereafter compromise her with her husband and Mr Dugdale, but told her to cultivate her good graces in every way, so that in the time to come her aid might be sure; and she obeyed him. The result of all this was much more peace for Gertrude; and as Meredith kept himself out of her way, devoting himself to Mrs Carteret and Eleanor, and leaving George Ritherdon to her society, it had the additional effect of increasing and consolidating her attachment to George.

Major Carteret was habitually unobservant; his wife confined her attention to Robert Meredith, of whose wishes she was the delighted confidante, and Eleanor, whom she did not at present suspect of more than an incipient inclination towards Robert. Mr Dugdale—whose health had declined considerably since the autumn, did not leave his rooms, and saw the different members of the family singly —was totally unconscious of the drama being played out so

near him. Things were better between the sisters, and he
rejoiced at that. The favourable impression which George
Ritherdon had made upon him on his first visit to the
Deane was deepened during his second, and he greatly enjoyed his society. Gertrude passed many happy hours,
working or drawing, beside her old friend's sofa, while the
two men talked with mutual pleasure and sympathy. When
that happy fortnight ended and the friends had returned to
London, Gertrude found her greatest consolation in Mr
Dugdale's frequent allusions to George, and in the eulo-
giums which he pronounced on his mind and his manners,
the latter being a point on which the old gentleman was
difficult and fastidious.

During and since that time, Gertrude, who was singularly
free from vanity and quite incapable of pretence, had frequently asked herself whether she had not given her heart to
one who did not love her. Even if it had been so to her
indisputable knowledge, she would not have striven to withdraw the gift. She loved him, once and for ever, and she
would sanctify that love in her heart, if he were never to be
more to her than the truest and most valued of friends. She
was utterly sincere and candid in this resolution; she had
no foreknowledge of the difficulty, the impossibility of maintaining it. She was content, ay, even happy, in her uncertainty, which was sometimes hope, but never despair.
Such a possibility as that George should love her and refrain
from telling her so, because of her wealth, literally never
occurred to her, any more than that, if he loved her, and
told her so, the most unscrupulous calumniator in the world
could accuse him of caring for that wealth, of even remembering it. It had no place in her thoughts at all. She
lived her dream-life happily; sometimes her dreams were
brighter, sometimes more sombre; but their glitter did not
come from her gold, their shadow was not cast by cynical
doubt, by worldly-wise suspicion.

When the time came for their journey to London,

Gertrude was more sad than elated. Her best friend, the one on whom she leaned with the trusting reliance of a daughter, from whom she had ever experienced the fond in dulgence of a parent, was to remain at the Deane. Mr Dugdale's health rendered it impossible for him to accompany the family, and Mrs Carteret and Eleanor did not regret his absence. Their feelings were in accord on every point connected with the expedition. Eleanor foresaw no impediment to her frequent enjoyment of Robert Meredith's society, under the auspices of Mrs Carteret, who, on her part, had great satisfaction in the prospect of partaking in the gaieties of a London season, for which she still retained an unpalled taste, and maintaining a splendid establishment at the expense of her niece.

More than half the interval which had to elapse between Gertrude's attainment of her majority and Eleanor's reaching a similar period had now elapsed, and Robert Meredith's successful prosecution of his schemes with respect to the Baldwins was unchequered by any reverse. In other respects things were not progressing quite so favourably with him. He had been negligent in his professional business of late, since his mind had been full of the mysterious game he was playing, and the inevitable, inexorable result of this negligence was making itself felt. George Ritherdon, on the contrary, was getting on rapidly for a barrister, and was beginning to be talked about as a man with a name and a standing. The relations between the two had insensibly relaxed, as was only natural, considering that the strongest tie between them, their common industry, their common ambition, had so considerably slackened. Nothing approaching to a quarrel had taken place; but they were tired of one another, and each was aware of the fact. The sentiment dated from their second visit to the Deane, whence each had returned preoccupied with his own thoughts, his own preferences, and profoundly conscious that no sympathy existed between them.

Little had been said between the two relative to the Baldwins' sojourn in London; and when George Ritherdon, made aware of their arrival by the *Morning Post*, asked his friend when he intended to present himself at their house in Portman-square, he was disagreeably surprised by the cold brevity of Meredith's reply that he had been there already, had indeed seen the ladies on the very day of their arrival, and was going to dine with them the same evening.

George made no remark upon this communication, and left a card for Major Carteret on the following day. An invitation to dinner followed, and on his mentioning the circumstance to Meredith, George was surprised and offended by his manner. He laughed unpleasantly, and said something about the futility of George's expecting to be received on the same footing as he had been in the country, which made him decidedly angry.

'I don't understand you, Meredith,' he said. 'You brought me to the Deane, I owe the acquaintance entirely to you, and now you talk as if you resented it.'

'Nonsense, old fellow,' returned Robert with good humour, which cost him an effort; 'I only discourage your going to the Baldwins, because I do not want to hear you talked of as an unsuccessful competitor for the heiress's money-bags, and because I know, if you have any leaning in that direction, it will be quite useless. The young ladies fly at higher game than you or I.'

A deep flush overspread George Ritherdon's face as he replied:

'I beg you will not include me, in your own mind, in the category of fortune-hunters; as for what other people think or say, you need not trouble yourself.'

'As you please. I only warn you that Gertrude Baldwin is an interested coquette, determined to make the most of her money,—to buy rank with it, at all events, but by no means averse to numbering her thousands of victims in the mean time.'

' You speak harshly of this girl, Meredith, and cruelly.'

' I speak candidly, because I am speaking to *you*. You don't suppose I would put another fellow on his guard. I might have got bit myself, you know, if I had not understood her in time. However, we had better not talk about it. Forewarned, forearmed, they say, though I can't say I ever knew any good come of warning any one.'

Thereupon Meredith pretended to be very busy with his papers, and the subject dropped. But it left a very unpleasant impression on George's mind. 'An interested coquette!' No more revolting description could be given of any woman within the category of those whom an honest man could ever think of marrying. Had George Ritherdon thought of marrying Gertrude? No. Did he love her? He knew in his heart he did ; but he did not question for a moment his power of keeping the fact hidden from the object of his love, and every other person. He would have regarded the declaration of his feelings to an inexperienced girl, who had had no opportunity of choice, of seeing the world, of forming her judgment of character, to whom the language of love was utterly unknown, on the eve of her entrance upon a scene on which she ought to enter perfectly untrammelled, as in the highest degree dishonourable. He would have held this opinion concerning any woman whose wealth should have made her position so exceptionally difficult as that of Gertude ; but in her particular instance he had an additional motive for his strict self-conquest and reticence, which, if it ever could be explained, must remain concealed for the present.

George Ritherdon had no coxcombry or conceit about him, and he had not made up his mind by any means that Gertrude loved him, or was likely to be brought to love him in the future, should he find that the ordeal to which she was about to be exposed had left her still fancy-free, and his own circumstances be such as to enable him to believe he might try for the great prize of her heart and hand without dishonour. He did not deceive himself as to the obstacles and the rivals he might have to encounter; he gave all the fascinations of the new sphere in which Gertrude was about to shine their full credit and importance, and he contented himself with this conclusion :

'If, when she has had full experience, ample time, when she knows her position and her own mind perfectly, I can be sure that she prefers me to all the world beside, I will win her, and marry her, without bestowing a thought on her fortune, or caring a straw for any one's interpretation of my motives, caring only for *hers*.'

Steadily acting upon the plan he had laid down for himself, George Ritherdon frequented Gertrude's society not often enough to make his visits a subject of comment, not sufficiently seldom to induce her to think him indifferent or estranged. She and Eleanor were going through the ordinary routine of the life of London in the season; he rarely participated in its more tumultuous and irrational pleasures. But he kept a tolerably strict watch upon Gertrude for all that; and he had no reason to believe, at the end of the second month of her stay in London, that any one of the numerous admirers with whom rumour and his own observation had accredited her, had found the slightest favour with the young lady of the Deane.

Before the end of that second month, Robert Meredith and George Ritherdon had parted company. The former could perhaps have given a plain and conclusive reason for his desire that so it should be; but, in the case of the latter, the actuating motive was more vague. George felt that they did not get on together. The Baldwins were hardly ever mentioned between them, though each knew the terms on which the other stood with the family, and they not unfrequently met at the house in Portman-square. The dissolution of the old arrangement, once so pleasant to them

both, was plainly imminent to each before it actually occurred, and it might have come about after a disagreeable
fashion but for a fortunate accident. The gentleman who
had been George's university tutor, and with whom he had
always maintained intimate relations, died, and bequeathed
to George his numerous and valuable library. What was
he to do with the books? Their joint chambers would not
accommodate them. George took a large set in another
building, and the difficulty was solved, to their mutual relief,
without a quarrel.

The season was a brilliant one, and Gertrude and Eleanor Baldwin had their full share of its glories and its pleasures. They enjoyed it, after their different fashions, but
Gertrude more than Eleanor. In the heart of each there
was indeed a disquieting secret; but in the one case there
was no self-reproach, no misgiving, while in the other that
voice would occasionally make itself heard. As time passed
over, Gertrude felt more and more hopeful that George
Ritherdon loved her, though for some reason which she
could not penetrate, but to which it was not difficult for
her docile nature to submit, he did not at present avow the
sentiment. Her happiness was not lost, it was only deferred; she would be patient, and then she could always
comfort herself with the knowledge that her love for him—
pure, lofty, with no element of torment in it—could never
die, or be taken from her, while she lived.

Eleanor's lot was by no means so favoured, and she
proved more difficult to manage than Robert Meredith had
foreseen. She chafed under the restraint of her position,
and suffered agonies of suspicion and jealousy. The evil
passion which he had been quick to see and skilful to cultivate, for his own purposes, was easily turned against him, a
contingency which with all his astuteness he had failed to
apprehend; and Eleanor's daily increasing imperiousness
and distrust made him tremble for the safety of his secret
and the success of his plans.

Nothing made Eleanor so suspicious of the falsehood of his professions, nothing exasperated her so much, as Robert Meredith's imperviousness to the feeling which had obtained so fearful a dominion over her. If she could but have roused his jealousy, as she ceaselessly endeavoured to do, by such reckless flirtations as brought her into trouble with even her careless uncle, and furnished plentiful food for ill-natured tongues, she would have been more easy, less unhappy, more convinced. But Robert would not be made jealous, and his easy tranquil assumption of confident power, not laid aside even during the stolen interviews in which he bewildered her with his passionate protestations and caresses, sometimes nearly drove her mad. An instinct, which it had been well for her if she had heeded, told her that this man was not true to her. But she loved him madly. He had changed her whole nature, it seemed to her, in the few seldom-recurring moments in which she saw clearly into the past, and strained fearful eyes into the future; he had ruined the peace and happiness of her home, he had estranged her from her sister, he had taught her lessons of scorn and suspicion towards all her kind. But she loved him, him only in all the world.

Towards the close of the season, Haldane Carteret grew extremely impatient. He had been, he considered, quite an unreasonable time on duty, and he declared his intention of at once returning to the Deane. The men-servants would suffice for an escort for Mrs Carteret and her nieces; or, if they did not like that arrangement, he was sure Meredith, who was coming down for the shooting at all events, would make it convenient to leave town a week or so sooner, and take care of them on the journey. No one had any objection to urge against this proposal; and Major Carteret took himself off, hardly more to his own satisfaction than to that of his wife, who declared herself worn out by his ' crossness,' and disgusted with his selfishness.

On the following evening Robert Meredith had a guest

at his chambers, who, to judge by the moody and impatient expressions of his host's countenance, was anything but welcome. Meredith had dined at Portman-square, where he had met George Ritherdon, to whom Miss Baldwin, with her simplest and yet most dignified air, had given, in her own and her uncle's name, an invitation to the Deane for the shooting season. This incident was highly displeasing to Meredith, who, distracted by an uneasy suspicion that his friend had found him out to a certain extent, desired nothing less than his presence during any part of the critical time which must elapse before he could make his *coup*. Robert had returned to his chambers in a sullen and exasperated temper, which was intensified by the spectacle which met his view. An old man, shabby of aspect, and anything but venerable in appearance or bearing—an old man with bleared watery eyes, bushy gray eye-brows, and dirty gray hair— was seated in an arm-chair by the open window, smoking a churchwarden pipe and drinking hot brandy-and-water. The mingled odours of tobacco and spirits perfumed the room after a fashion which harmonized ill with the sweet autumnal air and the flowers which adorned the sitting-room, in accordance with one of the owner's most harmless tastes.

'What, you here, Oakley!' said Meredith, in a tone which did not dissemble his disgust. 'What are you doing here? What has brought you up from Cheltenham?'

'Business,' replied the unvenerable visitor quietly, without rising or making any attempt at a salutation of his reluctant host. 'Business,' he repeated with an emphatic nod.

'With me?' Meredith threw his hat and gloves upon a table, and sat down, sullenly facing his visitor.

'With you. Look here, I'm tired of all this. You see, I am not so young as you are, and at my time of life I can't afford to play a waiting game. You can't, if you would, make it worth my while to do it; and as the case actually stands, you *don't* make it worth my while to play any game at all—of yours, I mean. Of course I should, in any case, play mine.'

'I don't understand you,' said Meredith, making a strong effort to keep his temper and speak with indifference. 'I have kept the terms I made with you to the letter. What do you mean by *your* game, as apart from mine?'

'Just this. I have no interest whatever in your marrying this girl rather than in any other man's marrying her. It does not matter to me where my price comes from; I'm sure of it from her husband, whoever he may be, and I don't believe you're sure that she *will* marry you. You have tried to keep me dark, and in the dark, cunningly enough; but I have found out more about them than you think for, for all that; and I know she has more than one string to her bow, and at least one of them more profitable to play upon than you are. If you can't persuade the girl to marry you before she's of age, and raise money for me upon her expectations, or if you can't in some way make things more comfortable, I shall try whether I cannot carry my information to a better market. Indeed, I am so tired of living respectably upon a pittance, paid with a dreary exactitude which is distressingly like Somerset House, I have been seriously contemplating an affecting visit to my relative Mrs Carteret, and a family arrangement to buy me off at once at a long price.'

'And *my* knowledge of the affair; what do you make of *that*, in your rascally calculation?'

'Not quite so much as *you* make of it in *your* rascally calculation, my good friend; for it is not knowledge at all, it is only guess-work; and you have not an atom of proof without my evidence, which I am quite as willing to withhold as to give, for Mr Trapbois' omnipotent motive—a consideration.'

For all answer, Robert Meredith rose, opened an iron safe let into the wall of the room, and hidden by a curtain

—greedily followed the while by the old man's eyes, which watched for the gold he hoped he had extorted—and took out a red-leather pocket-book, with a clasp of brass wire-work. He came up to the old man's side, and opening a page of the memorandum-book, pointed to an entry upon it.

'No evidence, I think you said. Not so fast, my faithful colleague. What is *that ?*'

'Initials, a date,—a guess, Meredith, a mere surmise, not an atom of proof.'

'And this?' Robert Meredith took an oblong slip of paper out of a pocket in the book, and held it up to the old man's eyes. 'An attested copy of the marriage-register is evidence, I fancy.'

'Yes,' said Mr Oakley reluctantly; 'that's evidence of one part of the story, to be sure; but not of the material part, the only part that's profitable to *you*. You can't do without me—you can't indeed; but I can do very well without you. You will save time and trouble by acknowledging the fact, and acting on it.'

'What the d—l do you want me to do?' said Meredith fiercely, as he threw the pocket-book back into the safe and locked the doors in a rage. 'I can't marry the girl till she is of age. I tell you I am perfectly sure of her. Do you think I am such a fool as to allow any doubt to exist on that point? But I don't choose to change my plans, and I *won't* change them, let you threaten as you will. You old idiot! you would ruin yourself by thwarting me. You don't know these people—*I do;* and you could as soon induce them to join you in robbing a church as to buy you off in the way you propose. You had much better stick to the bargain you've made, and have patience. I think if *I* can find patience, *you* may.'

Mr Oakley reflected for some minutes, his bushy gray eyebrows meeting above his frowning eyes. At last he said:

'Then I'll tell you what it is, Meredith. You shall give

me £20 extra now, to-night, and introduce me at once, to-morrow, to the family, and we'll go on playing on the square again.'

'No,' said Meredith; 'it won't do. I can't give you £20; I can't spare the money. I'll give you £10, on condition you don't show yourself here until I send for you. And as to introducing you to the family just yet, it is out of the question. It would only embarrass our proceedings, and do you no good.'

'What do you mean?' said Oakley furiously 'Why should you not introduce me to my own relative? I choose to partake of the advantages of her capital match. I intend to be Mrs Carteret's guest at the Deane this autumn, whether the prospect be agreeable to you or not.'

Meredith smiled, a slow exasperating smile, carefully exaggerated into distinctness for the old man's dimmed vision, as he said:

'*I* could have no objection to do my good friend Mrs Carteret the kindness of reuniting her with a long-severed member of her family, and to introduce you as a visitor at Portman-square, during the few days they will be in town, would not be any trouble to me; but as for your being invited to the Deane, the idea is *too* absurd.'

'And why?'

'Because Miss Baldwin, and not your relative, is the mistress of that very eligible mansion; because you are not the style of person Miss Baldwin admires; and because, you may take my word for it, you will never set your foot within those doors while the Deane belongs to Miss Baldwin.'

The old man's face turned a fiery red, and the angry colour showed itself under his thin gray hair.

'While the Deane belongs to Miss Baldwin!' he repeated low and slowly. 'Well, then, there's no use talking about it. Hand over the £10, and I'll be off.'

In a few minutes Robert Meredith was alone, and as he

24

listened to Mr Oakley's heavy tread upon the stairs, he muttered:

' It's a useful study, that of the ruling passions of one's fellow-creatures. An expert finds it tolerably easy to work them to his advantage. Avarice and pride ! eh, Mr Oakley ? and pride the stronger of the two. You won't give me much more trouble. No danger of your being bribed to abstain from saying or doing anything that can harm Miss Baldwin.'

CHAPTER XXXI.

THE MINE IS SPRUNG.

TIME sped on, and no fresh obstacle opposed itself to Robert Meredith's designs. His venerable colleague gave him no farther trouble. He had calculated with accuracy on Gertrude's nobility and delicacy of mind preventing her seeking to prejudice his friends in the household at the Deane against him, leading her to keep her promise of secrecy in its most perfect spirit. Thus, he pursued his design against her undisturbed, under her own roof, and with all the appearance of a good understanding existing between them.

Meredith was, however, mistaken in supposing that Gertrude was ignorant of her sister's attachment to him. She was much too keen-sighted where her affections were concerned to be deceived as to the state of Eleanor's mind, even had it not painfully revealed itself in the altered relations between them. She knew her sister's infatuation well, and she deplored it bitterly. The sorrow it caused her was all the more keen, because it was the first of her life in which she had not had recourse to Mr Dugdale for advice, sympathy, and consolation. Now, she asked for none of these at his hands. She could not have claimed them without divulging the secret she had pledged herself to keep, and grieving the old man by changing his regard for the son of his dead friend into distrust and dislike. So Gertrude suffered in silence; and as she became more and more isolated—as she felt the sweet home ties relaxing daily—she clung all the more firmly to the hope, the conviction that George Ritherdon loved her; though for some reason, which she was content to take on trust, to respect without understanding, he was resolved not to tell her so yet.

George Ritherdon passed three weeks, that autumn, at the Deane; but Meredith avoided him—making an excuse for selecting the period of his visit for fulfilling another engagement. During those three weeks the regard and esteem of old Mr Dugdale and George Ritherdon for each other so increased by intimacy, that Gertrude had the satisfaction of seeing them occupy the respective positions which she would most ardently have desired had her dearest hopes been realized. When George's visit had reached its conclusion, Mr Dugdale took leave of him as he might have done of a son, and the young man left his old friend's rooms deeply affected. Gertrude was not much seen by the family that day, and it was understood Mr Dugdale had requested her to pass the afternoon with him.

'Why does he say nothin', when any one that wasn't as blind as a bat could see he dotes on the ground she walks on?' asked Mr Dugdale's faithful friend and confidante, Mrs Doran, when they compared notes in the evening, after Gertrude had pleaded fatigue and left them.

'I don't know, indeed,' was Mr Dugdale's answer. 'I suppose he thinks she has not had a fair chance of choosing yet.'

'Hasn't seen enough of grand young gentlemen just dyin' to put her money in their pockets, and spend it on other people, maybe!' said Mrs Doran ironically. 'Bad luck to it, for money it's the curse of the world; for you don't know which does the most harm—too little of it, or too much! However, it's only waiting a bit, and they'll find each other out. Sure, he's a gentleman born and bred, and every inch of him, and made for her, if ever there was a match made in heaven.'

So Gertrude's best friends were silently waiting for the fulfilment of her hope. Mr Dugdale had asked George Ritherdon to write to him frequently,—a request to which the young man had gratefully acceded; and his latest letter had informed Mr Dugdale that he found himself obliged to leave London, for an indefinite period and at much inconvenience, owing to his mother's illness.

The time was now approaching when Eleanor should attain her majority, and Gertrude had resolved that the event should be celebrated with all the distinction which had attended her own.

To Eleanor and to Mrs Carteret the birthday-fête had the surpassing attraction of a charming entertainment, rendered still more delightful by the presence of the lover of the one and the particular friend of the other. To Gertrude, though she strove to be bright and gay, and though she sought by every means in her power to evince her affection for the sister who turned away with steady coldness from all her advances, the occasion was a melancholy one. It furnished a sad contrast to the fête which had welcomed her own coming of age in every respect,—above all, in that one which had become most important to her: George was not present.

Robert Meredith caused his manner to be remarked on this occasion by more than one of the guests at the Deane. To Miss Baldwin he was scrupulously but distantly polite; with Mrs Carteret he assumed a tone of intimacy which she seconded to the full; but to Eleanor he bore himself like an acknowledged and triumphant lover. Every one saw this, including Mr Dugdale, during his brief visit to the scene of

the festivities, and Haldane Carteret, not remarkable for
quickness of observation. The fact made both these observers uneasy, but they did not make any comment to one
another upon their suspicions.

The sisters, who had each been dancing nearly all night,
did not meet on the conclusion of the ball. The old familiar habit of a long talk, in one of their respective dressing-
rooms, after all the household had retired, had long been
abandoned; and when, on this occasion, Gertrude—resolved
to make an effort to break through the barrier so silently
but effectually reared between them—went to her sister's
room, she found the door locked, and though she heard
Eleanor moving about, no answer to her petition for ad-
mittance was returned. Full of care and foreboding,
Gertrude returned to her room, and it was broad day before
she forgot her grief, and the presentiment of evil which
accompanied it, in sleep.

The ladies did not appear at breakfast the next morning,
and the party consisted only of Major Carteret, Robert
Meredith, and two harmless individuals who were staying
in the house, and in no way remarkable or important. On
the conclusion of the meal Robert Meredith requested
Major Carteret to accord him an interview, which the latter
agreed to do with some hesitation. They adjourned to the
library, and there Meredith, with no circumlocution, and in
a plain and business-like manner, informed Major Carteret
that he had proposed to his niece Eleanor Baldwin, been
accepted by her, and that she had requested him to communicate the fact to Major Carteret.

Eleanor's uncle received the intelligence with awkwardness rather than with actual disapprobation, and acquitted
himself not very well in replying. Something of unpleasantly-
felt power in Meredith's tone jarred upon him as he used a
perfectly discreet formula of words in making the announcement. Haldane Carteret did not dislike or distrust Meredith,

and he was not an interested man. He had married for love himself, and he knew his niece had sufficient fortune to deprive her conduct of imprudence, if she chose to do the same. It was not fair to take it for granted that Meredith was not attached to Eleanor, that he was actuated by interested motives; and yet Haldane Carteret, an honest man, if not bright, felt that all was not straightforward and simple feeling in this matter. He said something about disparity of age; then admitted that, in referring Meredith to him, his niece had merely treated him with dutiful courtesy, as his guardianship and authority had terminated; and finally, on being pressed by Meredith, said he perceived no objection, beyond the evident one that his niece might have looked for more decided worldly advantages in her marriage, and that he thought the proceeding had been somewhat too precipitate for the best interests of both. All this Haldane Carteret said, because his native honesty obliged him to say it; but heartily wishing he could bring the interview to a close, or hand Meredith over to his wife, who would probably be delighted.

Meredith received Major Carteret's remarks with calm politeness, but hardly thought it necessary to combat them. He could not see the disparity in age in any serious light, and he ventured to assure his Eleanor's uncle he and she had understood one another for some time; there was no real precipitation in the matter. As for the advantages which such a marriage secured to him, he was most ready to acknowledge them, and to admit their effect on the general estimate of his motives, but he did not mind that. Secure against an unkind interpretation by Eleanor and her relatives, he was indifferent to any other opinion. He flattered himself Mrs Carteret would learn the news with satisfaction. This was ground on which Major Carteret could meet him with cordial assent; and he got over his difficulties by referring the happy lover to Mrs Carteret; and having summoned her to the library to receive Meredith's communication from himself, he left them together.

Mrs Carteret was expansively and enthusiastically delighted. She declared she felt herself quite a girl again in contemplating the happiness of her beloved niece and her old friend ; and it may be assumed that Robert Meredith had evinced very nice tact and discretion in the method by which he conveyed the information to her.

It was no small portion of the suffering which Gertrude Baldwin had to undergo at this time, that she heard the news of her sister's engagement—not from Eleanor herself, not in any kindly sisterly conference, but from Mrs Carteret, whose light gleeful manner of imparting the information to Gertrude was far from conveying any sense of its importance to the agitated girl ; and who filled up the measure of her congratulations to everybody concerned, by remarking that in 'poor dear Eleanor's invidious position, it was most desirable that she should marry early, and before Gerty had made her choice.' This speech chilled Gertrude into silence, and she left her aunt—having uttered only a few commonplace words—with the well-founded conviction that Eleanor would believe her either envious, indifferent, or prejudiced against her and Meredith. Gertrude was quite alone in her distress of mind, as she purposely avoided Mr Dugdale— being unwilling to awaken a suspicion in his mind of its cause—and Mrs Doran, who she instinctively knew would penetrate and share her feelings.

In the course of the day both those members of the family were made aware of Eleanor's engagement. Old Mr Dugdale took the intimation very calmly, as it was his wont to take all things now, since he had ceased to feel keenly save where Gertrude was concerned. Mrs Doran heard it, with a sad foreboding heart and a gloomy face. She had never liked, she had never trusted, Robert Meredith ; and she could not forget that the man her dear dead mistress's daughter was about to marry was the same who, as a boy, had hated Margaret.

Robert Meredith and Gertrude did not meet alone. They mutually and successfully avoided each other, and the elder sister was pointedly excluded by Eleanor and Mrs Carteret from all the discussions which ensued relative to the arrangements for the marriage, which was to take place soon. Gertrude heard that her aunt and her sister proposed to go to London, to purchase Eleanor's *trousseau*, to select Eleanor's house, without a word of comment. But when something was said about the marriage taking place in London, she interposed, and in her customary sweet and yet dignified way remonstrated. Eleanor, she said, ought to leave no house for a husband's, but her own.

'Mine!' said Eleanor. 'I presume you mean yours— you are talking of the Deane.'

'I am talking of our mutual home, Eleanor, where once no such evil thing as a divided interest ever had a place.— Uncle,'—here she turned to Major Carteret, and laid her hand impressively upon his arm,—'speak for me in this. Tell Eleanor I am right, and that our parents—I, at least, have never felt their loss so bitterly before—would have had it so.'

'I'm sure I don't know what to say,' replied Haldane Carteret forlornly. 'I can't conceive what has come between you two girls; but I must say I do think Gerty is in the right in this instance.—Lucy, my dear, the wedding must be at the Deane.'

So that was settled; and afterwards, until Eleanor and Mrs Carteret, accompanied by Robert Meredith, went to London, things were better between the sisters. There was not, indeed, any renewal of the intimate affection, the unrestrained cordiality, of other times; and Gertrude felt mournfully that a complete restoration could never be—the constant interposition of Meredith would render that impossible. Under ordinary circumstances, the marriage of one by involving separation from the other must have loosened the old bonds; but this marriage was indeed fatal. They were young girls, however, and the evil influence which had come between them had not yet completely done its work, had not spoiled all their common interest in the topics which fittingly engage the minds of young girls. Gertrude strove to forget her own wounded feelings, to conquer her apprehensions, and to disarm the jealous reticence of her sister by frank interest and generous zeal. She succeeded to some extent, and the interval between the declaration of the engagement and the departure of Mrs Carteret and Eleanor was the happiest time, so far as she was individually concerned, that Gertrude had known since the first painful consciousness of division had come between the sisters.

Everything went on quietly on the surface of life at the Deane when Eleanor and her aunt had left home. Mr Dugdale was a little more feeble, perhaps; his daily airing upon the terrace was shorter, his period of seclusion in his own rooms was lengthened; but he was very cheerful, and seemed to desire Gertrude's presence more constantly than ever.

The visit to London was as prosperous as its purpose was pleasant. Mrs Carteret's letters were quite exultant. Never had she enjoyed herself more, she flattered herself Eleanor's *trousseau* was unimpeachable, and Robert Meredith was the most devoted of lovers and the most delightful of men. She had had an agreeable surprise, too, since she had been in London. She fancied she had chanced to mention to Gertrude that a distant relative of hers, whom she had only seen as a very young child—a Mr Oakley—had gone out to Australia, and, it had happened oddly enough, had there known Robert Meredith's father and their beloved Margaret's first husband; indeed, he had known Gertrude's

dear mother herself. This gentleman—a fine venerable old
man, 'quite a Rembrandt's head, indeed,' Mrs Carteret
added—was now in London, having made an honourable independence; and he naturally wished to find friends and a
little social intercourse among such of his relatives as were
still living. Mr Meredith had brought him to see her, and
the dear old gentleman had been much gratified and deeply
affected by the meeting. Mrs Carteret went on to say that,
knowing dear Gertrude's invariable kindness and wish to
please everybody, and also taking into consideration her
characteristic respect for old age combined with virtue and
respectability,—so remarkably displayed in the case of their
dear Mr Dugdale,—she had ventured to promise Mr Oakley
a welcome to the Deane, on behalf of Miss Baldwin, on the
approaching auspicious occasion.

To this letter Gertrude replied promptly, expressing her
pleasure at having it in her power to gratify Mrs Carteret,
and enclosing a cordially-worded invitation to the Deane to
the venerable old gentleman with the Rembrandt head; who
received it with a chuckle, and a muttered commendation of
the long-sightedness which had made Robert Meredith defer
his introduction to Miss Baldwin until the present truly
convenient season.

On her side, Gertrude was making preparations on a
splendid scale for the celebration of her sister's marriage in
her ancestral home. Nothing that affection and generosity
could suggest was neglected by the young heiress, whose
own tastes were of the simplest order, to gratify those of
Eleanor. She lavished gifts upon her with an unsparing
hand, and, indeed, valued her wealth chiefly because it enabled her to obey the dictates of a most generous nature.

Mrs Carteret and Eleanor returned to the Deane, attended by Mr Oakley. Robert Meredith was to follow the
day before that fixed for the wedding. The old gentleman
did not impress Gertrude particularly as being venerable, as

distinguished from old, in either person or manner ; and she quickly perceived that Mrs Carteret was aware and ashamed of his underbred presuming manners. This perception, however, was only another motive to induce Gertrude to treat him with the utmost courtesy and consideration. She must shield her aunt from any unpleasantness which might arise in consequence of her relative's evident unfitness for the society into which she had brought him. At all events, it would only be putting up with him for a short time, and he certainly could do no harm. So Gertrude was perseveringly kind and gentle to Mr Oakley, and actually so far impressed the old gentleman favourably, that he believed Robert Meredith to have lied in imputing disdainful pride to her, and almost regretted the part he had undertaken to play. There was no help for it now, however ; he might as well profit by the transaction, which it was altogether too late to avert. Thus did the faint scruples called into existence in Mr Oakley's breast, by the unassuming and graceful goodness of the girl he had undertaken to injure, fall flat before the strength of interested rascality.

The wedding of Eleanor Meriton Baldwin presented a striking contrast to that of her mother, which had excited so much contemptuous comment among the 'neighbours' in the old, old times at Chayleigh. People of rank, wealth, and fashion assembled in gorgeous attire to behold the ceremonial, which was rendered as stately and imposing as possible. The dress of the bride was magnificent, and her beauty was the theme of every tongue. The bridegroom was rather less insignificant than the bridegroom generally is, and looked happy and contented ; as well he might look, the people said, getting such a fortune. Miss Baldwin's own husband would not be so lucky in some respects ; for this gentleman might do as he pleased with Miss Nelly's money —she *would* have it so, and she could leave him the whole of it—whereas in Miss Baldwin's case it would be different.

The wedding-guests were splendidly entertained; all agreed that the whole affair had been exceptionally prosperous. The leave-taking between the sisters was not witnessed by any intrusive eyes; and in the final hurry and confusion no one noticed that Robert Meredith did not shake hands with Miss Baldwin, that he spoke no word to her. Gertrude noticed the omission, and with pain. It was over now, and she would fain have made the best of it —have been friends with her sister's husband, if he would have allowed her to be so. That he should have been thus vindictive on his wedding-day, that he should have had place in his heart for any thought of anger or ill-will, boded evil to Eleanor's peace, her sister thought. But it never occurred to her to fear that it might also bode evil to her own, otherwise than through that sister whom she loved.

In Scottish fashion, a ball wound up the festivities of the Deane, and proved, in its turn, a successful entertainment. Miss Baldwin, indeed, looked tired and pale; but that was only natural, after so much excitement and the parting with her sister. The dreamy look that came over her at times was easily explicable, without any one's being likely to divine that the absence of one figure from that brilliant crowd had anything to do with its origin. And yet, as the hours wore on, Gertrude forgot the fresh pang the day had brought her—forgot Meredith and her forebodings, forgot all save George Ritherdon and that he was not there.

Three weeks had elapsed since Eleanor Baldwin's marriage. Mrs Carteret had received two short letters from the bride, but Mrs Meredith had not written to her sister. Mr Oakley was still at the Deane, where his presence had become exceedingly unpleasant not only to Miss Baldwin, but to Major and Mrs Carteret, to whom he had dropped one or two hints relative to Meredith's character and probable treatment of Eleanor, which had made them vaguely, though

unavowedly, uncomfortable.   Gertrude was keenly distressed, and had found it impossible to keep the knowledge of
her trouble and its cause from Mr Dugdale.   Some un-
named undefinable evil seemed to be brooding over the Deane.
It was not known exactly where the newly-married pair
were.   Eleanor had given no address in her last letter, and
Gertrude and Mrs Carteret (the latter most unwillingly)
admitted that it seemed constrained and strangely reticent.

The fourth week had begun, when one morning, as the
family party were dispersing after breakfast, a servant announced the arrival of a gentleman from London, who desired to see Miss Baldwin on urgent business.   He placed a
card in his mistress's hand as he delivered the message.

' Mr Sankey ! ' read Gertrude aloud ; ' I don't know the
name.   What can his business be with me ? '

' *I* know the name,' said Mr Oakley hurriedly, ' and I
fear I know the business he comes on too.   Meredith has
sent him.—Major Carteret, you had better see this gentleman first—you had, indeed.   Miss Baldwin cannot be
spared *much ;* but do you come with me and see him, and
let us spare her all we can.'

CHAPTER XXXII.

THE RIGHTING OF THE WRONG.

SOME years have passed since the blow fell on Gertrude
Baldwin which deprived her of wealth and station, which
struck away from her her home, and left her to face the
curiosity, the ill-will, the evil report of the world which had
envied and flattered her, as best she might.   The story of
the interval does not take long in the telling, and, considering its import to so many, has but few salient points.

No resistance was made by Gertrude or counselled by her advisers ; no resistance to the hard cold terms of Robert Meredith's claim on his wife's behalf. It was all true : Gertrude was an illegitimate child and Eleanor the rightful heir. The proofs—consisting of Mr Oakley's evidence concerning Godfrey Hungerford's death, and the attested certificate of the date of that occurrence, and the testimony of the certificate of the second marriage ceremony performed between Mr Baldwin and Margaret—were as simple as they were indisputable, and Gertrude made unqualified submission at once.

She suffered, no doubt, very keenly, but much less than her friends Mr Dugdale and Rose Doran suffered for her. So much was made plain to her, so much was cleared-up to her now. She knew not why it was her father had left her nothing by his will ; she understood now from what solicitude it had arisen that he and her aunt, whose loving care she remembered so well, had bequeathed everything within their power to Eleanor. Thus they had endeavoured to atone for the unconscious, unintentional wrong done to the legitimate daughter and heiress. And all their efforts, all their care, had failed ; the invincible inexorable truth had come to light, and the result of all these efforts was that Eleanor had everything—yes, everything. The young girl who had risen that morning absolute mistress of the splendid house and the broad acres of the Deane, and the large fortune which could so fittingly maintain them, stood in that stately house the same night a penniless dependent on the sister who had placed herself and all she possessed in the power of Gertrude's only enemy.

It was long before Miss Baldwin, or indeed any of the party, realized this—long before the full extent of the truth presented itself to their minds ; but when it came, it came with terrible conviction and conclusiveness. There was nothing for Gertrude. Her father's loving care had indeed been her undoing. The situation was a dreadful one, escape from it impossible. Robert Meredith had no longer anything to gain by either dissimulation or temporizing; on the contrary, he now felt it to be his interest that every one concerned should be cured of all their illusions concerning him as soon and as effectually as possible, and should arrive at a clear comprehension of his powers, motives, and intentions. He assumed at once the name that his marriage with the heiress of Mr Meriton Baldwin imposed upon him; and his letter to Haldane Carteret was simply a reference to the bearer as qualified to give all needful explanations and proofs, and in the event, which he took for granted, of the young lady known as Miss Baldwin not disputing the facts, he begged it might be understood that she could be suffered to remain at the Deane only a very short time. He hoped no farther communication on this subject might be required. The young lady would best consult her own interest by abstaining from making any such communication necessary.

It is unnecessary to dwell on this portion of the trial appointed to Gertrude. Its bitterness came from Eleanor, not from her triumphant enemy. Her sister made no sign —not a word of kindness, of sympathy, of regret came from her whose life had been almost identical with that of Gertrude for so many years. Even Mrs Carteret—who, the first shock and surprise over, was characteristically disposed to keep on good terms with the new Mr Meriton Baldwin, and in reality an extreme partisan, endeavoured to get credit for impartial fairness, and 'a 'no business of mine' bearing—even Mrs Carteret was indignant with Eleanor. Her shallow nature did not comprehend the growth and force of such evil feelings as she had nurtured in the mind of her niece. Gertrude suffered fearfully, but anger had little share in her pain. A deadly fear for her sister possessed her; a fear which suggested itself speedily, when she found that Eleanor made no sign, and which grew into conviction under the influence of Rose Doran's manifest belief in its reason and validity. Eleanor's silence was her husband's doing; she was under his influence and dominion, she was afraid of him. When Gertrude, who had striven to hide her feelings on this point from Mr Dugdale, could not hide them from Rose Doran, that faithful friend said sadly,

'It's true for you, Miss Gerty; she's in the grip of a bad man, my poor child, and she's not to be blamed.'

Then Gertrude, in the depth of her love and pity for her sister, forgave her freely, and never did blame her more, but mourned for her, as she might have done had she been dead and laid beside their mother beneath the great yew-tree, only more bitterly. All it is necessary to record here is, that Eleanor's silence remained unbroken—unbroken, when her sister, with Mr Dugdale and Mrs Doran, left the Deane for ever, turning away from all the associations and surroundings which had been mutually dear to them—unbroken, when some time after Gertrude wrote to her to tell her that she was well and happy, and more than reconciled to all that had befallen her, except only her alienation from her sister's heart.

Much time had now gone over, and Eleanor's silence still remained unbroken. There was absolutely no communication between the sisters. Major and Mrs Carteret were living at Chayleigh, in a style which at first Lucy had found it not easy to adopt after the pleasant places of the Deane. But she had hit upon a consolation which, if imaginary, was likewise immense; this was the notion of independence. To be her own mistress, the mistress of her own house, her own servants, and her own time, was discovered by Mrs Carteret to be a blissful state of things. Besides this consolation, she had soon 'brought round' Major Carteret to an acquiescent form of mind respecting the state of things at the Deane, and they made frequent visits there;

but not even in this indirect way was the separation between the sisters modified. Mrs Carteret was given to understand on the first occasion of her meeting Mr and Mrs Meredith Baldwin—and a very awkward meeting it was—that it would be for her own interest to abstain from speaking of Gertrude to Eleanor, and, indeed, that her retaining the valuable privilege of an *entrée* at the Deane was contingent on her strict obedience to this hint. Mrs Carteret proved worthy of her old friend's confidence; and the former life at the Deane might never have had existence for any reminiscence of it that was to be traced now.

The intelligence which reached Gertrude of her sister through her uncle and aunt was too vague to satisfy her. Eleanor was very popular, very much admired; Eleanor's entertainments were splendid; and Mrs Carteret felt convinced she and Meredith Baldwin lived fully up to their income, large as it was. She really could not say whether Eleanor was *happy*, according to dear Gertrude's strange exaggerated notions. She had at least everything which ought to make her so, and she was always in very high spirits. She was rather restless and fond of change, and no doubt Meredith *was* a good deal away from her; and then poor dear Eleanor had always had a strong dash of jealousy in her disposition, and she never was remarkably reasonable. No doubt she did occasionally make herself unpleasant and ridiculous if her husband stayed away when she thought he ought to be with her; but she got over it again, and it did not signify. As to Meredith's ill-treating Eleanor, Mrs Carteret begged Gertrude not to be so silly as to believe anything of the kind, if such ill-natured reports should reach her. Why, everybody knew Meredith was no fool; and if Eleanor (who was very delicate—and no wonder, considering her restless racketing) did not make a will in his favour, he would have nothing at all in case of her death. There was no heir to the Deane—two infants had been born, but each

25

had lived only a few hours—and Mrs Carteret knew positively that Eleanor had made no will. Meredith was not likely (supposing him to have no better motive—which Mrs Carteret, though her tone had become greatly modified of late in speaking of her quondam admirer, could not endure to suppose) to endanger his chance of future independent wealth by ill-treating the person who could confer it on him.

This was poor comfort; but it was all Gertrude could get, and she was forced to be content with it. The old life at the Deane had faded away; no change could bring her back the past; she never could have any interest in it. She sometimes speculated upon whether it would add to her grief, if her sister died, to think of her father's property, her own old home, in the possession of total strangers. She had hardly ever heard anything of the next heir—a bachelor, already a rich man, living in England. This gentleman's name was Mordaunt, and he had a younger brother, who had assumed another name on his marriage, and to whose children the Deane, failing direct heirs of Eleanor, would descend. The sisters knew nothing more of these distant connections, nor had there ever been any acquaintance between them and Fitzwilliam Baldwin.

Though Gertrude sometimes pondered on these things it must not be supposed that she brooded on them, or that the irrevocable past filled an undue place in her practical and useful life. The misfortune which had befallen her had from the first its alleviations; and there came a day when Gertrude would have eagerly denied that it was a misfortune at all—a day when she would have declared it was the source of all her happiness, the providential solution of every doubt and difficulty which had beset her path. What that day was the reader is soon to know.

The first act of Mr Dugdale when the truth was made known to him—when he clearly understood that once more the foreboding of the woman he had loved and mourned

with such matchless and abiding constancy had been fulfilled
so many years after its shadow had darkened her day—was
to declare his intention of immediately leaving the Deane,
and forming a new home for Gertrude. How devoutly he
thanked God then for the life at whose duration he had
been sometimes tempted to murmur, the length of days
which had enabled him to profit by the impulse which had
prompted him to decline to add to the ruin which, in their
blindness, they had all accumulated to heap in Gertrude's
path! When he explained this to her, and made her see
how her father and mother had loved her, great peace came
to Gertrude, and much happiness in the perfect confidence
between her and her aged friend, owning no exception now.
In his zeal for Margaret's child, Mr Dugdale seemed to find
strength which had not been his for years. He bore the
journey to the neighbourhood of London, whither Mrs
Doran had preceded them for the purpose of engaging a
house for them, well; and he settled into his new home as
readily as Gertrude did.

In a neat small house in a western suburb of London,
George Ritherdon found Mr Dugdale and her whom he had
last seen in all the lustre of wealth and station, when he returned from the long absence which had been occasioned by
his mother's illness and subsequent death. George was
perfectly conscious that neither his voice nor his manner,
when he was introduced by the faithful Rose with manifest
satisfaction, conveyed the impression which might have been
considered suitable to the occasion, whether regarded from
their point of view or from his. He knew his eyes were
bright and his cheek flushed; he knew his voice was thrilling with pleasure, with happiness, with hope; and he
abandoned any attempt to express a sadness he did not feel,
to affect to grieve for a change in Gertrude's circumstances
and position which rendered him exquisitely happy, and for
which he, though by no means a presumptuous man, felt an

inward irresistible conviction he should be able to console her.

In less than a year from the falling of the long-planned blow on Gertrude Baldwin's defenceless head, the day before alluded to had dawned upon her—the day on which she recognized the seemingly insurmountable misfortune of her life as its greatest blessing and the source of all its happiness. It was her wedding-day. There was no need for waiting longer for equality in their fortunes; there was no need to think of what the world might say of George or of her. The world she had lived in had ceased to remember and to talk of her; the world he lived in would respect him, as it had ever done, and welcome her. Theirs was a quiet, happy courtship, a peaceful, hopeful time, blessed with their old friend's earnest approval and loving presence. A rational prospect of the best kind of content this world can give was opening before them—a prospect of neither poverty nor riches, of no distinction in mere name—the meaningless legacy of others—but of a position to be worthily won. Mutual love, confidence, and respect, and such experience of life as, leaving them the power of enjoying its good, should save them from its illusions—such was the dowry with which these two began their married life.

Major and Mrs Carteret attended the quiet wedding, at which they and two friends of George Ritherdon's were the only guests. Gertrude had hoped that Mrs Carteret would have been the bearer to her of some communication from her sister, that the barrier, which she felt no doubt had been interposed by Meredith's authority, would on this occasion be broken down. But Eleanor still made no sign; and Mrs Carteret could tell Gertrude no more than that Eleanor had heard the news of her sister's intended marriage with agitation, but in silence, and that she was then in London, *en route* for the Continent, where she was to pass the winter. This was a cloud; but it was the only one upon the bright-

ness of Gertrude's wedding-day, and it soon passed over.
It had quite passed when the bride and bridegroom were
bidding farewell to Mr Dugdale, before they went away on
their brief wedding-trip. It was to be very brief; for they
would not leave him alone for any length of time ; and in
the mean time Mr Dugdale was to remove into the larger
house in the same neighbourhood which was to be the home
of George and Gertrude.

The farewell words had been spoken, and Gertrude had
risen from her kneeling position beside the old man's chair,
when the servant entered and handed Gertrude a parcel addressed to her by the name not three hours old, addressed to
her in Eleanor's hand. She broke the seal, and the contents proved to be a flat case containing a suit of beautiful
pearls. A scrap of paper lay among the jewels. Gertrude
seized it eagerly and read :

'*Wear these, darling, for the sake of old times, and of me.
Forgive me, and make your husband forgive me, and love me a
little even yet and after all, as I love you for ever and better
than all.*'

As Gertrude's tears fell fast upon the precious words,
and George and Mr Dugdale looked at her, distressed and
yet glad, Rose Doran came to her side, and said, while she
dried her eyes as if she were still the child she had nursed :

'There, there, alanna, didn't I tell you it wasn't *her* fault
at all, but *his?* and now you see for yourself it's true, and
you'll go away with an easier mind. And, mark my words,
it's coming right—it's coming right by degrees, and it will
all come right in the end.'

Mr Dugdale still kept late hours, as he had done all his
life. Mrs Doran left him at the usual hour in more than
his accustomed spirits, and not apparently fatigued by the
unusual emotion of the day. When he was alone, the old
man passed some time in reading ; then he closed his book
and gave himself up to thought. His thoughts were seemingly very peaceful, and not sad ; for there was a calm and

patient smile upon the worn face, to which old age had brought a serene dignity. His large deeply-cushioned arm-chair moved easily upon its castors, and, after a period of profound stillness, he rolled himself in the chair towards a writing-table, on which a lamp was burning. He unlocked a deep drawer, the lowest of a set on his right hand, and took out two objects. One was his will, which he spread out upon the table and read attentively. Then muttering to himself, 'A few kind words to Nelly,—God help her, poor child!' he wrote half-a-dozen lines on the reverse of one of the pages of the document, and appended his initials in a clear and steady hand. This done, he replaced the paper in the drawer, and turned his attention to the other object he had taken out.

It was the portrait of Margaret, in its beautiful setting of passion-flowers in jeweller's work of enamel and gold. There was reverential tenderness in the old man's touch as he placed the picture upright before him, opened the screens of golden filigree, and ' fell to such perusal ' of it as had been familiar to him since the coffin-lid had closed over the face it feebly shadowed forth. The minutes fled by as he gazed upon the likeness of the beautiful spiritual face which had gone down to the grave in untouched loveliness ; and a glass upon his dressing-table alongside reflected his bowed head, sunken features, bent shadowy figure, and thin gray hair. Now and then a few unconnected murmurs escaped his lips, but rarely ; while his gaze remained fixed, and a solemn peacefulness spread over his face.

' The same eyes in heaven,' he whispered, ' the same smile. How many years have I looked for them, and longed for them—how many, many years ! I shall go to her ; but she has not been waiting and watching for me. No, no ; heaven has been full enough to her all this time with him there.'

He changed the position of the picture slightly, and leaned his head back against the cushion in his chair, looking at the face from a greater distance; then stretched out his folded hands and rested them upon the table.

'A long, long time—but nearly over, I think—and I have not murmured over-much, for your sake, Margaret. But now, now I think I may make the *Nunc dimittis* my evensong.'

A little longer the old man's gaze remained fixed upon the picture; and then his form settled down amid the cushions, his hands fell gently from the edge of the table upon his knees, and his eyes closed softly. Through the hours of the night the lamp burned, and lighted up the picture with its golden trellised covers unclosed, and lighted up the old man's serene face. But with the morning the flame in the lamp flickered and died, and the sunshine came in, and gleamed upon the walls and the floor. Voices and footsteps stirred in the house, and soon Mrs Doran came to Mr Dugdale's room, as she did every morning. Then she knew, when she looked at the old man and touched his passive hands, still clasped and resting on his knee,—so gentle had been the parting between the body and the spirit, —that his sleep was never to know waking until the resurrection morning.

The blinds are closely drawn in Gertrude Ritherdon's house, and she sits alone, dressed in deep mourning. There is a touch of sadness upon her beauty; but she is more beautiful than she was in her girlhood, and for all the sorrow in her face to-day, one can see she is a happy woman. She is so. A happy wife, loved, trusted, honoured; her husband's companion and his friend. A proud and happy mother too, untroubled, when she watches her boy's baby glee and hears his laughter, with any remembrance of a great inheritance which was once to have been the birthright of her first-born son. A happy woman in her house, and popular with her friends; one whose life is full of blessings and void of bitterness. It is not for her faithful old

friend Gertrude Ritherdon wears mourning to-day. That
wound has long been healed, and she and her husband have
none but sunny happy thoughts of him. Death has come
nearer to Gertrude this time even than he came when Mr
Dugdale answered his summons—they have received formal
notice of Eleanor's decease. The event has been long looked
for, and Gertrude has well known that life has had nothing
desirable in it for Eleanor. The sisters have never met,
and of late Eleanor has lived abroad altogether, her husband being rarely with her; but Gertrude knows that her
sister's former feelings have long ago returned, and there is
sorrow, but not anguish, in this definitive earthly parting.

George Ritherdon has been summoned to Naples, where
Eleanor Baldwin died, by Major Carteret, and Gertrude is
now expecting his return. Her thoughts have been busy
with the past; and when they have rested upon Robert
Meredith, it has been without any anger for herself, but with
some wonder as to how he will take the passing away to a
stranger of all the wealth and luxury he bought at such a
price, and enjoyed for so comparatively short a time. He
will be a rich man, no doubt, with all Eleanor had to bestow
on him; but he will have to see a stranger in the place he
filled so pompously, and to feel himself once more a person
of no importance. For Eleanor has died childless, and the
Deane passes away to the eldest son of the late brother of
that Mr Mordaunt who was the next in the entail, and who,
strange to say, died only two days before the death of Mrs
Meredith Baldwin occurred. Gertrude has heard this
vaguely, in the hurry of George's departure, and during the
first bewilderment which death brings with it.

A carriage stops, and Gertrude lifts the end of a blind
and looks out. Two gentlemen enter the house, and in a
few seconds she is clasped in her husband's arms, and sees,
standing behind him, her uncle, Major Carteret. She greets
him affectionately, and then loses her composure and bursts
into tears. The two men allow her to give vent to her

feelings without remonstrance, and when she is again calm, they talk a little of their journey, and then approach the subject of Eleanor's death. Gertrude knows the particulars of the event, and they go on to speak of the will.

'I thought it better to tell you than to write about it,' says George. 'You must prepare for a surprise, Gertrude. Eleanor has left her entire fortune—it is much wasted, but still large—to you.'

'To me!' exclaimed Gertrude, 'to me! And what has she left to Meredith?'

'Nothing,' replied Major Carteret. 'Precisely what he deserved. She makes no mention of him, his name does not occur in the will. She probably explains her motives and tells the sad story of her life in a letter which she left directed to me, that I may give it unopened into your hands. You shall have it, but hear first what we have to tell you. She has left you everything in her power to bequeath, and left it all at your absolute disposal.'

Gertrude seemed stupefied. At length she said slowly:

'What must he feel? What did he say?'

'I don't know what he felt,' replied Major Carteret. 'What he said quickly deprived me of all inclination to pity him, the scoundrel! I hope we have all heard and seen the last of him. His worthy associate, Oakley, made me understand his character long ago; but while poor Nelly lived it would have served no purpose to resent it, and we had nothing to gain by exposing him. Now it turns out she has avenged herself and us all, and we can afford to dismiss him from our minds. You must allow me to congratulate you, Gertrude, on poor Nelly's handsome legacy, and then on something much more important still.'

Gertrude looked from her husband to her uncle nervously, and her lips trembled.

'What is it? I can't bear much more.'

George put his arm firmly round her, and placing her on a sofa, took his place by her side. At this moment Mrs

Doran came quietly into the room and approached the group. Haldane made her a sign to be silent, while George spoke to his wife :

'While I was staying at the Deane, when I first went there for your birthday, Gertrude, my mother wrote to me, and told me it was a curious circumstance that I should be a visitor at Miss Baldwin's house. Why? Can you guess?'

Gertrude silently shook her head.

'Because, as I then learned for the first time, my father's old bachelor brother, Mr Mordaunt, was in the entail of the Deane, and in the very improbable event of there being no direct heir, that which has come to pass might come to pass. Do you understand what has happened now, my darling?'

'No,' stammered Gertrude; 'I—I do not.'

'This is what has happened: my uncle, Mr Mordaunt, is dead. I am his heir. My father took my mother's name in consequence of a family quarrel about his marriage, and, as you know, he died some years ago. I am the next in the entail, and Eleanor's dying without a child, makes me the possessor of the Deane. You now know why I did not ask you to be my wife when I believed you to be the lawful owner of the property ; you now know how doubly joyfully I made you my wife when you lost it. Gertrude, my darling, I think you will prize your old name and your old home more than ever now that it is your husband who gives them back to you.'

'I said it would all come right, Miss Gerty, didn't I, alanna?' exclaimed Rose Doran, as she in her turn caught Gertrude in her strong arms, and rocked her to and fro like an infant. 'But I never thought it could come *so* right. Honest people and rogues have got their due in *this* world, once in a way, anyhow.'

THE END.

JOHN CHILDS AND SON, PRINTERS.